TEA LEAVES AND TAROT CARDS

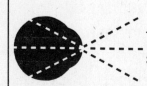

This Large Print Book carries the
Seal of Approval of N.A.V.H.

TEA LEAVES AND TAROT CARDS

JACQUELINE SEEWALD

THORNDIKE PRESS
A part of Gale, Cengage Learning

GALE
CENGAGE Learning™

Detroit • New York • San Francisco • New Haven, Conn • Waterville, Maine • London

GALE
CENGAGE Learning™

LIBRARY OF CONGRESS CATALOGING-IN-PUBLICATION DATA

Seewald, Jacqueline.
  Tea leaves and tarot cards / by Jacqueline Seewald.
      p. cm. — (Thorndike Press large print romance)
  ISBN-13: 978-1-4104-3292-6
  ISBN-10: 1-4104-3292-0
    1. London (England)—History—19th century—Fiction. 2.
Large type books. I. Title.
PS3619.E358.T43 2010b
813'.6—dc22   2010035069

Published in 2010 by arrangement with Tekno Books.

Printed in the United States of America
1 2 3 4 5 6 7 14 13 12 11 10

This novel is dedicated to my husband Monte who supports me in every way possible.

ACKNOWLEDGMENTS

I especially wish to thank Jayne Ann Krentz (Amanda Quick), wonderful, best-selling author and former librarian, for both reading and endorsing this novel.

My thanks also to Mary Balogh, a queen of Regency romance, for generously reading my novel far in advance of publication and offering encouragement, valuable suggestions and feedback.

A note of appreciation as well for my excellent, multi-talented editor, Alice Duncan.

I want to thank Five Star's Tiffany Schofield and Tracey Matthews who diligently help authors like myself.

Last, but not least, a special thanks to fellow librarians from all over the United States, Canada, the U.K., Australia and

New Zealand who have ordered my previous Five Star/Gale romantic mystery novels *The Inferno Collection* and *The Drowning Pool.* I greatly appreciate your support and hope it will continue.

"Mutual Forgiveness of each Vice
Such are the Gates of Paradise . . ."
                    William Blake
For the Sexes: The Gates of Paradise

CHAPTER ONE

London 1816

"My mother's death is surrounded by mystery, shrouded in secrecy, and as such, it troubles me. I should like very much to be attuned to her spirit. You see, I never knew her and that grieves me. I would wish to learn the circumstances of her life and death. As you are knowledgeable in such matters, it seems likely that some greater force may have seen fit to bring us together."

Maeve thoughtfully studied the young woman before her. Lady Caroline Grenly was a striking blond beauty of seventeen, pleasant natured and mature for her years. Caroline and her Aunt Amelia had visited Maeve's lodging only this afternoon.

The vague eyes of Caroline's aunt took on a glow of warmth. "It would be splendid if you could help my niece. You have certainly done well by me. When God chose to take my dear vicar's mortal being, we were both still young. I have mourned my husband ever since. It is a great solace to know that he can now be at peace because you were able to join the two of us however briefly. I pray that you may offer Caroline similar comfort and solace."

"I can try," Maeve responded sympathetically. She would not promise, because there was no way to know for certain that she could penetrate the veil of darkness surrounding the dead. Sometimes the power was gifted to her; other times it was denied.

"If it is acceptable to you," Lady Caroline said, "I would very much like to visit you on the morrow and attempt to commune with the spirit of my mother." The girl's lovely face was flushed with excitement and eagerness.

There was no further opportunity for private conversation as several gentlemen now joined them. Maeve recognized Caroline's brother, James Grenly, the Earl of Southford. Although they had not been formally introduced, Caroline had pointed him out to her earlier. He was a handsome man. Like his sister, he was of medium height, slender and blond. His eyes were a much darker shade of blue than those of Caroline, but there was a definite family resemblance.

"Caroline, may I present Sir John Simmons, an army friend of mine. John, my sister, Lady Caroline." With the earl was a short, stocky gentleman whose right eye twitched slightly.

"How nice to meet you, sir," Caroline said politely, offering a graceful curtsy.

Maeve observed the man's ruddy complexion redden like a rare roast beef in response to Caroline's charm and beauty.

"A pleasure," he said with a nervous pull at his neck cloth. He gave her an awkward bow. "Perhaps you might dance with me later, that is, if your card is not already filled." He cleared his throat.

"Of course," Caroline said. She offered him a kind smile.

Two more gentlemen joined their little group. Maeve recognized the notorious Duke of Rundwall, whose silvery hair framed a face as narrow as it was lined. His rheumy eyes were watery and myopic. He was dressed in the fashion of a young buck, which seemed inappropriate to his years, most particularly since he had the air of a jaded rake. The gentleman who accompanied him was much taller, indeed the tallest man in the room, well proportioned and outrageously handsome, but handsome in a hard way, a dangerous way. This aristocratic gentleman instinctively caused Maeve to feel uneasy when he stared at her. She quickly glanced away as he scrutinized her.

Sir John Simmons also appeared uneasy and moved on, his right eye twitching again as he took a furtive backward glance at Caroline.

Clearly, the duke saw only one person in the group and that was Lady Caroline. He demanded an immediate introduction from Southford while the other gentleman stood by, observing with silent interest.

"Caroline, may I present His Grace, the Duke of Rundwall, and his cousin, the Marquess of Huntingdon."

"So you are the Lady Caroline that Southford has described. By God, James, you did not overshoot the mark. Your sister is a remarkable creature." The duke's eyes glittered as his head moved to one side in a look of shrewd appraisal. He reminded Maeve of a sly, silver fox.

Under the gaze of these worthies, Lady Caroline's face flushed hotly. Maeve felt instant sympathy for the young girl. The duke examined the tender debutante as if she were prime cattle for sale at Tattersall's. His cousin actually had the temerity to hold up his quizzing glass and stare at the girl in a studied manner of aloof elegance. Maeve found him grievously lacking in sensibility.

Caroline rose to the occasion and curtsied gracefully. Southford then introduced Amelia Wingate, who was his sister's aunt and chaperone. Since he did not know Maeve, he could not introduce her, which was, in her opinion, just as well.

Maeve felt awkward and out of place. Unlike Caroline, she was not having a Season, nor would she have wanted one. The attention of these exquisites was fastened on Caroline, and Maeve much preferred it that way. Maeve had wanted to view the *ton* firsthand and it had been arranged for her, but she was finding the experience more than a little distasteful and disappointing.

"You are the loveliest girl in this room," the duke said to Caroline. "Is she not so, Huntingdon?" he asked, turning his dissipated face to the tall, impeccably attired aristocrat standing beside him.

That cool sophisticate raised his quizzing glass again and surveyed Caroline without the slightest hint of emotion. "The perfect china doll," he drawled languidly.

Then his sharp gaze again drifted toward Maeve and seemed to probe deeply into her soul. Maeve was riveted by the keen eyes of the marquess; their intensity and perception indisputably gave the lie to his effete, world weary manner. Behind his facade, she sensed a keen intellect. While their gaze was locked together, she felt sudden acute pain and let out an involuntary gasp. It was his pain she felt, his past suffering and lingering sorrow. Her second sight, a form of intuition, told her that he was sensitive but ashamed of displaying such unmanly emotion and so chose to hide behind a veneer of cynicism. The marquess was most assuredly by turns puzzling and fascinating, but certainly a man of whom to be wary.

Rundwall and Huntingdon moved on; others were demanding their attention. The earl attended the ladies. Maeve observed Caroline breathe a deep sigh of relief and then begin to fan herself.

"Since the Duke of Rundwall has seen fit to pay you his compliments, sister, you can expect to be a social success," the earl said with an air of satisfaction.

"He frightened me. I do not like his grace or the marquess. There is something most intimidating about them."

"Your nerves are overset," Aunt Amelia said, patting the girl's hand in an affectionate, soothing gesture as if she were a pet poodle.

Caroline shook her head. "The *ton* is overwhelming. The beau monde is not what

I expected, although I allow that my expectation was based on ignorance and naiveté. For months since you told me I would have a Season, I have dreamt of coming to London to meet the fine, beautiful and witty people that inhabit Camelot. But this is nothing of the sort. All is affectation here."

The earl's eyes narrowed. "You are in a room filled with some of the greatest, most notable people in England and therefore the world. As to Rundwall and Huntingdon, they are peers of the realm. They are sophisticated and cultured. It is only natural that a young, country-bred chit should feel inadequate and overwhelmed. You are but an inexperienced child. Strive for amiability, girl, neither giggle nor whine. Excuse me, I see some old friends." The earl was clearly displeased by his sister's reaction to the duke in particular and the *ton* in general. But Maeve quite empathized with the girl's feelings. She sensed decadence beneath the glittering façade, and it caused her to feel uneasy as well.

"This is your first real ball outside of Almack's Assemblies. It will get easier and better. You will see." Amelia's voice was gentle and comforting. Maeve was certain that Caroline's aunt was a simple, kind-hearted woman without a personal agenda.

"Why did you come here tonight?" Caroline asked Maeve pointedly.

"Curiosity, I suppose. It is also good for business. I have been accounted an original, an entertaining eccentric. I amuse those who suffer from *ennui*. In return, they come to my lodging as you and your aunt did today and avail themselves of my services."

"How odd. I have never known any woman brave enough to arrange her own business affairs, except perhaps for Madame Bessoire, the seamstress."

"Don't forget Mrs. Smith, the milliner, dear," Aunt Amelia reminded Caroline with a tap of her fan on Caroline's wrist.

"I know a great many women who must work for their bread," Maeve said, "but then I do not suppose they are accounted ladies." Although Caroline and her aunt gave Maeve questioning looks, she decided it was best not to elucidate. Her reasons for her behavior were her own, private and personal.

There was no further time to talk because Rundwall presented himself once more as the music began again. He leaned over and requested the dance of Caroline.

"Oh dear, it is a waltz. We do not waltz overmuch in the country, Your Grace, it is considered somewhat decadent. I am much better at the quadrille. Perhaps you should look to another partner, someone more accomplished. I fear I would only embarrass you." She fluttered her fan in agitation.

The duke laughed as if charmed by her ingenuousness. "Fustian, I am just the one to properly initiate you. And, my dear, you will soon discover the steps to this wicked dance quite pleasurable." In a moment, the duke had swept Caroline away in his arms.

"They make an attractive couple," the Earl of Southford said, returning to stand beside his aunt.

"The man's too old for her, is he not?" Aunt Amelia squinted at the dancers whirling around the floor.

"Too old? Why he's the finest catch on this Season's marriage mart. Rich as Croesus. Would I had his groats. He would still be a good match for Caroline if he had a score more years on him. I've taken the time and trouble to nurse the ground for Caroline, as you may know. I am persuaded they will suit famously. He has wealth and position, while she has youth and beauty. They will deal well together. Sorry to be vulgar, Aunt, but we must face facts: a man of means is fine husband material, no matter his age."

"Well, there is the duke's cousin," Amelia said, apparently not willing to yield her position. "He is much younger, nearly as wealthy and handsome besides."

The earl sniffed the air distastefully. "Even wealthier when he becomes a duke himself. I'm told he's been running his father's estates along with his own for many years and quite astutely. But be grateful he was not the one taken with our Caroline. The man has seen thirty summers and still shows no interest in marrying. He's an infamous rake. Never associates with decent, respectable women, only high flyers and the fashionably impure. Also, he did odd things in the war, I'm told." The earl looked around then lowered his voice. "Something to do with espionage activities, not at all fitting for a gentleman. I believe he worked in Whitehall at the War Office helping direct the army's covert activities. They say he is a hard fellow to deal with and a devil when crossed." Southford paused to take a deep breath. "Now Rundwall is another matter entirely. Had to bury two wives and he's got no heir. Plainly wants another wife as soon as possible. Perfectly straightforward, just what we're looking for, and he's clearly smitten with our Caroline. What could be better?"

In spite of his good looks, Maeve found the earl unattractive. She always trusted her instinct, and it told her that the Earl of Southford was mean-spirited despite outward charm and good looks. He could not have more than thirty years himself, yet he spoke with the assurance, authority and pomposity of one old and set in his ways. When he turned his attention to Maeve as if seeing her for the first time, she was less than pleased.

"Who is this lovely lady, Aunt?"

"Why Maeve, of course, did you not already meet?" The light blue, myopic eyes turned to him in vague confusion. "I vow we spoke of her to you."

"I vow you have not." He turned to Maeve. "The music implores. Shall we not dance?"

She saw no way of refusing his invitation without appearing rude. When she was in his arms, Maeve felt him studying her. She looked over his shoulder, watching the dancers glide to the music under the lights of myriad candles glittering in crystal chandeliers.

The earl moved stiffly, lost count and stepped down on her slippered toe.

"Madam, you seem to be dancing with an elephant. My apologies."

She smiled and ignored the momentary pain. "You are forgiven. I sense in you a reluctant dancer. Perhaps we might just end our exertions for now."

"If you will walk with me in the garden instead. I fear I have been ill-mannered in not obtaining a formal introduction. I would make amends."

"That is unnecessary."

He guided her through the ballroom doors into the cool spring evening, ignoring her protest. Torchlight lit the garden of Lord Damley's fine estate and displayed perfectly the well-tended shrubbery.

"I take it you are not comfortable at festivities such as these?"

"Quite observant of you, madam. I hardly measure up to the elegance of the cream of London society. Huntingdon and Rundwall, I warrant, spend half their time being measured by their tailors. I was not always titled, you see. I had no expectations until my older brother died unexpectedly. As an army captain, I had the pleasure of serving with Wellington and giving old Boney a trouncing. The fact is, I would not be here were it not for Caroline. I enjoy London, but I am no dandy. Tell me about you. You are surely not a debutante?"

She shook her head.

"No, I thought not. You are older than these girls. You do not dress in white or pastel, the virginal uniform. However, burgundy becomes your coloring better. You are most exotic." He studied her appreciatively.

She tried to turn the conversation back to him. "Do you miss soldiering?"

"In part I do, but my brother left the family finances in some distress, and I have been kept busy righting matters. Do you have a husband?"

She shook her head, hoping that would end his questions.

"Are you a widow?"

"No, I have never been married." She sensed he would ask more personal questions, ones that she did not wish to answer, and so in an effort to change the way his mind was moving, she took his hand in her own and lifted his palm toward her, gently following the lines with her fingertips.

"My God, you are a sensual woman." He trembled slightly.

"I am merely reading your palm. You have an interesting lifeline. It divides and may go in either of two directions."

He laughed. "You tell fortunes?"

"Occasionally." Her voice was cool, careful and composed. "We should get back to the others."

"Not yet, surely."

"I believe your sister is looking for you, Southford." The lazy drawl was not to be mistaken. Leaning negligently against a doorframe was the Marquess of Huntingdon, one golden brown brow raised in an air of amusement.

The earl frowned at him with undisguised displeasure.

"We should go," Southford said to her.

Maeve shook her head. "I will return shortly." After the earl left, she stood gazing out at the night, relieved to be alone. Then she heard a movement behind her and turned, half-startled.

"I am still here. You do recall me I presume? Did I frighten you? It was unintentional, I assure you."

Infuriated by the marquess's air of smug superiority, she faced him squarely and then saw the twinkle in his depthless dark eyes. He looked elegant and dashing in snowy cravat and black superfine evening coat, which displayed to advantage his wide shoulders and broad chest that needed no padding. His black breeches were so tight, every muscle of his powerful thighs and calves were delineated. She let out a soft sigh.

"I thought you had gone too."

"You looked as if you wanted rescuing.

The addresses of the earl did not please you." He observed her intently.

"The earl and I are strangers. I do not presume to encourage him, since he does not know me."

"I did not think gypsies possessed of such high scruples." His voice was deep, resonant and his eyes riveted her attention.

She had the distinct impression he was deliberately baiting her, but to what purpose? "Sir, we are also strangers. Let us remain so." She began to walk away from him, but he blocked her path. He was such a tall, well-built man that she was forced to stop. Doing so caused her to become angry. How dare he presume upon her, this arrogant aristocrat!

"Your Lordship, is there something you wish of me?"

"Indeed there is." He gave her teasing smile. "It is said that you are something of a seer. I wish to gaze on the face of one such as you." He spoke mockingly, but she sensed a seriousness behind his detached, studied manner.

Her eyes took in the square jaw, the strong, jutting chin, the imposing brow. She felt mesmerized by the forceful presence of the man, unable to leave his presence. Yet she knew he could be nothing but trouble to her. Like an onion, he had many layers. She was afraid what she might find if forced to peel some of them away.

The Marquess of Huntingdon found the female before him totally desirable. He had been struck immediately by her dark beauty. Although her gown was not excessively low cut, it showed to advantage the full, tantalizing bosom of the raven-haired temptress. He admired those firm, high breasts, wondering what it might be like to caress or kiss them. Although dressed in a fashionable yet subtle high-waisted empire gown, she showed to advantage a fine figure, a small waist and flaring hips that swayed provocatively.

But he was as drawn to the face of the woman as to her body. Her silvery eyes had a fey quality that seemed to dissolve into mist while her skin was unusual, a deep color like fine wine. Or was the bold color of the gown lending her complexion its hue? He could not be certain. Her eyes were large liquid pools in a well-boned face with prominent cheekbones, small straight nose and full, sensuous lips. This was not a woman whom men ignored. Yet she was here with no escort, leaving him to speculate about her position in society.

He knew that she was accepted as an original, but who had sponsored her entrance into society? Obviously, someone of consequence. Since she was neither wife nor simpering debutante, he was led to speculate if the woman was under the protection of some eminent individual. He decided to find out about her. Whose mistress might she be? Little about society interested him overmuch anymore. He was usually bored by the same dreary, superficial people, but this puzzle intrigued him.

"Were you mine, I should guard you jealously." He thought blunt words might surprise her into telling him something about herself.

She did not smile at his drollery, definitely a bad sign. "I should not be your creature."

"Why not? Who is your protector?"

She gave him a cryptic smile. "Perhaps I do not need one." Her soft voice had a husky, throaty quality he found sensually exciting.

"You are a challenge, but I shall contrive to unlock the gate to your secrets."

"What if I do not wish you to know them?"

"Then that would make you all the more alluring."

"Ah, the great aristo with no regard to the

sensibilities of those he deems his inferiors."
Her face burned as she jeered at him.

He had an overwhelming urge to kiss her
enticing lips. He drew closer as she stepped
warily away. "Where does a gypsy fit into
polite society? Have you many lovers or just
one? You are someone's mistress, are you
not?"

The slap caught him unawares and stung
his face. He was shocked rather than an-
gered. He grabbed her gloved hand as if to
prevent further incident, but she did not
seem inclined to repeat her action.

"I do not wish to be insulted. My affairs
are my own. You would not speak so to a
lady you deemed to be your social equal.
Do not take liberties with me."

"On the contrary, that is what I *must* do."
Her fiery nature enthralled him.

His fingertips gently rubbed the rose-petal
softness of her cheek. He drew her into his
arms and kissed her hungrily. He thought
she would fight him but she did not resist.
He found her trembling in his arms and it
caused him to deepen the kiss, to take possession of her. God but she was intoxicating, and he wanted more of her. One tiny
taste hardly seemed enough. His blood
began to hum in his ears. The wildness of
his need was potent. His passion was a fire

that ignited with primitive force. And then he heard it. A small, sensuous moan escaped from deep in her throat. She was responding to him; he was not alone in his desire.

Then quite suddenly, she was pushing him away. "I must return to the ball." Her voice seemed breathless, as if her heart were racing.

Ruthlessly, he controlled his passion, knowing that it would take a few minutes for his body to resolve itself. His arousal had pulsated from the mere touch of his body against hers. There had been many women in his life, but never one like this. He flitted restlessly from one female to another. No woman had ever affected him so powerfully. He resolved that he must know more about this beguiling dark lady, one way or another.

CHAPTER TWO

The Earl of Southford sought Maeve out the moment she returned to the ballroom. She had hoped to be rid of him as well as the intimidating marquess whose dark, penetrating eyes she felt watching her still.

"Do talk to my sister. I fear Caroline is going to become a watering pot and disgrace the family."

"What on earth is the matter?"

"I have no idea. I was simply emphasizing how taken Rundwall is with her and how honored she should feel that he has made her the object of his gallantry this evening, whereupon she became agitated and said she felt unwell. For some reason, Amelia thought I should send for you, that you could settle her."

Maeve followed the earl to where Caroline sat, off to one side with the chaperones, shrinking into a corner behind a gilded Dorian column.

"Maeve is here," James told his sister unnecessarily.

Caroline was biting her lower lip. "Might I talk to her alone for a few minutes?"

James seemed all too eager to oblige. "Yes, of course. I see old Johnny over there. I'll be back later."

Caroline breathed a deep sigh of relief. "When I danced with the duke, he told me he was looking for a wife and implied that I was just the right sort. It made me rather uncomfortable." She shivered slightly. "I know he is very rich and of the highest social rank, but he is dreadfully ancient. Why he must have fifty years at least. His stays creak, he paints his face, and his breath reeks most vilely. I was certain James would not even consider letting such a man pay his attentions to me."

Caroline looked so sad and young sitting dejectedly in her virginal white silk gown, Maeve wanted to reassure her. "Surely your brother will not try to force you to marry the first gentleman who shows an interest. You are here for the Season. Why worry? Try to enjoy yourself."

"According to James, Rundwall immediately spoke to him. James says the duke has formed a *tendre* for me."

"Oh, surely that cannot be. Why you and

31

he are barely acquainted."

The earl returned to where they sat. He pushed back a sandy lock of hair, which was styled in the windswept manner and furrowed his brow. "Are you hiding from Rundwall? Do not discourage him." The earl's expression was like a thundercloud.

"The man is old." Caroline wrinkled her nose. "He creaks and reeks."

"That does not signify, girl. He is still virile. I am disappointed in the shallowness you exhibit. I thought better of you."

Caroline pressed her hands together in a prayer-like gesture as if to solicit her brother's understanding. He sighed deeply, impatient with her.

"It is a lady's position in life to make the best match possible. You shall be the veriest success if you manage to snare the duke's affections. You will be the social success of the Season."

"But I do not like him. I do not want him for a husband."

"Then do not overly trouble yourself. The way you are carrying on, the duke will soon take you in disgust. You hold yourself too high, my girl." James turned to his aunt, who stood quietly beside Maeve. "Amelia, this is your fault. You and that foolish governess spoilt her. Caroline was given her way in all matters, and now look at her. Instead of being the sweet, biddable child she once was, my sister has turned into a conceited, headstrong brat."

Tears welled up in Caroline's eyes; she looked destroyed.

Maeve felt outrage rise within her. "Surely, a girl as lovely as Caroline may have a choice of suitors."

"Do not interfere." The earl gave Maeve a hard look.

"Loving is not spoiling," Caroline said, gathering courage from Maeve. "Perhaps I have had a taste of freedom, but I do not think it at all bad." She tried to touch her brother's arm in a placating gesture; however, he pulled away.

"Had you been raised in a household with a proper mother and father, you would have been beaten when you got above yourself. As it was, your aunt was little more than a poor relation grateful for a home. You were lady of the manor all these years and the servants deferred to you from the time you were but a small girl."

"Whose fault was that? You know well that Father shunted me away because he could not stand the sight of me. Only you, James, ever came to visit occasionally."

"I would have come more often but for

the army. Soldiering took nearly ten years of my life." Now it was he who was defensive.

"Perhaps Caroline is more mature than you realize," Maeve suggested. "She understands her own heart."

"We've not had a formal introduction, and yet you are meddling in my affairs."

"Well, we may remedy that," Amelia said quickly, as if to make amends for what James found lacking in her care of his sister. "Maeve is a seer and healer and our new friend. She has helped me communicate with dear Vicar Wingate and brought his soul blessed peace. And tomorrow she shall try to commune with the spirit of Caroline's long dead mama. Is it not wonderful?"

James's countenance darkened like a storm cloud. He looked at Maeve as if she were excrement in an open sewer. "You are that charlatan they talk of? I expected some toothless old hag." He laughed mirthlessly. "How easily you deceived me. Witch! You think to beguile me as you have these two green country yokels?" He turned a furious look on his sister. "You will no longer defy me! If the duke chooses to offer you his attentions, you will accept them graciously. You shall smile and flirt with him. There are other diamonds of the first water present.

Consider yourself fortunate that you have been chosen. And as for this creature . . ." He pointed to Maeve. "You are forbidden to see her ever again."

Maeve was mortified. Of course, she was not accounted an aristocrat, but her bloodlines were as good as those of anyone here and she had been accepted into society. She was as angry as she was insulted. How dare Southford behave in such a manner, calling her a charlatan!

Before she could either leave or make some retort, they were rejoined by Rundwall, Huntingdon and Sir John Simmons. Rundwall immediately asked Caroline for the next dance. Quickly, the girl looked about and, catching sight of Sir John's smiling countenance, told the duke that the baronet had the next dance. Sir John was all too eager to comply. Huntingdon watched Maeve thoughtfully and then inquired if she also wished to dance. She agreed, relieved to remove herself from Southford's hateful glance. But she had not counted on how Huntingdon's touch would make her feel. The mere whisper of his hand made her skin tingle.

"Your little friend does not seem overly pleased with Rundwall's attentions. Has she taken him in disgust?"

"I cannot answer for her." Maeve sought to avoid his piercing dark eyes and looked instead over his shoulder as they danced. She was aware of the grace of his movement and the firm, skilled manner in which he led her around the floor.

"It interests him that she does not become flustered and enthralled by his attentions."

"It does not offend him?"

"Not in the least. He is accustomed to women fawning upon him and chasing after him. His position and wealth are great aphrodisiacs. A woman who holds him in disdain, therefore, cannot help but prove a challenge. She is clever to use such a ploy. It is the perfect snare for him."

Their eyes met. "Caroline is a young, inexperienced girl. She is guileless."

He smiled at her as if doubting her words. "And you, of course, are very experienced and know the difference."

"Let us say I have excellent instincts when it comes to understanding people."

"And do you understand me?" A gold-tipped patrician brow lifted.

"You are far too complicated."

"But are you not possessed of second sight? Do you not read minds?" His hand tightened around her waist, and his eyes dropped to her lips as if he desired to kiss her again.

She gently pulled back, scarcely able to ignore the quiver in her stomach. "I believe that we are dancing closer than is deemed proper."

"Are you here with anyone who will redress such behavior?" His voice, deep, rich and cultured, could have charmed a cobra. But his face was hard, jaded and knowing. He was playing with her, amusing himself at her expense.

"I believe that was a rhetorical question."

He lifted the stone of her necklace and where his fingers touched her skin she felt as if on flame. Surely, she must have imagined that burning sensation.

"Is this a rough diamond that you wear?"

"Part of a crystal," she answered. She would not tell him more than that. He need not know about her.

"Unusual, like its owner."

He pulled her close again and she felt the raw power in him, the strong virile energy of the man. God help her, she found him as attractive as he was intimidating.

"Does Rundwall really consider Caroline exceptional?" she asked, trying to change the tone of their conversation.

"Both of his wives were of her type."

"What type is that?"

"Blond, blue-eyed, ice queens, both of them. Your friend doesn't like Rundwall, does she?"

Maeve would not answer, but he looked into her eyes as if to search her soul.

"No, she does not like him," he said, answering his own question. "No mind. Her distaste will only make him want her more. Ironic too. She is quite unfashionable." His indifferent tone implied he held the subject as being of little consequence.

"I don't understand. Caroline is beautiful."

"Yellow hair is not at all the thing."

"How silly. Who says it is not?"

"Dark women appeal to the romantic spirit. Ladies like yourself."

She was disturbed by the manner in which he regarded her. His eyes glided over her in a sensual, sweeping caress.

He gave her a small salute. "So happy I could clarify that minor matter for you."

"Sir John seems quite taken with Caroline. Perhaps others will not much object to her fairness either."

"I daresay Southford would not approve an alliance with Simmons, not when he thinks Rundwall is interested. A duke is worth ten baronets, to be sure." His tone of voice was coolly detached, as if the entire matter were nothing more than a passing diversion for him.

She felt anger well up within her. "How flippant you are, sir. I cannot comprehend you."

"And you are overly passionate about matters that do not concern you. I fear you are a Methodist and not a gypsy at all, for if you were a gypsy, you would seek to entertain and amuse me. I should be very grateful and generous to a passionate gypsy who sought to deliver me from the *ennui* that plagues my spirit." He touched her necklace once again and then gently drew her more closely into his arms.

Maeve found herself short of breath, nearly dizzy from the caress of his hand on her bare skin. "I believe those who are easily bored lack character. One should be able to amuse oneself, not expect others to provide diversion."

He gave her an infuriatingly tolerant smile. "It is the fashion to suffer from *ennui*."

"And you are so very fashionable?"

"I am among the enviable few who decide what is fashionable and what is not."

"How nice to have such influence."

"It is indeed. Brummell has said it best: 'I know I am fashionable because the people who once cut me now bore me.' I daresay had Brummell not fled to the continent to escape his debts, I would have shown up the fellow in the fixing of a cravat." He gave her an insouciant smile. "Tell me, gypsy, how will you choose to amuse me?"

He was deliberately provoking her. "I am afraid you misunderstand me. I try to help people, but I rarely entertain them."

"A pity. I am of the opinion that you could please me well enough if you wished to do so." His voice insinuated suggestively while his warm breath caused chills to form on her bare neck.

"Your Lordship plays a rude game."

"Call me Adam. I do assure you I play deep only at cards. However, I could be persuaded to do otherwise."

Was there a double entendre there? Of course there was. She refused to be drawn. "You have a reputation as a rake."

From his elongated forehead, he pushed back a lock of dark brown hair highlighted at the top like a newly minted guinea. His hair was so thick. She itched to run her fingers through it.

"I enjoy making love to women, but I give them great pleasure as well. If that makes me a rake, so be it. You are shivering. Are you cold?"

Her state was quite the opposite. His eyes

caught hers again and her heart began to beat wildly. She could see into the essence of his soul. There was a primitive wildness here, an untamed passionate nature lurking, a beast reaching out to seduce and beguile her. The trappings of a civilized gentleman were mere façade and artifice. Fortunately, the dance ended at that moment, and Maeve took it as her opportunity to depart from the disturbing proximity of his body. She could not imagine why she was reacting this way to the marquess. No man had ever made her feel so vulnerable and defenseless before. She reminded herself how strong she was, how much she had managed to endure to survive. He would not take away her dignity or self-respect.

Across the room near the doors that led from the ballroom to the hall, Maeve saw Caroline collide with a tall, handsome young man. He took Caroline's arms as if to steady her. It was Charles, Maeve realized, and he had come none too soon.

"Are you all right?" Charles was saying to Caroline as Maeve approached.

Caroline's cheeks flushed, her azure eyes blinking up at him. "Well enough, I suppose."

"You ought to watch where you step, girl."

Maeve could tell that Caroline was surprised by the broad, lower class accent.

"Why you insolent, rude man. Perhaps you walked into me!"

"Not likely." A feral light glowed in his amber eyes. Charles carried himself like a pugilist. He wore skin-tight pantaloons that emphasized his muscular thighs. His black Hessians were polished to a high gloss and he swaggered about in vast swathes of neck cloth. Maeve sensed his outrageous style, often imitated by the pinks of the *ton*, was pure affection. Charles was not as he appeared.

"I see you've met Lady Caroline. You should show better manners, Charles," Maeve chided.

He scowled at her. "Ready to leave these aristos?" His tone was derisive.

"Are you Maeve's footman?" Caroline studied Charles with great interest.

He crossed his arms; they rippled with powerful muscles across the expanse of his wide chest. "Do you see me dressed in livery, girl?" In Maeve's opinion, his tone was unnecessarily scornful.

Caroline's cheeks burned with embarrassment. Maeve understood the error. It was an honest mistake. Handsome, well-built young men were often employed as footmen by the wealthy of London.

"Maeve, I will see you tomorrow," Caroline said, turning away from Charles.

Maeve shook her head at the young woman. "You heard your brother. You are forbidden to visit me anymore."

"I do not care." Caroline's lower lip curled in a pout. "I shall get away without his knowing. He will be at his club in the afternoon and I will join you then."

They had no further opportunity for conversation. The Earl of Southford was suddenly upon them and took his sister's arm possessively. "Why are you talking with this person again? She is beneath your consideration. A pox on all 'Gyptians.' "

"Maeve is as good as anyone here," Charles said belligerently. He was taller than the earl, far more massively built.

"I'm ready to leave," Maeve said quickly, hoping to avoid trouble. She knew very well how explosive Charles's temper could be. There were many in London who feared him and for good reason.

"Perhaps this here gent would like to learn some proper manners." Charles began clenching his fists.

"I've seen you before," James said, and narrowed his eyes as if trying to remember.

"You have and will again." Charles spoke with cryptic malice.

The two seemed ready to exchange blows. Maeve knew Charles hated aristocrats, particularly those who assumed a superior attitude.

"Le Brun, isn't it? Who have you taken on recently?" The Marquess of Huntingdon smoothly inserted himself between the antagonists. "I saw you last sparing with the Brighton Bomber at the Fives Court on St. Martin's Street. Flattened the fellow in seven rounds, as I collect. Won a bit of coin betting on you that day." He spoke with studied nonchalance.

Charles was distracted by Huntingdon, who took the slightly taller young man by the arm and led him swiftly toward the outer hall. Maeve followed behind them feeling a sense of relief.

"Seems I've seen you around as well, guv," Charles said. He studied the marquess thoughtfully. "You work out, don't you? Got the look."

"I spar at Gentleman Jackson's. Wouldn't mind taking a workout with you, though."

Charles grinned at the marquess. "Reckon that can be arranged." He saluted Huntingdon as he escorted Maeve to their waiting carriage.

Adam de Viller observed his dark lady leave

and felt a peculiar emotion rise within him. He watched her with fascination as she settled back in the carriage. Her hair was a midnight black, swept up in classical Grecian style with glossy curls at the crown, her skin an opalescent apricot at this moment, while her large, wide-set eyes were luminous shards of quicksilver. She seemed fragile, vulnerable with an ethereal, otherworldly air about her. Yet at the same time, he knew her to be as volatile as an untamed lioness. His cheek still smarted from the unexpected slap she'd given him. He should have been infuriated, at the very least offended, yet instead, he longed to plumb the depths of that passionate nature. She made him feel incredibly alive. No one else had made him feel much of anything since the war ended. There was such coldness, emptiness inside of him. Sometimes, he was frightened by it. What a peculiar, introspective mood he was in, and she was the cause of it.

What did the great bruiser who took Maeve's arm with such familiarity mean to her? Was he one of her lovers? All sorts of outrageous stories circulated about the woman they called Princess Maeve, but no one could separate fact from fancy. She remained an image of romantic fantasy and mystery. He'd had a taste of her, but it was only enough to stir his hunger. He wanted a great deal more. He returned to the ball, lost in thoughtful speculation.

"Admiring Caroline?" Rundwall asked, joining him.

"Not I. I am not to be considered among her suitors. No, I was dangling after the gypsy this night, or at least I have heard her referred to in that manner. Do you know anything of Princess Maeve, cousin?"

Rundwall shook his head. "Very little. She is an enigma. Lydia might know," the duke said, indicating the rotund Duchess of Penworth. "I understand she was the one who sponsored the woman, brought her out into society."

"My curiosity is pricked," Adam allowed.

It took a bit of engineering to draw the duchess off by herself, but she seemed flattered by his attentions. A pudgy bejeweled hand came to rest on his. "You want to know about Maeve? Well, yes, I did introduce the girl about. Nursed the ground for her and got her the proper invitations, but as you see, she is all the rage quite on her own merits. It is all the thing to consult the spirit world through her. She is quite extraordinary. They say she converses with the dead. Perhaps you wish to use her services?"

The duchess eyed him speculatively.

"Actually, I prefer the living. Why did you feel it necessary to sponsor Maeve?"

The duchess avoided his eyes. "Let us just say I did it as a courtesy to someone who wished to please the girl."

"This someone is the girl's protector? Someone with whom you are quite familiar?"

He could not tell if the duchess blushed, since she wore so much blanc to hide the marks that denoted a bout with smallpox at a younger age.

"I cannot tell you the details. But I will say that the person in question has known Maeve many years. Since she was a mere child of eleven, in fact."

"Good God, you don't mean to say she's been kept by this fellow since she was a child?" He did not know why such a thing should surprise him. He, who was shocked by nothing.

"Maeve is quite acceptable, I do assure you. Her bloodlines are appropriate. I shall say no more."

The duchess moved quickly away from him, as if suddenly afraid she had divulged information that should not have been given but held in the strictest confidence. He had to wonder at her reaction.

Who was this rich, depraved man? Obviously someone of power and consequence or he could not have persuaded a great lady like the Duchess of Pemworth to do his bidding. The enigma intrigued him vastly. He knew that the tempestuous gypsy was beginning to consume his thoughts. Perhaps it was foolish, but he had to know more about her. With a start, he realized he was actually enjoying the challenge that Maeve presented, looking forward eagerly to confronting her again.

CHAPTER THREE

Maeve did not sleep well. First, there was a problem getting to sleep; her mind kept returning to the evening and the odd feelings the Marquess of Huntingdon had stirred in her. She envisioned the hard planes and angles of his face and thought that he was a man who would make a terrible enemy. He seemed formidable, invincible, a man who knew his own power and wouldn't hesitate to use it ruthlessly. And yet when he kissed her, had he not been a man consumed by passion? She had been boneless in his arms. Certainly, he set her on fire. Every inch of her burned. But he also tormented her. He could only complicate her life, a life that was already complicated enough. It was best to avoid Adam de Viller. She sensed he would bring her nothing but trouble.

That night she was plagued by frightening dreams. Several times, she woke abruptly sensing that something terrible was happening. When she was finally able to sleep again, she had a dream so real and horribly vivid that when she finally woke, Maeve's entire body was soaked with perspiration. Someone knocking at the door of her room caused her to stir.

"Miss Maeve, are you all right?"

"Yes, Ginny, I was having a bad dream, a nightmare. Did I cry out?"

The maid came into the room with a look of concern. "Oh, you don't look well. Have you a fever? Perhaps I ought to call Mary."

"No, don't bother any of the others. I know just what to do."

"But we want to do for you, Miss. You've done so much for us. Why, we owe you everything."

Maeve smiled at the adolescent girl affectionately. "We take care of each other. That's the right of it. I'm fine, Ginny. Just help me prepare my toilet so that I may go down for some breakfast. I believe I must go out this morning."

"It's near afternoon," Ginny told her.

"I suppose I must have slept late because of my restless repose. All the more reason for me to hurry. I have a client coming to the lodgings this afternoon, and I must see the Runners first."

Ginny looked at her in amazement and wonder. The girls knew something about her unusual activities, but they did not really understand. Maeve had no intention of explaining. Charles and Mr. Brockton knew; that was quite enough.

It was nearly one by the time her carriage arrived on Bow Street. Accompanied by Ralph Burns, their stalwart footman and bodyguard, Maeve went into the courthouse and asked for John Townsend. She had the most confidence in him; that Bow Street Runner had a reputation of the highest order and had even been trusted to escort the Prince Regent to Brighton.

"Townsend ain't here," came the abrupt response.

"Will he be returning today?" It was difficult being patient, but she had learned courtesy and politeness early in childhood from her mother.

"Not likely to return any time soon. He and some of the others are catching a gang of smugglers in Kent with the help of the troops."

The man facing her was short, with a puffed up chest and jowled mouth. She wondered if she could trust him, but decided that there was no help for it. She must unload her burden. After identifying herself,

Maeve told him what she suspected. She knew her story sounded absurd, but she had worked with the Runners before, and there was no question of her sincerity. Then she had to explain herself once again to the chief magistrate, Sir Richard Birnie, who remembered her from previous times she'd come forward to offer her help.

"I collect you located that fellow for us in Norwich, the one who'd been sunk in the pond, and you even found the pistol covered with the victim's blood and hairs. We couldn't prove the case without the body. Thurston's accomplice turned King's evidence, and Thurston was convicted at Watford and hanged. All thanks to you. They say you have the second sight."

He issued a search warrant without further comment.

Two Runners went with her to a rookery in the East End where poverty and filth reigned supreme. The house she led them into had the battered look of a domicile where little was ever done to alleviate the squalor. Paint peeled from the walls. Somewhere an infant cried. A woman looking sick and hungry-eyed viewed them with open hostility.

Maeve noticed these things. However, she was now back in her dream, returned to her nightmare world. Over the protests of the male occupant of the house, Maeve led the two Runners and Ralph, a man burlier than either upholder of the law, down to the cellar of the house where she found a large trunk. When the men pried it open, they found the body of a young woman recently murdered.

It wasn't long before the man of the house was confessing his crime before the head magistrate at Bow Street. The fellow's sister had refused to work the streets for him the previous night. In a drunken rage, he had slit her throat. This was what Maeve had experienced in her dream. The spirit of the dead woman had cried out to her, joined with her, if only for a brief moment.

On the drive to her lodging house near Fleet Street, Maeve shivered. She felt sick to her stomach. Why had this awful power been visited upon her? How much better it would be if she were able to prevent such horror. She put her hand to the crystal at her throat. It felt hot to the touch, and she clasped the gold chain instead. She wished she could talk to her mother, to ask if it had been the same for her as well. Such power was a terrible responsibility.

When the carriage pulled up in front of her

building, Maeve saw both Caroline and Charles. He was walking up the winding street while Caroline was standing in front of an overturned stall. Two Bucks were laying hands upon Caroline, one pulling off her shawl, the other trying for a kiss. "Let's have a go at this bit a' muslin," one fellow, dressed entirely in blue, was saying drunkenly as he grabbed at Caroline's arm.

Lady Caroline gave a hard slap to the blue boy's face, which caused his friend, another dandified fop, to pull her toward him.

"Pretty piece like you should learn some manners."

Caroline kicked him in the shin and then offered a blow with her reticule. By then Charles had joined the fray.

He intervened as Maeve stepped hurriedly from the carriage. "Just what are you lads about?" Charles looked quite menacing. "Let go of the young lady right now!"

"We were having some fun. You'd probably have done the same." The blue boy gave Charles a nervous smile.

"They've wrecked my business is what they've done," the street vendor said, pointing to nuts and gingerbread lying scattered on the ground. "This here young lady told them they was wrong and wanted them to right my stall."

Charles turned to the two dandies. "You heard the lady. Clean up, and then pay the man what you owes him."

The two Bucks studied Charles carefully then exchanged looks. "No harm done."

Charles gave the blue boy a hard kick in the rump. "That's for molesting the young lady."

"I am glad you came by," Caroline said with a tremulous smile.

"Shouldn't be out alone," Charles replied gruffly. "That's why they didn't think you was a lady." He took Maeve's arm with one hand and Caroline's with the other, leading them toward the stairs and into the building. "Where's your maid? You're supposed to always have one with you, ain't you?"

Maeve took a glance backward and had the impression that a man was watching them intently from a doorway across the street. He gave her an uneasy feeling.

"I took a hack over here so I could see Maeve. I could not use my brother's coach. I did not wish anyone to know that I slipped out. My maid is telling everyone that I have the headache and cannot be disturbed."

"I would rather you did not get into any trouble on my account," Maeve told the girl. Her attention had returned to Caroline. "Your brother is set against you being here."

"Yes, I know, but he is most unjust."

When they entered the plainly furnished rooms, Caroline removed her bonnet and silk shawl. Maeve smiled as Charles cast an appreciative eye on the girl. Caroline was dressed demurely in a blue muslin dress with a high waist and tiny puff sleeves. Her golden hair was worn in clusters of curls classically styled.

"Thank you for rescuing me," Caroline said to Charles. There was a look of adoration in her eyes.

"Be more careful in the future," came the harsh response.

"I merely told those two riotous, disorderly fellows that they were not living by the Golden Rule. How could I do less?"

"It don't pay to be too prosy with their kind."

Caroline cast her great cerulean eyes downward.

"Charles does not mean to hurt your feelings, do you, Charles?" Maeve gave him an appealing look.

He gave a curt nod of his head. He was rather rough edged, but a hard shell hid a tender heart. When they were children, she had teased him and called him her tortoise.

Maeve felt a sudden chill and closed her eyes against it. In her mind's eye, she saw the dead woman's face once again and began to shake violently. Charles held her.

"What is it?"

She explained about her experience with the Runners. "I heard that woman's scream. I keep seeing her bloody corpse."

"How horrid!" Caroline shuddered.

"I believe we could all do with a cup of tea," Maeve said, starting to rise unsteadily. "Tea makes everything better." Maeve turned to Caroline. "Indeed, there is nothing more restorative than a good, strong cup of tea. Afterwards, if you like, I shall read your future using your tea leaves."

"That would be splendid," Caroline exclaimed.

Charles put a hand on Maeve's shoulder to restrain her. "I'll see to the tea since the young lady's come to talk to you." He smiled at both Maeve and Caroline. "I'll also see if I can't get the landlady to provide us with some of her excellent scones as well."

After Charles left, Caroline turned a questioning look on Maeve and then spoke in a hesitant manner. "Is he your special friend?"

"You mean my lover?"

Caroline lowered her eyes, blushing deeply. "I should not have asked."

"Charles and I have always been very close." Maeve saw the dejection on Caroline's face. "He is like a brother to me. Charles and I have known each other many years. He is three years my junior. He has just begun his twenty-third year. No girl in particular has caught his fancy."

Caroline's expression brightened. "Then Charles is still unattached. That is very good to hear."

"He would not be considered suitable for you, as you must know." Maeve realized a warning was necessary.

"I collect hearing that a great lady eloped with her footman. It was the gossip at the ball."

"You heard of it because the matter was considered quite scandalous. And the lady in question had money of her own. Do you?"

Caroline shook her head, dejected once again. But Maeve refused to take pity on her. The world was a cruel place, and it was best the girl knew the pitfalls. She needed to be educated.

"Society forgives everything if one is rich enough. But it is not considered socially acceptable for a lady to marry beneath her."

"I take it that rule does not apply to gentlemen."

Maeve was reflective. "The man always has the better of it."

"Well, I should like to marry someone young, handsome and brave. Someone like Charles." Caroline spoke with both innocence and determination. The girl's chin lifted and her spine straightened.

"Let us talk of your mother instead. That is the reason for your visit, is it not?"

They sat opposite each other on the chairs set at the plain table in the middle of the room.

"I should perhaps offer some background and explanations. My mother was my father's second wife. He was much older than she, but he had a title and her family was impressed. That is as much as I was able to discover. No one at our house ever knew her. Not even a single servant. I was never allowed to visit the main estate. So I do not know if she died in childbirth or later. But I always assumed she died giving me life, because my father would have nothing to do with me. I believe he must have blamed me for his loss. Our older brother never visited me even after he assumed the title. Only James was ever good to me, but he would not talk of my mother either." Caroline touched Maeve's arm imploringly. "If only you could reach her for me. My aunt is kind, but I so long for contact with my mother."

"Have you anything that once belonged to her? A miniature perhaps? Pictures are often helpful."

"No, I have nothing of hers."

Maeve reflected on the sadness of Caroline's situation, for although she had lost her own mother at the tender age of six years, they had forged a bond that could never be broken, even by death. Maeve got up and went to close the heavy draperies at the front windows that overlooked the street below. The room became immersed in shadows. She rejoined Caroline and took her hand; her other hand she placed tightly on the crystal which hung in the valley between her breasts. Maeve then closed her eyes, shutting them tightly like coffins, and asked Caroline to do the same.

"Speak your mother's name. Then call her to you."

"Elizabeth Grenly. Mother, please come to me."

No sign came to Maeve. The crystal remained cold. There was no image, no special sensation in Maeve's consciousness. She asked Caroline to call forth her mother's spirit once again. Still nothing at all happened. Finally, she withdrew her hand from Caroline and reopened the draperies.

"I am sorry, but we could not make contact."

"It is hopeless then." Tears welled in the young woman's eyes.

"Let me cast the cards for you. We may learn something that way."

Caroline's face brightened. "Do, please."

As Maeve prepared her Tarot deck, Charles returned with a tray of tea things.

"The landlady is of the opinion I make a perfect butler. What do you think?"

Caroline laughed; the sound tinkled lightly, like a small bell. "The prospect of you as a butler is too absurd."

"Ain't I got dignity, girl?"

"Oh, it is simply that you are so virile." Admiration glowed in her bright eyes.

"Caroline is an orphan like ourselves. Charles, too, lost his mother," Maeve explained.

He looked momentarily sad and distracted. "She died too young. A curse on the man who broke her heart." A look of bitterness glittered in the amber of his eyes, and his lips tightened.

Maeve shuffled the deck of Tarot cards and then cut it three times with her left hand. She then cast the big cardboard shapes, spreading the cards on the hard-

61

wood table in a pattern so that she could interpret the meanings of the card symbols. The Tarot deck was very different from mere playing cards; its pictures included emperors, jugglers, fools, lovers, the devil and death. She studied the cards thoughtfully, drew forth the lovers and smiled at Caroline. "You will fall in love and be married soon."

The girl did not smile. "Will I marry the man I love?"

"I do not know," Maeve admitted. She was not always able to read the meaning of the configurations accurately. It was a tricky business, reading the cards.

Caroline chewed her lower lip. "I fear that James will try to marry me off to the Duke of Rundwall, if the man wants the match."

"Rundwall?" Charles knocked over the tea tray. "God, no!"

Maeve salvaged the tea as best she could and gave Charles a restraining look. She understood why the mere mention of the duke's name upset him, but it wouldn't do to burden Caroline. She turned back to the girl, who was studying Charles with a questioning look.

"What else may I do for you? I've been of no help so far." It was best to change the nature of their discourse.

"Not true, Maeve. I must pay you for your services. James gives me a small allowance, pin money really, and I have just received it." Caroline lifted her reticule.

"No, I will not accept it," Maeve said firmly. "I have not earned it."

"I should like us to see each other again." The girl spoke in a shy, tentative manner.

"Your brother will be out of countenance with you."

"Only if he discovers me. I do not intend that. I should like to spend time with you — and Charles. I have never seen the city of London. Perhaps I shall never have another opportunity. Could the two of you go with me?"

"I do not think we should get involved. Your brother does not approve of you seeing me. He has made that quite clear."

"Please, Maeve! It would mean much to me. You and Charles are so wonderful. And I am so alone."

Charles looked rather pleased with the suggestion. "It wouldn't do for a young lady to go about on her own. Maeve and I will be happy to show you London."

"Don't you have to work?" Maeve asked him pointedly.

He shrugged. "I can make my own hours. You know Mr. Brockton would never mind."

By the time Charles put Caroline safely in a hack for home, the girl was as elated and happy as anyone could be. Charles looked just as excited. Maeve supposed nothing could come of it, but their budding romance was indeed a pretty thing to watch. As Charles helped her into their own carriage, Maeve caught sight of the man watching them from across the street and again had the uneasy feeling of someone lurking, spying. The notion sent a small shiver slithering down her spine. If she saw him again, she resolved to mention the matter to Ralph.

Adam de Viller held a glass of Madeira in one hand and a lit cheroot in the other. He and his cousin sat together smoking thoughtfully at White's.

"I am going to offer for the girl within the next few days," Rundwall said.

Adam raised a patrician brow. "I cannot see why. The girl don't give a farthing for you."

"I am an endearing chap, not a wretched scoundrel like you. She shall learn to adore me."

Adam shook his head doubtfully. "Why not one of those pretty, plump little creatures who flirted outrageously with you the other night?"

"If you're talking about the one whose mother wore that ghastly puce turban, she had the smell of the shop about her. Can't stand people in trade. Beneath contempt."

"You are an insufferable snob."

"Quite right," the duke conceded with a complacent smile. "And do not expect me to change. I must uphold the standards of British aristocracy."

"I believe the chit with the chestnut curls has a father who is a barrister. That is acceptable, is it not? The man purports to be highly prosperous."

"Fustian. They are a family of social climbers. Nothing but mushrooms, I assure you. And the girl titters. Can't stand a giggler. No, Caroline is quite special. Mature for her age. I remember her mother's come-out. What a lovely thing she was. A pity I was already married at the time, or I would have offered for her. But the daughter will do quite nicely. She is not the Princess Charlotte, of course, but close enough."

Adam saw there was no hope of changing his cousin's mind or his prejudices.

"Help me, lad. You've got a diabolically clever brain in that head of yours. Plan a stratagem for me."

"I'll do what I can, Richard." What the

duke did not say was how much Adam owed him, or more precisely, what was owed by his father. But debts of honor were often the hardest ones to repay, because they were not tangible in the sense that money was. No, he could scarcely forget what was owed. "As to princesses, I have a man following Maeve."

The duke raised a questioning brow. Adam did not care to explain.

"My man reports that your Caroline visited the gypsy at her lodging. We might be able to use the girl's trust in Princess Maeve to our advantage."

The duke was immediately animated, excited by the possibilities. "Gypsies are clever. Perhaps we could pay the fortune-teller to sing my praises to Caroline. What think you?" The bloodshot eyes opened wider.

Adam nodded curtly. "I will talk to Maeve tomorrow and make suitable arrangements. Then I will suggest to Southford that he allow his sister to see Maeve. I will explain the circumstances."

"Excellent, my boy. A subtle means of persuasion is always best." The duke's florid complexion became more sanguine, and as his enthusiasm grew, he looked less the debauched roué. "Soon I will have a healthy young bride, and hopefully, at long last, a robust heir."

The two of them joined in a toast to the future. Adam was pleased to have found an acceptable excuse to see Maeve again so soon. He envisioned a very private, intimate meeting and felt the unmistakable stirrings of lust.

CHAPTER FOUR

Adam's meeting that morning with his man-of-affairs, Pritchard, raised more questions than it answered. Maeve still remained an intriguing riddle without an answer, a puzzle for which there was no solution. Pritchard's lad followed Maeve and Charles Le Brun to a fine mansion. Did she live there? With him? Le Brun seemed too young to be her protector. No, Le Brun must work for the fellow who kept her in some capacity. Today Pritchard assured him they would find out who owned the house where Maeve had gone the previous evening. Adam had every confidence in the man. After all, Pritchard had been exceptionally efficient in their intelligence-gathering work against the French.

It was nearly one in the afternoon. Pritchard had informed Adam that Maeve arrived at her lodging shortly before. And so Adam left his townhouse to seek her out.

Her lodging was located in a suitable area, leaning toward the commercial, but still respectable and clean. He walked up two flights of stairs and knocked at the door. As he waited for a response, he sniffed the homey, pungent odor of boiling cabbage from somewhere nearby.

"You're early," Maeve called out and answered the door with enthusiasm.

He did not know whom she expected, but it was certainly not himself judging by the look of surprise that crossed her face. He was again struck by her unusual beauty. She wore a high-waisted grass-colored gown that seemed to make her light eyes change to a shimmering green. He gave her an approving smile.

"You are in looks today, Princess."

She seemed unmoved by his compliment and stared at him askance. "Your Lordship, why are you here?"

"Do not view me with such alarm. I am not the big bad wolf come to gobble you up."

She offered a smile, but it was tentative at best. He knew his presence was making her uncomfortable, yet he had no intention of leaving.

"Perhaps I have come to have my fortune read."

"I find that highly unlikely since you think me a fraud."

"You do not know what I think." His eyes caught hers.

"I know you to be cynical."

"I accept that others believe in supernatural powers. Your friend Lady Caroline, for instance. She seems to value your opinion." He walked into the center of the room and looked about. He saw a stark room, a plain scarred table and four chairs, a thin Oriental carpet, dark window coverings, a single divan, no sign of ornamentation. It was clean, neat and impersonal. Nondescript was all he could think of to characterize this room. Did she live here? He could only doubt it. She was too vivid not to leave an impression of herself on any dwelling she occupied.

He glanced into another room at what must be the bedchamber. Looking into it, he saw no sign that anyone actually slept there. The wardrobe was slightly ajar, enough so he could see that it was made remarkable by the absence of clothing. Only a single cloak hung in it. For all intents and purposes, this lodging was nothing more than a business address. She was indeed a woman of commerce. Well enough, he would soon make her an enticing business proposition.

"Have you seen enough?"

He turned back to her. "Forgive my rudeness. I was curious."

"Someone mentioned that you spied for the government during the war. Have such habits become ingrained?"

He smiled wryly. "Just so. But I came to discuss business with you."

"Would you like me to arrange for some tea?" Her voice was polite but carefully guarded.

"Not necessary, I assure you."

"What brings you here, Your Lordship?"

"Do call me Adam." His eyes dropped from the thick black lashes that fringed her ethereal eyes to the full mounds of her breasts. The mere sight of her set his blood on fire. He would have liked to lay her across the table and bury himself in her soft warmth.

"What might I do for you?" she asked, folding her arms over her beautiful breasts as if in a protective gesture.

"Oh, there is quite a lot you could do for me." He gave her a suggestive smile that met with a frown on her part.

"My footman is a big, burly fellow and he is right downstairs. I will have him show you out if necessary."

"I am perhaps giving you the wrong impression about my visit today." He kept his voice calm and crisp.

"I am persuaded that you are the one with a wrong impression, Your Lordship." Her tone froze him.

"Do call me Adam. I assure you that I have come to see you on a business venture that will prove mutually beneficial." He realized that he must get to the point quickly. Her eyes were narrowed in suspicion. She was certainly not the most trusting of women. From inside his coat pocket, he withdrew a large purse and placed it in the middle of her table.

"For you," he said.

"What is it?"

"A generous amount of gold."

"No one gives gold without a reason, least of all an aristocrat."

"It is yours if you will grant but one favor."

"And that is?"

"You will continue to see Lady Caroline and dispose her to accept a proposal of marriage from the Duke of Rundwall."

"The earl has forbidden Caroline to see me."

"But she sees you anyway." His tone did not allow for argument.

Maeve did not reply; at least she did not

have the audacity to lie about what he knew to be fact.

"Rundwall will soon ask Southford's permission to pay his addresses."

"What have I to do with that?" Her suspicion of his motives was obvious.

"Use your influence with her. She will not accept him otherwise. That is quite apparent. Read her fortune. See happiness with Rundwall in her future. Convince her." He lifted the heavy purse and placed it in her hand. "Yours," he said with emphasis. When she did not respond, he continued, "Does not the gypsy love gold above all other things?" His voice was silk.

"I do not sell my honor."

"I believe the notion of honor is foreign to the female gender." He kept his tone indifferent and dispassionate.

"You are bitter toward women. Why?"

"I adore women. I simply do not trust them."

"Had you no mother to love you?"

"Just so." He knew how to keep his face a perfect mask. His feelings regarding his mother were a private matter; the old hurt ran very deep.

"I won't be put off by your heavy sarcasm."

"That is good to know." He placed his

hand over hers and pressed it tightly against the black leather purse. "Take this."

"I think you overestimate my influence."

Those otherworldly eyes gazed up at him through impossibly thick lashes and sent a lightning bolt of pure lust through his loins. "I do not believe I could possibly overestimate your powers." Barely able to control his desire, he leaned over and brushed her lips with a gentle, chaste kiss. But the sweetness of her nectar was too intoxicating and he found himself taking her into his arms while the purse of gold fell heavily to the floor between them.

He kissed her lips, her mouth, her cheeks, her chin, her neck and began to press his fingertips against the fullness of her breasts. She felt and tasted as exotic as she looked. She moaned in his arms, and he recognized that she was as enthralled as he was. Fever rose in his blood. "I am besotted with you, bewitched. I want to make love to you."

She shook her head violently, but he kissed her again, taking her mouth fully, his tongue probing entry into her mouth. Their tongues danced and mated with passionate abandon and it was wildly erotic. But then she broke free of him.

"Take back your coin, my lord, I want none of it. You know the cost of everything and the value of nothing." Her voice quaked with turbulent emotion. She was both fire and spice.

He shrugged as if vastly amused, although humor was far from what he was actually feeling. "Ah, a woman of wit. I do value a clever tongue."

A loud sound startled them both. Someone was knocking at the door. Maeve bolted from his arms. As she went to answer the door, nervously straightening her hair and the bodice of her dress, Adam discreetly took the leather pouch and placed it on a small bureau in the bedchamber.

He heard Lady Caroline's chirpy voice as he returned to the outer room.

"I am so eager to see the Town. I have heard there are beasts at the Tower of London. May we go there?" Caroline looked up and saw Adam standing there. Suddenly, she was no longer happy, but frightened.

Maeve saw the change in the young lady and took her arm for support. "His Lordship was just leaving," she said pointedly.

"I was, but I have changed my mind. Since you will not be able to give me a reading today, Princess, I shall escort you about the city."

"Charles will do that."

"And who is Charles?"

"That would be me." Le Brun stood in the doorway blocking out the light. "I've offered to take these two lovely ladies about town."

"Oh, it is you, Le Brun, old chap. Two beautiful ladies all to yourself? How greedy! No, I must insist on sharing in the bounty."

"Will you tell my brother that you saw me here today?" Caroline eyed Adam biting down on her lower lip.

"Not a word, for I shall be joining you as a co-conspirator. Besides, I have encouraged your brother to allow you to see Maeve as often as you wish, and he has agreed."

"Oh, thank you," the girl responded warmly. He could see that she was won over now.

Caroline gave Maeve an appealing look; Maeve shrugged her acceptance, which made Adam smile with satisfaction.

"Have you already made plans?" he asked Charles.

"I was thinking that the ladies might enjoy the afternoon performance at Astley's." Charles turned to Caroline. "Have you ever seen bareback riders?"

The girl's azure eyes opened wide in anticipation. "Never! Oh, do let us go, but don't forget about the Tower."

■ ■ ■ ■

Astley's was a grand success, at least for Lady Caroline. She was enthralled with the equestrian performances. He himself could remember enjoying such performances as a child. He'd seen Philip Astley when that great performer had done his own equestrian acts. The amphitheater had been burned to the ground and rebuilt several times since then. Now with Philip dead, Young Astley managed the property and sometimes rode himself in the manner of his father. Adam enjoyed good horsemanship, but his attention was drawn to other things today. Even the female performers in their skimpy sequined costumes and flesh-colored tights proved unremarkable points of interest. All he could think about was the extraordinary woman sitting beside him; Maeve was an amazing distraction.

"I do wish you had let us sit up closer," Caroline said to Adam. "We could see so much better up there."

"To be quite frank, only men sit on the front benches," Adam said.

"What he means, my girl, is that you never see a woman sitting up front unless she's a whore. Those lecherous bucks come around to ogle the females in the show and make lewd comments. They're the kind that sit on the front benches."

Le Brun could be astonishingly crude and vulgar. But Adam decided to reserve judgment. He preferred to think of himself as fair-minded. After all, the young man had obviously not been educated as an English gentleman.

Caroline's face reddened. "I had no idea. Oh, dear, look! How does she manage to ride so well standing on the horse's back that way? I'm sure I could never do it." Caroline seemed once again captivated by the combination of circus, melodrama and spectacle. Or had she merely wished to change the subject?

The gentlemen sat on either side of each lady. Adam slipped Maeve's hand into his. She appeared unmoved by his action, pretending to ignore him, but he saw the color rise to her face. When he was certain that Caroline and Le Brun were engrossed in the performance, Adam spoke softly and sensually into Maeve's ear.

"Have you decided to accept my offer?"

Her look was direct. "I do not accept bribes."

"Do not consider it a bribe."

"I do not want your money."

78

"I am accustomed to paying women for their services. The honest ones take my money and give me value in return. Make your demands known to me." His fingertips rubbed her palm.

"Has no one ever given you anything without exacting a price?" Her expression actually bespoke sympathy.

He gave her a cynical smile. "Men in my position are expected to pay well for favors received. I am rich as a nabob and everyone knows it. It is the way of the world to pay for what one gets. I am resigned to it. Why not turn it to your advantage?"

She shook her head.

"Will not a gypsy do anything for gold?"

When she did not answer, he continued, "But you are not a true gypsy, are you?"

"My mother was a gypsy."

"And was she a princess?"

"Her mother was the queen of her tribe."

"Ah, a woman with magical powers no doubt."

"I realize you are mocking me. But as a matter of fact, my grandmother did have powers. She was a healer and a seer. So was my mother. She taught me a great deal in the short time we had together."

"Maeve is an odd name for a gypsy."

"My father named me."

"For Mab, queen of the Celtic fairies? Cu-chulain's Maeve was an evil goddess who destroyed men with her sexuality." He studied her and thought she too could destroy men if she wished.

Maeve did not respond and kept her eyes scrupulously fixed on the stage before her.

"Your father, what became of him?"

"I do not know." Her lips narrowed into a thin line.

"And his family?"

"I have no family." She managed to keep her husky voice devoid of inflection.

"Are you telling me that you are an or-phan?"

"I lived in an orphanage until I was eleven."

"But before that time?"

"I was allowed to live in the servants' quarters of a great house . . . until my mother died."

He heard the rancor in her voice and saw the pain in her eyes. But it was only momen-tary, and then she regained her composure. Still he would not relent. He wanted to know her, to reach her essence.

"How old were you when your mother died?"

"We had six years together."

"Who are you, Maeve? I want you to tell

me about yourself."

She did not look at him. "What if I do not wish it?"

"You can trust me."

"I cannot imagine that to be so. And you do not trust me either." Her eyes flashed with wild lightning.

He began again to caress her hand, to rub her palm with a gentle, circular motion of his fingertips. She closed her eyes for a moment, seemingly lost to the erotic stimulation.

"Is Le Brun your lover? Will he be jealous of my attentions to you?"

She snatched her hand away from his grasp. "Charles is my friend." She would say no more.

"Did I insult you? I did not intend it. You are a gypsy. I expect that your blood runs hot. As a civilized man of my century, I accept that a woman may take lovers just as a man."

"How very tolerant you are." Now she was mocking him. "But in your ignorance of gypsy customs you are probably unaware that the Romany are neither as civilized nor as open-minded as you. They are a primitive people who expect their women to remain chaste. Otherwise they are cast out of the tribe."

"I see. Is that what happened to your mother?"

He saw her eyes momentarily flash with anger, looking like the sea on a stormy night. "Cease your questions. I do not wish to answer them."

"Why will you not trust me?"

"What precisely is it that you want from me, Your Lordship?" Her voice showed exasperation, but her skin was hot to the touch.

"I want you to open yourself to me in every way. I wish to plumb your depths."

"Impossible!"

"We shall see."

"You deliberately provoke me." Her spine stiffened.

"Do I indeed? Perhaps I wish to test your mettle just a bit."

"Although you claim to love women, I sense in you a bone deep anger."

"And do you feel hostility toward me?"

"I do, Milord." She folded her arms across her luscious, full breasts.

Her passionate nature excited him, aroused him more than any woman he'd ever known. He was certain of only one thing: he must have her at any cost. He would have her!

"We shall find suitable means by which to

deal with these feelings lest they undermine our good health and well-being." Through hooded eyelids, he stared at her lush, pink lips with deep sensual longing. By God, he hungered for her, like a starving man beholding a magnificent feast. He longed to strip her naked and bury himself in her softness. Nothing short of that would satisfy him.

The rich wine color of her face seemed to deepen, as if she knew precisely what he was thinking. She tried to ignore him, concentrating on the performance.

"Where does Mr. Astley get such clever horses?" Caroline called across to Adam.

"I understand usually at Smithfield. Old Astley told Prinny once that he cared little for shape, make or color. Temper was the only consideration. Hardly did he ever pay more than five pounds for a horse. Best horse-tamer any of us ever saw. Man had a rare gift. Young Astley's nearly as good as his father." Talk of horses seemed safe and neutral. He saw that Maeve had relaxed and was now listening to him with interest along with Caroline and Charles. He sensed he dared not probe more deeply for the present for fear of alienating her entirely.

Le Brun's carriage was waiting for them when the performance ended. He realized how much he'd been enjoying himself and that he didn't want the afternoon to end.

"Oh, do let us go to the Tower of London now," Caroline said. "I have heard so much about it."

"The Tower of London," Adam agreed.

"I should like to see the beasts. Are the lions most ferocious? Oh, and the Crown Jewels! They must be ever so magnificent. Have you seen Anne Boleyn's ghost there? Squire Reed, our neighbor back in Noscombe, insists that he sighted her atop a tower on his visit." Caroline stopped only to catch her breath. Her excitement was infectious. Adam could not help but enjoy her youthful exuberance.

But Le Brun put up his hand as if to call a halt. "Hold there, my girl, the Tower ain't just one building but many. It will take a rare bit of time to see all that you want. I think it might be best to wait for another day."

Caroline immediately looked forlorn. "Charles, I do not wish to be prudent."

"He is right," Maeve said. "We haven't the time now."

"But shall we ever have another day like this? I fear not." The girl looked ready to cry.

"We could all do with a bit of refreshment," Adam suggested. He gave the coachman directions to a tea shop that he was certain the ladies would like.

Over cream cakes, chocolate biscuits, and hot tea, Caroline resumed her former optimism. Le Brun's eyes never left the girl's pretty, flushed face. No doubt there was something developing between these two, and it did not bode well for his cousin.

"You are not a pugilist by profession I take it," he inquired of Le Brun.

"No, that is my enjoyment. Keeps the body fit and hardy. But then, you know all about that yourself," Le Brun responded indicating Adam's hard, muscular frame.

"Are you a gentleman of leisure then?" By looks alone, Le Brun could easily pass for one of aristocratic background, until he opened his mouth.

"No, I work for a living. I am no aristo." Charles spoke the last with derisive emphasis.

Adam decided not to take personal offense at Le Brun's comment because he recognized it wasn't intended that way. The young man was obviously hostile toward the nobility in general, not himself in particular.

"How are you employed?"

Le Brun exchanged a meaningful look with Maeve. Their relationship was a curious thing, and he wondered at it.

"I dun people, collect what's owed."

"Owed to whom?"

"My employer," came the terse response. It was clear the young man would not say more. His eyes were shuttered.

It did not matter; Adam knew that he would learn the rest through the endeavors of Pritchard. No one had ever been a better spy.

"Do you collect debts from the wealthy?" he inquired smoothly.

"Yes, and I've learned one thing for certain. Aristos are an arrogant lot. The richer they are, the less likely they are to pay what's owed. They need special reminding." There was something almost savage in Le Brun's look of satisfaction. Adam decidedly would not wish to owe that fellow's employer any great sum of money. Le Brun's intimation of violence was all too evident.

"I suggest a walk in the park to digest this excellent repast." Adam rose to his feet.

"We should really be going," Maeve said. "We are expected, and I would give no cause for worry."

He wanted to know who expected her and Le Brun, but he knew neither one of them would give him a satisfactory answer. They did not give their trust easily. However, neither did he.

"Too lively a day not to walk in the park," he said. "Not many glorious spring afternoons like this one to be had. Mostly, rain, damp and fog. *Carpe diem.*"

No one would argue with that. Even Maeve finally agreed, though with some reluctance. She was so wary, he could not help but wonder why.

They walked into Hyde Park in a leisurely manner. The fragrance of new grass and the beauty of budding flowers surrounded them.

"It is nearing the fashionable hour when the beau monde will be riding along Rotten Row. Do you not wish to be joining them?" Maeve asked him.

"Not I. Do you?"

"I am not one of them as you are. Perhaps you should be with someone more suitable to your station." She refused to look at him.

"I believe you and I are perfectly matched."

Le Brun and Lady Caroline were well ahead of them. He could see affection growing between the two. He felt like a traitor to Rundwall, but he would see to his cousin's interests soon enough. At the moment his own interest in Maeve was very strong, his unruly body placing potent demands upon him. He did not want this time to end. Just like Caroline, he felt this day was special. The fact was that he wanted to be with Maeve, wanted her as he had wanted no other woman in his life. His fascination grew in proportion to his lust.

He took her hand as they walked along the path and thought of how he would delight in making her his mistress. Glossy black curls peeped out from beneath a natural straw bonnet trimmed with an edging of *eau-de-nil* green silk. A small green bow at the back matched her gown of silk muslin. She looked so fresh and lovely, so delightfully vital. They were nearing a tall hedge, and he saw his opportunity to be alone with her if only for a few moments. The large growth provided a brief opportunity for intimacy, a shelter from the curious.

"What are you doing?" she asked in a breathy voice.

"Truthfully, I want to kiss you. Do you object?"

"How can you ask it?"

"You're right. A wise man never asks, he acts."

He kissed her gently, brushing his lips against hers. She tried to pull away but his arms enclosed her tightly. "You should

88

come away with me. I would treat you better than your so-called protector does. I should treasure you above all else. Ask what you want of me. You will find me to be as generous as I am rich. I wish to lavish gifts upon you."

"The only thing I wish is to keep my freedom."

"I am not known as a slaver."

He kissed her with the deep passion he felt. She was so warm and alive; the cold, empty place within him was suddenly filled. He no longer felt hollow. His lips grew more demanding, hot and hungry for her; his tongue captured hers and moved sinuously, suggestively. He felt her respond in kind.

His mouth began to move, to trail kisses from the lobe of her ear to her neck. Then his hand spread over her breast, cupping her, gently fingering her nipples with a fiery touch. He felt the peaks stiffen against the thin fabric of her bodice. She shuddered and moaned in his arms.

"No more, please!" Then she pushed him away with shaky hands.

"Just when we were having a most uplifting interchange." He spoke in a teasing manner.

She insisted on her release, and he behaved the gentleman, but he knew they weren't done with each other. Far from it. The more difficult she was to obtain, the more he wanted her. The challenge she presented was irresistible, the prize worth any price.

CHAPTER FIVE

"Now I understand why they call it a crush," Caroline observed to Maeve. "But why would the Treethams invite so very many people to their rout when their townhouse is not very large?" She fanned herself diligently.

"The party would hardly be considered a success if there were no crowd," the Marquess of Huntingdon said as he handed each of them a glass of ratafia.

"The ubiquitous marquess," Maeve said. "It seems we are constantly seeing you these days." She spoke lightly in an attempt to hide the fact that his proximity was disconcerting her.

"I thought you both looked dreadfully thirsty." His hand brushed Maeve's arm and made her skin burn. The sensation had nothing whatever to do with the warmth of the room.

She found herself staring at him, although

she did not wish to do so. His was a compelling visage, long, bold nose, forceful, square jaw. Everything about him suggested a man of strength and power, a man accustomed to getting what he wanted. The paradox was that he still managed to be a modish Corinthian. His high, starched cravat was an immaculate snowdrift of perfect style, a contrast to the severe elegance of his black evening clothes, just as his inky eyes were a powerful contrast to the gold tipped highlights of his rich chocolate hair.

A woman with a full-blown figure and heavily painted face deliberately pressed her body against Huntingdon. She gave him a slow, seductive smile over her fan. "Hello, Adam. How are you?" She waited hopefully for a reply.

"Tolerable, and you, Suzannah?"

"Oh, well enough. You must visit us again soon." She gave him a look that promised everything and then fanned herself vigorously.

Maeve found she was feeling rather irritated with the woman who, she observed, wore a damped down bodice with a décolletage barely concealing her nipples. Was she jealous that this person obviously had carnal knowledge of the marquess? She had no right to be. But logic did not prevail over emotion.

Suzannah moved on, much to Maeve's relief. She had hoped that Huntingdon would move on, too, but that was not to be. In fact, they were joined by the Duke of Rundwall who seemed very pleased to be in Caroline's company again.

"My dear Lady Caroline, I called on you the afternoon after the ball promptly at three and was told that you were not receiving guests." His heavily lidded eyes gave him a dissipated air.

"I am sorry we were not available," Aunt Amelia quickly said as she joined them. "I have been playing cards with friends these several afternoons and Caroline has been indisposed." Maeve realized that Caroline must have confided her distaste of the duke to her aunt.

"I would have expected someone of your distinction to merely send a servant with a card, your Grace," Caroline said.

"You do not know your power," the duke responded with a wide smile. "I wish to talk with you privately."

"This hardly seems the appropriate place."

"Quite true," he agreed, observing the milling crowd of people. "I will visit you tomorrow."

"I have plans with friends for the afternoon," she said in a high, nervous voice.

"Then I shall come early. For you, my dear, I am prepared to rise at noon. No discomfort is too great." He took her hand and kissed it in the continental manner. The duke moved on then, but Huntingdon remained.

Sir John Simmons was soon beside Caroline, along with her brother James.

"You are looking quite lovely," Sir John told the girl.

Maeve observed that Caroline was truly regal in aspect today. She wore a thin, white muslin shot with gold, a broad lace pattern around the hem that floated about her lithe body. The bodice and sleeves were done up with seed pearls, and she wore one strand of luminous pearls around her swanlike neck with matching pearl earrings. Her hair was dressed *a la Greque* with soft golden curls dangling.

Maeve knew that her own appearance was in sharp contrast to Caroline's classical mien. She had chosen to wear black silk, a gown that featured spangles and looked sophisticated, while Caroline appeared the perfect innocent.

Maeve felt Huntingdon's eyes upon her, those depthless eyes, which missed nothing. *"She walks in beauty, like the night/Of cloud-*

less climes and starry skies; And all that's best of dark and bright/Meet in her aspect and her eyes."

"You flatter me," she said, not quite meeting his gaze.

"I prefer to think Byron wrote that for you rather than Lady Horton. I daresay he would have done so had he but seen you first." His voice was a silken caress.

"Byron won't be seeing us anymore," Sir John said. "Of course, you must have heard: his wife has left him after only one year of marriage and he's gone off to the continent in a huff."

"Poor fellow, I shouldn't wonder," Huntingdon observed. "He was cut by too many, ostracized by the very society that adored him for so long."

"I love his poetry," Caroline said dreamily. "So romantic. His heroes are dark, handsome and brooding, just like himself."

"The man was scandalous," the Earl of Southford said. "I cannot believe you would idolize such as he, sister."

The earl's look of disapproval brought a defiant rise of Caroline's chin. "I would have been honored to meet such a talented artist."

"Byron's affairs were shocking. Why the fellow flaunted his infidelities. There is not a shred of decency in him."

"Fustian," Huntingdon drawled lazily. "George has style. How many chaps do you know who would drink their wine out of a human skull?"

"Precisely," the earl argued. "He broke all of society's conventions and rules. No sense of propriety. Byron is a shameless profligate."

"The fact is he did nothing that others do not do except that he made the mistake of being too open about it. One can get away with anything if one is discreet." Adam studied his long, well-boned fingers. Maeve couldn't help thinking they were wonderfully shaped. Then she remembered how those very fingers had caressed her flesh and quickly looked away, afraid the rising heat in her face would betray her thoughts.

"Good Lord, Huntingdon, don't talk so in front of the ladies," Southford said. "I understand you libertines will defend one another, but you are shocking my sister and aunt."

"Quite right. Perhaps we should discuss politics instead," Sir John said staunchly.

"And pray, what would you like to discourse? Britain's load of debt, our disordered currency, our slumping markets or rising unemployment?" The marquess's tone was pure mockery.

"Ain't much of interest there, Huntingdon," Sir John observed. "All boring news now that the war's at an end."

"Actually, I believe there is cause for concern. The poor seem more plentiful than ever, and the government hardly concerns itself with their welfare." Maeve knew she should not have spoken even as the words tumbled out. Both Southford and Sir John gave her a scandalized look, while Huntingdon merely smiled in tolerant amusement. Women were not expected to have an interest in current affairs. The fact that Maeve did made her seem unladylike, but then she wasn't considered a lady, was she? So it couldn't matter.

"Point well taken," the marquess said. "The misery of the masses is obvious. My fear is that it will breed violence and insurrection. We've seen it in Ireland. And those demmed Luddites have again taken to smashing machinery in the Midlands. Next there will be rioting in London if we're not careful."

Maeve was impressed with his knowledge and insight. "You appear to be more than a mere dandy, Your Lordship."

"I have always considered it a family responsibility to attend the House of Lords.

Fact is, I've been urged to stand up for the Commons."

"You, Huntingdon? Why I thought your lifestyle would not allow such a thing." The earl looked at the marquess with skepticism.

"If anything, it would be family responsibilities, such as my duties in running our estates, that would stop me. However, I am giving the matter some thought."

He was as serious as she had ever seen him. As if suddenly aware of this and embarrassed by it, he determined to change the mood of the conversation. "And so, when will the mysterious gypsy read my fortune?"

"Oh, that is all the thing, is it not?" Sir John said amiably. "I should like an appointment myself."

"You may come tomorrow if you wish, Sir John," Maeve said quickly.

Huntingdon raised his brow and smiled at her. "I believe I have just been put in my place."

"It was not my intention to give you a set down." She kept her voice devoid of inflection. But she could feel that his hot eyes were still fixed intently upon her.

"Indeed." Huntingdon gave her a small, disbelieving smile.

Why did he make her feel as if she were

standing naked before him?

Southford went on to complain that the laws were not being properly enforced and that sentences for criminals were simply too soft. "All they do is transport these devils nowadays. Bring back mass hangings like we had in the last century, I say! Let the low element see executions as an example. That would end all the nonsense quickly. It's no wonder the Prince Regent is so unpopular. He's much too full of the milk of human kindness and so is the government."

Maeve did not like Southford's thinking. "I believe it is good that our times are far more humane than those of the last century. There were few murders but too many executions in those times. You, Your Lordship, could have been executed for associating with me, since being found in the company of gypsies was a hanging offence."

"A lady of intellect and knowledge. How rare you are, Princess." Adam lifted his glass as if to toast her. But she was certain that he was mocking her.

Her intuition told her that she was not safe. "I believe someone is trying to catch my attention. If you will excuse me."

She quickly moved on to another group of people but soon tired of the frivolous conversation. The *Gorgios,* as her mother referred to non-gypsies, had all sorts of rules of polite behavior that she found to be hypocritical as well as repressive. Mr. Brockton had warned her the *ton* would not be as interesting as she seemed to think. Now she could agree with him.

The time dragged until Charles came for her. She was relieved to see him signal to her from the hallway to the drawing room. Caroline reached Charles before she did. Maeve realized that the girl must have been watching for him too. They exchanged a few words, and it was clear that Caroline was loath to see him leave.

"I'll come around your lodging again tomorrow afternoon, Maeve. Charles, will you be there too?"

"Well, I suppose I could stop by for a little while, but it can't be for long."

"Oh, that's quite all right," Caroline said eagerly.

When they were in their carriage, Maeve turned to Charles. "Caroline is very young and innocent."

"I know that," he responded irritably. "I'm not planning to take advantage of her, if that's what you think."

"No, I never thought that at all. It's just that she seems to have romantic notions about you."

Charles looked out the window moodily and refused to discuss the matter further. She could only wonder what he was feeling about Caroline. This was the first time in all the years she'd known him that Charles had shut her out. One thing was certain. Lady Caroline, young though she might be, knew her own mind and was clearly determined to become involved with Charles. Maeve worried that such a relationship could only bring with it difficulties and ultimately sorrow for both Charles and Caroline.

On the following afternoon, Sir John Simmons called at her lodging. Maeve left the door ajar and gave Ralph orders that he was to remain out in the hall. She was cautious and mistrustful of strangers.

Maeve offered Sir John a reading of the cards, but he seemed to prefer a palm reading instead. She began by studying the fingers and palm of his right hand.

"Can you really tell anything by examining my hand?" he asked.

"The gypsies believe that a strong, long first finger is a sign that the person will have good luck. Each finger and each line on the palm has a meaning." She did not tell him that the length of his lifeline indicated a short life. Taking both his hands in her own, Maeve felt a turbulence, a sensation that Sir John was not actually the pleasant person he outwardly appeared, but someone hiding a violent inner nature. A force was pulling her. This was not what she expected, not at all. She dropped his hand.

"What is it? What's wrong?" He looked as upset as she felt.

"You have killed people."

"Oh, that. Yes, of course I have. Wouldn't be much of a soldier if I hadn't, would I?" He pulled at his neck cloth.

She'd been aware of the battlefield, of fear and death surrounding the man there. "Perhaps that is what it was," she agreed.

Sir John looked at her carefully. "But you sensed something else, did you not? There was a girl once, dark, pretty like you. She was from Portugal. Met her during the Peninsula Campaign. We were very passionate, she and I. Perhaps I might have loved her. I do not know."

"What happened to her?" Maeve asked, fearing that she somehow already knew.

"Why the poor girl died. An accident. Very sad." He gave her an odd smile that unnerved her. "I do like dark women. You are quite a lovely creature."

"I believe you are enamored of Lady Caroline."

"Oh, she would be a perfect wife, but there are other types of relationships between a man and woman. We can have a bit of fun together, you and I." Suddenly, he was grabbing her, pulling her by the chain around her neck. A hand went over her mouth to prevent her crying out. When he inadvertently touched her crystal, it was Sir John who gave an astonished yelp. "Damn this thing, it's burned my hand!" He let her go abruptly.

She sensed another presence in the room. Someone seized the baronet. She was more than a little surprised to see the Marquess of Huntingdon deliver a sharp blow to Simmons's midsection, knocking the wind out of him.

"Are you all right?" he asked, turning to her. She saw genuine concern in his eyes.

"Yes, thank you."

"What is wrong with you, Huntingdon? We were just about to have a bit of amusement!" Simmons's round face was red as an apple.

"I believe you were leaving, Simmons. Oh, and don't forget to pay the lady what's owed, although I have a doubt you could ever really do that."

The baronet left in a fury. She found herself trembling. Adam's arms came tightly around her, pressing her face against his hard, muscular chest. One hand stroked her hair.

"You can let me go," she told him. "I am quite all right now."

"Certainly." But he didn't let her go right away; he just kept holding her against him with his strong hands, and she felt oddly consoled and terribly comfortable, as if this were quite natural and she would like to remain in his arms for eternity.

Yet she realized this was a foolish notion even as she thought it, and she struggled to free herself from his arms. She looked up into the face of the marquess, who stared down at her with concern.

"Really, I am all right," she told him. "It was just a bit of a scare."

"Foolish woman, how is it you allow yourself to spend time alone with a man unchaperoned? I see you give no regard to your reputation. But does your protector have no concern for your safety?" His eyes narrowed and glittered.

How dare he be angry with her! "Ralph was nearby. Sir John merely surprised me, prevented me from calling out." Why should she have to defend herself from his verbal assault?

"Next time, keep a maid with you. I presume you have one?"

She was surprised by the vehemence of his anger. "Many, as a matter of fact. But when I talk with a client, it presumes a certain amount of discretion and privacy. People do say things that might prove embarrassing. And what are you doing here?"

"I wondered what Simmons was up to, and it appears I had cause for concern. Like you, I observe people and seek to understand their motives." He looked so very handsome that it was hard to remain out of countenance with him.

"I suppose you meant well enough. Thank you again."

"Pray, do not over-concern yourself with graciousness." His manner was infuriating. "If you'll allow me to say so, this business venture of yours is not a good one."

She was angry with him again. He had no right to presume to know what was best for her. "I need the freedom to try, even if I fail." Why did she feel the need to explain herself to him?

Maeve was relieved to hear Charles's familiar knock at the door. She called out to him to enter.

"Glad you are here, Le Brun. I have a matter to discuss with you regarding Maeve's well-being."

She quickly touched the marquess's arm. "Please don't. I am fine and quite able to handle my own affairs."

"I am not at all convinced of that." The marquess frowned deeply.

"Has she been helping the Runners again? It's getting to be too much, Maeve."

Not Charles, too! Both of them were acting as if she were a small child in need of protection.

"Bow Street Runners?" Huntingdon asked with curiosity, an expressive brow lifting.

"I help them with their cases occasionally. It is nothing."

"Maeve has the gift of second sight," Charles said with some pride.

Huntingdon viewed her with skepticism. "I've always considered that sort of thing nonsense."

She did not bother to acknowledge his remark. Let him believe as he wished.

"Le Brun, I am concerned that Maeve is alone when she deals with her clients. I refer to the males of the species particularly. There are those who are not the gentlemen they may claim to be. They may, in fact, seek to take advantage of her vulnerability."

"By God, did some bastard try to lay hands on you? Just tell me who he is, and he'll be picking up his teeth." Charles clenched his fists.

Maeve met Charles's temper with an air of calm. "Lord Huntingdon, Charles has taught me principles of self-protection. It is something he does for all of our girls, in fact. So you see, I don't need help from either of you. I can take excellent care of myself."

"As you did today?" Huntingdon asked pointedly.

She stiffened. "That was unusual. Besides, I am no concern of yours." Their eyes confronted each other; she would not look away, but neither would he. "Sir John's behavior was unexpected. I will take better precautions in the future." She turned to Charles. "Perhaps I had best warn Caroline about that man." What she did not say was that she intuitively knew the man was guilty of murder and capable of murdering again.

Without any concrete evidence, the marquess would certainly think her mad if she made the accusation. He already viewed her abilities in a dubious light. Charles, with his volatile temper, might easily decide to beat the man viciously. She did not want Charles in trouble on her account. She vowed to handle the matter in her own way.

Her thoughts were interrupted by the arrival of Caroline, who rushed excitedly into the room much like a storm hitting the seacoast.

"Maeve, the most dreadful thing has happened, just what I most feared. The duke has formally asked James to be allowed to pay his addresses to me. James has most eagerly agreed. He and I had the most horrid quarrel over it. I cannot bear it!" Caroline took a moment to catch her breath.

Distraught, Caroline had not looked around the room until now. Catching sight of the marquess standing off by himself near the window, Caroline let out a gasp. "Oh, goodness, I did not know *you* were here."

"Apparently not." The marquess faced her squarely. "My dear girl, you are quite forgiven for being out of countenance. Consider that I am not your enemy. I am persuaded that we often do not know what is best for us. On that score, experience is the wisest teacher. I shall leave you to converse privately with your friends, although I confess to being an interested party." Huntingdon spoke in a dispassionate manner, all cool nonchalance; then he quickly departed with a final, lingering look at Maeve.

When he was gone, Maeve felt oddly empty and let down; the feeling confused her. She should have felt relief, but that was clearly not her emotion. She turned back to Caroline in an effort to put the man completely out of her mind.

"What can I do to help you?" she asked.

Caroline sat down wearily on a chair and wrung her hands. "I am not certain. I just needed to talk to someone other than my aunt. She is a wonderful person, but James quite intimidates her. He said awful things today. He told me that he was out of pocket for my Season. I must marry and marry well. He believes I owe it to him. A matter of family loyalty."

"Perhaps this is just the earl's way of pressuring you into what he considers a good match."

Caroline shook her head desolately. "No, he says there are debts. Not his, to be sure. However, it would seem that our father and brother were profligate in their spending. According to James, they bled the estates dry so that they might continue their gambling habits. Everything is heavily mortgaged."

Charles took Caroline's hand and patted it in a comforting gesture, his expression grave. "The reason the earl thought he recognized me was because I had come to him to collect on gambling debts. Your father played deep and usually lost. And your brother who was earl after him was often in his cups and would bet on anything."

Caroline held fiercely to Charles. "I often wondered why our household allowance was so meager. Sometimes we were forgotten about entirely. Aunt Amelia had to write and request funds. We were very frugal and always supplemented our diet by planting our own garden. We even made most of our own clothing. Besides my governess, our only servants were a housekeeper/cook and general groundsman. I'm afraid they stayed with us only out of loyalty, since we could not always properly pay them. So you see, I am not in need of a rich husband. I have not been spoilt as James seems to think." Caroline looked worriedly into Charles's eyes. "Oh, what am I to do?"

Maeve remembered Huntingdon's fat purse. She would have liked to claim it. There was a very worthy cause to put that coin toward, but Maeve could not bring herself to encourage Caroline's acceptance of the duke, not even to further her own charitable work or to please the marquess.

"There is a ball tonight that everyone will attend," Maeve said with slow deliberation. "Perhaps if you make your feelings known to the duke, the matter will be ended once and for all."

"If I do, I am afraid James will beat me."

Maeve saw genuine fear in the girl's face.

"Has he threatened you?" Charles balled his large hands into fists; a muscle worked in his angular jaw.

Caroline lowered her eyes. "James said if I did not obey him, I would pay the price. He has a monstrous temper."

"Then the duke must be made to cry off without you taking the blame," Maeve said.

"I have a better solution," Charles said. "I'll deal with Southford." There was a chilling grimness in his manner.

Maeve shook her head. "No, you would end up before the magistrate. I won't have it. I'll talk with Huntingdon. Perhaps, he may get the duke to be reasonable."

"There is another way, a better, surer one," Caroline said. Her countenance brightened. She stared at Charles hopefully. "Would you consider — what I mean is, well, I do like you awfully much. I believe we could be very happy together. I should make a good wife. What I mean, Charles, is that I would like it very much if you would marry me."

Charles stared at Caroline in shocked amazement. "I must be touched in my wits. I thought I heard you propose to me."

"And so I did!"

He ran his fingers through his dark, curly hair. "Total madness! You're all of, what — seventeen? It wouldn't even be legal without your guardian's consent, and you're not bloody likely to get that, my girl."

Caroline gave him a sunny smile. "Precisely what I think as well. That's why we must elope to Gretna Green. My age will not matter when we are over the border in Scotland. Oh, it would be so romantic. Why we could leave today."

Charles stared at her incredulously. "I thought you different, but you're not. Another typically irresponsible aristo. You want to use me to escape. What you want is all that really matters, ain't it? No doubt you plan to leave a letter behind for your brother so he will follow us. He catches up with us and horsewhips me, and you get your way about not marrying Rundwall. But think again. Who will want to marry you if such a scandal got out?"

Caroline's eyes filled with tears and her lower lips trembled. "Do you think so badly of me?"

"I don't believe you really care for me. You don't even know me. I believe you're a silly, selfish chit." He folded his muscular arms stiffly over his chest.

"Not care for you? How little you know *me!*" Caroline ran sobbing from the room.

Maeve stopped Charles from going after Caroline. "Do not talk to her again until your anger cools. You have hurt her and done her an injustice."

"How could I marry an aristo, Maeve?"

"If you and she love each other, then that should not be an impediment."

"We've known each other such a short time."

"With love, it is not always a question of time."

"You women with your foolish romantic notions! You know nothing of the real world."

Maeve found Caroline weeping in front of her building. She put her arm around the younger girl in a gesture of comfort.

"I humiliated myself," Caroline said. "And now Charles hates me."

"Ridiculous. Charles is very taken with you. But men like to feel they are in charge. You took him by surprise. Give him a chance to think the matter through." She looked around to make certain no one was standing near them. "I believe there is something you should know about Charles. He is a bastard by birth. His mother was an émigré, a woman of high rank, who left France just ahead of the Revolution. Her parents were not so fortunate. She found herself penniless and took a position as a seamstress. An aristocrat saw her one day as he brought his current mistress to fit a gown. He was very taken with Mathilde Le Brun and sought to win her affections. The story is an old one, I suppose. Mathilde became the man's mistress. When it was evident that she was with child, he lost interest in her. Mathilde was crushed. Another man soon loved her and took care of her and her son, but she was never the same. Charles remains bitter to this day toward the nobility."

"Poor Charles," Caroline said with a deep sigh.

"There is something even worse."

Caroline's eyes opened wide as the ocean.

"You see, Charles's father is the Duke of Rundwall."

Caroline clasped her hands together and gasped in surprise. "Then I have brought Charles further pain. But I should never have guessed the two were related."

"Charles favors his mother, with the same

olive skin and dark hair, but the eyes, they are as the duke's. Do not despair of Charles," Maeve said gently. "He appears hard outwardly, but his heart is good and gentle. Give him some time. I believe his affection for you is genuine."

The large azure eyes filled once again. "I am afraid the one thing I do not have is time."

"Tonight at the ball, I will talk to the marquess and explain matters. I believe he may prevail with the duke and make his Grace listen to reason. If the duke withdraws, the earl cannot blame you. And there will be other bachelors tonight. Perhaps you will meet just the right one for you."

"No, I want Charles and no other." Caroline appeared very certain. "My suggestion of elopement was not so thoughtless as Charles believes. Thank you for helping me, Maeve. I do appreciate your kindness. Whatever happens, I will remember that I have made one good, generous, true friend in London."

Maeve had Ralph find an appropriate hackney coach for Caroline. Maeve could not help but worry about the girl. Was Caroline a headstrong child destined for ruin? Her instincts told her that was not the case. Caroline might be young and inexperienced, but she had clearly left her childhood behind her.

How was Maeve to win Huntingdon's support? And what might he expect of her in return? Maeve was plagued by uncertainty. But she touched the crystal at her throat and felt its restorative warmth suffuse her with strength. Maeve knew that her mother's spirit was with her. It was a great comfort. She would find a way to help Caroline. The girl had called her a true friend and Maeve had every intention of being one. Maeve bit down thoughtfully on her lower lip. Life was fraught with difficulties.

CHAPTER SIX

They met in a place of frivolity and fun, but neither of them was laughing nor so much as smiling. Why did she not flirt and giggle as the other women did? Why was she so solemn when everyone knew gypsies were frolicsome creatures? But she was never what one expected. And that, of course, was why she so fascinated him. His eyes ensnared hers the moment she entered the ballroom. He was drawn to her as if she were a lodestone. He wanted to go to her immediately, but was certain she would see this as a sign of weakness on his part. There was no point in letting her think that he valued her so highly. Self-control was always best.

"Well, Huntingdon, I see Princess de Lieven's ball has drawn you hither. Never thought to see you at one of these Russian Embassy affairs, though it promises to be one of the outstanding events of the Season.

Lud knows, the woman's proved a genius of invention in the past. Her parties sate the most jaded of appetites." Lord Howard Randall studied him with interest.

Adam shrugged indifferently.

"Wife hunting?" Lord Randall gave him a wink.

"I've not reached that auspicious moment yet."

"Glad to hear it." The younger son of the Earl of Caulbridge removed a small silver snuff box from his jacket pocket, expertly took a pinch, and sniffed deeply. "Wellington complained t'other night about you."

"Odso? And what have I done to offend that worthy?"

"We were at Harriette Wilson's salon and old Arthur up and says 'By Gawd, where's that coxcomb Huntingdon? Haven't seen him since my return from Cambrai. Miss that deuced wit and drollery.' The ladies heaved great sighs of agreement. Have you given up on demi-mondaines, old man?"

"Hardly that."

"Unfortunate, you've spoilt every high-class doxy for the rest of us."

"It's not my person that is in demand so much as my well-filled purse."

"Courtesans like Harriette and her friends are all the best. One may buy love without responsibility."

"Love is but a euphemism for what Harriette provides."

Lord Howard snorted indelicately, sounding very like the horses he loved to race; unfortunately, Adam observed, although Howard's face did have a horsy look, it was not so handsome as any of his thoroughbreds.

"Why are you here, Huntingdon?"

"Rundwall is shopping the marriage mart and feels in need of moral support."

"As I recall, there's nothing particularly moral about that roué."

Huntingdon allowed himself a look of displeasure at his dandified friend. "Were you not such a rattle, Howard, I might take exception and call you out for assassinating the character of my cousin."

Lord Randall eyed Huntingdon nervously. "Said in jest only, old chap. Would I insult the cousin of such an august marksman? I'm guilty of many things, but being a fool isn't one of them."

Huntingdon nodded his head imperceptibly.

"That gorgeous gypsy is casting glances in this direction. I do believe she is watching your every move. You sly dog, have you begun a liaison with her?"

"Not I. Perhaps it is you she is looking at."

"Not bloody likely, Huntingdon. I would offer her *carte blanche* if I thought she would accept, but she hasn't moon-eyed any man present. Haven't you noticed? I venture she's someone's fancy piece though. He probably set the whole thing up for a lark. It must amuse him vastly to watch who gives her a try and fails. All manner of decadent voyeurs among our ranks. A clever game, I own."

Lord Howard's words brought a visceral reaction. What if his friend was correct? Then again why should he care? But he found that he did. To hell with Howard, who had been a clown at Eton and was demonstrating that he still had silly notions! Besides, he would know all about Maeve soon enough when Pritchard made contact with him again. And then he would set about eliminating his competition. Adam found that he was impatient with anticipation.

"I say, Huntingdon, where did you get that superb waistcoat? Weston's I expect. As always, you are in the first stare of fashion."

"I would prefer to leave that distinction to the ladies, old man."

They chatted inconsequentially for a time

and then the music began. Lord Howard moved on to try his luck with one of the debutantes. Adam wondered why he hadn't felt much like visiting Harriette's establishment of late, but when he looked across at Maeve, all thoughts of other women left him. He desired only her. His self-control had kept him resolute long enough. Her steadfast gaze was fixed on him as he moved toward her, and he saw no one else.

Vaguely, he observed how well the rose color of her gown set off the dark wine of her complexion. He thought her a full-blooded beauty like no other and felt himself captivated as if by witchcraft. Had she cast some sort of spell on him?

"You should wear bright, red roses in your hair," he said. It took Herculean effort not to touch her.

"I doubt I would find any that exactly matched my gown."

"Who said anything about you wearing a gown?"

Her color deepened. "My lord is a randy goat."

"Indeed, I hope so. One could not look on such beauty and not be moved."

"Let us talk of serious matters."

"I can think of nothing more significant." He took her hand. "Do you wish to dance?"

"It is warm in here."

"The princess has several marquees set up on the grounds for dancing."

"Perhaps we may just walk together and hold a polite conversation."

He took her arm and they went out into the open air. Small lamps marked the walks and the night was warm, but a gentle breeze was blowing.

"The gardens here are impressive," Huntingdon said. "The Princess has spread out refreshments in the hothouses. If you wish anything, please say."

Maeve shook her head. "No, I came this evening really to speak with you."

"The evening has already improved. I am flattered. But surely you will stay? Prinny intends to come. He and Princess de Lieven are close friends."

"Is the prince regent out in society a great deal?"

Adam looked into the large doe-shaped eyes and had to force back the desire to kiss them. "The fearful old rip doesn't go out as much as he used to. Last I saw he was weeping in a maudlin manner to Lady Conyngham. He's taking it hard that Princess Charlotte won't marry his choice of husbands."

"One cannot help but admire his daughter's courage, do you not think?" She was challenging him again; that was clear as window glass.

"I think the young princess quite obstinate and not at all a dutiful child. But we are not actually talking about her, are we?"

"No. You are perceptive as always. I will be blunt. Lady Caroline does not wish to marry your cousin, as you know. You have asked me to use my influence, such as it is, to convince Caroline otherwise. I find in all conscience, I cannot do as you ask. I would return your gold."

"Keep it as one would keep a trifling bauble." They were by themselves for the moment, and he wanted to take advantage of the situation. He touched her cheek with the palm of his hand, then pulled her toward him to steal one brief kiss from her full, sensual lips. "I should like to give you a great deal."

The kiss overwhelmed him. He felt as if a volcano had erupted in his veins. One taste of her would never be enough.

But she pulled back from him. "Lady Caroline really will not have the duke. Perhaps if you could convince him that she is not suitable, then he would end his suit." Her voice sounded breathy, and he realized she was not unaffected by their brief intimacy.

Adam dropped Maeve's hand. "Rundwall wants Lady Caroline very much. He's even told Southford he expects no dowry."

"He knows of the earl's straightened circumstances?"

"Gossip is the *ton*'s most indubitable hobbyhorse. Without a substantial dowry, Lady Caroline cannot marry well. The duke does the foolish twit quite an honor. Rundwall is also prepared to pay all wedding costs and provide Southford with substantial, generous loans to set him financially aright."

"And the earl is more than willing to sell his sister."

"He is eager to arrange the match. Not all marriages are of the romantic variety that you ladies so delight reading about in the novels of Mrs. Meake or Mrs. Radcliffe."

"How coldly unaffected you are," she said, her voice edged with anger. "Without affection or attraction, no match is suitable."

He sighed dispassionately, striving to keep his own temper cool. "Rundwall is quite a good fellow. Can you not make the girl see how fortunate she is? It would be an excellent alliance for her. He desires to indulge her. Surely, if the girl has any sense at all, she can be moved."

Maeve thought of her last conversation with Caroline and the girl's desperate proposal to Charles. Perhaps Caroline's behavior would not seem logical to the marquess, but her feelings should not be ignored.

"You think with your head not your heart. There are those of us who find wisdom in what the heart tells us. I regret that we must remain opposites in opinion on this matter."

He brushed his hand against her cheek once more with a gesture of longing and kissed her forehead ever so gently. "We will speak soon again, I assure you. I am not without feeling, not where you are concerned." When he smiled, his face changed; he became less aloof and severe, almost boyishly handsome, in fact. It was an appealing transmutation, like an alchemist turning lead into gold. She studied him with fascination.

He must have sensed what she was thinking, because he drew her close to him again. His thumbs skimmed the sensitive bare skin just above the bodice of her gown. Then he held her against him and began kissing her throat. She tried not to moan. But something stirred within her, something hot and needy. Then his lips joined with hers and she melted. He tasted of tobacco, port wine and exciting masculinity. Liquid fire roared through her veins. Her lower body felt heavy, where molten lead was being transformed into pure, precious gold. His mouth was soft and hard at once, ruthlessly plundering her own. His tongue joined with hers as his hands caressed her breasts. She nearly cried out from the pleasure of the aching passion he was rousing in her. But then there were voices. Others were approaching through the darkness.

"I must apologize," he said, his voice thick.

She could scarcely manage to speak at all. Dazedly, Maeve discovered Adam had walked her back toward the ballroom. Inside, all was bright and gay. But sadness weighed upon her heart; his leave-taking made her feel as if she had sustained an immeasurable loss. She chided herself for a fool. The man was nothing but a jaded rake. Therefore, nothing good could ever come of an association with such as he. She knew this. But why then did her body so easily respond to him?

This was the last ball she wished to attend. Perhaps she amused these people, but they did not amuse her. She was tired of being viewed like a two-headed freak at a carnival.

The Duchess of Pemworth joined her along with other notables, several ladies deemed bluestockings who were also known to dabble in the occult. One theory or another regarding the supernatural was discussed. The time seemed to drag on. And Maeve was well aware that the marquess was staring at her with disconcerting directness from across the room. His gaze made her blood run hot and cold all at once.

"Is it true, my dear, that you know secrets of the healing arts?" the duchess asked her.

"Like all gypsy girls, I was taught by my mother, who was taught by her mother, a renowned healer among her people."

"I collect being told that you were an orphan from a tender age." All of the duchess's chins bobbed as she spoke.

"My mother taught me everything she could about herbal remedies before she died. Even now, her spirit comes and guides me when I most need help."

This caused something of a surprised stir and murmur among the other ladies.

"How very extraordinary. You mean to say that you can consult the ghost of your mother when you wish?"

"Not exactly. Her spirit is not yet at peace. And we are also connected through this." Maeve pointed to the milky crystal she wore. "It was part of a larger piece that belonged to her."

Eyes opened wide, staring in curiosity.

"I have had trouble in digestion for some weeks. I find I can hardly eat a thing," the duchess said. "What would you suggest?"

It was all Maeve could do to keep from saying that the duchess should be more moderate in her appetites. Instead, she responded politely. "The Romanies simmer the leaves of wild carrot and drink a little of the water for stomach troubles. I myself find that sprinkling ground ginger into one's cooked food is also of benefit."

"Famous," the duchess said. "After I have sampled the Princess de Lieven's delicacies tonight, I shall have my cook prepare your carrot drink with ginger."

"What about pain in the joints?" another elderly lady asked.

"Crush the seeds and leaves of burdock and place them on the painful part of the body."

"Rest assured, you shall have many new clients," the duchess said, patting her condescendingly on the head as if she were a favored pet lap dog.

By midnight, she was waiting impatiently for Charles to come for her. Maeve noticed Caroline dancing with Rundwall and that the girl was talking to him in an earnest manner. The next time she had occasion to observe them, the duke was escorting Caroline out to the embassy grounds. At that moment, Maeve had the awful feeling that all was not well, that something terrible was about to happen to Caroline. Her fingers absently went to her crystal which felt hot to the touch. She knew then that her premonition was true.

Charles made his way around the throng of dancers and came toward her.

"I am relieved you have come. As Rundwall walked Caroline out to the gardens, I had an intuition that some harm would befall her. I believe we must find her."

"Where is she?" Charles seemed genuinely concerned.

Maeve took his arm, closed her eyes and concentrated. She could see it clearly: there was a gazebo in the center of a maze. "I believe I can find her," she said.

Charles held her arm as she led him from the ballroom into the gardens. She needed his support to move safely forward because Maeve's mind was now with Caroline in the gazebo. Locked inside the vision, she held Charles's hand securely in her own and guided him to a high wall of shrubs that signaled a labyrinth. Inexorably, they moved through the bewildering maze, Maeve knowing the way with unerring comprehension. She could hear Caroline cry out and see the duke laying his hands on her slender young body.

"Oh, let us hurry!" They must not be too late to stop what she knew was happening.

And then they were in the center of the maze running toward the gazebo and Caroline's strangled screams were no longer part of a vision but reality. Charles ran forward and forcefully thrust the duke from Caroline.

"By God, if you've violated her, I'll kill you!"

Caroline's gown was torn, her hair loose; she sobbed uncontrollably. Maeve hurriedly took the girl into her arms and held her. Soon she was stroking Caroline's back in a gesture of comfort as a mother would an injured child.

The duke backed away from what he clearly feared was a madman. "It is just a lover's quarrel, a misunderstanding between myself and my betrothed. Please be on your way and do not interfere. You are not needed or wanted."

"Defiler of innocence!" Charles accused. Maeve had never seen Charles so enraged. His face, even in the dim light, appeared a mottled purple. He raised his fist toward

Rundwall but was quickly staid by arms equally as strong as his own.

"Le Brun, you will not touch his grace." Huntingdon's deep, rich baritone was commanding and powerful, the sort of voice other men obeyed without question.

Charles drew back, but he still shook with fury. "Do you have any idea what he tried to do?" Charles's outrage and indignation were not to be denied.

"I am certain his grace was carried away by passion and did not in the least mean to harm or upset Lady Caroline."

"The bastard tried to rape her!"

"His grace is ever the gentleman."

"How can you defend him that way?" Maeve asked incredulously.

"You do not know the circumstances. You condemn without knowledge. Your prejudice rules over reason." His eyes were cold and remote. Certainly he was not the romantic lover she had so recently known.

"Prejudice? That is your flaw, not mine." She was furious with him. They faced each other antagonistically, fire and ice.

Maeve only came to Huntingdon's shoulder; however, she was not in the least intimidated by his size. She was much too enraged.

"Charles and I will take Caroline home.

As you see, she is in no condition to return to the ball. Please make our apologies to the earl. Tell him what you wish. Perhaps that Caroline has the headache."

Caroline clung to Maeve pitiably, pulling together the bodice of her gown and rising unsteadily to her feet. She turned hot, accusing eyes on the duke, who had shrunk into a far corner of the gazebo.

"How could you attack me like that?" She choked back her sobs, her words barely coherent.

"My sweeting, I implore you to understand. I merely intended to make you see that you care for me as I do for you. Had I compromised your virtue, it would only have been for your own good. You would have been forced to accept me then, and I have every intention of honorably marrying you."

"You would ruin me?"

"On my honor, that was not my intent. Huntingdon knows it to be so."

Maeve looked from the duke to the marquess, eyes opening wide. Had Huntingdon known what the duke planned? Had he been a party to it? The thought brought her palpable pain, as if a knife thrust deep into a vital organ. Why hadn't she seen him for what he was, self-centered and arrogant?

Instead, she allowed physical attraction to cloud her good judgment.

Caroline moved to Charles and took his arm. "This is the man I wish to marry. This is Charles and he is exceptional. High time you knew him, knew who he is."

Maeve was horrified, for she realized that Caroline was about to tell Rundwall that he was Charles's father. She could not allow it. A terrible mistake to tell Caroline about Charles. The matter was one of the utmost privacy. Charles did not want his parentage made public knowledge. Most of all, he did not want the duke to know of their relationship. Just as she was about to stop Caroline from continuing, the duke interrupted.

"Don't be such a peahen, girl. You wish a misalliance with a common footman? You must realize what a silly romantic notion that is."

"But you are so wrong . . ."

"Caroline, no more! We must be going." With that, Maeve abruptly steered Caroline away. With Charles leading the way, they walked around the side of the mansion to where their carriage waited. Charles gallantly covered Caroline with his jacket.

"I should have throttled him," Charles said as the carriage began to move. He was shaking with outrage.

"You saved me," Caroline said. "You are ever my champion." She pulled his dark jacket tightly around her. "The duke lured me into the garden by informing me that he had known my mother. He said that he could tell me all about her. I was such a fool."

"Damn him! I'll take you both home and then I'm going back." He looked ready to commit murder.

"No, you won't," Maeve said in a firm voice. "Besides, the prince regent will soon arrive, and they will be very careful about who is allowed to enter after that."

"Very well, I expect Rundwall and I will have another time of reckoning."

"Perhaps, but not tonight."

"No, I do not wish it," Caroline assured Charles.

He took Caroline's hands, rolled down her gloves, and tenderly kissed each palm.

Adam handed his cousin a snifter of brandy. Rundwall did not look well; his hand trembled and the liquor sloshed out of the glass and onto the Aubusson carpet in his study.

"I must have her. I will not have another." Rundwall took a swallow of brandy.

"Let the girl have Le Brun. *If of herself*

she will not give, the devil take her."

"Trust you to quote a cavalier. You do not value any woman overmuch."

"I learned well at my mother's knee what to expect from the fair sex." He smiled sardonically and lit a cheroot.

"More's the pity."

"On the contrary. What happened to my father will never happen to me."

"I need your help. You could find a way for me."

"I am not certain I like the sound of that."

"Your father received my help, now I would ask you for yours."

"My best advice is to forget the silly chit."

"No, she is the one I want. I cannot let her throw herself away on a fortune hunter."

"Le Brun is a young hothead but no mercenary. Besides, there is no money. The girl is not an heiress. No, they believe themselves in love, God help them."

"We must deal with the lad. I have been thinking. I have devised a plan I want you to implement."

Adam did not like the grim expression on Rundwall's face. "I do not wish to be involved in any dishonorable scheme, and I would advise you to reconsider, cousin."

"You did worse in the war, I am certain."

"An entirely different situation. Le Brun

is not Napoleon. Forget what you plan."

"Let me explain it to you."

Adam rose to his feet. "I will help you in any reasonable way, but this is not proper, not to my liking. Frankly, though I defended you, I was ashamed of your behavior tonight."

The duke viewed his disdain with surprise. "A rake such as you prosing at me?"

"I do not deflower innocent virgins."

"Someday perhaps when you are older, my boy, you will understand the dire need that possesses me."

Adam merely shook his head, unclear as to Rundwall's motives. The behavior of Richard puzzled him. It was so unlike the duke. He left his cousin and could only hope that Richard would act sensibly hereafter, but he was far from certain. His mind returned to Maeve. He had wanted very badly to make love to her tonight, and all he managed was to secure her enmity. However, there was tomorrow, and he determined that it would be different.

CHAPTER SEVEN

Maeve received a note from Caroline the following day. She had just arrived at the lodging house when a liveried footman appeared. He stood at attention, waiting for a reply. Maeve examined the letter.

Caroline wrote of something extraordinary happening and that she had sent the coach in hopes that Maeve would come to her house. Could Maeve please come at once?

Maeve wondered at Caroline's cheerful assertive tone in the missive. Perhaps Caroline was a trifle self-centered, but that was understandable. Until recently, Caroline's world had been a small, simple one, and she had always been at the direct center of it. Maeve's own experience of life had been very different.

That fateful night when Maeve ran away from the orphanage, she had hoped to find her mother's people. But she was weak from illness and hunger; too soon her mind had become clouded with fever. She was fortunate to have survived. Now she was bound, locked in by loyalty, duty and honor to serve the needs of others.

Caroline was waiting impatiently for her when Maeve entered the drawing room of the Southford townhouse. The room was dark with no suggestion of elegance. In fact, the furnishings looked shabby, as if redecorating had been postponed indefinitely.

"I have the most wonderful news and I want to share it with you." Caroline seemed miraculously recovered from her ordeal of the previous night. There was a light in her eyes, a spring to her walk, and her complexion glowed.

"I daresay you will never guess. A gentleman arrived to see me today, not one of those boring fops from the ball, but a man who has come all the way from Italy. What do you think of that?"

"What should I think?"

"Consider: who would I know in Italy? Why, no one of course! So I sent Burgess, our butler, back to the hall to inquire further. The gentleman, a Mister Frederick Layton, said he wanted to see me on a most delicate and personal matter that concerned my mother."

"Did he explain?"

"Yes. I spoke with him at length in the library where he remains now. A pity Aunt Amelia had already left for her card playing. But I knew you would be interested." Caroline took her hand with an excitement that was barely contained. "I also wish you to ascertain whether or not the gentleman tells the truth. I would trust only you to verify his words."

Caroline then led her to the library. The girl was too distracted to make anything but perfunctory introductions. Mr. Layton rose to greet them. He was a trim, unpretentious man with carrot red hair, although traces of white showed at the temples. His face was pleasantly lined, smile marks crinkling the firm mouth and clear eyes.

"Sir, would you be so kind as to tell my friend what you have told me?"

They sat down on aged, uncomfortable chairs that creaked under their weight and then faced each other. Mr. Layton looked from Caroline to Maeve.

"I told Lady Caroline that I was sent by her mother to find her. I brought a letter from Lady Elizabeth, which she has read. It explains why Lady Caroline was told that her mother was dead." Mr. Layton cleared his throat nervously. "You see, Elizabeth and

I loved each other from childhood. We lived on neighboring properties. But Elizabeth's parents considered that I was unworthy of her because I was but the third son of a baron and stood to gain no great fortune or title. Older though he was, the Earl of Southford was her parents' choice. They thought him good marriage material, but he was not. Elizabeth dutifully married the wretch, only to be abused. She was his second wife, and he cared little for her. He was often drunk and beat her for sport."

"My poor mother," Caroline whispered.

"Indeed. I do not wish to overset your sensibilities, only to have you understand why Elizabeth could not remain in that intolerable situation. You were but an infant and we had every intention of taking you with us. Unfortunately, our plan was discovered. Caroline's maid overheard our conversation and reported back to Southford. Needless to say, he was furious. He told Elizabeth to get out, but he would not relinquish you. He said that we were free to leave the country. However, he would not be publicly held up to ridicule. I believe his behavior was a matter of revenge. He concocted the story that your mother was dead. He swore if she returned, her family would be told that she was an unfaithful whore, and you would grow up with the stigma and shame of having it known that your mother cuckolded your father. Let me assure you that it was nothing of the sort. The man was a swine. But Elizabeth's parents would not have understood or accepted her back.

"When we found out that your father was dead, we tried contacting the present earl. Your brother vehemently refused any connection. He wrote that you did not know of your mother's existence, and he would make certain you never did."

"I have always wanted to know about my mother. James is well aware of that." Caroline's eyes were brimming with tears and Maeve patted her hand in a gesture of comfort.

"We want to know you, too. I am not especially rich, but we have a comfortable life. You have a brother and two sisters whom you have never met, and your mother thinks of you always. If you will come to Italy, I am able to pay your expenses. Your mother and I are now legally married, so there can be no moral objections from anyone."

"Yes, I would like to go to Italy. James lied to me, as did my father. James expects me to marry a man I detest. I very much want to go to Italy to meet my mother." Caroline turned to Maeve. "But what do you think, dear friend?"

Mr. Layton struck Maeve as being honest. It also seemed quite clear to her now as to why she had been unable to contact the spirit of Caroline's mother. The woman was not dead. But just to be certain, Maeve walked over to the man and held his hands tightly in her own. Then she looked deeply into his eyes. A positive energy force emanated from him. No, there was little doubt that he was telling the truth.

"I believe him."

"Then I intend to go. There is nothing but pain for me here. But, Maeve, please tell Charles that I truly care about him. I do not want him to believe that I am flighty in my affections toward him. Nothing could be farther from the truth. And he has been so good to me, even if he cannot love me." She let out a deep, sad sigh.

"I am not convinced that Charles lacks affection for you, Caroline. Do not despair of him so easily," Maeve said.

"If only that were so," Caroline said, new hope causing her eyes to beam.

Maeve visited for nearly another hour, and then the Southford coach returned her to the lodging house. She expected to see some clients from the contacts she had made at the ball. The duchess had fulfilled her promise.

How would Charles react to Caroline's news? She could only wonder. She could not speak for him, and so it was wise for her to remain silent. It was not her place to interfere in their lives.

Adam's conference with Pritchard was held in the privacy of his study, a small room in which he kept his escritoire and often lounged comfortably on leather chairs. The ducal townhouse was a large mansion with many servants and little privacy. This room suited his personal needs better than any other.

"What have you discovered?" he asked the balding, diminutive man.

Pritchard cleared his throat. "Wasn't as easy as it might seem to gather information on the young lady, Your Lordship. Had to be quite generous with the blunt, if you get my meaning."

"I shall be happy to reimburse any additional expenses incurred. Now get on with it, man." He found himself becoming impatient.

"Well, Miss Maeve lives with none other than William Brockford, the fellow who runs the queen of gambling clubs. Prince Regent himself favors the place and is partial to Brockford. Needless to say, they live very well."

Adam recalled Brockford but could hardly put the man together with Maeve. By any standards, he was homely and common and far from young. Still, he was wealthy and could buy what he wanted. "How long has she lived with him?"

"Quite some time. Here's an odd bit. The house is loaded with pretty young girls."

"Are you telling me Brockton runs a brothel as well as a gaming club?"

"Miss Maeve chooses the girls."

Adam felt suddenly ill. A whore and a madam. Could it really be? Was Maeve nothing more than a jade? How could he be so wrong in his assessment? "So she is not just his mistress as I thought."

"Oh, as to that, I wouldn't know. The girls are all trained as domestics."

"What?" He stared at Pritchard without comprehension.

"Seems Miss Maeve selects the girls from an orphanage and brings them to Brockton's home where they're trained for service. As one is placed, another is brought in."

"So then it is something of a school that she runs." He breathed a deep sigh of relief.

"Seems so, your Lordship, though I

couldn't say for certain. The girl our man talked with couldn't speak highly enough 'bout Miss Maeve. It seems she's very well liked and respected." Pritchard ripped at a hangnail. "That Le Brun fellow you asked about lives at the house too. They've all got separate bedrooms, though I don't know that means anything, if you take my meaning. Anyway, Miss Maeve is definitely mistress of the house. As to Miss Maeve's past, there wasn't much I could find out. She keeps her business private. Maintained a low profile until recently. Sorry I couldn't discover more. Will that be all for now?"

Adam indicated that it was and told Pritchard he would be in touch. He sat back in his favorite chair and thoughtfully contemplated what he should do. A mistress complicated a man's life, but he wanted Maeve. The fact that she obviously belonged to Brockton did not deter his intent. How to proceed? He drummed his long, elegant fingers thoughtfully.

He would eventually have to approach Brockton. The man was powerful because his friends were of the most influential. He could offer to pay Brockton for her. The matter would require some delicacy. But first he would woo Maeve, make certain she would have him. He could not imagine otherwise; no woman had ever rejected him, but one never knew. Maeve was certainly not conventional. Yet he had felt her passion and knew she was far from indifferent toward him.

A long-necked lady with a receding chin was leaving Maeve's lodging as he came to the door. He'd had to announce himself to the burly footman downstairs, who looked as if he had an excellent knowledge of fisticuffs, but the fellow remembered Adam from his last visit and so there was no problem.

Adam knocked at the door and Maeve called out to come in. Her voice sounded the way fine brandy tasted, warm and smooth. Her look of surprise was duly noted. He studied her for a moment. He could not look at her without admiration. Today she wore a white muslin frock, which gave her a girlish, innocent air. Her glossy black curls were held up in a knot by an ornamental pin. It was all he could do to keep from touching her.

"As Shakespeare said of Cleopatra, you are a woman of infinite variety." He somehow managed to keep his tone of voice nonchalant.

She raised her chin mutinously. "Did you know what the duke was planning to do?"

"How can you think it of me? You cut me to the quick. Of course not. I am persuaded that he is not himself."

"There we disagree. The man is arrogant and self-serving. He does not even consider that others have rights, especially not women."

Her angry expression frustrated him. "I did not come to argue with you. I have provided a peace offering. Will you oblige me by accepting?"

"That depends on the offering." She eyed him suspiciously.

He smiled at her in what he hoped was a disarming manner. "I had a picnic in mind. I thought to take you to the park. The hamper is bulging with good eating. Can I not tempt you?"

Her ebon brow furrowed. "Charles will arrive soon. I am expected at tea time."

"Perhaps neither Charles nor Mr. Brockton will mind overmuch if you leave a message with your footman. I promise not to keep you out late."

She looked at him in alarm. "How did you know about Mr. Brockton? I did not tell you."

"I have my sources of information. You need not be ashamed of your liaison. I assure you I am a man of the world." He saw color flame in her cheeks.

"You really understand nothing."

"That is quite true, and I won't know about you unless you choose to tell me. Otherwise, you will remain a fascinating, mysterious woman of many secrets." Who was Maeve? How he longed to plumb her depths.

"I do not have a maid with me at present."

"Then I must be the perfect gentleman." He studied her thoughtfully. "Besides, I rather thought you cared little about convention."

She was pensive for a moment. "Upon further reflection, I will have that picnic with you," she said. She raised her chin defiantly, which he found rather attractive.

He was not at all certain why she had changed her mind but he was too happy about it to care overmuch.

The park was lovely. Maeve spotted several deer, much to her surprise. One did not expect to see such creatures in London.

"I love the grass and flowers," she said. "It is so peaceful here."

"I would like to take you to a true pleasure garden, Vauxhall or Ranelagh. They have many attractions. You would love the fireworks, I am certain. Of course, you have likely been there already." He lifted a patrician brow inquiringly.

"No, I have not." He appeared to be testing her, playing some sort of game. He must know, just as she did, that such places had unsavory reputations for lewd behavior. She had to remind herself that he thought her a doxy.

He laid out a large hamper replete with cold chicken, strawberries, cherries, crusty bread and wine. Suddenly, she felt terribly hungry.

"We shall eat, walk and enjoy this marvelous day. How does that sound?"

When he smiled as he was doing now, the marquess did not look nearly as sharp. A lovely dimple appeared in his cheek. Strange, but she felt as if she would like to kiss it. Where had such a naughty thought come from?

"I have always liked the outdoors," she said. "And there are such charming walks here."

"We shall explore them in a leisurely manner," he told her. The seductive caress of his deep baritone voice promised much more than an ordinary walk. She pretended not to notice.

He had never looked more strikingly handsome. He stood there in the elegance of starched white linen, loose-fitting shirt without coat or cravat, garbed in black buckskin breeches that clung tightly to the strong muscles of his thighs and calves and shod in Hessians shining like black glass. He was truly magnificent.

She glanced around and realized the location he had chosen for their picnic was quite secluded. She saw no one else in the vicinity.

"It occurs to me that you have chosen a rather isolated place for our picnic. Why are we not near the lake where there are other people?"

He appeared offended by her words. His dark eyes flashed and his mouth turned downward in a frown. "I assure you my intentions are not nefarious. Would you prefer that I took you to the Italian opera so that you may be well displayed to all and sundry upon my arm?"

She shook her head. "I wish you no embarrassment."

"How little you think of me and yourself."

"No, on the contrary. It is you who think little of me." She turned away from him.

"I think very much of you."

Suddenly, he was pulling her into his arms and kissing her. The heat of his body unnerved her. She could smell the clean, manly scent of him as he pressed against her. He rubbed her arms sensually, sending chills down her spine. But his kiss was restrained and she was certain that he was holding back. Then he released her. Maeve realized that she was scarcely breathing.

"I could not help that," he said. "Perhaps we should have our picnic now. Otherwise, I may be forced to indulge in another sort of feast."

She couldn't tell if he was teasing or serious, but she suspected a little of both.

The food was wonderful, and she ate with pleasure. All the time, he watched her and took very little for himself.

"Why do you stare at me that way?"

"I have never seen a woman so honest in her delight of food. You eat with great passion. I wondered if you make love the same way."

Heat rose to her cheeks. He said the most disconcerting things, but then he considered her a whore. Perhaps that was the way men spoke to strumpets. She'd seen little of that world. Although it might have been otherwise, she reminded herself. She had not forgotten that terrible time in her life and never would.

"I have something for you," he said. A moment later he placed a black velvet box in her hand. "A small token of my esteem."

She stared at him in surprise. "I cannot accept gifts from you."

"Just open the box," he urged.

When she refused, he did it for her. A jeweled bracelet caught the light of the sun. "Allow me to place this on your wrist. I thought rubies were just the thing for you. They go so nicely with your coloring. Pidgeon's blood rubies from India, the jeweler informed me, very rare and exotic, just like you."

"It is splendid. No one has ever given me a gift of such exquisite quality, but I cannot accept it."

He studied her thoughtfully. "I admit that one wants to give a mistress jewelry, but I assure you there are no demands attached to this gift. I have no expectations. It would simply please me to see you wear this, even if it were just in my presence. I take it your protector has been less generous than he ought to be."

He kissed her hand and implored her with his eyes. She shook her head, firmly placing the bracelet back in his hands. He gave her a sad sigh and then caressed her cheek.

Huntingdon made her feel very odd indeed. "Let us take a stroll," she said with the hope of changing the course of the conversation.

The walks were paved with gravel bounded with high hedges and trees. It was a picturesque and spacious garden. There were striking lawns with a riot of beautiful flowers everywhere. They walked along companionably, admiring their surroundings, although it seemed that Huntingdon spent more time studying her than the scenery.

"Will you tell me more about yourself?" he asked. The tip of his finger traced the line of her nose.

"I don't think there is much to tell."

"On the contrary, I believe there is a great deal."

"I lived with my mother until I was six, and then she died. After that, I was sent to an orphanage until I ran away at the age of eleven. The rest you seem to know."

"That you have lived with Brockton since you were eleven? How did that come about?"

She looked away, not comfortable with the intense look in his eyes. "Beedle's was a nasty place. At a certain age, young girls were sold to whoever would buy them. I was to be sold to a brothel. In fact, most were. I knew it was time to run away. I had thought to join a tribe of gypsies. I looked for a *patrin.* My mother told me where I would find it. But the night was so cold and I was ill with a touch of the quinsy, I believe. In any case, a fever descended upon me and I could not think. I wandered the streets of London somewhat delirious. I remember stealing some oranges and running away. For a time, I was quite lost and confused. If I slept in the street, I feared I would die. Certainly, I could be tossed in the workhouse or even worse still, thrown in jail. A man took pity on me and brought me to his home. The rest, you know."

He gave her a puzzled look. "I think there is much more to your story, but you do not choose to tell me."

She shrugged; as usual, he was entirely too perceptive. But there were things she sensed he would not understand.

They were concealed now by a pavilion of Greek design, and the marquess brought her into the circle of his arm. "How shall matters proceed between us?"

Glancing up into those mesmerizing fathomless eyes, Maeve could not think very clearly. His arms came around her waist, his lips hovered over her own.

"I don't think my coming here with you was a very good idea," she said.

"I think it was the only thing we could

154

do." The rich, deep baritone of his voice was now little more than a husky whisper.

His arms embraced her, and a warm, searching mouth took possession of her own. His lips were tender but insistent. She found herself unable to keep from responding, and then the kiss deepened. His tongue sought her own in a sensual rhythm. His arms supported her, for she was suddenly dizzy, lost to this strange moment of longing and passion. Her heart beat wildly. His tongue plunged and then retreated in erotic movement. His kisses drugged her.

Then his hands began to move along the sides of her breasts until he was caressing her fullness. His mouth began making love to the hollows of her throat and neck. Gradually, his lips moved to the rounded tops of her breasts. Then he was hotly kissing her breasts through the thin white muslin of her bodice. Her breasts swelled; her nipples rising in anticipation. She let out a soft moan.

He moved her back against a large tree, pressing his body against hers. Suddenly the bodice of her frock was pooled around her waist, as was the top of her chemise.

She felt his eyes on her naked breasts.

"Beautiful," he said. "You are just as lovely as I knew you would be." He did not wait for her to speak. He lifted her slightly in his arms and brought his lips to bear on her nipples. She could hardly stand the erotic thrill. Now his tongue was circling her hardened nipples creating a pleasure and excitement so overwhelming that she could scarcely endure it without crying out. She arched her back in anticipation, running her hands through his thick gold-edged hair.

She could feel his lower body pressing against her, his hardness against her softness. His hands slid down and squeezed her rounded derriere, bringing her firmly against his erection. His arousal was granite hard. Her body shuddered in response.

"I want you," he said. "I am mad for you."

His words brought her back to some semblance of sanity. She pulled out of his grasp and stumbled away from him.

"I cannot," she said, panting. She righted her clothing as best she could and started to run from him, awkwardly, uncertainly, not sure where the path was. There were tears in her eyes and she could barely see.

He caught up with her quickly and stopped her, his hands on her shoulders. "What is it? You think you would betray *him?* Is that it?" When she wouldn't answer, he continued, "Brockton has had you long enough. I want you to be mine now. Have no fear of disloyalty. I will talk to him. We shall come to an accord. We will decide the matter amiably."

He kissed her again and this kiss was as much one of promise as passion.

CHAPTER EIGHT

Adam knew that William Brockton was very prosperous. There was no easy intimidation of a fellow in his circumstances. He could have gone to Brockton's club and met the man on more neutral territory, but he preferred the privacy that calling at the house would offer. Pritchard told him Brockton seldom rose before two in the afternoon. That was to be expected, since the man operated a gambling establishment until nearly dawn each day.

After announcing himself to the butler and handing over his card, Adam observed that Pritchard was right about the number of pretty maids that worked in the house. They certainly added ambiance to the decor.

However, there was a tasteful elegance about the furnishings that surprised him. What had he expected? He supposed vulgarity and garishness, a general lack of good taste, but such was not the case.

He was led into a well-appointed drawing room. A striking painting of Maeve hung over a fireplace mantel delicately carved and inlaid with colored marble. He noted that the marble was of the same exquisite design as that in the main hall. The walls were of damask in a robin's egg Wedgewood blue. The furniture was all done in fine mahogany inlaid with satin wood.

A young maid who now replaced the butler led Adam into the room and indicated a comfortably upholstered settee. Adam gave her a smile that brought a flush to her cheeks. "Mr. Brockton says he will be with you directly, sir." She dropped him a quick curtsy and hurried out of the room.

He hadn't asked for Maeve because he was certain that she was already gone. Actually, he had hoped not to see her here at all. His business was with Brockton and no other. Maeve's odd behavior of the previous day had only served to confuse and frustrate him. She had responded to him with great passion at first and then suddenly frozen and run away as if she were some innocent frightened virgin. No, he did not understand. But the answer had to lie with Brockton.

The gambling entrepreneur joined him in

short measure. Another maid brought refreshments. Brockton drank a cup of tea and nibbled on biscuits. He offered Adam the same.

"Thank you, but I've really come to talk to you about Maeve."

"Do you require her services?"

"In a manner of speaking."

Adam studied Brockton thoughtfully. The man was very ordinary in looks. Middle-aged, with a paunch and a thinning hairline. Brockton looked like someone's benign, aging father. His homely features and broad lower class accent did little to improve Adam's opinion. What could Maeve possibly see in such a fellow?

"Maeve is a very gifted young woman, but I suppose you've noted that, Your Lordship." Brockton seemed to be sizing him up as well.

"Yes, I find her quite extraordinary." Adam stared up at Maeve's portrait, as did Brockton. Her presence seemed to dominate the room.

"She decorated this house for me. Done quite a job, wouldn't you say? But that's nothing to what she's brought into my life. I owe all my good fortune to her and I ain't ashamed to admit it."

This was going to be even more difficult

than he first imagined. "Believe me when I say that I wish you well. And I fully comprehend your affection for the young woman. In fact, I have developed a *tendre* for Maeve. I should like to have her. I realize that you have been her protector for many years. She seems very devoted to you and I admire that sort of loyalty. But I should be quite good to her. I am prepared to make you a generous offer in order for you to part with her services."

Brockton stared at him, eyes narrowing. "Are you saying what I think you are?"

"Perhaps I have been indelicate?"

Brockton rose to his feet. "I'm not a man of delicacy, my lord, never was, never will be. I started out as a costermonger, became a fishmonger and then had the luck to move up in the world. But I've not forgot who and what I come from. You ought to understand that you can't pay me for Maeve."

"I believe I may make a most agreeable offer, sir."

Much to Adam's surprise, Brockton shook his head vigorously and then began to laugh. "By Gawd, not everybody and everything has a price."

Adam tapped his fingertips thoughtfully on an end table. "I am willing to play a high stakes game of chance for her if you prefer it done that way."

"As I said, some things are not for sale."

"I have found just the contrary. Name your price and you shall have it."

"Demme, I don't believe this conversation. You really don't understand, Your Lordship. I don't own Maeve. I didn't buy her. She's always been free to do as she likes. What holds her to me has little to do with material things."

Adam felt increasingly bewildered and uncomfortable. "Exactly what does hold her to you? I believe I have a right to know the situation."

Brockton shrugged. "If Maeve hasn't told you, then I have no right to do so. I'm sorry, your Lordship. I do not wish to offend you, but this conversation must end."

Adam was shown out of the elegant house by yet another lovely girl. Just now, he hadn't the slightest bit of interest. She might as well have been part of the furniture. He was frustrated and bewildered. The conversation with Brockton had been totally unsatisfactory.

Where was Charles? It was well past tea time, and Mr. Brockton would be expecting them. It was something of a daily ritual that the three of them were together for high tea. Of course, Maeve had missed being with them yesterday because of the marquess. Never should she have gone with him to the park! She knew that he was dangerous, yet she had allowed herself to be lured by him. Never would she let that happen again. It would not do to end up in the bed of a rake, and she did not have the willpower to resist him if they were ever alone together again. He was too devastatingly attractive. She'd melted in his arms. Yet she must resist the desire he inflamed in her. She did not wish to end up as her mother had, abandoned by an aristocrat.

At the first knock, she threw the door open, assuming it was Charles. Caroline bustled into the room.

"Thank heavens you are here! Maeve, I have just received this epistle. Please read it."

Maeve assumed that Caroline had received another letter from her mother or stepfather. She almost refused to read the note since she considered it a private matter, but Caroline's look implored her.

"Read it aloud and then tell me what you think."

Maeve did as Caroline asked. "My sweeting, please know that I have no desire to cause you undue concern, but you must understand that I have no wish to marry another. Your friend has been detained. Please oblige me with a visit so that we may decide his fate and ours." The note was not signed, but it did not have to be.

"Where is Charles?" Caroline asked.

Maeve shook her head. "He is late in arriving today."

"Just as I feared. The duke has abducted him!"

"Calm yourself. We cannot be certain."

"I am certain. Rundwall is a madman. You read the missive. He implies that Charles is in danger. I must go and confront the duke, but I fear going alone." Caroline's eyes beseeched her.

"That is what he wants, to lure you to him. Do not go yet. Let us make certain that this is not some idle threat, a nasty hoax."

Maeve sent Ralph to find out about Charles. If anyone was capable of doing so, it was her stalwart footman and bodyguard. An hour passed very slowly, and although Maeve offered to have tea sent up by her landlady, Caroline was too upset to want any. When Ralph returned, his lined face was cast in a deep frown.

"He's gone, Miss Maeve. Never showed up for the coach today. His bed weren't slept in last night. No one noticed till now. Thought maybe he'd had an affair d'amour. But he wouldn't disappear without a word. Mr. Brockton's right concerned, he is. You know our Mr. Charles don't go off without telling folks where. It ain't like him."

Maeve's mouth felt suddenly dry, her stomach a vortex of nausea. Caroline had told the duke that she loved Charles; no doubt, he had thought to do away with his competition. "Ralph, we need a hack."

"No, Miss Maeve, your coach is waiting outside. I knew you'd be wanting it."

It was not long before she and Caroline were on their way to the Duke of Rundwall's townhouse. They spoke very little, each absorbed in her own troubled thoughts.

Rundwall did not make them wait. In fact, it appeared that he was waiting on them. "Lady Caroline, I see you have brought your friend for support." When he tried to touch her, Caroline cringed. "I should not harm you, my dear one."

Maeve thought he looked awful, as if he had been drinking a good part of the night. His clothing was wrinkled and his eyes bloodshot.

Maeve decided to be forthright. "We are concerned about you harming Charles Le

Brun, Your Grace."

He gave her a small smile that did not reach his eyes. His yellowed teeth reminded her of a wolfhound. Then he turned to Caroline. "No permanent injury has befallen your friend. He is held only until after our nuptials are celebrated."

"You would coerce me into a marriage I do not want?" Caroline shook with outrage.

"For your own good, my dear. And your young man suffers only a temporary inconvenience."

"What if Caroline refuses to marry you?" Maeve asked.

The duke narrowed his hooded lids. "That would be unfortunate for the poor fellow. But let us not dwell on such unpleasant thoughts. I am obtaining a special license and we will marry shortly."

"How long do I have to decide?" Caroline lowered her eyes.

"I would like an answer now, my love."

"Then I suppose I must accept." Caroline sounded defeated.

Rundwall gathered the girl into his arms. "You will not regret your decision. I will call on you tomorrow afternoon." He tried to kiss Caroline's lips but she turned in disgust and he brushed her cheek instead. "Until tomorrow when we may spend some time in greater intimacy."

After Caroline pulled free of him, the duke took Maeve's hands in his own. "Your friend will be fine. I am a man of honor."

She looked deeply into his eyes, hoping to seek out the core of him, and there found something disturbing. She saw it; she felt it; her hands tightened around his. The awareness and the vision frightened her.

The duke dropped her hands. "How odd," he said in a shaken voice.

"Have you seen a physician?" she asked.

"Quacks, the lot of them."

"Not all. What you are doing is outrageous, and it will not serve to solve your problem. I implore you to be reasonable and release Charles."

"My malady makes me ever more desperate. I have no time to waste." He turned back to Caroline. "Until tomorrow then."

Maeve found it necessary to support Caroline as they walked to the carriage. Several times, the girl shuddered. Maeve thought Caroline might fall down in a faint.

Once on their way, Maeve spoke to her. "You cannot marry him."

"You are Charles's dear friend. Would you have me let him die? You heard the duke. I have no choice."

Maeve held Caroline's hands. "Listen to

me. The duke has a serious illness. I felt it when I touched him. He may die shortly. His mind has been affected by his fear. There's something else, another reason why you should not marry him. I believe his wives may not have died of natural causes."

Caroline's eyes widened in horror. "You cannot mean you believe he murdered them!"

"There were visions when I took his hands in mine, ugly visions of past deaths. Sometimes the spirits of the dead, women in particular, call out to me. I do not know exactly how or why it happens. I can only say these women were not at peace when they died. Something was very wrong."

"Dear God, this is a nightmare! And it is all my fault. I should never have told the duke about Charles. I should have left for Italy immediately, and then the duke's suit would have ended."

"There is no sense dwelling on past mistakes. We will rescue Charles. His spirit and mine are kindred. I am certain I will find a way to reach him, and in so doing, discover where he has been taken. Go home, Caroline, and speak to no one of this, not even your aunt."

"Only if you promise that when you go to rescue Charles, you will take me with you. I could not bear it otherwise."

The promise was given and Maeve deposited Caroline at her family's townhouse. She had tried to reassure the girl, but her confidence was not as great as she led Caroline to believe. On the drive home, she closed her eyes and concentrated on Charles, mentally reaching out to him, but nothing came to her. Maeve's mind remained perfectly blank. She was afraid that something was very wrong.

Mr. Brockton was waiting for her when she arrived home. "Any word about Charles?"

She proceeded to tell him what she had learned; his concern equaled her own.

"I will contact the runners at once," he said.

She placed her hand on his. "That is a good idea. I will go to bed early tonight and try to reach his spirit with my own. Perhaps I shall reach him through my dreams."

True to her word, Maeve prepared a special herbal potion her mother had taught her to brew. The dream-filled sleep that ensued was just what she needed. Her mind traveled a dark, twisting path and she awoke early in the morning with a clearly delineated vision. She now believed she knew where Charles was.

■ ■ ■ ■

Two carriages were necessary. The runners came in their own, two strong men who were well paid to accompany them out of London. Maeve, Mr. Brockton, and Caroline traveled in their closed coach with Ralph sitting up in the box beside Simon, their coachman. Both men were well-armed.

Mr. Brockton had grimly prepared a brace of pistols; he was the sort of pragmatic man who always knew what was needed and never shirked from responsibility. He took an immediate liking to Caroline, while his presence did much to calm and reassure her. Maeve spoke to neither of them on the ride out of the city. Her concentration was total; she could not allow it to be broken. Distraction might cost Charles his life.

The old farmhouse was just as it appeared in her vision. At first it seemed deserted, but on closer inspection, they saw several horses tethered at the back. The runners carefully positioned themselves at the front and rear of the building respectively. They kicked in the doors simultaneously and shouted out that those inside were under arrest. A great alarm went up within, and as the men came running out of the building, all three found themselves looking down the barrel of Mr. Brockton's pistols. Surrender was instantaneous.

They located Charles in a state of semi-consciousness lying on a bed in a back room.

"Thank God he's alive!" Caroline cried. She began to sob with relief.

Maeve found towels and clean water, made a compress and applied it to Charles's head. She felt a large lump there and hoped that he wasn't seriously injured.

"They must have hit you very hard," she said.

He moaned softly. "Coshed me with something. I was doing well against the lot of them, but one of the wretched cowards mashed me from behind. Lucky I've such a hard head. Though I didn't have my wits about me for a time I'll warrant."

"You must be seen by a physician," Caroline said.

"Maeve's the best healer I know."

Caroline leaned over and kissed his forehead. "Poor Charles. All this because of me. I will leave for Italy within the next few days. Then you will be left alone by the duke, that dreadful villain. I want you to know before I go that I do love you. Your suffering afflicts me."

Charles smiled for the first time. "I'm a lucky fellow then with so many to love me."

Caroline kissed his cheeks and fingers. "I love you more than you can know. I am dreadfully sorry for the misery I have brought down upon you."

Charles took the golden-haired girl into his arms and kissed her passionately. "My seraph, we shall not be parted again. If you will have me, I will marry you."

Caroline exclaimed excitedly and returned his kiss with exuberance. "We could be married in Italy. Only think how romantic that would be."

Mr. Brockton returned to find Charles and Caroline locked in an embrace. "The runners have taken those rogues off. They swear they were hired by another criminal. They will name him, but say they know nothing of the duke."

"No doubt Rundwall did purchase their services through an intermediary," Maeve observed.

"We had best be on our way back to town if you are well enough to travel, Charles." Mr. Brockton looked worried. "I would not want this young lady's brother to suffer unnecessary concern."

"I want nothing more to do with James," Caroline told him. "My brother has lied to

172

me, and I fear he does not love me as he claimed. My mother is in Italy, and I have promised to go there to meet her."

"It is decided," Charles said. "We will go together. You may have your mother attend your wedding."

Mr. Brockton clapped Charles on the back. "An excellent notion, and I shall pay your expenses. You must honeymoon in grand style. And when you return, I am thinking that a country estate might be just the thing."

"You are too generous," Caroline said; happiness shone in her eyes.

"The lad deserves the best."

"Caroline, you must take your aunt with you. I am afraid Southford will be furious when he finds out you've eloped and will take out his anger on her."

"You are right, Maeve, and it is only proper that Charles and I are chaperoned."

"I've spoken to the runners," Mr. Brockton said. "They will be discreet about the matter and keep things quiet for at least several days."

The sound of a carriage pulling up made all of them apprehensive. A handsome black phaeton was now in view.

"Ralph and Simon are without," Mr. Brockton said and drew his pistols again.

Maeve had the shock of her life when the Marquess of Huntingdon walked into the farmhouse. His arms were confined on either side by Ralph and Simon.

"Did you arrange for the duke to abduct Charles?" Caroline pointed an accusing finger at Huntingdon.

"I assure you, I only found out myself this morning and came to put an end to Le Brun's captivity."

Maeve wanted so much to believe him, but her mind was racked with uncertainty.

"Now that I see all is well, I shall return to London. It seems my help was unnecessary after all. I am glad Le Brun is all right. Rundwall led me to believe that it might be otherwise."

"I'm afraid you cannot go back, Your Lordship, at least not for a few days. We don't want the duke to know what's happened here for a time. You'd feel it necessary to tell him."

Maeve realized that Mr. Brockton was right; Huntingdon could not be trusted to go off on his merry way.

"What do you suggest?" Huntingdon didn't seem to be taking the matter seriously at all. There was an amused smile on his face.

"You'll have to take Charles's place for

174

now. I regret your inconvenience."

"And who will be my jailer?" He looked from one to the other.

"Ralph will stay with you. He'll tend to your needs."

"I shall make a grand fuss over this unless Maeve remains here."

"Impossible," Mr. Brockton said. His face reddened.

Huntingdon nonchalantly examined his fingernails. "Then you will be charged with kidnapping a peer of the realm. I believe it to be a hanging offense."

"Ralph and I will stay," Maeve said quickly. "It is best that way. The rest of you must return."

"Maeve, the fellow might overpower you and do you some harm." Mr. Brockton threw Huntingdon an accusing look.

"Not with Ralph here. Besides, Huntingdon is a gentleman. Do you give us your word to behave honorably?"

"Don't I always?" he asked dryly.

Charles and Caroline kissed Maeve goodbye and thanked her. Mr. Brockton glared at Huntingdon, but the marquess only gave him a cool smile in return. Her benefactor took Ralph outside for some final private instructions.

Maeve was left alone with the marquess.

She felt his warm breath on her neck and then he whispered softly in her ear.

"This promises to be a most interesting confinement. What will you do with me, Maeve? Perhaps I could make a suggestion or two?"

The skin on her arms was suddenly in gooseflesh.

"Or we might go off together in my phaeton, frolic in the countryside at an inn and then back to London."

She did not face him. "We must keep you here, your Lordship, for several days. Charles and Caroline need that time to be on their way."

"Famous, but I must be on my way as well. Perhaps another time then?"

Something in the tone of his voice caused Maeve to turn and look at him. She let out an involuntary gasp of disbelief. Huntingdon was pointing a pistol at her.

CHAPTER NINE

"What about your promise to behave as an honorable gentleman?" Maeve demanded. "I am very disappointed in you. It appears you cannot be trusted."

"Fustian. I have no intention of harming you, Maeve. I merely no longer find this place amusing and wish to leave."

She was furious with him. Had the man no character whatsoever? It seemed he took nothing at all seriously. Ralph entered the room at that moment and took quick stock of the situation.

"Now, Your Worship, you hadn't ought to be threatening Miss Maeve with a pistol like that. You might do her an injury." As Ralph spoke, he was moving. For a man his size, he was remarkably agile. His powerful ham hock of a hand came down with a chopping motion to disarm Huntingdon with one quick, decisive movement.

The marquess let out a groan that expressed both surprise and pain. Ralph's large, meaty hand smoothly scooped Huntingdon's pistol.

"If you'll oblige me, sir, by walking into the other room?"

Huntingdon shrugged with cool disinterest. It amazed her how he managed such sangfroid in the face of adversity.

"My dear fellow, this is an error. Suppose I gave my word not to reveal what I have discovered for the next few days?" Huntingdon turned his most charming smile on Ralph.

"Sorry, sir," came the gruff response. "Your error it would seem to be."

"I assure you, I had nothing whatever to do with hatching this cork-brained scheme." The marquess turned an imploring look to Maeve, who merely shook her head.

"You have proven your loyalty to Rundwall before. You have also shown that you cannot be trusted. I apologize for your inconvenience, but it does appear necessary."

Ralph wasted no time in securing Huntingdon. He was tied around the midsection to a chair, his hands roped at the wrists.

"There, sir. You won't be too uncomfortable, now will you?"

The marquess seemed annoyed by Ralph's

solicitous manner. "If you really want me comfortable, you'll untie my hands."

Ralph laughed as if the marquess had made a joke. "You're a cool, clever one, ain't you, your worthyship?"

Ralph followed Maeve out to the kitchen where they examined the store of foodstuff left behind by the kidnappers. It was depressing in its deficiency.

"These rogues lived on little but gin from what I can see."

"It does appear that spirits were freely imbibed and little else," Maeve agreed. "We are going to need some supplies, something more substantial."

"I could go to the village hereabouts and purchase what's required."

"I don't have money," Maeve realized.

"Mr. Brockton took care of that before he left. Not to worry, Miss Maeve. Just be careful of his magnificence."

They heard sounds of movement from the other room. Someone was striding rapidly and opening a window.

"He's trying to escape," Ralph said. Already he was running into the other room.

Maeve hurriedly followed and observed that Huntingdon had somehow managed to free himself. He was halfway out the window when Ralph caught him by the legs and pulled him back down.

"No, you don't, guv!"

Although Huntingdon was a tall, lean, well-muscled man, Ralph was even taller, and his broad build was pure muscle. His large, barrel chest and powerful limbs built like tree trunks made it fairly simple to wrestle Huntingdon to the ground. Had the contest lasted a little longer, Maeve was of the opinion that the wily marquess might have found a way to prevail, but Ralph simply overpowered him.

"Here's the answer, Miss Maeve, his greatness had this dagger tucked in his boot. My fault for tying him up so poorly. I underestimated him. Afraid we're going to have to strip you down, sir, and then tie you to the bed."

The countenance of the marquess did not change. He seemed to view his captivity with nonchalance and well-mannered courtesy. Maeve discreetly turned her back as Ralph did a thorough search of Huntingdon's person.

"What? Not watching, Maeve? How disappointing. That would be my only pleasure in this absurd situation."

She ignored his sardonic tone of voice and decided it was best to leave the room and let Ralph to do whatever was necessary. In the meantime, she set aside empty gin bottles and went about finding whatever food there actually was with the intention of cooking a meal. It had been a long time since she herself cooked but she had not forgotten. After all, she had mostly lived in the servants' kitchen until her mother died, and afterwards worked hard, long hours helping to feed the other orphans at Beedle's. Making something edible out of almost nothing was one of her specialties.

Ralph returned shortly. "The fellow's too clever by half. Slippery as an eel he is." Ralph handed her a small dagger with a jewel-encrusted handle. "Keep his sticker for your protection. I'll hold on to his pistol. I've made certain he's got no more fancy weapons to surprise us with. Now mind, he'll trick you if he can."

"I'm a survivor. You know that. And we do need provisions."

Ralph looked at her worriedly. "I don't like leaving you alone with him, but I'll borrow his eminence's carriage and tell folks I'm shopping for a fancy gent. That ought to get us good victuals right quick. You take a care now. I'll be back as soon as possible."

After Ralph left, Maeve looked around the abandoned main room of the ruined farmhouse. Her exploration convinced her that no one had lived here for a very long time. There were dust and cobwebs everywhere. She cleaned a little to make the room more acceptable to herself. Then she heard Huntingdon call out and went to see what he wanted.

"Where's your brutish friend?"

"Ralph? He's hardly a brute. He's merely protective of me. You should like him. Ralph was once a professional pugilist."

"Quite a watchdog."

"It is the job he was hired for," she said.

"Perhaps I should offer to pay him a handsome amount to work in my employment."

She gave him a small, weary smile. "I shouldn't think he would do it."

"Brockton commands amazing loyalty. Perhaps then I should offer to buy you. Name your price."

She knew he was not talking merely about the present situation. "Freedom is always bought dearly."

"I concur. I prize my own freedom very highly."

"As I do," she replied in a quiet voice.

His eyes were dark, depthless quicksand. "I visited your Mr. Brockton just the other day and offered him any amount he wished for you."

"You did what?"

"I wonder at your reaction of surprise. I thought you perceptive. Surely you realize I am besotted with you."

"I am most flattered. What did Mr. Brockton say?"

"After he laughed in my face? He gave me quite a set down. He said that you were free to do as you choose. Are you?" Now his eyes were searching torches.

"In a manner of speaking."

"I made quite a cake of myself, didn't I?"

"You don't seem overly perturbed. I shouldn't worry."

He gazed at her body with a hungry look. "Two days as your prisoner. Perhaps I should just lie back and enjoy the experience. Come closer, Maeve, sit here beside me."

She had to smile. Here he was, his hands tied to the bedpost overhead, his long legs spread slightly and tied to the bottom posts. His fine lawn shirt was loose, the cravat crumpled on the floor; he wore only hose and pantaloons, his boots removed as well as his jacket. The position was clearly uncomfortable and demeaning, yet he still maintained his aplomb and thought about seducing her.

"If there's nothing the marquess requires, I will return to my humble kitchen chores."

He gave her an insouciant smile and languidly raked her from head to toe. She rolled her eyes.

"Besides the obvious, Your Lordship."

"Adam, if you please. Intimacy such as ours requires some familiarity. Do sit by me for a time. I am in dire need of your company."

She shook her head uneasily. Being close to him confused her.

"What? Are you shy, Maeve? I would not have thought it."

"You are a very disturbing man."

"Am I?" He studied her thoughtfully. "That I have the power to disturb you is a hopeful sign. I am very thirsty. Would there be some water to drink?"

She was grateful for an excuse to leave him for a time. She found a pitcher in the kitchen and took it outside. There was a well not far from the house and she filled the pitcher there. Then she brought that along with a relatively clean glass into the bedchamber.

"You'll have to lean over and hold it for me — unless you're willing to untie my hands?"

She shook her head and smiled. "How cunning you are. I shouldn't think you are really thirsty at all."

"Indeed I am, and I will prove it to you."

As she leaned over him, he managed to drink some of the water. Then suddenly his cheek was nuzzling her breast. She let out an involuntary gasp and dropped the water on his chest. She pulled back from him and set down the glass on a small nightstand.

"Do come back and dry me off," he said. His eyes were very dark and his voice very deep.

"I should be going."

"I'll catch a chill. Please, I need you." His voice had a hypnotic, seductive quality.

"I will not untie you. I know I cannot trust you. Perhaps you even arranged for Charles to be abducted."

"You think so little of me?"

"I know you think well of Rundwall. I assume you have your reasons. But you must realize that he is seriously ill."

"Of what illness are we speaking?" Adam frowned with concern.

"It is the wasting sickness."

Adam stared at her in total shock, and she was convinced it was not a feigned reaction. "How could you know such a thing?"

"I have seen people with it before. Remember, I am requested as a healer as often as a seer."

"Rundwall has not said anything of this."

"People often do not. For men in particular, there is a stigma attached to illness. Perhaps he fears to be pitied or avoided. But his illness may well be the reason he has not fathered a child in so many years."

"He has never fathered a child to my knowledge," Adam said. His mood was far more grave and thoughtful now.

"I refer to his illegitimate children."

"What intelligence have you of that?" He stared at her in perplexity.

"More than you have, I should imagine." She kept her remark purposely cryptic. It would not do to tell him about Charles. "There is also the matter of the duke's two previous wives."

"What about them?"

Maeve looked down at the dirty floor, not wishing to meet his sharp gaze. "You must have known about them, about how they died. Can you tell me?"

He shrugged. "Short, sudden illnesses I believe. The first wife was most unhappy. Her babies were always stillborn. She died following childbirth. The second never conceived at all. There was some suggestion that because she was barren, the woman might have taken her own life, but I cannot say for certain."

"I thought they died unnaturally."

186

"How can you say such a thing?" His tone of voice suggested outrage.

"Yesterday when I took the duke's hands, I felt it. I knew he was ill, and I knew that he was in some way responsible for the demise of his wives. There were turbulent images of death surrounding him."

"Forgive me, but I believe you suffer from an overactive imagination." His tone was stiff and tight.

"I do not blame you for being skeptical. How can you understand something of which you have no experience? There are more things in heaven and earth than are dreamt of in your . . ."

He interrupted her. "Yes, I am familiar with Shakespeare. However, he too had a fantastical mind. Perhaps you should take up the writing of plays or novels."

"Perhaps so. The tutors Mr. Brockton hired to teach me claimed that I had an intuitive talent for the creative arts."

"Brockton educated you? Why did he not do the same for Charles?" The patrician brow rose.

She shrugged uneasily. "Charles was offered an excellent education, but he rebelled against the notion of being molded into a gentleman."

"Curious. Why would he not long to better himself?"

She sat down beside Adam on the bed, lost in thought. "Charles hates anything that smacks of the aristocracy."

"And why would that be?"

She quickly changed the subject. "Do you want more water?"

"No, thank you, but if you would be gracious enough to remove these ropes from my hands and feet, I would be much more comfortable."

"You know I cannot do that."

"Are you so afraid of me? Do I intimidate you?"

"Yes and yes again." His patronizing demeanor infuriated her. "Not long ago you held me at gunpoint. Have you so soon forgotten? I certainly have not."

"We both know I had no intention of harming you."

"How relieved I am to hear that," she said dryly.

"Now who is the skeptic?" He gave her a tolerant smile.

"I best leave you to your thoughts."

"Not yet," he protested. "Have mercy on your captive. Cool my brow with your fingertips."

She leaned over and touched his forehead but immediately regretted it. The mere

188

touch of her hand against his skin caused a wave of heat to move through her. He raised his head and pressed his mouth against her breast, his warm, moist lips sucking on her nipple right through the wispy muslin bodice. She let out a gasp and moved away even as a peculiar sense of excitement rippled through her.

"Straddle me, Maeve. Ride me. Let your hunger and mine join together."

She shook her head, backing nervously away, even as her traitorous body yearned for him. She ran from the room and tried to put the outrageous man from her mind. Yet the terrible aching need inside her would not soon go away.

She would go back to cooking; that was her only hope of forgetting that he was in the next room. She found some cheese and cut away a moldy portion. Some stale bread could be improved by warming it near the hearth. She built up the fire, which was little more than embers. Perhaps there remained something of a garden?

Outside it was a beautiful day and that cheered her considerably. She looked around to see if there were some wild vegetables growing, something from which to fashion a stew perhaps. There was not a great deal, but she found wild mushrooms and young nettles that would do. There were also dandelions from which she took the tender leaves to make a salad. Farther into the woods, she saw some blackberries growing wild on a prickly bush and picked all the ripe ones, carrying them in her skirt, which she lifted around the precious finds so as not to lose any of them. She kept looking and finally found wild garlic that she could use for seasoning. This was the Romany way that her mother had taught her long ago. She had never forgotten those lessons.

She was just coming back into the kitchen when she heard Huntingdon call out to her again. Carefully, she put down her treasures.

"Where have you been?" he asked as she came toward him. "I've been calling you for at least five minutes."

"Ah, his lordship is impatient and petulant. Obviously you are unused to waiting."

"I am feeling nature's call. I must use the necessary."

She blinked twice in rapid succession. "Ralph should return soon and he will assist you."

"That may be quite a while and I cannot wait."

"I am certain you are wrong."

"There is no village close to this place or

had you not noticed? He will not soon return."

"Very well, I shall help you." She searched around the room and found a chamber pot in the far corner. The smell of it made her nose twitch.

He shook his head emphatically. "I prefer the woods to be my privy."

"You are quite impossible. You simply want me to untie you so that you can escape."

"I assure you the matter is most pressing and I shall lose more than my dignity if you do not soon assist me from this bed."

She folded her arms over her breasts and stared at him askance.

"I take it that attractive pose is to indicate that you are unmoved by my situation? Suppose I promise on my honor that I shall not run off."

"Since Ralph has your carriage and has also taken the liberty to hide your boots, I suppose you could not travel very far anyway." She went to the kitchen and brought back his small dagger then freed his hands and feet.

He let out a deep sigh of satisfaction, massaged his wrists and slowly managed to get to his feet. "You'll have to help me," he said. "My legs are sponges for the moment. Your

Ralph tied me too tightly this time. My hands and feet are numb." He put his arms around her without further ceremony and she helped him walk outside. "Ah, fresh air again. That room is more than a little stale." Without a further word, he disappeared into the woods.

She waited for what seemed a very long time and then finally called out to him. There was no response. Alarmed, Maeve hurried in the direction she'd seen him move. Overhead, there was the music of birds and farther on, squirrels scurried up an ancient tree, but no sign of Huntingdon. She listened for him as she continued to walk. Had he escaped because she had been foolish enough to trust him? An odd knot formed in her stomach. She could not bear for him to be so dishonorable.

Then she saw him and a surge of relief swept over her. In reality, she heard him before she actually laid eyes on the man himself. There was a loud splashing sound. She found herself in a woodland glade with a beautiful, green stream before her. In the middle of the water was Huntingdon swimming around happily.

"Do come in and join me. The water is most refreshing."

She shook her head. "We must go back."

"You'll have to come in and get me if you want me," he taunted.

"I cannot swim." But the water did look cool and inviting, and she was so hot and tired. "I'll put my feet in," she conceded. She removed her kidskin slippers, silk stockings, and lifted her skirts gingerly. She slipped her feet into the water. Heaven!

Adam swam toward her and then stood up in the water. Maeve had the shock of her life. There was the most perfect Adonis, perhaps Michelangelo's David, only on leaner proportions, a downy mat of dark hair on his broad, muscular chest, powerful muscles in his thighs and calves. His manly part began to engorge in its nest as she studied him and she quickly turned away in embarrassment.

"Never seen a naked man before?"

She did not answer but swallowed hard. He was so magnificent, how could she not have stared?

"Take off your clothes and join me in the water, some water sport would serve us both well." Although his tone remained teasing and lightly jovial, she sensed the tension beneath.

"Ralph will return soon."

"Afraid of shocking the fellow? Or worried that Brockton would be devastated if he found out?"

She turned her back to him and hoped her face was not as red as it felt.

With a deep sigh of resignation, he agreed to leave the stream and get dressed again. "For a gypsy, you do not have a very daring disposition. I expected a wild, impetuous nature."

She turned back, trying not to look at his magnificently virile body. Water gleamed in rivulets down his broad chest and she felt the absurd urge to lick them away. "I am only half gypsy, as you have observed. But I have told you before that gypsy girls are modest, contrary to what you may think. However, I do know a gypsy trick or two."

"Really?" He gave her a lewd, suggestive smile which was more teasing than serious.

It made her laugh. "While you dress, I will try to provide the main course for our dinner."

She walked quietly along the side of the stream and studied the water. Finally, she saw what she was looking for. Ever so quietly, she lay down close to the water.

Slowly, her arm went into the stream. Her hand silently followed in harmony with the total concentration of her eyes. Ever so gently, her fingers stroked the trout she had located. With a quick movement, she flipped the fish on the ground beside her.

"Good God, what have you done?"

She looked up at him with pride. "I've tickled a trout."

He studied her in a bemused manner. "You mean you actually know how to catch fish without using a rod?"

"Roms don't need fancy *Gorgio* equipment to catch fish. My mother taught me how it was done. When she was little, her father let her go along with her brothers because she begged so. The things my mother taught me, I never forgot."

"It would seem you forget very little." Did she imagine a grudging admiration in his voice?

"If you are patient, I will teach you how to tickle your own trout."

They stayed and fished long enough to catch a generous dinner. She enjoyed being with him. In spite of the current of sexual tension that ran between them, there was an easy enjoyment of each other. She did not think it especially her doing. It was his wry sense of humor that she enjoyed and the convolutions of his clever, witty mind. She felt herself relaxing in his company for the first time.

Maeve actually regretted when it was time to return to the farmhouse. She walked back barefoot, as did Adam. The sense of freedom was a good feeling, but she did stub her toes once on a tree stump. When she began to hobble, he handed her the fish and suddenly lifted her into his arms. Her protests went unheeded.

"Hold on tightly or we shall both fall over."

Her face was pressed against the hard male chest, her arms entwined around his neck. He felt and smelled wonderfully masculine in spite of the fish. When he finally set her down, one hand caught around her waist, while the other tangled in her raven tresses. He brought her to him and kissed her gently. The taste of his lips was like a potent wine.

"Let me love you," he said. His eyes were darker than midnight in a Roman catacomb, his voice mellifluous and sensual.

She could hardly catch her breath, dizzy and drunk on his words and his touch. "You gave your word of honor that you would return and allow me to retie you."

"Did I? Sometimes being a gentleman is quite a tiresome bother."

She watched the sunlight arabesque off the gilt highlights of his hair. Strange, he no longer looked sinister to her. The strong features that had seemed chiseled out of granite now took on a more human incarnation. Did she actually see warmth in those fathomless dark eyes? He was cajoling her, of course, and it was proving hard to resist.

"Must you tie me up again this minute? I am still on my honor. Let me help you prepare dinner."

At that she could not help but laugh. "Have you ever been in your own kitchen?"

"I've inspected the kitchens." He looked offended.

"It isn't the same thing. All right, you may sit in that chair and not move while I prepare our meal."

He watched every move she made intently. His scrutiny made her self-conscious and she tried to ignore his intent watchfulness.

"Do tell me about what you were like as a child."

He laughed as though the question were a source of amusement. "I was never a child, dear one. I sprang full grown from the head of Zeus."

"That would make you Minerva."

He looked perplexed. "Dear me, I thought that was Hercules." A wicked smile passed across his lips. The dimple showed attractively in his cheek. At that moment, he might have been mistaken for a pirate.

"You are funning me," she said. "Perhaps

you are like Minerva. She was wise, while Hercules had only brawn."

"Which is better in your estimation?"

"Both are useful, but I should think wisdom more important."

"Then we are in agreement." His eyes followed her as she roasted the trout in the glowing embers of the fireplace, seasoning it with the mushrooms, garlic and young nettles. "You are the one who is wise."

"Certainly not, or I would have you all trussed up like a Christmas goose again and out of my way."

He smiled at her and pushed a lock of hair back from his forehead. "Clever girl."

No, if she were clever, she wouldn't let herself feel anything for this handsome aristocrat when only heartbreak could come of it for her. Hadn't her mother's fate and that of Charles's mother taught her anything? If only he weren't so appealing!

"I hope no accident has befallen Ralph. I thought he would be back by now."

"That stalwart fellow can take care of himself. As I collect, one of my wheels was a bit wobbly. I drove rather quickly to get here. He may have found a problem with it and had to repair it. Don't worry overly."

They ate together in companionable silence, looking deeply into each other's eyes from time to time. He took her fingers and kissed each one until she began to shiver and pulled her hand away. Later, Adam drew a fresh bucket of well water for them to drink and wash up with. Neither wanted any of the gin.

"A superb repast." He complimented her culinary skills and told her that the fish was the best he'd ever eaten. She was pleased with the compliment but merely lowered her eyes and did not reply.

Day turned into evening and Maeve searched for candles. There were precious few; she lit one and then, as shadows began to fall, insisted that Adam go back to the bedroom.

"Very well," he said with resignation. "I wouldn't want you scolded by your own servant. It wouldn't do at all. You may do with me what you wish." There was a wicked glint in his eye and she knew he was only half-serious.

He lay down on the bed and stretched out to his full and not inconsiderable length. His smile, slow and languorous, seemed a clear attempt at seduction.

Leaning over to tie his arms to the bed-post, she felt his warm breath upon her throat. The next thing she knew, he had tumbled her on top of him. His powerful arms caught her around the waist and pressed her body against his.

"Don't do this," she said. Her voice was barely more than a whisper.

A hand lifted her skirt and moved along her thigh. "You've beautiful legs. I want to caress them." His fingers began to knead and rhythmically undulate the flesh of her upper thighs. Higher and higher his fingers silkily swept until he was touching her most private places. She felt too paralyzed to move and could in fact hardly breathe.

"This cannot continue," she said in a shaky voice.

"I desire you," he said simply.

She shook her head and removed his hands from her body. "It is quite impossible."

"Pardon me if I don't understand why."

She finished binding him with the ropes; a great sadness weighed on her heart. She refrained from looking at him but felt his dark, intent gaze upon her. Why did she long so to give herself to him? How could she be such a foolish peahen? Surely lust had addled her mind. Attics to let, as Ralph would say. God, grant her the willpower to remain strong in her resolve!

CHAPTER TEN

Adam watched Maeve walk into the room and sit down on the chair. It had grown dark and the evening was chilly, as was often the case in late spring. She rubbed her arms with her hands.

"Ralph still hasn't returned."

"I shouldn't worry. He must have been delayed. Why don't you lie down beside me for a while and get some rest?"

"No, I shall remain in the chair."

"Rest here with me," he persisted. "You've got me trussed up like a capon, remember? You're perfectly safe, except from the linens. I cannot vouch for them."

She laughed lightly. He liked the soft, throaty sound of her laughter, liked the way the dim candlelight illuminated her pale eyes, touching them with unearthly beauty. He liked everything about her really. But there were those dark, secret places in her soul where she would not allow him to trespass. Perhaps he understood such things better than most, since he was no different. There were dark places in his soul as well. And like her, he kept his own counsel.

The truth was he had behaved damnably, holding her at pistol point earlier in the day. However, he could not help but rebel against the notion of being held hostage. He supposed he wanted to show her that he wasn't some helpless fop who would allow others to force his compliance. But the incident had only served to increase her mistrust of him.

He was in no hurry to escape now that he could be alone with her for a time. Let her have her way with him; later it would be his turn. He smiled involuntarily, imagining what he would like to do to her body. Then he saw a shiver take her.

"Come here," he said firmly. "You're cold and I'm very warm. That thin muslin frock won't do at all."

He watched as she came toward him; the provocative swing of her hips caused an ache in his groin. He longed to remove every bit of her clothing and explore every inch of her luscious femininity. It still surprised him how hungry she made him feel. He must have a care to maintain his control, not to let her see the power she exerted over him. She came hesitantly and ever so slowly lay down beside him.

"Closer," he said. "I'll turn on my side and you can move your back against my chest. It will keep you warm."

Maeve squirmed against him quietly. He knew she had qualms, but finally she accepted the comfort he could provide. Leaning into him, she began to relax. A short time later, she fell asleep. Her breathing stilled, her chest rose and fell in a natural movement. The full rounded globes of her derriere pressed into the lower portion of his belly, causing his half-arousal to become a granite hard erection. A wave of raw, aching desire swept over him. The sweet womanly scent of her filled his nostrils. There would be no sleep for him, not for a very long time. He endured his torturous state with equanimity, aware that he had chosen it. But there was no ease for him, only a building need. He wanted her; God how he wanted her! Finally, he turned away, offering her only his back and tried to float off on a wispy cloud of dreams.

He awoke to the sound of her voice. She was singing a song in a strange language — the tongue of the gypsies?

"Wake up," she said in a cheerful voice,

"Ralph has returned."

"What time is it?" His tongue was thick.

"Morning, and not early either."

He groaned at her and kept his eyes closed. "Wake me in the afternoon. I was woken early yesterday because of Rundwall's idiocy. If I must be a prisoner, I wish to be allowed to sleep quite late."

"Very well." But he did open one eye just to peek appreciatively at her as she walked back toward the door. He fell asleep again and dreamt about Zeus and Leda, only he became the swan and Maeve was Leda; then he mounted her and entered her sleek tightness with a powerful thrust, which she welcomed. They were a perfect fit.

He woke much later, rock hard once again, and let out a deep groan. He was excruciatingly uncomfortable. Something would certainly have to be done if he were to maintain his sanity.

"How's his worship doing this morning?" Ralph asked.

Maeve smiled at him. "It's his lordship, as you well know."

His eyes twinkled. "Can't seem to remember what to call them top-lofty folk. Were you all right without me, girl?" His expression grew serious with concern.

"Of course. Huntingdon is not an evil man."

"That remains to be seen. Can't trust his kind. Haughty they is. Thinks folks like us is nothing better than the dirt under their boot heels."

"I do hope you are wrong about him," she said. Maeve realized that Ralph was only watching out for her, but it actually hurt deep in her heart to know he considered Huntingdon cruel.

She began fixing the good country food Ralph had brought back. There were large brown eggs and bacon that she sizzled on a skillet over the hearth. Thick loaves of rye and wheat bread were still warm. Unable to wait a moment longer, she broke off a large chunk of rye and slathered rich butter on it.

"This is so good," she said through mouthfuls. "But why did you not return last night?"

"His gracefulness's carriage nearly bounced me on my head. I had to leave it behind and walk to the village. Once there, I found the cartwright was already abed and wouldn't make the bloody repairs until early this morning. So I slept in his barn for the night."

"I am sorry, yet you seem none the worse

for it." She tried to soothe Ralph's injured dignity.

"Aye, missy. I'll go now to chop more wood for the fire. Looks like we'll soon be out."

Ralph left her to her breakfast and her thoughts. If he knew how much she had enjoyed her time alone with Huntingdon, Ralph would truly be annoyed with her. She could not stand anyone lecturing her, not even a faithful friend like Ralph. Of course, the marquess was completely wrong for her, but she was immensely attracted to him. If he was dangerous, then perhaps she reveled in walking a perilous path.

Huntingdon awoke in the early afternoon and called for her. Ralph insisted on going along. The marquess looked almost comical in his consternation.

"Not you, my good man. I want only Maeve."

"Well, you will have me besides. I expect you need to clean up a bit after being tied to that bed for so long." Maeve knew Ralph was being delicate for her sake and smiled.

"I will fix you your breakfast, Your Lordship, while Ralph takes you to *clean up*." She turned then and left them to their own devices.

When they returned to the farmhouse, she

insisted that Huntingdon be allowed to eat before the hearth as he had on the previous evening. He was again appreciative of her cooking skills, but his manners were formal and correct in front of Ralph and there was no intimation of their former closeness. That was as it should be, and yet she could not help but mourn the change. She made an effort to concentrate on kitchen chores and not to watch him closely.

But for just a single moment as Ralph led him back to the other room, she caught an unguarded look on Huntingdon's face which spoke of longing. It comforted her to know that he still wanted her, though why it should, she did not comprehend.

Later, Ralph returned and sat down beside her. "He says he wishes to take a nap. Can you imagine? Doesn't want me to disturb him. Says if he must be a prisoner, he'll sleep the sentence away." Ralph sniffed, his wide nostrils spreading even further in annoyance.

"Well, let us do as he asks," she said. "We are inconveniencing him, are we not? I do hope Charles and Caroline are making good progress."

"With Mr. Brockton to ease the way, they'll be just fine." Ralph patted her arm reassuringly.

She was certain Ralph still thought of her in terms of the sick, starving waif that Mr. Brockton had brought home so many years ago. In those days, there were only two servants, Ralph and Mrs. Wiggins. That sweet old woman had long since gone to her reward, but Ralph was still a bull of a man, and though he too was getting on in years, he protected those he served with vigor. It was a very good thing that she had risen early before Ralph could find her sleeping beside Huntingdon. She knew it would have upset him mightily to know how friendly she and the marquess had been, in spite of the fact that the marquess was bound.

"I hope Mr. Charles will be happy with that bit of fluff," Ralph said, his voice dubious.

"Caroline is really of strong character. Did you notice how well-mannered he was with her?" Maeve laughed. "He actually called her his *seraph*. I didn't think Charles knew such a word, let alone had it in his vocabulary."

Ralph smiled cheerfully and winked at her. "Aye, now that you mention it, I believe the lad's been properly leg-shackled."

"Love draws the best from people."

"If you say so, Miss Maeve."

There wasn't any point arguing with Ralph. He was a skeptic in such matters. She was a romantic, who believed that real love had the power to bring out the best in each lover. Charles and Caroline would be the better for loving each other. But what of her? Would there ever be love in her life? She sighed deeply.

The afternoon dragged on. She wanted to go to Huntingdon but didn't dare. She had no excuse. Ralph remained on guard duty, sitting on a chair outside the crude bed-chamber. Finally, she left to take a brief walk in the woods. There was a restless feeling in her that made her unable to sit still. She collected some wild herbs for medicinal purposes so the walk should serve a useful purpose, then continued to the glade where they had caught trout yesterday. With a smile, she remembered her time with Huntingdon and yearned for more.

How clean and quiet the country seemed after London. She realized she would like to live again in the peaceful beauty of nature as she had as a child. However, that great house had not been a real home for her, and it was best she never forget it. She again felt anger toward the people who had so badly mistreated her mother and herself.

Ralph ran toward her as she emerged from

the woodland. His face was red as a rare roast beef, his teeth bared.

"What's wrong?" she asked but feared she already knew.

"It's that damned lordling. He's gone, rode off in his phaeton after I went and fixed it!"

She felt a sense of loss; she would probably never see Huntingdon again. "I don't understand how he got free."

Ralph balled his hands into fists. "The sneaky bastard slipped a knife into his shirt while he ate. I'm certain of it. Them ropes was cut through. Then he waited for just the right time. I suppose I must have dozed off for a while. It was a warm afternoon and I didn't sleep much last night. Damned uncomfortable I was. Anyway, he sneaked away, he did. I've failed you and Master Charles. I'm that sorry, I am." Ralph lowered his head in shame.

She hugged the bear of a man as best she could. "No need," she told him. "Huntingdon will not betray them. I am certain of it. The truth is, he most likely could have escaped before if he chose. I was not a particularly assiduous jailer either. And I am the one who insisted he be allowed to eat in the kitchen with his hands untied. I accept the blame. But do not worry. I have a strong intuition that he will not tell the duke a thing until Charles and Caroline are well on their way. He is in sympathy with us despite what we did to him. It will all be fine."

Ralph was reassured by her words. He set off across the countryside once again to hire or purchase some means of conveyance for them. When this failed, they walked to the closest posting house and caught a coach headed back to London. They were both exhausted on their return but stayed up half the night talking with Mr. Brockton.

Everything had gone well at his end. Charles had accompanied Caroline to the earl's townhouse in Berkeley Square at a time of day when Caroline was certain that her brother would not be at home. Luckily, her aunt was there, although in a terrible state of worry. They packed and left hurriedly, leaving a brief note behind to announce the elopement, but not where they were going. The worst did not happen, and there was no need to deal with the earl.

On hearing this news, Maeve breathed a great sigh of relief. Southford would assume that Caroline was on her way to Gretna Green. If he went there looking for the young lovers, so much the better. She feared what the earl might do to them if he got the opportunity. However, she was very sure that would not happen. Caroline and Charles would be on their way to Italy. She prayed that they would find happiness there.

Several days later, Maeve resumed her accustomed occupation of going to her lodgings. Ralph remained outside to tell their coachman when to pick them up again and Maeve went directly upstairs. The door was not closed, and that was peculiar because she was under the impression she left it locked. As soon as she opened the door, she had a sense of another presence. She called out but no one answered. Hesitantly, she walked into the room. A sudden jarring sensation overtook her. Someone caught her from behind, grabbing her around the throat so she could not cry out. She tried to fight her attacker, jabbing backward with her elbow. She sensed a strong man, comfortable with violence. Fear strengthened her power to resist but the chokehold tightened. Her struggling grew weaker as blackness peeped around the corners of her consciousness. She managed another hard jab to the solar plexus and was satisfied to hear a groan. Then blackness closed in.

"Miss Maeve! Are you all right?"

Her eyes flickered open and she saw Ralph. When she tried to talk, her throat hurt terribly and all she could manage was a croaking sound.

"No, don't try to speak. I don't know who he was 'cause he went through the window in the bedchamber and down through the back alley. I ran after him a ways, but he were quick. It was a man though. I'm certain of that. He tried to strangle you but he heard me coming and scurried off. Damned cowardly bastard!"

Ralph was holding her in his arms now and patting her back. She could not seem to stop crying, even though doing so made her throat and neck hurt more.

"I'll keep a closer eye on you, I vow. This won't happen again. If it was his Lordship claiming revenge, he'll be sorry for this."

She shook her head vigorously. Huntingdon would never do such a terrible thing — would he?

It had been several days since Adam made good his escape. It amused him to think of what Ralph's reaction must have been; the old guard dog probably had a fit of apoplexy. What of Maeve? What had she thought and felt? Her only concern would be for her friends. It was foolish to think otherwise.

He wanted to see her again. But she had refused to leave Brockton for him. Still, there was no harm in trying a second time. Like his cousin, he was prepared to behave shockingly to win his advantage. The difference was that he refused to harm or endanger anyone else in his pursuit.

The door to her lodging was open and he could hear Ralph talking inside. He was less than eager to see Ralph but walked in anyway. The sight of Maeve lying on the floor held in Ralph's arms astonished him. Ralph turned a malevolent look on him.

"You! Did you do this to her?"

It was then that he saw the marks on Maeve's throat and the tears in her eyes. He got down on his knees and pulled her away from Ralph into his own arms.

"Good Lord, man, how could you think it?" He kissed her damp cheek. "Maeve, are you all right?"

She nodded her head. Her eyes met his own and he could see that she was frightened and in pain.

"Someone tried to kill her just a moment ago. The man got through the window and away before I could catch him."

"It wasn't me, Ralph. I care about Maeve, and I would never harm her intentionally."

Ralph studied him thoughtfully. "No, I

don't suppose you would, sir. But who would do such a thing?"

"I don't know either. Maeve, I want to take you to a doctor, a very good one."

She shook her head.

"Miss Maeve does her own doctoring."

"I have my phaeton downstairs. I'll drive you anywhere you wish."

Ralph wanted to help, but Adam preferred to carry Maeve in his arms. He pressed her body against his and slowly took the steps. The shaking that had gripped her began to subside as she clung to him. He wanted very much to protect her from harm. It infuriated him that someone had attacked her in such a vile, dastardly manner.

On the ride back to Brockton's townhouse in Belgrave Square, Adam held Maeve in his arms and alternately kissed and caressed her, not caring who should see them. He had Ralph drive for them, but the open carriage allowed for little in the way of privacy or space. He promised Maeve that he would take care of her if she would allow it. As they drew up to the house, he gave her one gentle final kiss on the forehead.

"I have a man who will investigate this incident. He is very good, and we will see what we can discover."

She managed a small smile. Ralph did not

let him carry her into the house, but Adam watched vigilantly as they disappeared inside. As he rode away, Adam could not help but ask himself who would do such an awful thing to Maeve. Then he thought of Rundwall and wondered. But surely his cousin was above taking such revenge, especially on a woman?

Rundwall appeared to have taken the news of Caroline's elopement better than expected. Adam realized that the duke actually did look ill. Maeve, it seemed, truly knew about such things. Adam urged his cousin to visit a physician, and the duke finally acquiesced.

"I'll see Witherspoon. He's done creditably with your father. How was Simon when last you visited?"

"As well as can be expected. Witherspoon has prepared us for the worst."

The rheumy eyes of the duke were reflective. "I thought surely Simon would die after his suicide attempt, but he survived miraculously."

"Survival was no favor. He only half lives." Adam found he could not keep the bitterness from his voice.

The duke nodded his head solemnly.

"Someone tried to strangle Maeve today."

"The gypsy girl?" Rundwall looked surprised. "Why would anyone do such a thing?"

"My sentiments precisely. She did, of course, help Caroline to run off."

Rundwall turned and stared at him directly. "Lad, you don't think I am responsible? Have I ever given you the impression that I am vindictive?"

"You were obsessed with the girl."

"As you said, the matter is done." The duke's expression was grim.

"Let's hope it is," Adam agreed.

Rundwall rang for his butler and requested port for each of them. "I believe we will both benefit from some refreshment."

The matter was no longer discussed, but Adam could not help wondering how well he really knew his cousin. He thought of what Maeve had said. Surely, Rundwall could not have been responsible for the deaths of his wives. It wasn't possible — or was it? Adam realized he no longer felt completely at ease in the man's company. What Rundwall had done for his father would always be there, uniting them, but now there were other considerations as well. What Adam cared about most right now was Maeve and her well-being. Whoever tried to harm her might well do so again.

His hand tightened around the glass he held. The glass shattered.

CHAPTER ELEVEN

That night Maeve dreamt of her mother, dreamt of a time when she was small and sheltered sitting on her mother's lap.

"I am afraid," she said.

"Afraid of what?" Mama hugged her. "You are the baron's grandchild. You are safe and secure here."

"Only if you are with me."

Her mother's smile was benign. "It will all be well. I will stay and watch over you."

But suddenly her mother was gone. Maeve looked everywhere and still could not find Mama. Again and again she cried out for Mama. The terror made her throat hurt; the danger would not go away. Then she heard her mother's voice calling to her as if from a far off place.

"I am still with you, my dear one. My spirit is one with yours. Return to our people and no harm will come to you. Leave the *Gorgio*. Free yourself of their influence."

Maeve woke abruptly, her nightrail soaked with perspiration. Sunlight swept through her window and she blinked at it. She felt the pain in her throat and the bruises on her neck and relived the memory of the assault.

Her mother's words came back to her. It would not be easy to leave her life here, yet soon she must do so or always live in fear. Who would want to kill her? Ralph suspected Huntingdon, but Maeve refused to consider such a thing. The tender way he'd held her, the solicitous manner in which he'd kissed her cheeks and forehead; that caring was surely genuine. After his fashion, Huntingdon cared for her. Surely, he did. She would not torture herself with doubts regarding his sincerity.

Besides, there were those who had better reason to hate her. Rundwall, for one. Charles would not have been found so swiftly after Rundwall kidnapped him but for her intervention. However, did Rundwall know about that? It was doubtful.

There were the criminals she helped the runners catch, each one a murderer. Had any escaped? Did they have family members or friends who were vindictive? There were many possibilities.

A knock startled her out of her reverie,

and Ginny entered the room carrying a tray. The unruly red-gold hair was, as usual, pulling free of its pins.

"How are you, Miss Maeve? I've brought a soothing gruel Cook says will be easy for you to swallow. It's got honey in it. Oh, and there be quill and paper to write out what you require. We're all anxious to do whatever we can for you."

Maeve gave Ginny a smile more reassuring than she felt. She reached for her writing supplies. Others were relying on her, and it was time to start her day.

Adam kissed the Duchess of Pemworth's hand in the continental manner.

"Oh, you are a charming fellow, and ever so dashing. Indeed, I cannot see why you are regarded as intimidating, an unfair reputation, I am certain, as I find you the soul of amiability."

"In all modesty, I agree entirely," he said with a smile.

"Now why have you come to see me today, dear boy?" Her small eyes were greedy with anticipation.

"Why, to share the latest *on-dit* with you naturally."

"Do not fun me, Huntingdon. Everyone knows how close-mouthed you are."

He let out an artful sigh. "Very well, I see there is no fooling you. I wish you to hold a small dinner party within the next few days and invite certain guests."

"May I ask why you do not invite these certain guests yourself?" The duchess's chins bobbed like aspic.

"A fair question. Let us just say that if I were the host, it is doubtful that they would all attend, while no one declines an invitation from the premiere hostess of the *haut ton*."

She patted his hand. "Such flummery. Shakespeare said Caesar was caught by flatterers and so shall I be."

"In a sense, you will benefit William Brockton. He is your friend, is he not?"

"Yes, he has proven a good friend."

"Is that why you sponsored Maeve?"

The duchess's lips pursed; even under the thick coat of paint, her discomfort was visible. She looked around as if to make certain that they were completely alone in the salon and no servant was eavesdropping. "Promise never to breathe a word of this, Huntingdon."

He quickly gave his assent.

"Well then, I must admit that I am fond of playing deep. One evening at Brockton's, luck seemed to turn completely against me.

I lost five thousand pounds at a single sitting. The duke, that miserable purse pincher, would have made a dreadful bramble. I approached Brockton, and he was very understanding. He told me to forget the debt. Some weeks later, he asked if I would return the favor by nursing the ground for Maeve. It seemed she was curious about society. I considered it a small request. Maeve has been a success all on her own account, really."

"Then it will please you to know that you are further helping Maeve in a matter of greater significance." He left the duchess having solicited her promise of full cooperation in dispatching his plan.

It was true that he was always looking for other opportunities to be with Maeve, but now he was also quite determined to discover who had attacked her in order to prevent such a horrible thing from happening again. He especially did not want her to have further cause to mistrust him.

The dinner party could prove dangerous, but he would be present to protect Maeve from harm. A thought occurred to him. He ought to visit Manton's Shooting Gallery. He was considered a deadly marksman, but practice was crucial. New dueling pistols were definitely called for. Joe Manton had improved hammer and breeching in weaponry. His elevated rib was the talk of sportsmen. Nevertheless, Adam thought that the game he hunted was a great deal more predatory and savage than anything Manton had in mind.

The dinner invitation from the Duchess of Pemworth surprised Maeve. She wanted to refuse, but Mr. Brockton insisted that she go.

"You need some diversion. You ought to get out again. You're looking a trifle peaked. Besides, we can hardly refuse your patroness. To do so would be an affront."

Mr. Brockton was working as usual, and she was forced to go alone. But Ralph promised that the coach would be waiting outside so she need only send a footman if she grew weary.

Her dove gray gown with a matching scarf artfully arranged around her neck set off her eyes to perfection. The bruises on her throat were not as obvious now and were well hidden by her scarf; her voice was nearly normal with only a slight hoarseness.

The duchess welcomed her warmly and asked after Mr. Brockton. "Come into the drawing room and meet our other guests. Most you already know, but I believe you are unacquainted with my niece's daughters. There was a death in the family, and they were not obliged to come for the start of the Season. They have just arrived in London."

Maeve was immediately introduced to the Misses Jane and Belinda Whitehead. Jane was older than Maeve, a thin, nervous woman. Belinda had not yet come out and was immature and giggly, plump and dimpled. Maeve soon ascertained that she had little in common with either of them.

"How nice that you are out in society again." Huntingdon's deep voice startled her.

"I did not expect to see you here," she said.

"Was that what you hoped?" His eyes had a penetrating edge.

"I should have said so if it were true." His dark gaze unsettled her, as it always did.

They were joined by the Duke of Rundwall. "And how is Caroline?"

She lowered her eyes. "Gone away, as you know."

"With your friend, the footman."

"He is nothing of the sort. Charles is a fine young man and no one's lackey. It is a shame that you cannot know him." She quickly walked away from Huntingdon and

Rundwall, afraid that she would soon be out of countenance with both if she were forced to remain in their company and would end up saying more than she should.

Beverages were served as the guests gathered and mingled. Maeve took only lemonade; she did not think herself capable of managing anything stronger. As she stood and spoke with several other ladies, out of the corner of her eye she caught sight of the Earl of Southford and Sir John Simmons. She felt sick to her stomach. Each of these gentleman shot hostile looks in her direction. She was fully aware that she was the subject of their discussion. Of course, they would blame her for Caroline's defection. She glanced over at Huntingdon and saw that he, too, was watching them with interest.

Although she sought to avoid him, Sir John came to her several minutes later and pulled her rudely aside.

"Do not put your hands on me," she said in a firm but quiet voice.

"You need not take that haughty tone with me, slut. I have come to tell you that James is in a taking over the elopement of his sister with that servant of yours. You should be punished for your treachery." His fingers dug painfully into her wrists.

"I am with friends, as you may see. Let me go or I shall scream loud enough to deafen a deacon." She tried to free her hands from his grip.

"Those Friday-faced chits are no friends of a whore like you."

"Apologize to the lady and leave her be." Huntingdon's voice was low and menacing. "Otherwise, I shall be forced to call you out."

"My abject apology, madam." Sir John's sarcasm gave the lie to his spoken words. But his bluster was gone, and he quickly stepped away from her.

Belinda joined them at that moment while her sister drew Adam's attention. "Oh, Sir John, such dark looks. I swear you scowl prettily." She let out a nervous giggle. "Her Grace has suggested you as my dinner partner. I hope that pleases you as much as it does me."

"Perhaps he will tell you of his war experiences in the Peninsula or how he murdered a girl in Spain. Or did you strangle her in Portugal? I do not seem to recall, Sir John." Maeve's words turned his coloring purple with rage.

Belinda giggled again. "Oh how amusing. Sir John, you must tell the most amazing tales to all the ladies. I can hardly wait to hear them." She fanned herself in a flirting manner and flounced away.

"Witch, do not dare to speak of such things again." Sir John's soft voice insinuated anger. The round face was red as a blood sun.

"Have you not already tried to kill me and failed?" She confronted him with more courage than she felt, refusing to give in to the sick feeling of fear that nauseated her.

Huntingdon was again at her side. "Do you believe it was he, Maeve?"

"I cannot be certain."

"But it well could have been. He attacked you before. Simmons, I intend to call you out for your treatment of Maeve." Adam placed himself directly between her and Sir John.

Simmons stared at Huntingdon in disbelief. "You cannot be serious."

"Indeed I am. The lady has been insulted, and I intend to uphold her honor."

Maeve turned to Huntingdon. "Please, this is not your affair. I would not have you endanger your life on my account."

"There is much more than insult involved here." He turned back to Simmons. "You have threatened Maeve. You have hurt her. I will not permit it."

"I have hurt no one. This is a misunderstanding. And everyone knows you are an exceptional marksman. Would you murder me in cold blood?"

Huntingdon smiled grimly at the pathetic figure before him. "Simmons, you were a soldier. You must be as accustomed to the use of weapons as I am. Besides, it is time I got some use out of those new dueling pistols Manton made for me." On the surface, the marquess was now treating the matter as if it were a source of amusement, but one had only to look at the deadly intensity of his eyes to know differently.

Simmons was sweating openly. Others had noted the tension building between them. There were hard stares in their direction and quizzing glasses were raised. The duchess touched the shoulders of each man.

"We are to be seated for dinner. Is everything quite all right?" She looked questioningly from one to the other.

Huntingdon smiled broadly. "Certainly, all is extraordinarily well. Simmons and I have something to settle between us on the morrow. But it is nothing that cannot be postponed for discussion until then. In the meantime, I shall take Maeve in to dinner."

As he took her arm, Maeve spoke in a quiet voice. "I won't have it, Adam. You cannot duel with him for my sake."

"I am persuaded dueling will prove unnecessary. Calm yourself, Maeve. I will visit
you tomorrow afternoon and we will speak
on it further. I have offered you my protection, and whether or not you seek it, it shall
be bestowed upon you."

"Your Lordship, you are quite mad."

He gave her a broad smile, his dark eyes
lighting with mirth. "That may well be, but
tell me, do I bore you?"

"Never."

He gently squeezed her hand. "Then all is
as it should be."

On the following morning, Maeve took
chocolate in bed, which was not usual for
her. But she had a great deal to think about.
Although the duchess served an excellent
table, she'd been nearly unable to swallow a
bite of food. Complaining of the headache,
she'd left the dinner early. Ralph and the
carriage were waiting for her, and she was
grateful for their dependability.

She thought of Huntingdon and wondered
what he was about. His recklessness terrified her. He could easily get himself killed.
Sir John was an awful fellow. He'd probably
hoped to marry Caroline himself. Had he
been the one who tried to strangle her?
Clearly, Huntingdon thought so. She was

not as certain. Unfortunately, in regard to her own affairs, Maeve rarely had the clear intuition that helped her understand other people's situations. Emotions muddled her perception in regard to personal matters.

Huntingdon came to see her in the afternoon, just as she was planning to go out. She had already tied her bonnet and arranged her pelisse.

"What's this, you cold-hearted wench, going out without a thought to my visit? Have you so soon forgotten that I have offered to duel for the sake of your reputation?"

"You make light of everything," she said. "Of course, I am concerned, but I did not think you would actually come here."

"I cannot imagine why. I do generally keep my word."

She turned to him with concern. "I do not want you to meet Simmons. Besides, dueling is illegal."

"So it is, but this is a matter of honor."

"Suppose you kill him? Would you have to flee to the continent?"

He gave her cheek the gentlest caress, and yet even that slight touch set her body quivering.

"I am pleased by your concern, dear one. However, all will be well. I shall merely cripple him. Does that meet with your approval?"

She ignored his cocky air. "When and where will you meet?"

"One's seconds arrange those matters. However, it will likely be at dawn at Chalk Farm." He put his hand beneath her chin, forcing her to raise her eyes. "I want to do this. Do not interfere."

She did not answer, finding that she was too choked to speak. He seemed to sense her distress. His arm encircled her waist and then pulled her body against his. His other hand tangled in her hair and pulled her head toward him until they were face to face. Then his eyes became dark pools on a moonless night. Their lips met and she felt his longing. Her hand trembled as she caressed his cheek. His mouth pressed urgently against hers. Her own need answered his. His tongue invaded her mouth and explored the velvet interior before joining and mating with hers. There was so much passion in his kiss that she felt overwhelmed.

"I must go," she said breathlessly. Somehow she managed the strength to break free of him, but it was not easy.

"My phaeton awaits, mistress. Where shall I take you?" He again managed to sound lighthearted.

"I am going to visit a sick friend. I am certain you would find it boring."

"On the contrary, I find nothing you do boring. I insist on coming along, unless you fear Brockton will object?"

His challenge pricked her pride. "Certainly not. I have complete freedom."

"Alas, none of us is completely free. That is pure mythological belief. And if we did have total freedom, why then we should soon be pursuing our own enslavement out of dread of something so awe-inspiring. As to your need for freedom, we shall see, shall we not?" He took her arm.

"Your skepticism is one reason I doubt the wisdom of you joining me."

"Let us say that I offer my protection and my friendship."

She looked at him and tried her best not to tremble. The Marquess of Huntingdon was many things but he could never be a mere friend to any woman. His raw masculinity contrasted with his careful affectation of the man of fashion. His thick hair was carefully dressed; he wore a blue silk frock coat of Weston's elegant tailoring, fawn pantaloons fitted tightly over his muscular calves and thighs and mirror-shined Hessians on his feet. Diamonds twinkled among the snowy folds of his neck cloth and sparkled on his fingers. And his eyes sparkled brighter than any jewel.

Ralph approached them as they walked down the stairs of the townhouse. "Miss Maeve, the carriage is waiting for you."

"She will be going with me."

Ralph gave Huntingdon a mutinous look. "Miss Maeve would be best off traveling in a closed carriage."

"It's a beautiful spring day. I believe some fresh air would do her good."

The two men stood glaring at each other until Maeve stepped between them.

"Ralph, I will be fine. The marquess is visiting a friend with me. Tell Mr. Brockton when he wakes that I shall be joining him for high tea later."

"If you're certain, miss." Ralph allowed himself one last threatening look at Huntingdon.

Adam gave him a brief, mocking salute and then helped her into his phaeton, which sported a team of two dappled bays.

"What fine horses," she said.

"Prime blood cattle," he agreed. "Saw them at Tatt's and knew I had to have them." He took up a multiple-caped driving coat and tossed it on carelessly, placed his tall, curly-brimmed beaver on his head, then pulled on his riding gloves and handed her his ebony walking stick to hold while he drove the phaeton, and off they went at a rapid pace. Obviously, he was a notable whip, skilled in handling the ribbons. She wondered if there was anything at which he was not skilled. Her thoughts turned disturbingly carnal, and she found her face flaming with heat.

CHAPTER TWELVE

"And what ailing friend are you visiting?" he asked in a casual manner.

"His name is William Blake."

"Yet another William among your admirers?" Adam tried to keep his tone light so that she would not guess that he felt jealous.

"It is not he who admires me but rather I who admire him." Her smile was so angelic and her eyes so ethereal, he was captivated. He was also very curious.

The address she'd directed him to find was in a poor area of town where he could not safely leave his magnificent phaeton or his fine horses. But a group of urchins quickly came to admire his gig. He reached into his pocket and pulled out a half crown and flipped it to the oldest boy, who appeared the leader.

"Take good care of my carriage and cattle and there will be a sovereign as well."

The boys exclaimed loudly and rushed to do his bidding.

He helped Maeve down from the phaeton and took the heavy basket she'd brought along.

"What is all this? Are we feeding the entire British army today?"

"You'll see soon enough," she said with an enigmatic smile and walked past him.

Adam was fascinated. Maeve truly was a woman of infinite variety, a seductive mystery.

William Blake was not at all what Adam had expected. He estimated the man's age at around sixty years. He appeared to be in declining health but welcomed them warmly to his cramped establishment.

"Have you worked on anything new since I last saw you?" Maeve asked. Her voice carried an aura of unabashed enthusiasm.

The man's visage brightened markedly. "I've had a vision of Jerusalem I plan to work on soon."

Mrs. Blake was an amiable elderly woman who thanked Maeve for the generously laden basket. She joined them almost immediately. It was clear to Adam that the old couple lived near poverty.

"I brought the marquess to see some of your wonderful work, Mr. Blake. Perhaps you might consider selling him a book?"

"I would be honored." There was no mistaking the look of gratitude.

Adam raised a questioning brow. Mrs. Blake quickly brought out some of her husband's books and Maeve attempted to explain the nature of Mr. Blake's art to Adam.

"Mr. Blake is an engraver by trade, but he is also a poet and artist. In fact, he is the most spiritual of artists. He represents eternal truths through earthly materials."

"My dear Catherine observes that I spend most of my time seeing God or the angels."

Mrs. Blake gently touched her husband's shoulder, then turned to Adam, offering a beatific smile. "I have very little of Mr. Blake's company. He is always in paradise."

Adam thought that making love to Maeve would be his idea of paradise, but given present company, it was best not to dwell on that notion. He began instead to look at the books of poetry and engraving. He admired *Songs of Innocence* and *Songs of Experience* in particular. But the work was not much to his taste, and the fact of the matter was that he would never have considered buying any of it except that it was obvious how much his doing so would please Maeve. He admitted candidly to himself that there was not much he wouldn't do to please her.

"Your work is quite unusual," Adam said. "I do not believe I've ever encountered anything like it." That was true enough, he owned.

"It is amazing, is it not? Oh, do not think me immodest. These poems are not my own inspiration and so I may praise them. Perhaps I should explain. You see, when I was four, I had a vision of God, and when I was ten years, I had a vision of angels. It seems I have always had metaphysical powers. My brother Robert and I had an engraving shop, but he died in '87, and without him, I was forced to give it up. He was very dear to me. But all was not lost. He became my communicator. I converse with his spirit hourly and daily. I hear his advice and write from his dictate."

Adam stared at the man in disbelief. Surely, Blake was mad. But Maeve looked at the fellow placidly, as if what he said were nothing out of the ordinary.

"Robert was brilliant. I learned the technique of engraving text on copper plate from him. I now write daily and nightly under the direction of messengers from heaven. I do not pretend to be any other than a secretary to the authors who are in eternity."

"Mr. Blake has the most moving of mystical experiences," explained his wife with a gentle smile.

Surely, these people must be quite insane. Yet Maeve thought highly of them. Adam supposed he understood from the beginning that she was something of a mystic; however, he'd assumed that her mysticism was merely part of the persona she chose to assume for business purposes. After all, it was quite fashionable if one were a gypsy to claim fortune-telling powers. It was quite the thing for her to claim second sight. He'd never considered that she truly believed herself endowed with such abilities or thought others might have them too.

He turned to her. "I would very much like to benefit an artist. Would you please select a work for me? I am quite willing to pay whatever is asked."

Maeve chose a book entitled *The Gates of Paradise,* which she termed prophetic. She spoke of the richness of finish of the engravings. It was all one to Adam, who much preferred the poetry of Byron and the novels of Scott, but he was determined to impress Maeve. He'd always prided himself on being a man of good common sense; yet where Maeve was concerned, he was lost. If she wanted him to be a patron of this particular artist, he would be one.

After they left the Blakes, he flipped a sovereign to the boys who waited for him eagerly. They were driving before Maeve spoke again.

"You do not have a favorable impression of Mr. Blake, I take it?"

He wanted to lie but found himself unable to do so. Maeve would see right through any charade. "I believe the man is odd."

"Dicked in the nob? That's what Ralph would say. What if I told you that I, too, converse with the dead? Would you consider me gifted with second sight or simply muddle-headed?"

He cast a sideways glance at her and found Maeve's eyes fixed on his face. "Must I answer that question? I find you enchanting and unusual. I would not have you any different, although we do not perhaps see the world in the same way."

She seemed hurt by his comment. "I knew you were a skeptic. I should not have made you buy that book."

"Nonsense, it is quite diverting."

"Someday, it will be valuable. Great artists are often unappreciated in their own time."

He was not about to argue with her when she seemed so set on the matter. Maeve was a woman of strong opinions, and he admired that quality in her.

"May I take you for a ride in the park?" he asked.

"I should like that, but I must be back home for tea."

He took her hand in his, guiding the reins with only one hand, and glanced over at her. "I find I do not wish to part with your company."

"Mr. Brockton also wishes my company."

"You should not remind me of that." He watched the rise and fall of her exquisite bosom and realized how hungry he was for her. "I must see you tomorrow," he said.

"Yes, you must. You will tell me about the duel. I pray that you will end the matter without violence or harm."

He reached the edge of Hyde Park and turned in. "Just for a moment," he said. He rode away from Rotten Row and chose a secluded place devoid of other people. "I need to have you in my arms if only for a few seconds. I cannot bear the thought that Brockton has you whenever he wants."

"I have told you that you do not understand." Her look was sad.

"And you will not explain."

She turned away from him. "Because you would not comprehend."

"My lovely girl, you give me so little credit. I would give you the world if you let me."

"I don't need or want the world."

"Do you want me even just a little?" He removed first his gloves and then hers. He kissed each of her fingers in turn. Then his hands caressed her hair; his lips moved on her neck. He found the hollow at her throat and felt the pulse that pounded rapidly there. He pulled back her pelisse as his mouth trailed burning kisses to the fullness of her breasts. His arousal was already stark, turgid with need and desire for her. "How soft and sweet you are. Do you have any idea how badly I want you?" he spoke thickly, unable to do otherwise.

She trembled in his arms as his kisses trailed back to her lips and grew more passionate and demanding. His hands cupped and then caressed her breasts. Her hands clasped tightly around his neck. She let out a shudder and a cry then pulled away.

"You must take me back at once. We can't. I can't."

He said nothing as he resumed the reins of his bays. Adam resolved he would not let matters go on as they were. He knew what he must do on the morrow once this business of the duel was finished.

Maeve hated to admit it, but she was anxiously waiting for Huntingdon to arrive the following afternoon. It was no good pretending that she did not want his company. The fact was, she could think of little else but him. She hardly knew the man, yet he was quickly becoming the center of her existence. This would not do. Perhaps it would be best if she ended whatever relationship they had. She realized that no good could come of it and had told herself that a thousand times. He could not love her, but would only use her and end up destroying her. Yet she felt only agonizing pain at the prospect of parting with him. What a fool she had become.

He arrived at two in the afternoon, looking just as dashing and handsome as ever, the hard planes of his face softening as he gazed on her.

"I have news about the duel," he told her, clasping her hands in his.

She waited expectantly.

"There will be none after all."

Maeve breathed a deep sigh of relief. "He apologized for his dreadful behavior?"

"Better still, he's left for the continent. Lord Randall, who was to act as my second, made the discovery. Apparently, Simmons could not run away fast enough. I had my fellow Pritchard collect intelligence of him. The baronet was a cowardly officer who in no way distinguished himself in battle. He is still a coward. We are well shut of him, and I believe this will end any danger to you."

"Perhaps," she said.

His patrician brow lifted. "You do not think he was the one who attacked you?"

"I am not certain of it. My intuition does not help me in this regard. Perhaps because I am too emotionally involved. When things become personal, matters become confusing."

"I suggest that we take a long ride today. I believe we have much to discuss."

She agreed with him. She stiffened her resolve. In spite of what she felt, today it must end between them. She would tell him so. But Sir John was not the only coward. Turning the marquess away was not something she could do easily. And so she got herself ready to go riding with him, her mind torn by conflicting feelings.

Before they could leave, Ginny came bustling into the room with a very young girl in hand. "Oh, Miss Maeve, I wouldn't bother you for the world, but this new one, she just don't listen proper." Ginny held up one of Maeve's silk evening gowns. It was the rose-colored one that Adam had admired as setting off the coloring of her skin.

"What is it, Ginny?"

"Ain't it true, Miss Maeve, that we don't brush out a silk gown, but use a piece of merino to gently rub it?"

"That is just so," Maeve agreed. She turned to the new girl. "Effie, each girl here is educated by the others. There are many things to learn in service, but when you finish your training, you will be a fine maid, and we will be able to place you with a good family. Ginny is an excellent teacher. You must listen to her and do exactly as she says."

"Everyone orders me about and criticizes what I do." The girl cast hard eyes downward, her demeanor surly.

Maeve took her hand. "It is always difficult in the beginning, but you will learn. Try not to be too sensitive. I am certain it will get easier. We will talk again."

"Thank you, Miss Maeve," Ginny said. She looked toward Huntingdon and blushed. "Sorry to have bothered you."

"Not at all."

They were in Adam's phaeton before he spoke to her again. "I must say you have an unusual household."

"I suppose so," she agreed. "We regularly buy girls from Beedle's just so they won't have to be sold to brothels."

"Brockton can well afford it, I daresay."

She lowered her eyes. "True, but I don't like asking him to do it. That was why I thought to open my own business."

He grew thoughtful. "You would like money of your own. Yes, that does seem reasonable. But I still believe this business venture of yours only creates more problems."

Maeve was not about to argue with him. The difficult situation with Sir John had grown directly out of her efforts to establish herself as a clairvoyant. The attempt had failed miserably and put her life in some jeopardy besides. The only good thing was that Caroline and Charles had found each other. How could she not sympathize with Caroline's desire to be free to choose the man she would marry? She could not regret helping the girl, no matter what the cost to herself might be.

It occurred to Maeve that Adam was not taking her directly to the park for their drive as she had expected. "Where are we going?"

He gave her a smile that lit up his face and made his features look less harsh. "I've arranged a little surprise for you. I believe it will prove diverting."

She never quite trusted him when he took that superficial tone with her; it meant he was hiding something, but what?

Huntingdon stopped his phaeton in front of a small townhouse in Curzon Street. "I want to show this place to you and see what you think of it. I intend to buy it."

"I am honored that you value my opinion so highly."

Maeve was surprised to find that the house was devoid of servants. The downstairs rooms were covered with dust clothes.

"I shall be your guide, and you must tell me what you think."

"It is unusual that there are no servants about."

He gave her a wicked smile. "They have been on holiday. The owner left London abruptly because of bad debts, I was given to understand. Actually, I think the fellow was challenged by an irate husband. I may have to acquire new servants for this house if I do settle on it. Perhaps you might be prevailed upon to assist me in acquiring staff."

She was getting a strange feeling, as if she

ought to turn around and leave, but he took her arm and led her toward the stairs.

"The rooms up here are of particular consequence."

Her steps slowed but he urged her forward. "Your Lordship, what are you about?"

He seemed to all but pull her down the hallway into the large master bedroom.

"Pleasant room, don't you think? Look around."

She walked across the room and glanced out of the windows as Huntingdon hovered by the door. She heard him shut it firmly. The chamber was at the rear of the house where a small, charming garden full of blooming red roses was on display from the windows. She could not help but admire the view.

"Try the bed. Huge and comfortable." He crossed the room with a panther's grace.

She stood where she was, hands on hips, chin raised and turned to face him directly. "You have planned an assignation."

"Give me more credit, my dear. I merely wish your opinion of the house. Oh, Randall was asking after you. He said you were the sweetest damsel he'd ever seen. He salivates for you, as I do." He walked to the bed and stretched out on it. "Shall you join me? You can advise me of its comfort."

"I am leaving," she said. There was no need to bid him farewell. She would call down a hack in the street. She felt hurt and angry. He only thought to use her, and well she knew it. How could she have dreamt otherwise? Why would she so often deceive herself regarding him?

"Afraid you won't be going anywhere. I've locked the door to this room and I have the key." He held up the key and then placed it into his coat pocket. "If you want to leave, you will have to come and get the key."

"I will not play childish games with you." She folded her arms furiously over her breasts.

He gave her his most supercilious smile. "Naturally not." Then the smile faded. His eyes turned dark and the look he gave scorched her very soul. "I assure you, this is no game. I want you. I have decided that the only way to win you away from your current protector is to have you to myself for a time. This establishment will be yours if you decide you want it. For now, consider that I have abducted you and am holding you here."

She stared at him in shock and amazement. "Surely, I did not hear you correctly."

"Indeed you did." His voice was smooth satin but quite clear.

"Is this a form of vengeance you are exacting because once I held you prisoner?"

"Revenge has nothing to do with my plans. Think of me as you would a pirate who has found a beautiful maiden and carried her off to his ship."

"To ravish?"

"To reverence with his passion."

She could not help but smile at his analogy. "As a pirate, may I say you are decidedly not up to crack."

"How so? You will wound me, madam, with your bold insults." He looked more amused than hurt.

"Where is your patch over one eye, Monsieur Pirate? And I would expect a billowing shirt open to the navel at the very least, and perhaps a parrot on one shoulder and a gold earring dangling."

He let out a melodramatic sigh. "My beloved cuts me to the quick."

"You are being very foolish, my lord."

"Am I? I must find a device to win you from Brockton."

"I do not wish to be your mistress, as you know."

He got up from the bed and moved to a large chair. "Come to me," he said. His eyes were all that was mesmerizing.

She shook her head. "Then I would be

251

the foolish one. I am not a Cyprian."

"Did I ever suggest I thought you common? Have you never known a man who wants you so much that he would risk being the complete fool to win your favor? I am such a man. Come let me love you. Let us know each other. I implore you." The look of dark longing in his eyes was impossible to ignore or resist.

She went to him and sat down on his lap as if in a trance. He took her hands and turned them palm upwards kissing each sensitive hollow in turn.

"I won't hurry this," he said softly, "but God knows I must have you. Consider yourself well and fairly kidnapped by one whose passion for you can no longer be contained."

"What if I refuse to be a party to your seduction?" Their eyes met and held.

He removed the key from his pocket and placed it firmly into her hand. "Let it be your decision then. But you must forgive me, my love, if I do my best to persuade you."

Chapter Thirteen

She knew in her heart that she could not, would not fight him anymore; she simply wanted him too much. He would not force her; she was certain of that. There was a basic generosity and goodness in him that he tried to hide from the world, but she knew it was there. Her intellect warned her not to give herself to him, yet she found it impossible to stop the heavy desire that was gathering in the depths of her being.

He wanted her and she wanted him. She realized that she wanted him to make love to her now and perhaps forever. Suddenly, nothing else seemed to matter. His lips pressed against the curve of her neck then moved to her mouth. Reason ceased to exist as his tongue explored the recesses of her mouth. She tasted the manly essence of him and shivered. He was lifting her into his arms and carrying her to the bed.

"Shall you tie me as I tied you?" she asked.

"With silken cords if you request it." He lay her down as if she were some precious treasure that might break. He removed his coat and cravat and lay down beside her on the tester bed with its furnishings of rich satin and damask. The dark drapes were drawn in the room and there was little light but she could see the brightness of his eyes like two candles reflecting darkly in a mirror.

"I am frightened," she said.

He took her hand and kissed each palm ever so gently. "What if I were to promise you the greatest pleasure?" His tongue licked her ear playfully.

She found herself unable to speak.

"You do not believe me? Let me show you." Then he was kissing her again; this time his mouth sought hers deeply, passionately. The taste and texture of his mouth were so dear to her that she could not help but enjoy the intimacy of his exploration.

His hands moved on her body, and she found her breasts were bare to his touch. She hardly noticed him push down the bodice of her gown and chemise. He cupped one breast with his hand, teasing the nipple of the other with his fingertip.

She gave a soft cry of pleasure as his tongue began to move rhythmically around the swelling bud. Then he was pressing each nipple and sucking them in turn. The pleasure was not to be borne. She felt it deeply at the very core of her being.

He slipped off every shred of her clothing and looked at her in admiration. Slowly, his eyes traveled down every inch of her body. "Just as beautiful as I imagined. Magnificent." Then he was kissing her again.

His lips sucked her breasts, licking her nipples while his hands burrowed through the silken curls at her apex. His fingers rubbed and caressed the small nub he sought. The pleasure intensified although she could hardly imagine it would.

"More?" he whispered in a husky voice.

She could not answer, but he understood. Her need for him was so great. His mouth trailed downward to the place his fingers rubbed so erotically. She guessed what he would do and wanted to deny him such intimacy, but it was impossible to deny him anything. His mouth took the nub of flesh as if it were some ripe, delicious fruit upon which he wished to feast. She trembled and moaned with delight. And then, when it seemed she could stand it no longer, she shattered into shards of crystal purity. The pleasure fragmented into spasms of ecstasy whirling her out of herself, out of time and space. She must have cried out, but she hardly knew it.

When she came to herself, her heartbeat began to quiet and the dew on her skin slowly cooled. "What was it?" she asked in wonder.

He looked at her with the dark intensity she had come to associate with him. "You've never known that pleasure before, have you? I cannot believe he could be so selfish. By God, I ought to thrash him!"

She realized suddenly that Adam was still dressed in his pantaloons and fine lawn shirt. She was embarrassed at her nudity and sought to pull the covers around her. What if he saw all of her? Saw her from the back? Surely, he would develop a disgust of her.

"Don't do that. No false modesty, madam. You are truly breathtaking as you are. I want to gaze on your lushness." He smiled and kissed the tip of her nose. "Besides, now it is your turn to do what you wish with me."

She found herself blushing deeply. "I think perhaps I best get dressed and go."

When she moved as if to rise, he took her around the waist and held her in his arms.

"Stay as you are. I shall join you." Then he began to undress without the slightest hesitation or modesty.

His body was just as magnificent as she remembered. The room suddenly seemed to grow hotter. She found herself reaching out to him, wanting him with a need she hardly understood. He came to her, and she felt the hair of his chest press against her breasts, the hard muscle of his sinew coiling around her. Her breathing was one with the rise and fall of his and the throbbing of his heartbeat sounded wild and passionate against her own.

His mouth began slowly kissing her body, exploring every part of her skin. He was kissing her everywhere, driving her wild with want. Heat started to build within her and heaviness formed at the juncture of her thighs. Need. Desire. Longing. All for him. Then he brought her hand to touch him, to feel his erection, pulsating like a hard, velvet fist. God, it was maddening. She was on fire and could hardly draw a breath. She felt him quake as she touched him and rubbed him the way he had her. He began to groan.

Then his mouth found her most intimate of places once again. His marauding invasion built convulsive shudders of need. His fingers gently pressed inside of her.

"You are hot and tight and liquid and ready for me," he said in a voice that ached with desire.

She could not deny him. She gasped and writhed against him, arching her back as he began to stretch and fill her. His fingers continued to rub the tiny nub deep within the petaled folds. His mouth took hers, his tongue erotically invading and joining with hers as he probed within the hot liquid volcano of her body.

As Adam plunged and then retreated, he felt the barrier. It startled him, coming unexpectedly as it did. He held himself over her and looked down. For a moment he hesitated, but his need for her was too great. He didn't tell her that it would hurt. What would be the point? It would only make her tense and frightened and therefore he would hurt her all the more. She cried out as he plunged into her and shattered the fragile barrier forever. Then he stayed in her, barely moving for a time, but still taut, hard and in dire need.

"The pain will subside," he promised. "Then you will feel the pleasure again. I will open the gates of paradise for you. First the pain and then the pleasure. Trust me?"

He felt the imperceptible nod of her head. He suckled her splendid rose-tipped breasts and whispered how wonderful she was and how much he desired her. Then he was moving again — wild, throbbing, the sensations built, crescendoing. He controlled himself as best he could, giving small, erotic strokes to her core. But he was caught in a maelstrom of rapture and soon he surged into her with an intensity beyond anything he had ever known. She moved with his every thrust. The feeling spiraled and whirled. It seemed that she cried out just when he did. He was lost, locked into a world of feeling and limitless passion. She opened herself completely to him, and he was touched by her innocent trust.

Later, he felt her in his arms, holding tightly to him.

"You were incredible," he said. "I adore you."

"You spoke the truth. It was beyond anything I could have dreamed or imagined." She looked at him with a sense of awe.

"Why did you not tell me that you were a virgin?"

She turned her eyes away from his. "You would not have believed me."

He ran his fingers through her hair. "You should have trusted me, though Lord knows I've given you little enough reason." A disturbing thought occurred to him. "I do not understand, Maeve. You have been with

259

Brockton all these years and he has not touched you in that way. Has he been unnatural with you?"

She turned an angry look on him. "Oh, you would think such a despicable thing! Nothing of the sort. The man has treated me like a daughter. He has never been untoward in any regard."

"All these years? Perhaps at first you were a child, but you are hardly that now."

"Charles's mother was his only mistress, the love of his life, and gladly would he have married her if she'd been willing but she was not. I think she believed him too lowly at the time. He has loved no other woman since. I think of Mr. Brockton as I would a father and kind benefactor. I am sorry if your mind is too vile to think in terms of other kinds of relationships. I forget that you are a jaded aristocrat."

He tried to placate her anger. "Perhaps you are the slightest bit unfair to me?"

She wound the sheet tightly around her body and turned away from him. He turned her around and held her in his arms. "I only meant I could not conceive of a man faced with so much loveliness not being moved by it. Since I myself am overwhelmed with the strongest desire for you, I cannot imagine any other man, be he natural, not wanting you as much as I."

What he did not say was that he was filled with a fierce sense of satisfaction, knowing that he was the first man Maeve had ever made love with. The very first man to love her! He had thought it didn't matter. What difference to a sophisticated man of the world how many lovers she'd already had? He wanted her regardless. But dear Lord, the elation he felt knowing that he was the first and only man who ever truly possessed her and initiated her in the ways of passion. It overwhelmed him. It humbled him. It also surprised him how primeval his feelings were in regard to her.

He had thought making love to her would end his obsession and desire once and for all. Yet the hunger was still there, if anything, stronger than ever. Her untutored passion had been so giving; he'd never known the like. Never again would he be satisfied with the studied artfulness of the courtesan, which now seemed nothing more than pure mechanical technique, and a poor, pitiful substitute for real emotion. He longed to bury himself in Maeve's earnest passion once again, but knew it was too soon.

He rose and went to the washstand, where he found a full pitcher of fresh water, scented soap and towels. He'd sent his own servants early this morning to make preparations and was well satisfied that they had done so.

"Stay where you are," he said when she began to move. "I'm going to wash you."

She began to protest but he refused to let her rise from the bed. "Don't be missish now. You must allow me to do this for you."

Maeve flinched when he moved the cloth between her legs. Gently, he washed away the evidence of their coupling, the blood and seed, the stickiness, were all soon gone.

"I confess I've never made love to a virgin before. Have I hurt you badly?" He put away the cloth and gently massaged her shoulders with his hands.

"I will be fine," she said. "I did want you."

Her husky voice, the glow in her eye and on her skin made him desire her all over again. A few pins remained in her hair, and he pulled them free so that he might bury his face in the ebon locks. He inhaled deeply of her rosewater scent.

"You stir me to such wild excesses of passion."

She put her hand against his chest. "I should go."

He sensed her reluctance. "There is a cold collation in the kitchen. Share it with me."

She looked downward, the thick, black

lashes hiding her eyes. "You know I must leave."

He took her hand in his. "You forget that you have been properly kidnapped. This time, you are my prisoner."

Her head snapped up. "Adam, Mr. Brockton will worry."

"I left him a note. It states that you will be with me for some time."

"That may worry him even more. Mr. Brockton has expressed to me his mistrust of you. He told me you have a certain reputation."

"Has he?" Adam watched as she snatched her clothes from the floor and moved toward the connecting chamber, quite literally backing away from him.

"He thought you wished to seduce me."

"And so I do."

He followed her into the smaller bedchamber. She had slipped behind a painted screen and was beginning to put on her clothing. The sun caught her shadow against the cloth of the screen and he watched her silhouette moving gracefully. He had the strongest desire to walk behind the screen seize her in his arms and rip off every shred of clothing that she put back on. However, he was a civilized a man, a man of propriety, although propriety could be such a dreadful bore at times.

He forced himself to sit down calmly and quietly on a shield-back Hepplewhite chair, vaguely observing its neo-classical elegance and utility. He studied his fingernails. "What else does Brockton say of me?"

"That you will soon marry and completely forget about me."

"A wife and a mistress are two entirely different things. A titled gentleman should have one of each, because a wife, you see, is merely a necessary evil. A proper mistress is a man's delight."

"You are a dreadful cynic."

As he watched her lushly curved body writhe into her white gown through the shadowed light of the screen, his own body felt a rush of hard desire. He began to think about touching her intimately again. Perhaps it was time to put his clothes back on. He did not want to frighten her into thinking that he was nothing more than a rutting swine, although the evidence of that was all too apparent at the moment. He went to the other room and quickly dressed.

She was fully clothed when he returned to the smaller chamber, but she had left her hair down and that pleased him. He ran his hands through the silky, raven tresses and then kissed her full, sensual lips that were sweetly rosebud pink and swollen from his passionate overtures.

She pulled away from him. "You will feel differently about wives once you choose your own. You will adore her and forget all other women. Why should it be otherwise? What will she be like I wonder?"

He groaned. "I do not wish to talk or think about that eventuality for many years yet. But let me explain for your edification. An aristocrat's wife is not selected by fancy. She must be a lady of impeccable lineage, of breeding above reproach."

"Like a race horse?"

"Quite so."

"Do you examine her teeth?" Her eyes twinkled mischievously.

"I vow it has likely been done."

Suddenly, she looked troubled. "So someone of disreputable heritage, a gypsy for instance, could never hope to be a lady. Such a one could only aspire to provide some temporary diversion for a gentleman of quality."

He saw the stricken look on her face. "That was not the intent of my words. It seems I may say nothing right. I cannot placate you."

"You have no need to please me." Her voice was aloof, distant.

"Have I not already pleased you?"

The color deepening in her face satisfied him. She moved toward the steps as if ready to flee and he quickly took her arm.

"Milady, our repast awaits."

"No, thank you, Your Lordship." She was being formal again, damn her.

He felt like shaking her. "What? I have worked myself to the veriest limits of endurance making these preparations for you."

She gave him a slight, grudging smile.

"Don't believe me, do you? Well, you are quite right. I am a liar when it suits me. But I did condescend to visit the kitchen this morning and tell Cook what I wanted. Now come talk to me and share my humble fare or I shall be devastated."

"Knowing you, there will be nothing humble about the fare."

They sat together cross-legged on the Aubusson carpeting in front of a marble-manteled fireplace in which no fire had been lit, nor was any needed.

"Do have a care for the ants. They have not your reticence I fear." He pretended that they were picnicking in the park, which made her laugh. He seemed almost boyish.

"Good, my bit of fustian seems to amuse you." He poured a glass of champagne for her.

"I expect your parents will want you to marry soon, despite your wishes." She nibbled thoughtfully on a roasted leg of pheasant.

He let out a deep sigh, feeling quite put upon. "That again? I assure you, love, that my parents are not the least concerned about my marital status."

"I thought a main concern of the aristocracy was begetting heirs. Rundwall certainly seems obsessed with it. Aren't your parents? What are they like? You have never spoken of them."

He gave her a small shrug, lifted her free hand and kissed it. "My parents are unworthy of discussion."

"You frighten me when you talk so," she said. "There is a hardness that comes into your voice and the expression of your face is so closed."

"You will plague me with curious questions until I tell all, won't you? You are an impertinent, saucy wench who will not allow a man to have any peace or privacy. Very well, I will discuss the matter but once, and then I wish never to have it brought up again. You will oblige me in this." He gave her a look that brooked no argument.

She folded her hands in her lap and watched him pensively.

"My mother, now there is a woman of excellent lineage. How unfortunate that she is also a whore. My father, I believe, was fascinated by her. Unfortunately, he did not satisfy her appetites. I was their only child. Her other children she had with various lovers, but that was after." He stopped talking and took a long swallow of champagne.

"After?"

He gripped the delicate stem of his glass so tightly that it shattered. "An involved and exceedingly nasty story. But then I suppose you might as well know, since you are so curious. I was at Eton when my father walked in on my mother in bed with a lover. I am certain that Father was previously aware of her wanton behavior. Rundwall assures me that she was notoriously profligate. However, that is not the same as being openly cuckolded in your own bed.

"The two gentlemen fought with their fists at first. I am told my father took the worst of it. Apparently, my mother taunted him, mocking and jeering his lack of prowess at manly diversions. Whereupon His Grace left the room, went to his library, drew out his pistol and attempted to kill himself. He did not succeed. What I failed to mention was that he was inebriated at the time, a condition most usual for him. The bullet entered his head in such a manner as to impair his ability to function in a normal way. And so he lives on more dead than alive. He exists, or the shell of him does, but he can do nothing for himself. He drools like an infant and is cared for as such."

Adam took a deep breath and let it out slowly. It pained him terribly to discuss the matter even with Maeve, who eyed him with the utmost sympathy. But he did not wish sympathy from anyone, least of all the woman for whom he felt so much passion.

"You questioned my loyalty to Rundwall. You should know that it was he who called out my mother's lover. He killed the bloody bastard, put a ball through his perfidious heart. It was brave of Richard, since his opponent was possessed of a formidable reputation."

"What happened to your mother?"

He smiled sardonically. "She left my father and went on to new lovers. I have not seen her since, nor do I wish to do so ever again."

Maeve's fingers caressed his face. "I am very sorry. You obviously had to assume a very heavy burden of responsibility at a young age."

"Again, Richard helped. He taught me a great deal about managing the estates. He made certain my agents were reputable and honest. I owe him more than can ever be repaid."

"I am so sorry. I did not understand your loyalty toward him."

He saw tears form in her eyes.

"I hope I have not been too unkind or unfair to him."

"It was Lady Caroline who hurt him, not you." He brushed away a tear that fell down her soft cheek. "A gentleman should beware of offering his heart to a lady of quality."

"Surely, not all ladies of quality lack morals."

"And I am certain that they do." His voice sounded harsh even to his own ears, but he meant what he said. "In the *haut ton,* a wife may be expected to be faithful, but only until she has been delivered of heirs. Then she may discreetly go her own way. It is the accepted thing. I will take my pleasures where I choose and expect that a wife will do the same."

She regarded him steadily. "How cold and disagreeable that sounds! If I were to marry, I should want someone who loves me and whom I can love in return. A contracted arrangement sounds so lonely and empty. I should want to be loved by my husband or I would not be willing to marry."

"If love is all you require of a man then

take mine." It was time to press his advantage. "Brockton will give you what you ask for and that is well and good. But I will give to you without you having to ask for a thing. Isn't that better? And I assure you, I would put you above any wife I might be forced to take."

"For how long? You would soon tire of me and go on to another mistress."

He lifted her hand and kissed the palm. "Tire of you? Never!"

"You are in lust with me, not in love. I cannot believe you."

Nevertheless, she looked confused. He could see that his words were persuasive and having an effect. This was the proper moment. He had waited to make certain, but he knew now what he wanted. There was no question in his mind; he was not willing to part with her. If he bought his gypsy with gold, so much the better. He rose and found the bank draft in his coat pocket then handed it to her.

"What is this?" She stared first at the draft and then at him in surprise.

"It is in your name. Do with it as you wish."

"But this says ten thousand pounds!"

"Too little?"

Her eyes opened wide. "What is it for?"

"For you, for anything you choose. Save it, spend it, invest it. There will be more."

"I cannot accept this," she said, and tried to hand the check back to him.

He moved away. "I told you, it is already yours."

She came toward him. "And what are your expectations?" She eyed him with suspicion.

He came and took her in his arms. "Have faith in me. I expect that I have bought nothing. This is a gift." He moved his fingers back and forth along the line of her jaw. "I do want you," he said. "I expect I have made that plain. At heart, I am just a simple man with simple needs."

"You are the most complicated person I have ever known."

"That does not sound like a compliment." He kissed her lips with gentle restraint and nuzzled her neck.

She withdrew from his embrace. "You are too generous, but I cannot possibly take your money."

He pulled her close once again. "You can and will accept it. It is what I wish. If you decide to accept me, then I will establish you in this house. You will have to leave Brockton, but this house shall belong to you always. And I will endeavor to be generous in all respects. I will delight in presenting you with beautiful baubles. You may depend on my continued regard."

When she did not answer, he kissed her again, this time with more urgency. "I am offering you *cart blanche*."

"You are very generous."

"I live by the golden rule. He who has the gold rules."

She knew he meant it as a jest, but the cynical remark expressed his materialistic philosophy perfectly.

"I believe I have told you before that I do not measure all things in that manner. You have many good qualities that make you the special man you are."

"Such as?"

"You are loyal to your friends."

"I remember my friends. That is true. But I never forget my enemies — or forgive them." He had once again slipped into the hauteur of the aristocrat.

How did he consider her, she wondered? Was she just to be a possession he wished to acquire?

"I shall wait upon your answer. I can be patient when it is necessary. In the meantime, do you wish to finish your dinner?"

"I am not very hungry."

He pressed his hand against her cheek. "But I am starving. However, I know I must go slowly. You must be sorely aching and I am the cause."

"I have made no complaint." Her eyes softened into mist.

He smiled down at her. "One of the things I adore about you. You are totally unspoiled. Pillow me against your delectable breasts and tell me a story of gypsies and their free, wild ways."

"You should finish your dinner."

His arms came around her, and as their lips joined in a deep, drugging kiss, somehow all thoughts of the rest of the meal were forgotten. Instead, they feasted on each other.

CHAPTER FOURTEEN

Adam was having an erotic dream. Garbed as a gypsy, Maeve danced before him. Her shoulders were bare; she wore a gypsy costume, a white peasant blouse with a brightly colored skirt cinched in tightly at the waist. A blood red scarf covered her hair but silky ebon locks escaped to cascade down her back. Large, gold hooped earrings caught the shimmering sunlight. She shook a tambourine and sang in a husky contralto voice. The gyrations of her voluptuous body were causing him to swell with lust. All he could think of was how badly he wanted her. He reached out for her but she disappeared.

He awoke abruptly aware of his need and aware that it was still very dark, perhaps only the middle of the night. He was lying on his side and could feel Maeve's firm buttocks pressed up against his erect member. The feel of her body covered only by the thin material of her chemise enflamed him with a desire unlike any he had ever known. He wanted to rip off her garment and enter her immediately. Instead, he gently edged her chemise above her waist and began tenderly rubbing the tiny nub at her apex with a rhythmically sensual motion. She moaned softly in her sleep.

His mouth kissed and nibbled the back of her swanlike neck. She snuggled in more tightly against him. He could feel her opening to him and positioned himself so that he could easily enter her sleek warmth. His fingers felt the warm liquid core of her bidding him welcome and he knew that he could wait no longer.

She gasped as he slipped into her, filling her with himself. She was awake now, aware that he was inside her. He moved ever so slowly, shifting so that she would be more comfortable. His fingertips circled her nipples and he felt them become taut under his ministrations. He moved in and out of her, accustoming her to the feel of him, coaxing her to respond, to tighten around him. Each time he thrust a little harder in sharp, short movements. She writhed against him and began to whimper. As the rhythm built, it felt so right and good. She was truly with him and they climaxed together as one in spasms of purest ecstasy.

"I love you," he heard her say in a soft, sleepy voice. Much later, he wondered if he had only imagined it. He should have felt guilty for insisting that she remain with him for the night, but he found he could not. He felt sated and satisfied as only the pleasure of making love to a good woman could bring to a man. He comforted his conscience with the thought that she really did want to be with him.

But in the morning when he reached for her again, she was gone. There was nothing beside him except a cold, empty space. He climbed out of bed and called her name. There was no answer. Muttering curses, he threw on his shirt and ran around the dark, closed house desperate to find her. But she was nowhere to be found and her things were gone as well. He realized that she must have returned to Brockton's house. The thought ripped at his heart. Perhaps she had only gone back to pack her things and tell Brockton that she was leaving.

Maeve hadn't left the bank draft behind, surely that was a good thing — or was it? He had told her the money was hers with no conditions attached. If she did plan to become his, surely she would have waited for him to rise, not gone off early in the

277

morning without a word. He was torn apart by doubts. He had not felt such a sense of grief and loss since he found out about his mother. No, this was far worse. His mother had visited him only occasionally in the nursery and although he had adored her and looked forward to spending any bit of time she might offer him as a child, the truth was, she'd always kept him at arm's length. There were nurses and servants he knew far better and who had shown him a good deal more affection and attention.

The following day, still not having heard from Maeve, Adam went to the Brockton townhouse where he was told by the butler that Miss Maeve was not at home. He asked when she would return and was told that no one knew. Had she told the butler that she was out to him? Or was she truly not at home? If so, where was she? What was she doing? His mind was tortured by uncertainties. He realized with painful clarity that she meant too much to him. He should never have allowed that to happen.

With growing anger and misgivings, he called at Maeve's lodging only to find out from her landlady that Maeve had not been there either.

The following day, he called again at

Brockton's and met with the same response. He left his card with shaking hands, barely able to contain his rage. He put Pritchard on the matter immediately. He felt like a damnable fool.

On the third day, he demanded to see Ralph. After all, Ralph was Maeve's devoted watchdog. When the butler did not instantly respond, Adam lost his temper, lifted the man off his feet and threatened to beat some civility into him. That was when the butler went scurrying for Ralph.

"Now, sir, no need for violence," Ralph said in a placating manner. "I know you're handy enough with your fives, but it ain't necessary to show off here."

"Where is she?" He practically snarled at the solid figure standing before him planted like a sturdy oak tree.

"Gone away for a time."

Adam was too furious to accept that vague explanation. He could only think that she had made an ass of him and that he had encouraged it.

"Damn it, man, do not lie to me! I am no flat to be tricked."

"I've been many things in my time but I'm no liar. Ask Mr. Brockton, he's the one to tell you about Maeve."

"Exactly what I intend."

Actually, he had no desire to see Brockton but he knew there was no place else to turn for information if he ever hoped to see Maeve again.

That evening, he entered the plush gambling club on St. James's Street that bore the name of Maeve's benefactor. Brockton's was all the rage. Celebrities such as Prinny and Wellington down to the youngest ensign of the guards hastened to enroll themselves as members whether they cared for play or not. Many great foreign diplomats and ambassadors belonged to Brockton's as a matter of course. It was simply *de rigeur*. Adam was indifferent to gambling and played only occasionally. He enjoyed belonging to a club but preferred White's. Deep play was not his style, although he owned it quite fashionable. It seemed to him that Englishmen would foolishly bet on anything at all.

He looked around Brockton's posh establishment and saw many familiar faces. Card tables were regularly placed and whist was played to some extent. But the greatest attraction was the hazard bank at which the proprietor took his nightly stand prepared for all comers. The old fishmonger was seated comfortably at his desk in the corner of the room vigilant as Cerberus guarding the entrance to Hades. Adam watched for a time and saw huge amounts of money changing hands. Wellington was there losing heavily, too absorbed to even notice Adam's presence.

Adam waited for the right moment to catch Brockton's attention. He half expected the man to gloat in his face. But when he noticed Adam, his face contorted with anger.

"You! How dare you show your face in my establishment!"

Adam ignored Brockton's outrage. "Ralph says Maeve's gone away. Is it true?"

"Damn you, man, it's true all right and you're to blame."

"I do not understand. Where has she gone? I wish to bring her back."

"You think you can, do you?" Brockton signaled one of his employees to take over for him and led Adam to his private office in the rear of the club. Then he firmly shut the door.

"When she came home that morning, I myself was just returning from here. I was shocked. Asked her where she'd been all night, and God help me, she looked me straight in the eye and said she'd been with you. She was never one for falsehood. I lost my temper with her. Told her that she'd been ruined, that I'd lost respect for her. Acting like a common tart. How could she? She didn't cry but I saw the pain in her eyes."

"So you threw her out, is that it?" Adam was furious, his hands pressed into fists, eager to punch Brockton in his homely, square jaw.

"Throw Maeve out? Never." Brockton slumped into the chair behind his desk, his face as gray as his thinning hair. "Why would I do such a thing? I'd be killing the golden goose, wouldn't I? It was the dear girl that brought me all my good fortune. All of this." Brockton raised his hands indicating their surroundings.

"I do not understand."

"She never told you about our arrangement?"

"She has not been forthcoming about her background. Perhaps you best tell me under the circumstances," he urged.

"I met Maeve on a cold, damp autumn evening. A scrawny waif came running up to me out of the fog and begged me to buy an orange from her. I told her in no uncertain terms that she was to get away from me. It was a bad time, you see. The only woman I ever loved had just died and I'd been out hoisting a pint or two of ale to drown my grief. I was just about to cross the road. Next thing I knew, the child grabs me and practically knocks me over. As she does, these two carriages comes charging out of nowhere. Two young fools were racing curricles on a dare. I would have been killed then and there if Maeve hadn't saved my life."

"She heard the carriage?"

"Nay, the fog was a pea souper, couldn't see nor hear anything until it was too late. She saw it in a vision. It's her powers, that special gift she has."

Adam shook his head; the man was simply superstitious, as all gamblers were prone to be.

"And so you gave Maeve a home in gratitude."

"Had to take her with me. She'd used her last bit of strength to save me. She'd of died out in that street, sick as she was. Taking her to live with Charles and me was the best thing I ever done. Once she was well again, she read my fortune. I downed a cup of tea, and she interpreted the grounds in my cup. Said I was destined to have great luck in a game of chance, and that was exactly what happened. I was comfortably established as a fishmonger but I always did like to play a bit. Never did I win much. But after Maeve's reading, I entered a big game with some wealthy coves, folks of quality like yourself. After a sitting of twenty-four hours I'm pleased to say I won the enormous sum of 100,000 pounds. That was when I opened this establishment. And it's done right well, just as Maeve predicted. 'Twas her notion to make the place luxurious in its decoration and turn it into an exclusive club with a regular membership. I never had much luck in my life before the girl come into it. She brought the luck with her. Now she's gone. The luck will turn against me again. I can feel it."

"You've made a fortune here. You needn't worry overly. Where's Maeve gone?" He studied the ordinary-looking, middle-aged man as he waited in tense silence for a reply.

"She said her mother told her to go back to her own people. There were things she had to sort out in her mind. I believe you upset her. You should have left her alone. She isn't what you think. Maeve's an innocent — or at least, she was." Brockton gave him an accusing look.

"I value her too," Adam said quietly. "I intend to bring her back and set matters right."

"Let's hope you do. Brave of her to go off

on her own like that. No milk-and-water miss is our Maeve. She did leave a note for you, asked that it be given to you in a few days' time."

His heart began to beat with a thud. "Lud, man, give it to me now!"

"It's at the house. You can pick it up tomorrow."

"No, I shall have it now." Maeve had become more important to him than anyone or anything else in the world. She had quickly become his obsession. He must find her. "Does Ralph know where the note is?"

"Probably not, but Ginny does."

Adam spoke no more to Brockton. Instead, he went running out of the gambling club. He rode through the streets of London with reckless abandon. At the townhouse, he found the pretty maid, Ginny, carefully polishing silver while instructing two other young girls in the technique. He wasted no time and immediately asked for his letter, which she rushed to get for him. He knew his manner was brusque but now was not the time for an excessive display of civility on his part.

Unable to wait, he sat down in the drawing room and tore off the wafer seal. *"Dear Adam,"* the missive began, *"You will wonder why I left so abruptly without a word and I will* endeavor to explain. I am aware that I have made a mull of matters. But there is one thing that I know, I cannot be your mistress. If ever I could assume such a role, it would be for you and no other. However, I do not wish to sell myself to any man. You would cage me and I would grow dispirited like those poor, wretched beasts at the Tower of London. I would soon bore you and you would dispose of me because I could no longer provide amusement. I am not a flighty female. I gave you my heart as well as my body, and it was not for a momentary fancy. In the meantime, I need to be free. When I ran from the orphanage so many years ago, it was to avoid bondage. I suppose I have not changed.

As to your money, you will find it well-spent, or at least I hope you think it so. Please do not remember me with bitterness or rancor if you choose to think of me at all. Someday, you will find a woman worthy of your name and lineage, and you will be properly loved. I have cast the cards for you and foresee a long life filled with happiness, prosperity and fine children. And if by chance a child should come into being because of our coupling, I will treat it with the love it deserves.

Goodbye,
Maeve."

Long life? Love? Happiness? Damn her!

She was playing her gypsy games on him. Tricks and lies. Did she think him that gullible? Well, he would not have it! What he would have was her in the flesh so he could wring her pretty neck. She would not off-put him with a prosy little note. By God, he would have her or at least move heaven and earth trying to find her!

A slip of paper had fallen from the letter. He picked it up and saw that an address was written in her handwriting. Was she there? He doubted it, but it seemed worth the effort to look since she obviously meant for him to visit. He thoroughly intended to exhaust all possibilities.

The house in St. Giles was on a depressingly poor street. Adam was glad he had taken a hack instead of his own carriage. Unfortunately, the driver was less than agreeable to the suggestion that he wait for his passenger's return. Adam promised a guinea extra and that finally convinced the fellow.

"Got me wife and babes to think about," the man said.

Adam ignored the sally and stepped out of the carriage. Dirty, ragged children played everywhere. He could hear the cries of street peddlers selling knives, eels, rat poison; ugly noise and nasty smells surrounded him.

The address he was looking for was a building as gray as a prison. He stepped inside the dingy, dilapidated structure and glanced around. The inside was no better. A thin, elderly woman, on seeing him enter, walked toward him with an awkward gait. She looked as worn as the building.

"Can I assist you, sir?"

"I'm looking for a woman named Maeve. I am persuaded that she has been here."

He was answered by a smile of recognition. "You must be the fine cove she said would be coming here to help us. Your name be Huntingdon?"

"I am so called."

"Then I have a letter for you, sir."

Another letter? What was Maeve about? Why all this aura of mystery? It was truly absurd. She had cast him as a bit player in a melodrama. He detested such things.

The woman went to a scarred secretary and removed a folded paper. Another missile. With no patience left, he hurriedly ripped open the seal and looked inside. Maeve had written to him again all right. This time to say that his money had purchased Beedle's Home for Orphaned Girls: *"Five thousand pounds was spent. Miss*

Forbes, who you have just met, will be in charge unless you decide on someone else. She is excellent with the girls. The rest of your money has been placed back in the bank under your own name. If you wish to spend some of it for the betterment of the Home, that would be very kind. I am certain you can see that improvements are necessary in the living conditions. In the past, I have bought up the girls one by one but this will be so much better. No longer will they live in fear of Beedle's cruel moods. I trust in your kindness and integrity."

Blast the woman! Now she was casting him in the role of deuced benefactor to poor orphan girls. What next? Yet at heart, he couldn't help but be impressed by the fact that she hadn't kept a pence of his money for herself. It also meant that he hadn't bought her passion. She'd given herself to him sweetly and without condition. Was she as strongly drawn to him as he was to her? She'd written of giving her heart to him, but how could she leave him without a spoken word if that were true? He was torn by doubt.

He promised Miss Forbes that she would be hearing from him soon and prepared to leave.

"I hope Miss Maeve will come around

again. The girls so admire her. You should have seen Miss Maeve set old bastard Beedle out of here after she paid him off for the place. She was a force of nature to be reckoned with I warrant. Her eyes fairly flashed lightning."

He smiled to himself. He could well imagine Maeve in the throes of righteous indignation. Perhaps his money was well spent after all.

His next stop was to Pritchard who was very surprised that His Lordship would condescend to visit a mere solicitor's office. They talked at some length and it was agreed that Maeve would be located as soon as possible. Adam considered offering a reward to the Runners, but Pritchard did not think it necessary.

"I'll put extra men on it. As long as you're paying, you'll get results."

"Very well then, an added bonus will be paid to the fellow who finds her."

"A fine incentive, Your Lordship," Pritchard assured him with an approving smile.

Adam did not know which group of gypsies she would have gone off with, but the trail began in the London area and so perhaps it would not prove difficult. He was confident that Pritchard would locate her, but that was not the real problem. Once she was found, how could he convince her to come back with him? She refused to be his mistress. What else was there? Marriage? How could he marry a gypsy? The notion was too absurd. Yet he wanted her, wanted her even more since they had been together. When he touched her, fire burned in his loins. He'd never felt anything like it with any other woman. If he admitted the truth, it went beyond the physical. He enjoyed being with her, talking to her. There had to be a way. He could not lose her. It would be unbearable.

CHAPTER FIFTEEN

Epsom was burgeoning with gypsies during Derby Week. They came to hawk their wares, tell fortunes, sell horses and turn over money in any way they could. Maeve found it exciting. She spoke with many of them, trying to decide with whom she might live comfortably. But no group seemed right. Then she met the old woman, Essmie, a nearly toothless hag, and her sweet young granddaughter Kata. Her intuition told her that these were good people and that it would be safe for her to join them. And so she went to the king of their tribe, a powerfully built man of middle years named Daris, and gave him a purse of gold sovereigns to insure acceptance. It was Adam's purse, but oddly, she felt no sense of guilt using it in this manner.

She wished to live simply. All she required was freedom from her tormenting desire for the Marquess of Huntingdon. Surely being at a distance from him would secure this. She would travel with these gypsies and perhaps the restlessness she felt would go away. If she had stayed with Adam as he wanted, she would have become nothing but a slave to the passions that he stirred in her. Even now when she thought of him, her belly clenched with need. She had wanted to remain with him but then she would have been divested of all dignity and self-respect.

She traveled with the gypsy tribe to Dorset in the Midlands, through beautiful farming countryside the like of which she had never seen. She sat beside Essmie and Kata on top of the old disreputable caravan which was pulled by a sway-backed roan, until they finally made camp beside a large stream.

Daris, like any true king, rode proudly at the head of the small group of wagons, his own cart pulled by two black stallions. Maeve was relieved to be with these people, her mother's people. She knew very well that her mother would have returned to her own tribe if she had been allowed. But Mama had been declared *marime,* which meant she was an outcast because she had married a *gadze,* an outsider. Mama had eloped with a young man of whom her own mother did not approve. She had been rejected from the tribe and could not return, even after the young aristocrat deserted her. Maeve thought of her father with bitterness. He had been the third son of a wealthy baron. She had not even known him. He ran off to seek his fortune in America after his family disowned him for marrying a gypsy. He had promised to send for her mother, but he never did. Instead, he ran away like an irresponsible child.

Her mother was a proud woman and would have managed to survive on her own but for needing a place for her child. The baroness had given them a home after Mama lowered herself to ask.

Mama had the legal papers, the proof of her marriage lines and the record of Maeve's birth. Although Maeve's parents had been married in a *Gorgio* church, Mama was consigned to clean the kitchen day after day, like a poor scullery maid, and in return for this so-called kindness, she was warned never to mention her connection to the family. This terrible life had destroyed her mother's spirit. But she had suffered it just to give her child a home. However, the loss of freedom had been too high a price to pay. A free spirit like her mother could not survive living as a slave. Maeve bitterly blamed her mother's early death on the weakness of her father's character. She and

Charles both had similar views regarding the English aristocracy.

Now Maeve was with Mama's people, where her mother had really wanted to be. This tribe accepted her in spite of her mixed blood. No one asked questions about her past or where she had come from. The old woman "adopted" her as a daughter and seemed grateful for another pair of hands. Essmie's own hands were mere claws gnarled with arthritis.

This secluded place in the country suited Maeve. Some boys had gone off to gather firewood. The dusky-complexioned, weather-beaten men were looking after the horses. The women pitched their tents with the help of the remaining children. They were dressed in shabby clothes, these people, but they looked healthy and strong. There was a happiness about them, for they had a sense of belonging with each other and it gave them a serene inner peace.

Before long, the aroma of stew from the big iron pots that hung over glowing coals wafted through the air. Everyone joined together to eat the evening meal. Afterwards, all gathered around the fire. Kata sang a sadly haunting song in her sweet voice while a young man played the fiddle. Then Essmie told them an old gypsy folktale, full of supernatural happenings. Maeve knew this could be a good life, just as her mother promised. She was safe here and she was free. Then why did she feel so unhappy? But she knew the answer to that question well enough: Adam de Viller was never completely out of her mind. She had to remind herself that there was no future possible with him; she could not be his mistress, and she could not be his wife. Yet the mere thought of him made her flesh tingle and grow warm. Without him, her heart was a cold, empty chamber with no hearth fire to heat it.

There was property here in the Midlands that belonged to his family. He would have to see to it sometime. Dorset was a charming place. Here in Central England Adam observed fine farmlands and rolling hills. He saw before him land planted with hedgerows blooming now in the springtime with the hawthorn's white blossoms and the red flowers of the dog roses. Long rows of fields with trimmed hedges made the shires seem highly domesticated in comparison to the wilder northern parts of England to which he was more accustomed. He'd been here before for the fox-hunting season as a boy with his father in that better time when the duke was a whole man. That was when he'd been an innocent child unaware of his mother's deceitful nature.

Was Maeve anything like the duchess? He shouldn't think so. Pritchard and his man had come with him in the large, closed traveling coach. They found out where she'd gone. It had taken only a sennight, which had, however, seemed more like an eternity.

He'd brought two good horses and sent the men back to London in his coach. He'd decided to settle the matter of Maeve quite on his own. In reality, he wasn't at all certain what he would say or do. He was conscious of a need to woo her back to him. But what had he done to frighten her off in the first place? He knew only that if ever he were to have any peace of mind, he must see Maeve and talk to her. He alternated between anger and yearning, a purgatory of emotions.

When he came upon the tribe of gypsies, exactly where he was told they were camped, the first thing that Adam did was find their leader. He told Daris that he would require to remain with them for a time and presented the king with a purse of burnished guineas and a horse. The horse made the greater impression, for it seemed Daris considered himself a fine judge of horse flesh and admired the quality of the gift. So pleased was Daris that he invited the English gentleman to live with the tribe for as long as he wished. Adam accepted the invitation.

Maeve heard his voice before she saw him. At first, she did not know it was him. The man's voice was deep, resonant, and held the cultured tones associated with wealth and privilege. He was talking with Daris, the two men discussing the lines of good racing horses. Adam turned and looked at her, his dark eyes searing her soul. At first, she thought he was very angry with her but then he began smiling. He came toward her and she felt a strong stirring in her blood.

"You cannot be here," she said, aware that she sounded foolish.

"I came for you." His eyes as always were far too dark and penetrating.

He wore a lawn shirt open at the throat, which strained across the great width of his shoulders, and form-fitting cream doeskin pantaloons that intimately hugged his muscular thighs. She jerked her eyes upward, embarrassed by the heat she felt coursing through her body, only to find that he was subjecting her to a thorough scrutiny of his own.

He came forward and took her hands. She felt a charge of lightning jolt through her at his mere touch and gasped. His scorching look of dark longing was not to be mistaken. He must have felt just as she did when they came together.

"You look beautiful. I was furious with you for running off, but now I can't remember feeling hurt or angry, only relief that you are well and secure."

"You should not have come." Those were her words but her body said something quite different.

He brought his hand to her face and caressed her cheek; heat radiated throughout her body again. She found herself trembling.

"I would have done anything to find you."

Daris was frowning at them.

"It is not proper for unmarried man and woman to exchange intimacies in Romany society."

Adam stepped away from her, but Daris was not fooled.

"You come to find this woman?" he asked Adam.

Adam nodded his head, his eyes never leaving hers.

"For what purpose?"

"I wish to marry her." The words surprised

her and from the expression on his face, they surprised Adam just as much. He must have spoken impetuously without prior thought, entirely unlike his usual tight self-control.

"You wish to marry?" Daris repeated Adam's statement as if to make certain he understood the Englishman correctly.

"No, he does not," Maeve said quickly. She did not want Adam trapping himself into making promises he could not possibly keep.

Adam turned to her. "Do not answer for me." He spoke again to Daris. "Yes, I have come to marry this gypsy woman. How do I go about it?"

Daris rubbed his chin, which showed a dark stubble of beard. "Well, you are not a gypsy but we can make you an honorary member of our tribe. Maeve has been adopted by old Essmie and so we will plan a Rom wedding." His black eyes sparkled with pleasure.

"Daris, you must excuse us. I require a few words alone with the marquess."

Daris looked from her to Adam and grinned. "I will give this fine beast some exercise." Then he took hold of the horse that was Adam's present to him, climbed on its back with ease, and rode away.

Maeve led Adam to a secluded place in the woodland where they could be entirely alone. This was as improper to Romany society as it was to English sensibilities but she did not care at the moment. Impropriety seemed the lesser evil.

"What are you about?" She turned angrily to face him.

He raised his brow. "Why are you in such a taking? I've decided to court you. Is that not evident? Are you not pleased by my declaration? I am quite a matrimonial catch, or so I am told." He put his hand out to take hers but she pulled away.

"You confuse me. You know a marquess may not marry a lowly gypsy. There would be such a scandalbroth."

"I thought the same nonsense at first. However, I do not wish to be deprived of you. It appears to me that I may do as I wish. You are deemed a delightful eccentric by the *ton.* May I not become one as well by marrying you? Society accepts originals. I shall own to being one."

"It is a put down for you."

"Nothing of the sort." He caught her then and began rubbing his hands up and down her arms.

She shivered, unable to think clearly when he touched her. "You would marry me in the way of the Romany?"

"If that is what you desire."

She could see that his emotions were in a similar state of upheaval as her own. He hadn't thought out what he was doing, not for a moment.

"My lord, I caution you to consider your actions carefully. Do not be impetuous. You will not long remain among the Romany and I do not want to go back to London."

"Why the deuce not?"

"English society would snicker to hear that we were married in a gypsy ceremony. I would be considered a light skirt who seduced an aristocrat. 'She's no better than she ought to be,' they will say. Perhaps I could tolerate that censure but it would hurt Mr. Brockton. He is already out of countenance with me for what he considers my immoral behavior."

"If anything, Brockton has been very selfish where you are concerned. He has kept you in his plush house as a talisman, a virtual prisoner, a hostage to his good fortune."

She was outraged. "How can you say such a thing? I have never wanted for anything since I came to live with him. I did as I pleased and I was able to help other orphans into a better life thanks to his generosity."

He drew her into his arms. "Let us not argue. I comprehend your loyalty. Perhaps it is jealousy that I feel toward Brockton. But the fact remains, I very much want to marry you. This is not the coil you make of it. I will marry you here and I will marry you again in St. George's Church at Hanover Square right in the heart of London society. So you see, I am not ashamed of our alliance. I am quite pleased to be leg-shackled." He spoke in a light manner, but his eyes were very serious.

"Perhaps I do not wish to marry." She saw and then felt his pain.

"You do not care for me?" His eyes probed hers.

"I told you that I want my freedom. When my mother married my father, it doomed her. He too was an English aristocrat, not even equal to you in rank. Yet his family treated us as dirt."

"But we are not they. Do you have so little regard for me that you would think me to hurt you were you to become my wife?"

"A wife is considered a man's property, his chattel, is she not? I do not want to lose my rights as a human being to merely be added to your collection of possessions."

"It does not signify. I am not making a purchase, Maeve." His spine stiffened with indignation.

"You have told me that the only women you trust are those you buy." She saw his dark eyes flash with anger.

"I have gone to great trouble to find you. Do you think I would do so if I did not care deeply for you? Now it seems the real question is how much you care for me. I have given you my trust. Will you do as much for me?"

She stared at him long and hard, not touching, only looking, and deep in her heart she knew that she did not wish to live without him. He had not said he loved her. She wondered if he were capable of such an emotion. She ought to make him leave. It would be wise and sane. It would be best for both of them, but she found she could not. Her love for him was too potent.

"I will become your wife in the way of the Romany. You need do no more."

Adam looked into those otherworldly eyes of hers and saw sadness and resignation, not the joy he had expected or at least hoped for. It infuriated him that she would trust him so little. Very well, she accepted that they would have a gypsy wedding; that would do for a start.

Later in the day, he sat with Daris and

explained the situation as best he could. "If I want to marry Maeve in the gypsy way, what would I have to do?"

The Romany king was thoughtful. "It is our custom for the father of the groom to ask the bride price of the father of the bride."

"And if a prospective bride and groom have no fathers?"

"Then they must call upon those nearest to them to act on their behalf." Daris leaned forward. "You may ask me to represent you. I say most humbly that I am a fine negotiator. Since Maeve has been adopted by Essmie, her nephew Ferenc will serve the bride." Darius lowered his voice. "Your Maeve will not cost much since she is neither young nor of pure blood. Now Kata will get a good bride price because she is a virgin and not yet even twelve."

"Maeve is the only woman I would want to marry."

"Then, my friend, she will be yours," Daris assured him with a brotherly slap on the back.

It went as Daris had promised. On Adam's behalf, he offered Ferenc a bottle of whiskey to which was attached a head scarf, and wrapped inside, a betrothal gift. The head scarf and gold necklace which constituted presents to the bride were accepted by Maeve, much to Adam's relief. Then the bride price was settled upon. This came to one hundred pounds, which was promptly spent for food and drink for everyone in the tribe to enjoy, and the celebration was a happy affair. There was dancing, singing, fiddle-playing and much drinking and feasting. Unfortunately, he was not allowed to be alone with Maeve, the only thing he really desired.

The wedding itself took place two days after the betrothal. Daris understood that Adam was very eager for the marriage and tried to be accommodating.

"You want to take your *bori* back to the *gadze* world soon," Daris said knowingly. "But remember, you will both be welcome here. We will ask no questions. We will not treat you as outsiders. To us you will always be family."

Adam could not say how much he appreciated the Rom king's generosity of spirit. Then the ceremony was carefully explained to Adam so that he would know what to do at the wedding. As it turned out, he had only to stand to one side and look embarrassed. That proved not difficult at all.

Maeve was dressed in a wedding gown made by Kata and Essmie from red silk cloth that by ritual he as groom had paid for. Maeve looked lovely and exotically mysterious. Ferenc and his wife sponsored her. The red bridal veil and a red rose were placed on a stick by Kata. Daris had told Adam in advance that the bride would not be garbed in white. Red symbolized happiness and good luck, just as the red rose symbolized virgin blood which it was expected would be spilled. Adam found their customs barbaric by English standards, but he could understand the thinking that hearkened back to a simpler and more primitive way of life.

Maeve was drawn into a circle by Kata and the other young girls of the tribe. They held hands and danced around Maeve. She was supposed to be weeping the whole time. Adam noticed with a small smile that she managed only the illusion of tears in her eyes. Maeve was not much of an actress. Soon, she was taken away, the *diklo* or bride's veil was removed from the stick by Ferenc's wife and carefully placed on Maeve's head. Now she was considered married.

The next part of the ceremony as Daris had explained it consisted of what was termed "bringing the bride home." Ferenc and his wife, Maeve's sponsors, brought her back to the others. Essmie and Kata gave her a goodbye kiss that spoke of affection and good will. Then there was a commotion and a great deal of shouting and confusion as the young boys tried to stop the wedding by preventing Maeve from joining Adam. Good Lord, they were actually ripping at her clothes! Adam started to go forward to assist her but was stopped by Daris.

"No, my friend, do not interfere. It is custom. The groom never enters the ceremony. He must be modest and not look at his bride or come near her. I shall bring her to you as is appropriate for your relative to do." Darius then went forward, pushed the boys aside with a thrust of his powerful arms and brought Maeve to Adam.

Maeve was flushed when Daris put her hand in Adam's.

"Now you are joined," he said.

An enormous feast followed; a whole roast suckling pig was turned on a spit over the open fire until its succulent pink flesh was black on the outside and the meat fell apart. Food and drink were lavish. But Adam found, much to his consternation, he was still not allowed to be alone with Maeve. He was beside himself with frustration.

"She cannot sleep with you until the second night," Daris explained. He seemed to understand fully what was in Adam's thoughts. "It is custom." Daris shrugged and gave a deep sigh.

Adam was taking their deuced custom in disgust at this point but remained civil since he was a guest among these people and they had been very kind and hospitable to both Maeve and him.

When at last they were alone in the tent set apart for them, he could barely restrain his enthusiasm.

"I thought that it would never end. I believe it is time I gave my wife a real kiss." He folded her in his arms and felt the heat envelop them.

His kiss began slowly, gently but soon deepened. His tongue searched for access to hers. Then it plunged in a sensuous rhythm only to retreat and plunge again until their two tongues mated in desire. He could not control his need much longer. He lifted her into his arms and carried her to the bed of cushions that had been made up for their lovemaking. His hands began sliding along and stroking her body. Unsteadily, he removed her garments and then his own.

She looked at him shyly and reached over

as if to cover herself.

"No, let my gaze on your beautiful body. You cannot imagine how much I desire you." His heart beat with a maddening rhythm. He took her hand and placed her fingers on his swollen organ so that she would know the absolute truth of his words.

She caressed him gently and he moaned, hardly able to stand even that. He was in dire need but he would see to her pleasure first. He knew how tight her passage still was and he was a large man. He began kissing her lips and then her neck, moving on to her breasts. His hands cupped the fullness of her orbs while his tongue teased the taut, ripe nipples. Her breathing became ragged and he could feel the heat emanating from her body. His touch went to the curl of ebon hair that adorned her mound. He began stroking her with a feverish touch.

Her hands moved to run her fingers through his thick hair then stroke his head. Trembling, her fingertips caressed his body. It made him wild with desire, desperate to sheathe himself in her. He slipped a pillow beneath her hips and then eased himself into her sleek warmth. Instinctively, Maeve arched her back and molded her hips to his lean, angular length. He rubbed the nub of her pleasure as he moved within her, while the tension continued to build between them, and when he felt her spasms convulse around him and heard her cry out, he began to thrust more deeply, lavishly, hotly pouring himself into her, plunging to the hilt, his seed into her womb. Before he collapsed, Adam buried his face in Maeve's silken tresses that cascaded like a waterfall at midnight. He had never felt so satisfied, so alive, so jubilant. The Marquess of Huntingdon had come home at last.

CHAPTER SIXTEEN

Through the night, they made love several times, each time more passionately than the last. Now in the dawn hour, Maeve studied Adam as he slept, admiring his virile form, the hard muscle of his back and buttocks. Maeve was happy that they were finally together. Adam had gone to some trouble to marry her in the Romany way and as far as she was concerned, this proved his love for her. Perhaps whether or not he admitted it in words was unimportant. They were sleeping naked together and she adored this intimacy with him. He was a tender and considerate lover. She would never have dreamed it when they first met, but it seemed that they brought out the very best in each other. On the surface, he might be hard and cynical, but beneath the facade was a kind, caring, generous man. She knew that she would love him with fierce devotion until the day she died.

He stirred beside her, opened his eyes and smiled. "Are you really here with me or is this one of my erotic fancies? I dream about you all the time, you must know."

She kissed his lips with tender regard. "I am most certainly here and willing to fulfill your every fantasy."

He gave her a contented smile. "Famous, then turn over on that flat, adorable belly and let me enter you like a stallion does a mare. I've had that fantasy of late too."

She was immediately alarmed. "No, you do not want to do that."

"Of course, I do. I swear to be gentle." He rolled her over before she could stop him.

He gasped when he saw what she had so feared would give him a disgust of her.

"Maeve, what caused this?" He delicately traced the lines along her back, and she shuddered.

She did not turn to meet his gaze. "I had hoped never to let you see them. Mr. Beedle used to beat me when he believed that I was disobedient. According to Mistress Sommes, his assistant, I often deserved that punishment. I tried to protect the younger girls as I grew older and my efforts led to extra punishments. You should know that your money made it possible for me to free the orphans from their cruelty. Beedle and

Sommes should never be allowed near children."

He began kissing her back, running his tongue along the raised scars. "I am sorry for your suffering. I cannot imagine such vicious treatment of a child."

"You do not find me repulsive?"

"I find nothing about you ugly."

"Along with her other healing gifts, my mother gave me a special salve and taught me how to make it myself. It saved my life, but the horrible marks will remain. I take them to mean I must always remember that when I am in a position to help those in need, I must do so. I know I cannot make the entire world right by my own hands alone, but I will do what I can."

"So that is why you bought the orphanage?"

"I see you understand."

"I will kiss away your pain as best I can." His lips held a promise of sweetest paradise and she was lost to all else.

Much later, they heard the camp begin to stir around them.

"Adam, they will expect the flag."

"What?"

She found herself blushing. "A bloody garment, proof of my virginity. But we both know that is no longer possible."

Suddenly, he began rummaging among his things and then lifted his knife from its sheath which rested with his clothing on the ground. Before she could stop him, he cut his arm and snatched up her chemise to rub the blood along it.

"Why would you do that?" she cried.

"A small price to pay for one's honor." He gave her a quick kiss.

"I have something that will make your cut heal faster," she said. She caressed his cheek. He was indeed a complex man.

"That salve of your mother's? All well and good, but there are other things that take my mind off pain far better." He teasingly licked one nipple into bold erection until she gasped with delight.

"You are insatiable." She tried to look stern and not smile at him but it was impossible.

He gave her a boyish smile that displayed his dimple and made him look years younger. "I am this way only with you." He buried his hands in her thick, midnight hair and held her close. "There was a cold, empty place within me that you have filled."

She knew it was the same for her, that she would never again feel whole or complete without him.

"I have been remiss. I should have asked:

are you with child?"

She shook her head. "Are you relieved? Perhaps I should have told you before." Was he frowning?

He moved back and looked deeply into her eyes. "I am neither relieved nor disappointed. I did not think about it when I married you. That was not the reason I wanted to marry you," he said. "Perhaps we shall have children together one day. I would like that, but being with you is all that really matters to me."

She did not want to leave the tribe; yet after two more days, Adam grew restless. He refused to let her stay behind when she made that suggestion.

"We are married, my girl. And I intend to repeat the same ceremony in a proper church just as I promised. Brockton may give you away."

"Are you sure?" she asked. "I could stay with the tribe and you could visit me when you like."

He let out an uncharacteristic snort. "This from the woman who refused to be my mistress? You still have so little faith in me. I have taken you for my bride. In any case, I will not leave you here. We belong together." His voice was rough, fierce and determined.

She found her eyes welling up with tears. "Whatever happens, please know that I love you more than anything else in this world."

Everyone wished them well before they left. Essmie gave her advice about satisfying a husband that had her blushing while Daris lectured Adam about the significance of having a wife.

"It is a woman's destiny to marry," Daris said and joined her hands to Adam's as he spoke. "Once she marries, she must be guided by her husband and accept his rule. This is the way to marital happiness. I bless you both." Then Daris turned and walked away.

Maeve wrinkled her nose in disdain while Adam watched her, then threw back his head and roared with laughter. "What? Already you are disobedient? Did you not say you wanted to live in the gypsy way?"

She sniffed at him. "It would seem that all men are alike. They wish to enslave women."

His expression grew more serious. "Not all men. I promise you respect and honor always."

She knew that he meant it and felt a warm glow deep inside. Still there was a dread in her, a foreboding. Her intuition told her that she would not be safe in London. However, she also dreaded sending Adam away without her. If she did, he would not understand and might well never return. The hurt would be too great. Returning to London with him was a sacrifice she must make.

Their first evening back in London was spent at the townhouse that Adam had bought for her. It was to be the house that they shared. It looked very different now. There were servants in it, candlelight everywhere and all the furnishings free of their dust cloths.

"Why, it's quite beautiful," she remarked after he had introduced the staff to her. "I know that we will be happy here."

"I wrote ahead when you agreed to marry me and had our ducal butler make the arrangements. I am glad you like it."

His face lit up in delight, and she thought he looked incredibly handsome. He seated her on a Queen Anne chair in the library and closed the door.

"Tomorrow morning, I will apply for a special license. Then we will celebrate our second wedding. In the meantime, so there is no talk, I will live at the ducal residence."

"We are to be separated again?" She cast a mournful look at him. "I do not wish it."

"Not for very long," he promised and kissed her lips with reverence. "We must have some regard for your reputation."

"My reputation does not signify."

He shook his head in a world weary manner reminiscent of the old Marquess of Huntingdon. "Society gossip can be ugly, and I would not want you to suffer unfairly for my lack of propriety."

That night Maeve slept alone and had horrid, frightening dreams. She awoke in the middle of the night, her body soaked with sweat, not certain where she was, but the terror passed and she remembered that soon Adam would sleep beside her always. She could not remember the dream, only that she was dying. There had been a great deal of blood. The dream had been very real; too real. She did not sleep again.

In the morning, she arranged to have the coach that Adam had provided take her to Mr. Brockton's house. He was not awake, just as she supposed, but she wrote a note for him so that he would know in general terms what had transpired during her absence from London. Then she visited with Ginny, Mary and the other girls, telling them about buying Beedle's, marrying Adam and how wonderful the marquess was. They were all very excited and happy for her.

"Imagine, Miss Maeve, you marrying a marquess! Why, it's like some wonderful fairy tale come true." Ginny got a dreamy look in her eyes, and Maeve knew that she was fantasizing about a prince charming who would come and carry her off to a castle in the mists.

The girls packed her things. She had taken very little with her when she left to join the gypsies, and the carriage was now loaded with baggage. Ralph wished her all the best and asked if she wanted him to guard her again. She remembered what Adam had said about Sir John Simmons no longer being a threat and decided that she had become too fearful. She had always believed in the prophecy of dreams, but perhaps this time she was being foolish. Besides, Ralph belonged here serving Mr. Brockton. She had no right to take him away.

After her things were unpacked at the new house, she found herself feeling restless. She decided to take herself off to Bond Street and do some bridal shopping, and so had the coach brought around once again.

She was soon exhausted by the selection of new nightrails and chemises with which she thought to please Adam. She indicated to the coachman that she would be stopping in a nearby tea shop. As she walked up the street, Maeve had the sense of being watched. She looked around, but there were so many people on the busy commercial street, and no one seemed to be looking at her in particular. Yet the back of her neck felt most peculiar, as if there were eyes focused vengefully on her. Around her neck, the crystal in her necklace felt hot.

Suddenly Maeve found that she had lost her taste for tea. The terrible dream of last night came back to haunt her in vivid detail. How she wished Adam were with her to help remove her fears. She turned and started back toward the waiting coach. As she did, Maeve felt a hand at her waist and something sharp pressed against her side. She let out a gasp.

"Do not speak," a male voice said into her ear. "There is a weapon ever so gently sticking you that can be made to cut much deeper. You will come with me and make no tumult, or I will kill you here and now. Do you understand?"

She nodded her head; the menace in the voice terrified her. The man drew her in a direction opposite where her coach was waiting. She had thought to alert her coachman, but she could see that both coachman and footman were lost in idle chatter. She missed Ralph terribly at this moment. At the very least, why hadn't she thought to take one of the maids with her?

Maeve looked stealthily around; there had to be someone who could surmise her situation. But if she screamed, this odious man would certainly stab her. His grip moved to her arm and was like iron; there was no freeing herself. Then she saw a familiar face on the opposite side of the street. It was Lord Randall, Adam's friend; she was almost certain.

She called out to him and waved. By the look of him, he did not immediately recognize her. The grip on her arm tightened threateningly but she refused to acknowledge it.

"Lord Randall, please tell the Marquess of Huntingdon that Princess Maeve sends her regards." Her voice was overly loud and shrill, but then, fear was not an easy thing to control.

His Lordship smiled pleasantly, nodded and moved on. A sudden pain as her arm was twisted caused Maeve to cry out. People turned to look but just as quickly glanced away and went about their own business.

"Don't speak out again or you may expect to die here and now." Then the man was pushing her into a closed carriage. She fought hard now that she had been released, aiming for his groin with the tip of her kidskin half-boot, but he was a man accustomed to physical combat and easily evaded her efforts. The coach door was quickly closed.

She stared into her captor's face. "I should have realized you were capable of anything," she said.

As he moved toward her, she tried to rip at his face with her fingernails, but he was too quick and strong. He overpowered her and the next thing Maeve knew, she was tied up and gagged while the coach moved rapidly forward.

"I wondered what you've been about," Rundwall said. "Haven't seen you in a fortnight."

"I am in the process of getting properly married. I secured a special license this morning."

Rundwall stared at him in disbelief. "A jaded rakehell like you getting caught like a fox in a trap? Who is the talented huntress? Anyone I know?"

"I am persuaded you know of my *tendre* for Maeve."

The duke shook his head and frowned deeply. "The gypsy? Nuptials with your *inamorata?* You catch me unawares. My boy, isn't this impetuous behavior on your part? She might make a suitable mistress, but a wife? Will you demand satisfaction of every fellow who remarks on the fact that the wife of the Marquess of Huntingdon was a past light o'love of a common gamester? Why you will forever spend your life on the field of honor!"

"She was never any man's mistress."

"A Banbury tale, surely!"

"Hardly. I had the proof of her innocence myself."

"She makes a May game of you!"

"You are becoming tiresome, old man. Please just wish me well."

Rundwall caught the look of danger in Adam's eyes and shook his head. "If this is what you really want, why then I suppose I must congratulate you. I believe this calls for a glass of port."

"A bit early for me," Adam said.

"Well, allow me to drink to your health."

They were sitting together very comfortably at White's. Rundwall looked no better than the last time they had seen one another.

"You are certain the gypsy woman will make a suitable marchioness?"

"She would make a suitable duchess or anything else she chooses to be. Maeve is exceptional."

Obviously, Rundwall did not entirely agree, but he was polite enough not to insult Maeve or demur. "She does have quite remarkable talents. She knew that I was ill, and so I am. She is fey."

"Brockton told me something similar. Claims she has second sight and so knew that he was in danger and saved his life. He believes she brought him all his good fortune. A bag of moonshine, that!"

Rundwall was thoughtful. Then he spoke hesitantly, "Actually, I would tend to believe it was true."

Adam studied the duke intently. "Maeve is an amazing woman, but you will pardon me if I do not believe she has such unusual powers, although she seems to believe in them herself. What has the doctor told you, by the way?"

"I have a wasting sickness. A slow, nasty death is what I may look forward to suffering. Who would have thought it? I have seen the best physicians available. I now believe there will be no heirs, no matter whom I marry." Rundwall gulped the rest of his drink and signaled the waiter for another.

"May I offer my regrets?"

"That damned profligate nephew of mine will be delighted. After I am gone, I venture to say he will go through everything in a few years, everything that it took my ancestors centuries to build. If only I had a son of my own."

Adam thought of something Maeve had said, or had it been merely a slip of the tongue from which he inferred more than was meant? He would have to question Maeve about that when he saw her later.

"Richard, are you aware of having any illegitimate offspring?"

"Strange you should ask. Of late, I thought often about one of my mistresses. I was a young rake myself at the time and a bit of a fool, I'll own. I was in between wives. This lovely creature was smitten with me and when she became *enciente,* I did what was proper and I married her. But I'm afraid she took umbrage, claimed we were not truly wed because we were not married in the Roman faith. She was a devout Catholic, you see. I tired of her rather quickly, ashamed to say. I took a new mistress. She was outraged. I believe our lack of affection was mutual, because she left me after only a few months had passed. I never knew if she had the child or not. I soon lost contact with her. It was her doing, her decision. Some years later, a mutual acquaintance mentioned that she was dead. That was when I decided to marry again. In hindsight, I fear I might have treated her rather shabbily."

"And now you wonder if she did have your child?"

"I don't deny it." Rundwall's voice was hoarse with regret.

"May I ask the woman's name?"

"It was Mathilde Le Brun. She was a French émigré."

"Le Brun, you say?" Adam felt a rush of excitement. He looked at his cousin carefully. Charles Le Brun had amber eyes, and they reminded him of Rundwall's. Maeve would have known all along, but for some reason had chosen not to trust him with the information. It troubled him.

"I believe Charles Le Brun is your son." He spoke in what he hoped was a dispassionate manner.

The duke stared at him in disbelief. "Surely not! That rude young man, the very one who ran off with my Caroline?"

"In point of fact, *she* ran off with him. She wanted him, you must know, in spite of his inferior station. Actually, Le Brun is not a bad sort of fellow at all. I can talk to Maeve about him if you wish. We can discover the particulars. She knows all about him, claims he was like a brother to her."

The waiter came with Rundwall's second

glass of port and the duke made short work of it. "Are you saying Le Brun is my heir?"

"It is a distinct possibility, Richard. In fact, it is almost of a certainty that he is your son. He does need polish and tutoring. However he is strong, intelligent, and healthy, and I believe of good character. Think of it this way. You wanted Caroline to breed your heirs. Well, this is one way of insuring it."

At that, the duke gave him a wide, wicked grin. "Lad, you have an interesting thought there. Perhaps you have solved my problem after all. But where is Le Brun now?"

"He and Caroline are visiting her family in Italy. They will be married there. I have no doubt that they will eventually return here. And then you may make your peace with your son."

"My son? That sounds very good to me. Perhaps just one more drink is in order?"

"I think not. You must not make a habit of being in your cups if you are to impress your heir."

"Quite right," the duke responded amiably.

Lord Randall joined them. He seemed in good spirits as well, and Adam welcomed him; he always enjoyed the company of an amusing rattle.

"You must congratulate Adam," the duke told the newcomer.

"Odso? What have you gone and done, old chap?"

"About to be leg-shackled," the duke said with some satisfaction, pleased to relate the latest *on-dit.*

"God, no! You've set such a fine example of debauchery for the rest of us. Surely, you'll not succumb so easily to a dampened petticoat or a bit of muslin." Howard's drollery was beginning to annoy Adam.

"He's going to marry Princess Maeve," Rundwall continued.

"It's obvious we don't need the *Times* anymore, cousin."

Rundwall laughed at Adam's barb. "I thought Howard would be interested."

"I daresay. That is most peculiar." Howard looked puzzled.

"Maeve is a wonderful woman," Adam said and felt his face flush with displeasure at both men. Why should he defend her? There was certainly no need.

"Oh, I would not suggest otherwise. Top of the trees and all that," Lord Randall hastily interposed. "No, what I refer to is that I just saw Maeve on Bond Street. She was carrying some packages and waved to me. There was some chap with her, but I couldn't make him out. His head was turned away and his hat pulled down. Come to think of it, he was walking on the inside, not at all the gentleman. In any case, Maeve called to me and said I should give the Marquess of Huntingdon her regards. Now what do you make of that? The message doesn't seem at'll right if you are engaged."

Adam leaped to his feet. "Something is wrong. Good Lord, I should have provided her with protection. She feared that someone was out to do her harm, but I thought that was all settled when Simmons left for the continent. Bond Street, you say?"

"Doubt she is there now. I believe I saw the fellow put her into a coach, but I cannot be certain. I was not paying close attention."

Adam's heart began to beat rapidly. Maeve was in trouble, and he must do something about it. He quickly left White's and took a hackney coach to the house that was to be theirs. As he feared, Maeve was not there. He found the coach still on Bond Street, driver and footman waiting restlessly for the return of their mistress. They told him she had mentioned stopping at a tea shop, but that had been a very long time ago. He had them help him look into every shop in the area and asked each proprietor if they'd seen her. The last person who had was Madame Legrande who'd sold Maeve "unmentionables."

He was beside himself now. Someone had kidnapped Maeve, someone who wished to harm her. Who would have done such a thing? Where was he to go? Where was he to look?

In desperation, he sought out Pritchard. The small, dapper solicitor was working with another client when Adam arrived, and he waited with little patience, barely able to contain his growing fear.

At last Pritchard was free, and Adam sat down opposite the cluttered desk in the cramped office.

"Didn't expect to see you so soon again, Milord."

"All was well for a time, but it seems someone has abducted Maeve right off Bond Street."

"What's the world comin' to, I ask? We can do our best to find her again. Does she have enemies? Is there someone who wishes her ill?"

He told Pritchard about Sir John Simmons.

"Doesn't seem as if he'd be involved in this. Though one never does know." Pritchard was thoughtful for a time. Adam knew his undistinguished features hid a rare, subtle intelligence.

"Might there be anyone else who would want to harm her?"

He thought of Rundwall, but could not bring himself to suggest that his cousin might hurt Maeve. Hadn't he just drunk to the marriage today? Still, Adam could not take a chance with Maeve's life. He realized that his first loyalty was now to her.

"Maeve was to help my cousin, the Duke of Rundwall, win the affections of a certain Lady Caroline, sister of the Earl of Southford. Instead, she assisted a young man named Charles Le Brun. The young couple have since eloped. I believe my cousin might harbor unpleasant feelings toward her." He'd spoken in a forthright manner, although he felt disgustingly disloyal.

"Well, Milord, then it seems to me that either the duke or the girl's brother might have reason to be angry at the lady."

"The girl's brother?" Adam hadn't considered Southford, but he should have. "Southford is in bad straits financially," Adam said, thinking aloud. "He wanted the match every bit as much as Rundwall. He was a soldier in the wars, and I do think him quite capable of violence. Pritchard, I believe we may possibly have solved the who. Now for the where."

CHAPTER SEVENTEEN

Maeve was terrified. She could scarcely catch her breath. To be here again under these circumstances was the greatest irony. The ruined farmhouse seemed the worse for disuse. Obviously, no one had been here since the day that she and Ralph left. Now she was tied up in a chair, legs and arms numb with loss of circulation. Why had he done this? What could he possibly hope to gain? Revenge perhaps? The thought sent a chill slithering like a snake down her spine.

He was staring at her now, rage on his face. She sensed a sickness in him, a malady of the mind. Perhaps he was planning to kill her. Another shiver shook her.

"Do not look at me like that, slut. I am no monster. Do not glance about either. It offends me. There is no one else hereabouts to whom you may appeal. I have sent my coachman back to London and am left with a horse."

One horse? She was not insensible to what that implied; for certain she was not to return with him.

"When I remove this rag from your mouth, you may scream if you wish, but it will be to no avail."

She could not help but notice how the rage that he carried within him transfigured what had been a handsome man into something not quite human. He removed the gag and she did not utter a sound. What purpose would screaming serve?

All the way here, she had concentrated on Adam. Could he receive her thoughts? Would he know that she was in danger? And if he did, how would he find her? But Adam did not believe in the metaphysical realm. He did not own to her special powers, and if one did not believe, then the brain could not receive. The ability had much to do after all with a credulous turn of mind and, much as she loved Adam, she knew him to be a skeptic. No, she could not depend on others; she must find a way to help herself just as she had always done.

He was talking to her now, and she made a concentrated effort to listen despite her fears.

"It was you who discovered where we brought that churl, you with your peculiar second sight. No one else could have known. You are to blame for ruining what would have been a perfect marriage for my sister."

"You and the duke abducted and hurt Charles. Of course, I was concerned. Caroline was just as desperate to find him as I was. They are in love and probably married by now."

He slapped her hard across the face without warning. Tears pricked her eyes. Speaking to him in a logical manner was obviously a mistake. One did not make explanations to such as he; they only escalated his anger.

"You were paid to help me convince Caroline that Rundwall was the one she should marry. You betrayed me, bitch. Now you shall pay well for your treachery."

She swallowed back the nausea she felt. It was best to try to keep him talking. Perhaps that might diffuse some of his fury, although she must have a care to what she said. "I understood that Rundwall hired those men to kidnap Charles."

He smiled in a nasty manner. "It was the duke's plan, but he had not the courage to carry it out alone. When he spoke to me of it, I urged him on, made him understand taking that brute was his only hope. I did all I could to help him. It was I who suggested that he seduce Caroline at the ball."

"You would have such a thing done to your own sister?" Maeve could scarcely absorb his words.

"The girl has no sense. I tried to reason with her. I should have taken stronger, sterner measures. She should have been beaten until she was biddable. Foolish, spoiled brat. I've done everything I could to hold on to the estates, but there is nothing left. It could all have been different if she had married Rundwall. He was prepared to be very generous. You will now tell me where she's gone off to with that guttersnipe, her and that old twit of an aunt. When I find them, I will kill Le Brun and perhaps Caroline as well."

There was no doubt that he meant what he said.

"I have no idea where they are."

He looked as if he wished to hit her again. She already tasted blood in her mouth, but she refused to cry or acknowledge in any way that his brutality had power over her. Maeve's thoughts traveled back to the stoicism she'd practiced during the punishments she'd endured at Beedle's. Her opportunity to escape would come, and she would see it if she kept her wits about her.

"You are a liar and I know it. I will beat

the truth out of you."

As he raised his hand, she spoke quickly. "They have left the country. That is all I know. They are gone."

Blue eyes narrowed to slits as he studied her, watching with interest the rise and fall of her breasts. "You are too afraid to lie now. That is good."

She closed her eyes and concentrated again on Adam, trying her very best to block out the pain and fear. *I am at the old farmhouse. Come here. Help me!*

"What are you about?" He sounded suspicious.

"Just wondering. How did you know about the abandoned farm?"

"From Rundwall, of course. We discussed where we would bring your footman. The place seemed a good choice. The plan would have worked but for you. It seems only rightful justice that you should die here. But before I kill you, I shall have you at least once. If you satisfy me well enough, whore, I shall let you live perhaps to please me some more. But you must be very good." He touched her cheek and smiled lecherously. His fingers felt icy cold, and it was all she could do to keep from shaking violently or retching.

"I watched Brockton's house for some

time and was very pleased to see you visit there this morning. I did not know you had a new address, but I should have guessed as much. You have left Brockton for a new protector I collect?"

She was relieved that he did not seem to know about Adam specifically.

"You do not wish to say? It does not signify. He will forget you soon enough, I own."

He took out a dagger and brandished it. "I could cut you into pieces with this, but for now, I choose only to cut these bonds. Perhaps I will let you live if you will please me with your excellent body. You understand?" His hand squeezed her breast with a hard, rough pressure.

She spat in his face. He hit her hard with his fist, and she slipped into the release of blessed unconsciousness.

Pritchard had hastily called together several men to begin the search. They accompanied Adam to the Earl of Southford's townhouse. However, it was soon discovered that the earl had gone off in his coach and not returned; neither his butler nor his housekeeper knew when he would be back. Adam and Pritchard questioned the butler as to the location of the earl's estates.

"Sir, I do not wish to be rude, but I fail to understand what business you have in making this inquiry."

Adam carefully controlled his temper. "I assure you that I have business with the earl. I must find him immediately. Otherwise, the Bow Street Runners will be dispatched here forthwith. There is a precious life at stake."

That was enough for the butler to provide the necessary information. Unfortunately, the earl's properties were a good distance from London. Adam thought it likely that Southford would look for a closer location to dispose of Maeve. It would also have to be isolated, since he would want no witnesses. Adam was desperate to take action, but where could Southford have taken Maeve?

Pritchard left one man to watch the townhouse so that if the coach returned with or without the earl, his servants could be questioned immediately, but Adam was concerned that they would not find Maeve in time. He was certain that the abduction would end in murder unless he was able to move swiftly. Time was getting away from him.

Through the afternoon, Adam had strange

thoughts entering his mind. He kept hearing Maeve's voice in his head, talking to him, telling him to find her and that she was terribly afraid. He could feel the fear and desperation as if it were a palpable object, like an orange, he could hold in his hand.

It occurred to him then that the duke might well know something that would help him find Maeve. If Rundwall and the earl had plotted together, Southford might have spoken freely in front of him. After all, they had both shared the same goals, hadn't they?

Aware of his cousin's habits, he thought Rundwall would have returned to his townhouse by this hour for tea and to take a nap before attending his evening activities. He found Rundwall in his library going over ledgers.

"Did you locate Maeve?" Rundwall asked at once.

"No, and I do not like the look of this. I believe that Southford may have abducted her and means her ill. Did he say anything to you about her, Richard?"

"Nothing that bears repeating."

"He may be planning to kill her."

"Good Lord, surely the fellow is not deranged?"

"Was he involved in planning Le Brun's abduction?"

Rundwall's face grew pale. "It was he who carried out the plan. I confess that I told him how desperate I was to have Caroline. He was just as determined as I. We conspired together. I doubt that I would have actually kidnapped the boy but for Southford's urging."

"As I thought. Do you know where he might take Maeve? It would be somewhere not too far from London, somewhere isolated."

"Like the abandoned farm where the boy was held?"

Adam felt his pulse beat rise. "Just so! Richard, did the earl know where the farm was?"

"I own all the land thereabouts and told him of the place. When Le Brun was taken, the earl was with the men to insure that they found the right location. In fact, he boasted that without himself, Le Brun would have broken free. He hit the boy over the head with an axe handle. When he told me the boy was unconscious, I became worried. That was when I decided to tell you of what had transpired. I wanted you to make certain that the lad was not ill-treated. I feared he might be dead. It was not what I intended, I assure you."

"Le Brun survived, no thanks to Southford. You should have told me about his part in it."

"He was only trying to help me."

"I think not. Southford is a selfish bastard with a dreadful temper. I fear his next victim is Maeve. I have no time to go back for my phaeton. May I have your racing curricle?"

"Of course, but will you be safe traveling on the roads outside of London in such a light conveyance?"

"I must ride swiftly. I'll take your fastest horses."

Adam sent a messenger to Pritchard so that he would be met with a proper coach, and then he was off, much like a charioteer must have felt in ancient Rome. He estimated that he could make the trip in under two hours without killing Rundwall's horses and prayed that he would be in time. Southford was either vicious, deranged or both. It did not signify; only saving Maeve's life mattered.

Maeve was somewhere in a state between unconsciousness and wakefulness. Her mind seemed clearer than it had ever been. She was totally without fear for the first time since the earl had forced her into his carriage at knife-point. Someone was talking to her. She realized it was her mother.

"I am with you, little one. Have no fear. I shall protect you. Your man is coming soon. You must trick this evil demon. Quiet yourself and let him think you are still unaware. Sleep deeply in a state of peace, for I am with you. All will be well."

Her mother floated insubstantially above her in a radiance of light. She was very beautiful. Her countenance was the benign, smiling face of the moon. Maeve would have reached out to touch Mama, but her limbs were much too heavy to move. She rested calmly and fell into a dreamless sleep.

Someone was shaking her, then slapping her cheeks. She moaned in protest against the discomfort.

"Wake up! You've been gone too long already. I can wait no longer. Open your eyes."

One of her eyes barely opened. It was swollen shut from the blow he had struck her. She wanted to find a weapon to use against him, anything at all, but his hands dug painfully into her shoulders. She realized that he had placed her on the bed in the other room. It made her feel panicky. She did not want him touching her intimately. He disgusted her.

That terrible smile was on his lips. "So you understand what will happen now? I could have taken you before, but I wanted to hear you cry out. I want you to suffer when I take you. Your pain will give me the greatest pleasure."

She did want to cry and forced back the tears, somehow understanding that this too would please him. His hands reached forward to tear the bodice of her gown. She fought him as best she could. At least he'd freed her hands when he moved her. She ripped at his face with her nails and heard his enraged cry. Pursuing her slight advantage, she caught sight of a water pitcher and lifted it in trembling hands to bring it down on his head. But his movements were quick. He caught her and wrenched the object away. The pitcher crashed against the floor. Southford was about to strike her again when a hand caught his in midair.

"Get away from her, you bastard."

It was Adam! She would know that deep, resonant voice anywhere. She had never heard him in such a taking. His voice was softly menacing and very dangerous. Southford turned and faced Adam, who raised a pistol, aiming it at the earl's chest.

"Lie down on the floor."

The earl did not move. "What do you intend?"

"Simply to tie you up and leave you for now. Attempted murder is a most serious crime. You shall have to appear before a magistrate."

"If you were any kind of man, you'd accept my challenge."

Adam was incredulous and laughed outright. "You amaze me! It is I who would challenge you, but I do not choose it because you are unworthy to be considered a gentleman. I want you treated as a common criminal. What say you, Maeve?" As Adam turned to look at her, through her good eye, she saw the earl reach for Adam's pistol. She screamed and pointed. Adam immediately turned back but not in time. Southford had dislodged the pistol from his hand with a hard blow. It fell to the floor, and they wrestled for possession of the weapon. Adam was the larger and stronger, and she hoped that would give him the advantage. Maeve saw the now cracked pitcher on the floor and lifted the largest piece to use against the earl, but the two men were too close together and constantly shifting position. She smashed the ceramic down on the back of the earl's head just as the pistol exploded.

Maeve was frantic. Had Adam been shot? But it was the earl who slumped to the floor groaning and holding his midsection where bright, red blood began to spot his snowy shirt. Suddenly he turned and set on Maeve a look of unrelenting hatred.

"You should have died the first time."

Both she and Adam went to the earl, but he soon passed into unconsciousness.

"Will he live?" Adam asked.

She examined the earl carefully. "I will do what I can for him. I can stop the bleeding but I am not a surgeon able to remove a ball in the body's interior."

"I'll see him to a surgeon," Adam said solemnly. "Though God knows it is more than he deserves after what he has done to you." Gently he took her into his arms and kissed her aching face.

Only now did she allow herself the luxury of tears. "Mama said you would find me. Did you hear me call to you?"

"I suppose I did." He kissed her forehead tenderly. "Do what you can for him now, Maeve. I'm going to pump cold water to clean your poor bruised face. You've been more than brave."

Mr. Pritchard arrived in a closed carriage. Wisely, he'd brought a doctor with him who attended Southford and pronounced that he would likely live.

"Good, for I would see that the earl get justice." Adam's voice was grim. "Transportation at the very least."

After the doctor attended to Maeve, Adam insisted that she lie down in the coach and close her eyes on the drive home. She fell asleep, her head resting safely on Adam's lap.

Adam insisted on waiting until Maeve was completely healed before they had their wedding. It was worth waiting for. There was a letter from Caroline telling them that all was well and she and Charles had married aboard ship. She promised to write soon again and tell them all about Italy. Maeve would write with news of her own. Not only were she and Adam married, but Charles was to be the Duke of Rundwall's heir. Charles might rail at first, but Maeve was certain that Caroline could convince him to accept.

As for Maeve, although the fashionable world was present at her wedding at St. George's Church in Hanover Square, the only person she was aware of was the Marquess of Huntingdon, handsome and resplendent in his finest evening attire. Her white bridal gown was a perfection of the

French dressmaking art, rich satin with seed pearls overlaying the bodice and shot through with silver threads that matched her eyes of pale mist.

As they finished saying their vows and kissed, their souls came together.

"I hope that I have opened the gates of paradise for you," Adam said. "You have certainly done so for me."

"I love you," she said, "with all my heart and being."

Their hearts were in their eyes as everyone could plainly see.

CHAPTER EIGHTEEN

The next several months were the happiest Maeve had ever known. She lived in a perpetual state of romantic bliss and idyllic fancy. Adam surprised her with a trip to the continent, a honeymoon in the elegant style that only he could have arranged.

"We shall take the grand tour together," he said. "And it will all be new and fresh for me as well, for I shall see it through your beautiful eyes."

And it was just that way. For the first time that Maeve could recall, Adam completely dropped his veneer of world weary cynicism. He seemed years younger, full of lighthearted enthusiasm.

Their days were filled with the pleasure of touring the great capitals of Europe. But it was the nights that Maeve felt mattered most, for that was when they came most alive. In those magical nights they truly learned each other's wants and needs. They taught each other the ways of passion in a slow, leisurely manner. Perhaps Adam did not say it in so many words, but Maeve had never felt so loved, protected or cherished. It was as if she were finally a complete, whole person. Gone were the terrible nightmares of the past. It was as though she had been reborn.

Adam told her that she would adore Spain. Madrid impressed her but it was Barcelona that made the greater impression. A city of around 80,000 people, it was the largest port of Spain. As such, there was life and bustle everywhere. At night, Adam took her to see the flamenco dancers and hear traditional Spanish music. She loved it. Such music struck a responsive note in her very being.

"It's wonderful," she told Adam, pressing her hand to his across their table at the cafe. "Have you been here before?"

He nodded, lips tight. "During the war on matters of diplomacy. Napoleon put his brother, Joseph, on the throne for a time. I had something to do with provoking the popular uprising that put Ferdinand on the throne. He was the rightful king. Of course, if Wellington were here, he'd tell you that he was solely responsible for driving the French from the peninsula."

"But of course he wouldn't be right."

He smiled at her mischievously. "Not in the slightest."

"I do not suppose you would want to tell me what you did in the war?"

"Don't suppose I would, dear girl. Maeve, turn back around. You are missing the best part." In his suave, sophisticated manner, he managed to divert her attention.

She let out a small sigh. Adam would always be something of an enigma. Perhaps that was what made being with him so exciting. One never knew what to expect.

The next afternoon in the plaza of Barcelona's largest square, Maeve was admiring the gardens and sculptures when she caught sight of a gypsy selling fans. Maeve brimmed with excitement as she spoke to the woman and selected a number of beautiful fans that she would give as gifts to her girls. For a time, they conversed together in the language of the Romany. Maeve felt wonderful. She told Adam she wanted to be on her own for a time, and they agreed to meet later for siesta at their hotel. This city was one in which gypsies were meant to wander freely.

"I feel somewhat left out," Adam said in

their hotel room later. "Have you tired of me already?"

She was abashed. "I am so sorry. It was just so wonderful seeing another gypsy."

"She did rather handsomely herself," Adam said, pointing to all of Maeve's purchases. "I daresay she'll not be forgetting you soon."

"I suppose I must prove to you how much I love you," Maeve said. She gave him a coquettish smile.

Then ever so slowly, she began removing her clothes. She didn't get very far before Adam began energetically helping her dispose of gown, chemise, stockings and slippers. His hands and mouth were everywhere at once.

"These Spanish have just the right idea. I say siestas are just what are needed in England."

"Every afternoon?" Maeve asked breathlessly.

"Better than tea time," Adam said. Then he began sucking on her lower lip and she forgot about everything but his lovemaking.

Adam took her to see a series of Spanish cathedrals and Gothic churches, some very old. "San Pablo del Campo was built in nine forty-one and destroyed by the Moors. It was rebuilt in the twelfth century, an interesting example of Catalonian Romanesque architecture with Moorish features."

Maeve was impressed by the depth of Adam's cultural knowledge and erudition. She decided not to tell him that she hadn't the faintest idea what he was talking about. Besides, she was happy just being with him.

That night in their suite at the hotel, Maeve decided to do something special for Adam. She had arranged with the gypsy woman to send a musician to their rooms. While Adam was downstairs after dinner having a smoke, Maeve changed her clothes to the special ones she'd purchased in the little shop where the gypsy sent her.

Adam did not believe his eyes. Maeve was dressed as he had seen her in his dreams. Her mane of long black hair, thick and lustrous, was loosely hanging around her shoulders and back, a skein of silk. She was dressed in an off-the-shoulder white peasant blouse and colorful full skirt. Gold hoop earrings gleamed at each lovely ear. There was a smile on her full, sensuous lips and a sparkle in her fey eyes.

He heard the music start from somewhere in the distance, a guitar playing softly at first, being strummed. Then Maeve began to dance and he saw nothing but her, heard nothing but the stepping of her dainty bare feet. Her enthusiasm seemed to grow and with it, the quickening rhythm of her steps. And as the rhythm increased so did his arousal.

Maeve danced with wild abandon. She tasted the freedom of the dance and became one with the sobbing flamenco. Hers was a wanton dance meant to inflame her lover's desire. The music claimed her soul even while he held her heart.

Adam pulled Maeve to him and kissed her hungrily with hot, wet open-mouthed kisses. His tongue mated with hers. In a hoarse voice, he called out to the guitar player that the performance was over. She was ready for him; her hands reached for him. She felt her nipples harden with uncontrollable pleasure under the ministrations of his clever touch.

He seated himself on a chair and pulled her into his lap so she sat astride him. Then he freed himself and settled her bare bottom against him.

"Ride me," he said. His eyes were darker than midnight.

With pleasure she took his hard, hot member into her weeping core. She clung

to him, lost in the languor of their shared
sensuality. She rode him slowly at first, but
then the rhythm built to a potent tempo.
The moment was magical and all caution
and sense were thrown to the winds. There
was only their wild, hungry passion for each
other, only this precious, special time. And
then it was as if a volcano exploded.

Athens proved a delightful experience.
Maeve had read Greek mythology and the
history of the ancient Greeks. It was quite
another thing to tour the ruins, to see the
Parthenon, the Acropolis, with her own
eyes. But it was Adam who made it all come
alive for her. His knowledge and wit meant
everything to her. It seemed as if there were
nothing he did not know.

The waters of the Aegean Sea were a
crystal blue-green as they cruised the Greek
Isles. Adam insisted on trying to follow the
route taken by Odysseus, and for a time she
feared they would be seriously lost. But it
was all such an exciting adventure.

"I have saved the best for the last," Adam
said when she inquired where they would
be going next. "You and I are on our way to
Italy."

"Where in Italy? Will we get to see Caroline and Charles?"

"I thought you would like a brief visit with them before we go on to see northern Europe."

She was elated. "Nothing would be more wonderful."

"You have no dire visions concerning our travel?" he said in a teasing voice.

She shook her head. "No dark premonitions. Everything is perfect. It is as if my special sensitivity has left me, at least for now."

"I am persuaded that is all to the good."

Maeve was not so certain; her gift, though both a positive and negative force in her life, was yet a significant part of who she was, an aspect of her identity. Adam was the dearest person in her life and she loved him totally. Yet it would not be good to give up on herself in accepting him. She forced the troubling thought from her mind. She would give herself completely to Adam; he was the love of her life. Her trust and commitment were total. But she would never forget who and what she was either.

She adored Venice and told Adam so.

"I knew you would. It is the most romantic city in the world."

"Why, there is water everywhere," she exclaimed.

"Indeed, Venice is situated on a great many islets separated by canals. Traffic here moves on water. There are no horses or carriages. Even the vendors transport their wares by gondola."

Maeve insisted that they take a tour by gondola on their first day in the city. The day was mild and perfect for boating. Adam hired the perfect gondolier. He wore a colorful shirt and ribboned straw hat. He also sang in a clear, beautiful tenor, which added just the right note of gaiety.

"It is quite fortunate we are married, else I might be very jealous regarding the way you look at that Italian lad, my girl." Adam spoke with joviality, but Maeve had the strange feeling that underneath he was serious.

"You are so far above other men, you need never feel jealousy."

He took her hand tightly in his own. "Ah, but you are my treasure, my dear. Other men will always admire you and want you. I am not fool enough to ever take my wife for granted."

Maeve suddenly realized Adam must be thinking about his parents. She sought to change the direction of his mind. "The Grand Canal is the main thoroughfare?"

"Quite so. It is lined with the palaces of

the rich and great."

As she had hoped, Adam began pointing out all the notable buildings. When they finally reached St. Mark's Square, he was in a much better mood. Maeve looked around in awe at the magnificent piazza that she shared at the moment with thousands of pigeons. On three sides, there were government palaces, on the fourth, the doges' private chapel. The basilica of St. Mark's was adorned with columns from the eastern Mediterranean and decorated with mosaics. Four antique bronze horses stood over the main portal. She was awed by the magnificence surrounding her.

"Spoils of war," Adam pointed out to her. "The Italians display the treasures of Byzantium. We're admiring the results of their looting."

"Just as cynical as ever, I see," she remarked.

"Just making an honest observation." He extended his arm to her and she took it.

That day they toured the city, the Old Library, the Bridge of Sighs, and the Rialto Bridge. By evening, her feet could scarcely hold her up. But it had all been worth it.

The following day, she bought presents of Venetian glass to bring home. "Aren't they magnificent?"

He laughed at her exuberance. "If you buy much more, we will scarcely have room in our luggage for our clothes."

They went on to tour Rome, Milan and Naples and finally sailed to a narrow coastal plain along the shore of the Gulf of Genoa to a place called Liguria, whose beautiful scenery and mild climate seemed to draw a great many tourists like themselves.

It was in Liguria that Adam found them a lovely villa with marble fountains at the front and rear that overlooked a private beach. It was also here that they made tender, passionate love even more spectacularly than before. And it was here that Maeve knew the sweetest moments of her life.

One morning Adam arrived with a letter while she sat in repose studying a leering marble Neptune frolicking with the naiads in the fountain.

"I have been in contact with Caroline and Le Brun. They are not far from here and plan to join us." He held the letter out to her. "This just arrived."

"That is wonderful news!"

"I thought you might be getting rather bored with just my company by now."

"With you? Never. But it will be nice to see them."

Adam sighed theatrically. "Well, if I must share you, so be it. What I endure to please you, La Belle Dame Sans Merci." He sprawled down in the grass beside her.

She laughed lightly and leaned over to kiss the golden hair on top of his head that had grown lighter from the sunlight. "How kind of you to indulge me so."

"Indeed, it is my mission in life to service you in any way I can." With that, he toppled her to the ground and settled his large body over hers.

She gasped and laughed. "Stop that, you brute. The servants are probably watching."

"But I exist only to serve your needs." He ran his hands over her.

She rolled away from him, still laughing, and got to her feet. "I do need a bit of exercise. I think a walk on our private beach is in order."

"Your wish is my command, though I believe I could offer you more stimulating activity." He rose swiftly and extended his arm to her.

She was enjoying his naughty, rakish air. They walked with a jaunty step down to the ocean where the sand felt like a velvet carpet beneath their feet. Then suddenly he was lifting her in the air.

"You wretch, put me down!"

"Very well, my dear, I prefer you down anyway."

The next thing she knew, Maeve was on her back lying beneath him. He began unfastening her gown, as his mouth rained kisses on her lips, neck and breasts. She tried to squirm away in protest but he held her fast.

"I haven't shaved this morning. Am I too rough for you?"

She kissed the day's growth of dark whiskers and ran her fingers tenderly over his face. He seemed to catch his breath at the sensuality of her touch. Then she felt his rampant erection press against the softness of her inner thigh.

"Will you soon tire of me, I wonder?"

"Impossible," he said in a husky voice.

He licked the tip of her breast and circled it erotically with his tongue. Then he did the same for the other. She moaned and arched her back trying to draw closer to him.

"How could I tire of this, woman? Are you quite mad?" He raised an imposing brow. "If anything, you are more addictive than opium, tobacco or tea. I would as soon forget eating or sleeping than do without you. I shall want to make love to you until I am old and decrepit."

"Prove it," she said.

And he did, beautifully.

Caroline and Charles visited in the late afternoon. The day was warm and beautiful, without a cloud in the sky. They were to stay several days. Maeve realized she had missed the company of other women, in spite of her joy at being with Adam.

For her part, Caroline hugged and kissed Maeve. Caroline had never seemed more relaxed and happy. There was a radiance about her and a new maturity. "I am so pleased that you are here in Italy and that you and Lord Huntingdon have wed! It is like a fairy tale come true."

"Do you know about your brother?" Maeve asked gravely.

Caroline's expression hardened. "My half-brother. Yes, though I could scarcely believe his cruelty. I am ashamed to call myself any sort of relation to him." Caroline sat down on a carved leather chair. "Let us speak of better things."

Adam came into the room, followed by a serving girl who proffered chilled glasses of a fruity wine. Charles joined them, too, and eagerly took a goblet. Maeve suddenly realized how warm the day had become.

"How have you found your mother and

step-father?" Maeve inquired.

"In the very best of health. They are established in a beautiful villa much like this one, not as close to the sea, but quite lovely all the same. They have been wonderful to us. I feel as though I am finally home, because I now have a real family. And Aunt Amelia is beside herself to know her older sister is alive and well. My mother is a woman of fine character and sweet disposition. My only regret is that I went for so many years without knowing of her existence." There were tears in Caroline's large, azure eyes.

"I am very happy for you," Maeve said.

"So Le Brun, how does it feel to be legshackled?" Adam said.

"I could ask you the same question," Charles retorted.

"Quite true, old man. I would have to say it is decidedly economical. I have a wife and mistress all in one. I am amazed by my own frugality."

"If your tongue becomes much more acerbic, I shall have to recommend its removal," Maeve said, deciding to tease him in return.

"But, my love, I can think of much better activities of which you might engage with said appendage."

Maeve found herself blushing.

"I believe you've married yourself a lustful devil," Charles said with some amusement.

"He is indeed playful," Maeve agreed archly.

"Ah, well, as to that, one can only try to rise to the occasion." Adam's eyes twinkled mischievously.

Charles laughed deeply while Caroline blushed. Maeve merely shook her head at her husband.

"You are quite naughty today," she said.

Adam took Maeve in his arms without warning and kissed the curve of her neck. "Indeed, I have not as yet been naughty today, and that is the problem."

"You are embarrassing Caroline." She broke free of Adam's embrace and placed her glass on a carved marble table.

"Very well, we shall speak of other things." Adam turned to Charles. "I have news of Rundwall."

Charles immediately stiffened. "What is he about now?"

"I assure you, nothing to give either one of you cause for concern. Rundwall wishes both of you the best. I told him that you are his son. The news meant a great deal to him, I can assure you. In fact, he informed me that he did in fact legally marry your mother."

Charles rose to his feet, knocking over his wine glass. "What? Are you certain? Is it possible?"

"They did marry. However, according to him, she chose to leave him before your birth. I believe that he had a new mistress. In anger, she left him, outraged at his behavior. She was apparently a woman of some pride. He never actually knew that you existed. You are Rundwall's legal heir."

Caroline gasped with pleasure. "I can scarcely believe something so wonderful could happen."

Charles looked much less pleased than his wife. "There's some catch to this, isn't there? Aristos don't just make strangers their heirs, especially after I took Caroline from him."

"It is not precisely what you think. Rundwall is dying. He knows there will be no more children whether he marries or not. And even if he could father more children, you would still be his heir regardless."

Charles sat down heavily beside Caroline, who seemed quite stunned.

"I could not like the man," Caroline said in a sad, thoughtful voice, "but I regret that he is ill."

Charles grunted in agreement. "I hated him for most of my life, wished him dead a score of times. And now I feel only a sense of regret, a sense of loss. I will never really know my father."

"You may know him yet," Adam said. "He will not die immediately as in some dreadful melodrama. Perhaps you will see him on your return to London. I know that would make Richard happy. He wishes to be reconciled to you."

Charles nodded his head. "I will see him, but I am not certain I want to accept any inheritance from him. And why did my mother never tell me that she and the duke were wed?"

"You will have to discuss the matter with him. But as I said, she felt quite bitter toward him."

Caroline rose to her feet. "Charles, you must take advantage of your good fortune. It is your birthright. It is only just."

"Caroline is quite right," Adam said. "My advice is to accept this turn of events with equanimity."

"The duke was no father to me." The sharp edge of bitterness in Charles's voice could not easily be ignored. "Mr. Brockton has been my father since I can remember. He saved me from a life of poverty and misery. He considers me his right hand. How could I forsake him for mere material gain?"

Maeve took his big hand in her own smaller one. "You cannot," Maeve agreed, "nor could I. However, Charles dear, might you not be allowed to claim two fathers? How can it be wrong to claim a double inheritance?"

"These women are a bossy lot, ain't they?" Charles said, turning to Adam.

"Indeed we are," Maeve agreed.

"And also very wise," Adam said as he turned an admiring, affectionate smile on his wife. "Besides, one does not mind a termagant too much if she is as beautiful as Maeve."

"I could cosh you over the head for that," she said with feigned menace.

Adam merely laughed out loud and then hugged her tightly.

"It cannot harm you to at least talk to the duke once we return to England," Caroline reasoned.

"Very well, I'll look into the matter and see what he has to say," Charles promised.

After Caroline and Charles left, Maeve and Adam stayed another week at their charming villa. But Adam was restless to continue their travels.

"I wish to show you Germany and Switzerland. I think we should visit a castle on the Rhine and perhaps climb an Alp or two. Possibly I will take up yodeling. Indeed, that will be the true test of our union, if you can tolerate my yodeling."

"Nothing could please me more, as long as you do not decide to do it in bed."

"And what should I do in bed?" He raised a gold-tipped brow insinuatingly.

"Do anything but snore," she said. "Come, let us take a walk along the beach."

"Where your wishes are concerned, sweetheart, I am prepared to be most obliging." He took her into his arms and gave her a long, lingering kiss that had her pulse rate beating rapidly.

They walked down the long beach away from their own villa to a place where there were other people enjoying the beauty of the blood-sun setting over the water.

"I wish that I might paint or watercolor tolerably," she said. "I would so like to capture the breathtaking loveliness of this scene. Memory does not signify. It leaves a most flawed perception." She sighed deeply.

"Ah, the lady wants art, does she? I shall find you a magnificent sunset on canvas."

"Adam, I do not mean to put you to such trouble on my account."

"On who else's account should I expend my efforts? It will give me pleasure to serve you in all possible ways." He seized her hand and kissed it passionately.

"I believe you will scandalize the people here."

"If I shock a few graybeards, it will doubtless be good for their digestion."

She laughed at his lighthearted jest. That only served to encourage him further. He bent her backward and leaned her over his arm then gave her a deep kiss. When she could breathe again, Maeve shook her head at him.

"You impudent, incorrigible brute!"

"Thank you. Let us return to our private beach. I have such thoughts as leave me a dire wretch in need of your gentle ministrations." Then he leered at her insinuatingly and completely spoiled the effect of his declaration and affectation of humility. She began to laugh, never having felt so happy or so appreciated.

"You are very good for me," she whispered. "I feel so jolly."

"So glad, my love, because I have every expectation that we will enjoy ourselves today more than ever before." His lips touching hers with a wisp of a kiss made an enticing promise.

CHAPTER NINETEEN

Maeve knew she would remember their special time in Italy and hold it in her heart every time she held her purple Venetian glass bowls in her hands. Every moment was precious.

They never managed their trip to northern Europe. As they prepared to continue their honeymoon tour, an important missive was delivered: Adam's father, it seemed, had taken a turn for the worse; the duke was dying.

"I am so sorry," Maeve said. She touched her hand to Adam's muscled shoulder, but it was as if he were a statue cast in bronze. He stood stiff and still, his face devoid of expression.

"We must go back to England with all possible haste. I promise to make this up to you sometime in the future. Will you forgive me?"

"There is nothing to forgive. I understand

completely. I will finish my packing immediately." She pressed her cheek against his wide expanse of chest, but he made no move toward her. Adam stood rigid and pale, clearly having difficulty in dealing with the message he had just received from his father's physician.

Perhaps she only imagined it, but Adam seemed to withdraw from her. Gone was the gaiety and lightheartedness of the past weeks. Worse was the lack of emotion, or even an expression of ordinary concern. His former manner was replaced by an aloof thoughtfulness, a reserve that bordered on preoccupation.

Maeve did her best to behave sympathetically. She was more than willing to offer comfort to Adam, but he made that difficult. He barely spoke to her at all. She could only mourn the loss of the Adam who had been her charming lover and regret the present manifestation. His behavior both worried and frightened her. Adam had spoken very little of his relationship with his father. However, she gathered that they had never been particularly close. She would try to understand his feelings, even if at present he chose to keep them bottled up inside of him.

■ ■ ■ ■

The climate of England on their return was chilly and damp; the weather had turned dreary. After the splendid sunny days they had enjoyed on the continent, England appeared a bleak place to be. It seemed that Adam's mood fit the depressing weather perfectly.

Edgefield was a grand ducal estate, an elegant, old manor house that had new additions tacked on every century or so. It was set back in the rustic countryside. Maeve had never seen a mansion so large and palatial. She felt a bit overwhelmed by the size. Everything about the manor spoke of formality and tradition, wealth and privilege. But she also had a sense of coldness and emptiness that made her shiver. She could not imagine actually living in such a place. Even the servants of the great house were as glacially impersonal as the building itself.

For the next week, Adam stayed close to his father's bedside. He rarely spent time with Maeve. Often he was gone by the time she awoke in the morning and did not go to bed at night until after she was asleep.

Maeve had been feeling very tired of late

and sleeping more than usual. In the past week, her stomach had not been well either. On the ship back to England, she assumed her nausea was caused by the constant motion and blamed seasickness, but the malady lingered on, much to her discomfort. She suspected what the problem might be but hoped she was wrong. Since there was no one she could discuss the matter with, she chose to ignore it for the present.

She almost talked to Dr. Hobarth, but he was her father-in-law's physician and at present quite busy. The duke hovered between life and death. Dr. Hobarth explained to Adam in her presence that little could be done for the duke.

"I am very sorry," the kindly old physician said. "I have served your family for many years, as you know. The duke does not have much longer." A gloom and darkness seemed to pervade the room and a chill set into Maeve's bones.

For the next few days the hushed household waited as time seemed suspended. Maeve walked in the park most afternoons. She loved the outdoors. The grounds were well-tended, the manicured lawns and shrubbery a delight. Each day she walked in another direction, exploring a little more of the grounds. There were horses in the stables, but she was a city girl and knew little of riding.

Much of the time, Maeve wished she were back in London where she had friends. Here in this strange house, she felt lonely and isolated. There really was no one to whom she could talk and confide her feelings. Even the neighbors did not visit. She would have insisted on returning to London alone, but she wanted to remain close by in case Adam needed her.

The night of his father's death, Adam did reach out to Maeve. "He passed quietly," was all Adam said to her. Then he sat down heavily on a carved chair in their bedchamber. Maeve got out of bed and placed her arms around him.

"You look exhausted. It is well past midnight. Come to bed."

He pressed his face into the valley between her breasts. "I do not believe I would be able to sleep. I will only disturb your rest."

"Please lie down with me. It has been so long since we have lain together," she implored. "I miss you so much. I ache for you. Please let me offer you some comfort."

In the firelight, he undressed slowly. She watched his every move with admiring eyes, adoring the beauty of his hard, masculine body. Then she held out her arms to him. Wearily, he came to rest beside her.

"I do not understand my reaction to my father's death, Maeve. He died a long time ago in reality. I should have grieved then."

"A delayed reaction perhaps?" She gently rubbed his back.

"His life was well and truly wasted. I cannot tell you how it pains me to know that."

"Darling, I do understand how you feel. Just remember that I love you always. I would do anything to help you."

"Can you love me even when I am morose like this?"

She kissed him sweetly on the lips and tasted brandy on his breath. "I love you for all time."

"You will love me through eternity?" He sounded like a child seeking reassurance.

"Forever."

He buried his face in her breasts and took the succor she offered. Slowly, gently, he made love to her, and it was a solace to both of them. In the early hours of the morning, they finally slept, both sated and exhausted.

There were many people at the old duke's funeral, a sea of strange faces for the most part. The important thing as far as Maeve was concerned was that Adam handled everything very well indeed. He was again the suave, sophisticated member of the *ton,* his mask perfectly in place. The ceremony was a long, formal service as befitted a man of the duke's station and rank.

As Maeve looked around, toward the back of the church, she saw Mr. Brockton; with him were Ralph, Ginny and Mary. She was touched that they had made the long journey from London just to be with her today.

The duke was interred in the family plot, where he joined centuries of eminent blue-blooded ancestors. There was no great outpouring of grief, for as Adam had observed, the man had really died a long time ago.

At the manor house, many came to pay their respects and offer condolences. Maeve felt rather awkward in the presence of the elite of English society. But her friends were there for her, although she could see that they felt every bit as out of place as she did.

"So many toffs here," Mary whispered to Ginny. "We don't belong."

Maeve was beside them and heard her. "You are my guests," she said. "I am very grateful you decided to come today. Your presence means a great deal to me."

"How are you faring, my dear?" Mr. Brockton asked as he took her hands and held them tightly.

Maeve lowered her eyes. "The honeymoon was wonderful. I intend to come back to London soon, and we will have a visit. Then I may tell you all about it. I brought back gifts for everyone."

"You need not have troubled yourself," Mr. Brockton said.

"You are my friends. It was my greatest pleasure searching for just the right things. You all mean so much to me." Maeve hugged each of them in turn. "I am so glad you came for me today." Maeve knew she was repeating herself, but it seemed important that they understood her feelings.

"Miss Maeve, how did you manage without a maid on your trip?" Ginny asked.

"Adam helped me. He acted a perfect lady's maid."

"I daresay he was probably better at helping you out of clothes than doing up your buttons," Ginny said, giggling.

Mary poked her, looking embarrassed.

"Quite true," Maeve agreed quickly.

She could see Ginny's comment had also made Mr. Brockton uncomfortable. He cleared his throat nervously. "I hope his lordship is treating you well. A fancy fellow, he is, and they are not always easy on their women."

"Adam is a fine man."

Mr. Brockton frowned deeply, as if in disbelief. "Nonetheless, if you're ever unhappy or he don't treat you right, you know you always have a home with me."

She kissed his cheek. "I do love you," she said.

The color rose in his face. "Well, we best be going back now. I've had my say." Then Mr. Brockton walked away.

Ginny turned to Maeve. "You are looking like a grand lady, Miss Maeve. Such an elegant gown."

"Adam had it made for me in Italy. He has fine taste."

"Oh, yes," Mary said. "Lovely silk. It's like a dream come true, you marrying his lordship and all."

"Come on now, we must hurry," Ginny said. "Mr. Brockton has no patience as you well know."

"Let's get your gifts then," Maeve said. "I cannot let you leave without them."

Maeve was sorry to see them leave and afterwards felt very much alone again. But then Howard Randall joined her, handing her a glass of wine which she put aside.

"I have already expressed my condolences to Adam, and now I wish to talk with a beautiful lady."

She welcomed his attentions, considering him a friend.

"You are in looks today, Lady Maeve, although a bit plumper than the last time I gazed upon your person." He noticed her look of discomfort. "Oh, it is quite attractive, I do assure you. You are most charming indeed. Has not His Grace observed as much to you?"

"His Grace?"

"Adam, of course. He is now the Duke of Clarmont with all the responsibilities that encumber that illustrious position of authority. You will henceforth also be referred to as Your Grace."

Maeve took a deep breath and let it out slowly. "I don't suppose I thought of that before."

Lord Randall patted her hand comfortingly. "Do not look so Friday-faced, my dear. It is all the thing to be married to a duke, you know. Besides, it is too late for you to cry off."

Adam joined them at that moment. "Are you flirting with my wife?"

Maeve was surprised to observe that Adam was not talking to his friend in a bantering manner. In fact, his mouth had narrowed to a grim line. Surely her husband could not possibly be jealous? Such an emotion was totally unlike Adam, but then, he had not been behaving much like himself lately at all.

"Me flirt with your wife? 'Course not, dear boy! You are much too handy with all weapons of execution — not to mention your flying fists. Don't wish to have you plant a facer on me. I only offer your graceful goddess friendship, since you appeared to be neglecting her. Not dangling after her, not at all."

Maeve felt a certain tension between the two men and decided to change the subject. "You look tired," she said, raising her fingers to run them along Adam's cheek. "How are you holding up?"

"I confess I will feel much better when our guests have departed."

"Ever the gracious host," Howard said, saluting Adam with his wine glass.

"One does one's best," Adam said coolly.

Maeve excused herself from the company after tea was served. The day had been long and trying for her, and she needed some time alone. She lay down on the large bed in what had obviously been Adam's room in his youth. It was clearly masculine in looks, with few frills but quality furnishings all in the best taste.

She must have slept for a time, for when she stirred, it was dark outside. She saw to freshening her appearance and then decided to go downstairs and find Adam.

All the guests appeared to have departed; that was her first observation. The butler, Wentworth, an ancient, arthritic fellow, approached her with a melancholy expression.

"Did you wish something, Your Grace?"

"My husband, Wentworth."

"He is in his study, Your Grace." Wentworth lowered his bald head deferentially. "Shall I announce you?"

All the formality in the great house served to make her feel awkward. "No, thank you, I'll just pop in."

"He is in conference," Wentworth said with a disapproving frown, his face a mosaic of wrinkles.

"Who is with him?"

Wentworth lowered his eyes. "It is not for me to say."

Maeve was bewildered, but she decided to find out for herself what was going on. She passed through the marble-floored hallway with its picture gallery that held a notable collection of paintings, including many portrait renderings of former formidable-looking dukes and duchesses. The hall was like a Roman basilica, formal and forbidding. Maeve shuddered involuntarily. Surely Adam would not wish to remain in this mausoleum of a mansion overlong.

Maeve found the study after looking into several sumptuous sitting rooms. She could hear Adam's voice, no difficult matter since he appeared to be shouting. Raising his voice was so totally unlike him that she was shocked. Then there was a woman's voice, not as loud, but clearly her voice was raised as well.

The study door was open a crack and she could look inside. At first glance, the lady Adam was shouting at appeared young, but when Maeve looked more closely she could see the woman was actually made up rather heavily with a good deal of rouge and blanc. Her gown was very fashionable with a low décolletage. She was a striking woman with golden hair, perhaps just a touch too golden for nature's own paintbrush, but lovely all the same. Her hairstyle was in the current, short style. She guessed the woman to be in her middle years, but her voice had a petulant, girlish quality.

"I cannot believe you have come here. Your audacity amazes me." Maeve had never heard Adam sound so angry, not even when he confronted the Earl of Southford.

"I considered your feelings, did I not? Was I at the funeral? No. I offered you no affront or embarrassment."

"You had no right to be there."

"I had every right!"

"He would not have wanted you present."

"He is dead, as you must collect. Besides, funerals are not for the dead. They are for the living."

"Why have you come here on this of all days?"

"Offer me a glass of sherry, and I will tell you."

"I prefer that you leave here right now. I do not want you seen by anyone."

"You are so thoroughly ashamed of me?"

"I do not know how you live with yourself."

Maeve could see the woman confronting Adam directly. She seemed every bit as furious as he was.

"You never heard my side of it."

"I will not listen now. I ask you to leave. I am grieving for my father."

"He was hardly a father to you."

"And whose fault was that?" Adam countered, his voice shaking with rage.

"His Grace was always in his cups, long before the unpleasantness."

"Is that what you call it? *The unpleasant- ness?*"

"What should I say?"

"In this case, mere words would hardly suffice. It is your actions that matter. And you are found wanting as both mother and wife."

"You would accuse me when you know nothing of the matter?"

"Oh, I know a great deal, madam. I am sorry to say, more than I wish."

It was then that Adam caught sight of Maeve. She decided to quietly knock at the door. In reality, she would have preferred to walk quickly away, but that was not an option.

"What is it, Maeve?" He sounded annoyed at the interruption.

"I did not mean to disturb you."

The woman immediately came forward and gave her a charming smile. "So you are Adam's wife. I have heard the *on-dit* regarding you. I see Adam is open-minded about some females." The woman gave her a superior smile, arching her brows in the same way he often did.

"Maeve, this person who is addressing you was my mother. She is no one to me now and was about to leave."

"Not yet. We have matters to discuss

385

between us." The lady sat down in a comfortable chair opposite Adam's well-appointed desk and folded her arms across her generously endowed bosom. Then she turned to Maeve. "I am your mother-in-law. You may call me Sophia. I am told you are a gypsy. I have no trouble accepting you, since we are a family plagued by scandal."

"Maeve, will you leave us?" Adam said. His expression was an emotionless mask. He was tightly controlling his temper. However, the tension in him was palpable.

Maeve said not a word and left the room, shutting the door behind her. When she walked into the hall, she noticed a young girl who stood peering at a marble bust of a Greek warrior that sat on a bronze pedestal. The girl looked up as Maeve came and stood beside her.

"Are they still arguing?" the girl asked worriedly.

"I suppose so. Who are you?"

"I am Brianna. Are you my brother's wife?"

Maeve was very much surprised. "I didn't know Adam had a sister."

"I do not suppose he is pleased about it." The girl spoke very well, with a lovely, cultured voice.

Brianna's face was heart-shaped. She was

taller than her mother, with a slender, willowy body. Her eyes were large and liquid, blue-violet in color, her hair a honey blond.

"I had a little brother, Nicky, but he died of the measles."

"I am very sorry," Maeve said.

"He was a sweet little boy," the girl said sadly. "We did not have the same father. Have I shocked you?"

"Not really. I do not shock easily."

"Good. Mother said you were not a conventional woman. She hoped you might intercede with my brother."

"Intercede how?" Maeve inquired.

Brianna lowered her large, bright eyes. "They will talk about it."

"Well, perhaps you and I might do the same? Have you eaten any dinner?"

"No, I have not, but I do not wish to impose."

Maeve decided the girl had very good manners; whatever else she might be, she was not rude.

"I am very hungry and I have not had my dinner, so you will please me very much if you will share supper with me. It is very lonely here, and I would like the pleasure of your company for my evening meal."

Brianna smiled brightly, a dimple much like Adam's showing in her cheek. "I am really very hungry too, but Miss Wilkins says a lady must never admit to such a thing."

"And who is this Miss Wilkins?"

"She was my deportment teacher at the young ladies' seminary school I attended in Switzerland."

Maeve led the girl into the dining room. Much to her relief, she saw that the table had been set. There were only two places, and so they sat opposite each other across the long table.

Maeve was pleased when Wentworth appeared and arranged for their dinner to be served immediately. They were both self-conscious, but hunger allowed them to share an excellent meal in companionable silence. Maeve lingered over the trifle that was presented for dessert. She was thinking what to say to this pretty young stranger. Obviously, Brianna felt just as awkward.

"I like this very much," Brianna said. "The cream is excellent."

"Tell me more about yourself," Maeve said. "I think we should become better acquainted."

"I should like to have you for a friend," Brianna said enthusiastically. "Outside of my teachers, I really have no friends. And you seem kind."

"No friends at all?"

Brianna again lowered her eyes. "The other girls would not associate with me."

Maeve was immediately sympathetic. "Children are often very cruel to each other."

"I imagine they were only reflecting the opinions of their elders. I do not condemn them for it. It was only that my life was often times very lonely. But I did have such wonderful teachers. And I learned so much." She stopped for another mouthful of brandy-flavored trifle. "My teachers were very kind, and I should have liked to become one of them. If only I had not written to Mother to ask if I could become a teacher, she would have continued to forget all about me, and we would not be here bothering you and my brother tonight."

Maeve wanted to ask why they had come but thought it might be rude to ask, and so she continued eating her dessert and wondering.

CHAPTER TWENTY

Adam kept a tight leash on his emotions. He had learned early the hard lesson of the need to be guarded and circumspect in his dealings with others; he practiced strict self-control. However, being in the company of his mother made him feel very much like a young child again, a very angry one. His hands were balled into fists.

He knew his voice had been raised and sought to lower it. He especially regretted that Maeve had overheard a portion of the argument. She had obviously been upset. Since Adam learned of his father's death, he had been unable to really speak with her in a meaningful manner. He knew she accepted his preoccupation, his distress, but could she understand it, particularly when he hardly understood it himself?

"Adam, are you listening to me at all?" His mother's voice was sharp with none of her usual effort at charm.

She appeared agitated, and he was glad of it, because she had certainly upset him very badly. Why had she come here on this of all days? Did she actually think he would welcome her with open arms after what she had done?

"Enough of this. Why are you here tonight? Certainly not to grieve or reminisce. I can only assume you want something of me."

"Nothing for myself, to be sure. Although my family disowned me after the scandal, I still have a small inheritance of my own from my maternal grandmother. You will collect I never asked a farthing of you, since I know what you think of me, however unjust your judgment."

He sighed deeply and poured himself another snifter of brandy. He rarely drank, and because he had hardly eaten all day, the alcohol went straight to his head. But he did not mind; in fact, he welcomed the heat in his throat and the numbing of his thought processes. It removed memory and pain, but only to a degree.

"I know what Rundwall must have told you regarding the incident. He turned you against me. That man was ever my enemy."

"I could never have managed without his help. Father was an invalid after you went off, as you well know."

"I did not choose to leave. I was given little choice in the matter." She held a handkerchief against her eyes as if to dab tears away, but he could plainly see her eyes were quite dry. "Rundwall murdered a good, gentle man, you know."

"You mean he fought a duel with your lover."

"Yes, I did love George. I do not deny it."

"And what of your husband, madam? Had you no care for his feelings, for his well-being?"

"Ours was never a love match. The marriage was arranged by our parents. Your father was a weak man. I thought I might grow to love him in time, but I found I could not. You are strong like me, Adam. You must understand. I did not bring your father to destruction. He did it to himself. I refuse to feel any sense of guilt or responsibility."

Adam could no longer contain his rage. The woman was without any shred of decency, totally immoral. "You are a whore, madam, a hard-hearted slut."

She turned away from him, gripping the oak desk as if she were about to faint. He remained unmoved, convinced she made the gesture for dramatic effect. He remembered all too well how gifted his mother was at manipulating others to get her own way.

"I promised I would not demean myself by quarreling with you. There is no need to wrangle. I hope only to put aside our differences that we may discourse on important matters of current expediency."

"Such as?" He knew he sounded impatient but didn't really care.

She sighed expressively. "Your sister's situation is a matter of utmost concern to me."

"You refer to your bastard, madam?"

She stared at him as if he had slapped her. "I refer to your sister. She is of an age where plans must be made for her future."

"Ever the doting mother," he said sarcastically, his voice cold and cutting.

"You can be most cruel. You have learned well from your father's cousin."

"I am only cruel to those who practice cruelty. You would do well to remember that."

She turned and looked deeply into his eyes, offering him her most ingratiating smile. With pain in his heart, he recalled how much he had once loved her, adored and doted on her, how beautiful he had thought her to be. And then she had betrayed both his father and himself.

"Let us not say hurtful things to each other. You have risen to greatness. Such pettiness is beneath you. The fact remains, Adam dear, that you have a sister, a lovely young girl. As you well know, I have nothing to offer her. But you have assumed your father's title and properties. You have an admired position in the *ton.* It would be nothing for you to arrange for your sister to have a Season. She needs a proper come-out."

"So that our family may once again be the source of gossip and general amusement? You wish to brew new scandalbroth?"

"You have it in your power to find a suitable husband for Brianna. The means are at your disposal if only you will employ them. As to scandal, it is well known that you have married a gypsy, a woman of questionable bloodlines, without either reputation or wealth. Surely scandal is not something you fear."

"I will ignore what you have said about my wife. Your words are not worthy of comment. The fact of the matter is, madam, I want nothing to do with you or your bastard. I would, however, wish you to leave this house and not return."

"Very well, you shall have your wish." Her face contorted with anger. "I will gladly leave this place. I was never happy here. As for you, you are an unnatural child. I want nothing further to do with you. I prepare to leave for Italy with Count Orsini."

"Ah, yet another lover. How many have there been? Do you even keep count? My mama, the queen of Cythereans."

"You are rude beyond belief! Brianna is my only concern, else I would never humble myself in this manner. Would you have the girl left to her own devices? She cannot come with me, you know. It would not be proper."

"Perhaps in being your daughter, she has already learned enough to manage by herself."

"Can you not understand that an innocent girl needs your help?"

Adam quickly poured himself another drink and gulped it down. "I saw my father buried today, but he died the day he found you in his bed with that child's father. He shot himself in the head, hoping for a quick death to end his misery."

"He was sick long before that. Perhaps I was not discreet, but his reaction was absurd in the extreme. I am not to blame."

His mother reached out to touch his arm, but Adam pulled sharply away from her as if she had the plague.

Maeve stood beside Brianna. They had

returned to wait outside the door to the study. The poor girl looked pale and frightened. Maeve observed Brianna was dressed plainly in a serviceable, high-necked gray gown that looked very much like a school uniform. Her dark gold hair was pulled back from her face but hung loose down her back in a child-like style. All in all, the girl appeared the very opposite of her worldly mother.

They could hear the raised voices through the door.

Brianna bit her lower lip worriedly. "Mother is here on my behalf. I am at fault."

"Why should you think that?"

Brianna wrung her dainty hands. "My mother will soon leave England again. She will go with her count to Naples, but she is concerned about me. She believes my brother should take responsibility for my well-being. However, he does not know me at all. I do not wish to be a burden to anyone. Yet, I confess I do not know what will become of me. I have been educated as a lady, which means I know a little of many things but have no skills by which to earn my bread. I would have taught at school, but Mother says we are of the aristocracy, and it is beneath such as we to teach school or act as a governess or companion." Tears formed in the girl's blueberry muffin eyes. "I must sound very selfish to you."

Maeve placed her arms around Brianna in a gesture of comfort. "It is a bitter thing to have no place in the world. I understand that better than you could know. I will help you as best I can. You have my promise, and I do not give my word lightly." At that moment, Maeve determined that Brianna would become part of her household. "I intend to convince Adam to invite you to live with us."

"Oh, thank you. You are so good." Brianna kissed her cheek.

"You belong here. I shall make him see reason. It will be resolved." Maeve took Brianna's hand, and the girl held to her tightly. Maeve felt the turbulence and fear that tore at the girl's soul and trembled as they bonded as sisters.

The door to the study opened suddenly and Adam's mother swept out of the room. "I am still the Dowager Duchess, and as such, deserve a modicum of respect and civility from my son. You will rue this day and come to regret your harshness and will-ful pride. Come, Brianna, we are leaving now. Your brother will do nothing for you."

The girl flashed a look of despair at Maeve, who turned to Adam's mother.

"Please do not go now in haste. Let me speak to Adam on your behalf and that of Brianna."

"To what purpose? I shall not further demean and humiliate myself." Her color was high. "He is heartless."

Adam stood in the doorway, arms folded across his chest. Maeve had never seen his eyes look so cold or hard. Still, she turned to him hopefully.

"Please allow Brianna to remain." Her voice was husky and imploring. "Do it for me. This is the only thing I will ever ask of you."

"Ask anything of me but that."

"Come, child, there is a coach waiting for us. It is hopeless. I have been a fool." The lady took her daughter's arm and pulled the girl forward away from Maeve. For just a moment she turned one last time to her son. "I said before that you and I were alike. I was quite wrong. You are weak, exactly like your father. He had no forgiveness in him either." With that she left, half dragging her sobbing daughter away from Maeve.

"Adam, please, I implore you. Let Brianna stay!"

He turned away from her.

When Maeve heard the coach pull away, she went and stood in front of Adam and shook her head, not trusting herself to speak.

"Do not look at me that way, Maeve. You must trust my judgment. Would you have me take responsibility for a whore's bastard?"

"The woman is your mother, no matter what offence she may be guilty of, and the young girl is an innocent, not guilty of anything. Brianna is not to blame for the circumstances of her birth. I am so terribly disappointed in you, Adam. What I most admired about you was your fairness, your generosity of spirit. This is so unworthy of you."

"Do not pretend to know what I am feeling or thinking. You do not know me that well. Do not accuse me." His voice was icy cold. She stared into his eyes and saw only darkness, emptiness.

She ran upstairs shaking, scarcely able to control her tears. Perhaps it was true that she hardly knew him. They had married quickly; theirs had not been a conventional courtship, to say the least. Yet she had felt she knew his heart and mind. Were her feelings all romantic illusion? No, her instincts had never failed her before. Surely she had not been wrong to love Adam so completely and give her heart over to him.

She sent for a maid to help her undress; the black crepe dress with its jet ornamentation was not only uncomfortable but had a row of tiny pearl buttons down the back, which was difficult to reach. The maid, a young girl named Jane, was all too pleased to serve her mistress, but Maeve quickly dismissed the girl and lay down on the bed. Although tired, she could not sleep. Over and over her mind relived what had happened. Could she have done something to change matters? Possibly, but what?

It was very late when she heard the door open. "Adam?"

"Were you expecting another?" His speech was slurred. She knew instantly that he was drunk.

She saw him undressing in the moonlight, none too steady on his feet. His magnificent body seemed unfamiliar to her as if he were a stranger. He climbed into bed beside her.

Then he pulled her close. "I would like a kiss from my wife," he said, his voice thickening.

"I am not of a mind to kiss you right now." Maeve struggled to free herself from him. She felt his breath hot against her skin and twisted in his arms.

"Don't fight me, sweetheart. I'll not harm you. I adore you."

"I want to go to sleep, Adam. I want to be left alone." She closed her eyes against tears.

"I see. I am a villain, a brute. Is that it?"

She shook her head, but he forced her to turn and face him.

"Won't even speak to me? Have I so offended you? Can you not consider how badly I was hurt? There was a cold place in me that knew no warmth until I met you."

"You are not yourself tonight. Your nerves are overset. Can we not talk in the morning?"

"Perhaps I wish to do more than talk tonight." His eyes were half-closed yet radiated sensual desire.

His lips skimmed the hollow of her swan's neck. She felt the warm flick of his tongue and then he was trailing a long, line of hot kisses along the swelling of her breasts.

"I do not want this now," she said.

"Liar! I feel your pulse beat quicken. You want me just as I want you. I must have you. I need you."

She fanned her fingers wide over his chest pressing her palms flat against the hard muscles.

His mouth tasting of brandy was firm against her own. He traced the contours of her lips with his tongue slowly, tasting the sensitive surfaces with erotic little circles until her body quivered in response.

She wanted to run away from him, to refuse him. She was still very angry with him and terribly disappointed by his earlier behavior. She must not let him do this to her. Then his hands began kneading her breasts and she heard herself moan with desire. Her breasts were so sensitive and full and his touch was so exciting. Soon his hands were moving downward along her thighs and he was stripping her nightrail over her head. He laid her bare and studied her in the silvery light.

"Beautiful," he said. Then his hands and lips began their exploration in earnest. "Such succulent fruits." His mouth dipped to her breasts and he began sucking at her nipples. "I'm mad for you."

It was more than she could bear. She was on fire for him, carried away by his raging desire. He took her hand and guided it to the source of his masculinity which shot out boldly from the rest of his body, pulsing and vital. His hand moved to the sensitive place between her legs where she was already moist and ready for him. She could not help running her hand over the turgid, silky strength of his virility as he groaned deeply in his throat.

Suddenly, he was over her, cupping her

derriere, positioning her. He entered her with a sure, powerful thrust that made her gasp. Then his hand came between them and he was touching that secret, special place that was folded within her like the center of a rose hidden by crimson petals.

As he moved powerfully within her, Maeve came alive with rapture. The velvet fist created a potent rhythm of primeval rapture. She was lost in wave after wave of purest pleasure as he spilled his seed within her.

In a few minutes, it was over. Adam moved free of her and turned over on his side. He was asleep almost immediately, as if their lovemaking had at least temporarily freed him of some dreadful demon.

But Maeve could not sleep. She wept silently. Everything seemed wrong to her. Adam, on taking over his father's title, had now become what he perceived his father to have been. There was no question in her mind that she still loved Adam. She believed that he loved her as well. And the physical attraction between them could not be denied. Nonetheless, she could not stay with him. Her conclusion was a question of principle, of honor. She came to a difficult decision as tears rolled down her cheeks. She rose and packed a bag. Perhaps he would come to his senses and eventually comprehend what she had done and why. There was risk involved, but it was necessary that she take a stand.

At dawn, while Adam slept like the dead, she had Wentworth rouse the coachman and ready the carriage. She left Adam a brief note by his bedside and hoped he would understand. There was no way she could continue to live with him if matters remained as they were. One thing was certain. She would have to return to London and see about finding Brianna. Maeve would not rest until the girl was safely with her. She had made Brianna a promise, and nothing would deter her from fulfilling it. The girl needed her help. As for Adam, he would have to come around, or their marriage could not continue.

CHAPTER
TWENTY-ONE

Maeve spent hours thinking during the coach ride to London, then finally slept the sleep of the exhausted for a short period of time. Arriving in the city at last, she felt a sense of comfort, as if she were finally home again.

Her first instinct was to go back to Mr. Brockton, but she thought better of it. Mr. Brockton's house was his home, not hers. And as much as she knew everyone would welcome her return, the distinction was an important one to her. Adam had bought her a townhouse, and it was her home to live in if she so chose. For the time being, she did choose to live in it, without Adam. She informed the coachman of her destination and sat back wearily against the red plush cushions.

She had in fact another reason for not immediately wishing to see Mr. Brockton. Maeve did not want him to know that she had left Adam. Not having fully thought matters out yet, she was not ready to discuss her situation with anyone, even those individuals whom she knew really cared about her.

She spent the next day recovering from the stress of her physical and emotional ordeal. But once installed in her own house, Maeve began to feel better, more in charge of herself and her life. She began formulating a plan for finding Brianna. If only her special talent was still available! She had viewed it as something of a curse in the past but now wished devoutly she had it.

Maeve knew that she could have found Brianna easily with her visionary power. She and Brianna were attuned to each other. She had realized it intuitively from the first moment they spoke. There was no question that her thoughts could have reached out to touch the girl's mind. But she was no longer possessed of that level of concentration. Second sight had been closed to her during the trip to the continent. Maeve knew why and could no longer ignore what it meant.

She was having a child, Adam's child, and the special gift had turned inward. It was as if all the energy involved in the process of seeing was now needed for nurturing, focused on the new life that was growing within her. It was also the reason she felt so tired all the time. This new life was draining her of vitality. But she did not begrudge it; if anything, she looked forward to becoming a mother, welcomed the prospect. She realized how much she loved Adam and how much it meant to her to have his child. If only Adam would become again the wonderful husband he had been on their honeymoon.

She would not think about that now. Perhaps her departure would shock Adam and return him to his senses. Locating Brianna was her immediate concern, and that would now prove more difficult than it would have been before she conceived. She must resort to the measures followed by ordinary people. And so, she reasoned, that to find the way to Adam's sister, her path must begin with Adam's mother. Where would Sophia take her daughter? Obviously, only someone who knew the woman well could answer that question for her. One possibility came immediately to her mind: the Duke of Rundwall. She disliked the idea of seeing him, especially without Adam, but there was no help for it.

The duke received Maeve courteously enough. It was clear that he was curious as to the purpose of her visit, but he asked no questions of her immediately, for which she was mightily grateful. He seated her politely in his drawing room and offered to have tea brought but she declined.

He looked pale and thinner than she remembered but seemed in good spirits nonetheless. "How is your health, sir?" That seemed the best way to begin.

"Your suggestion for further treatment proved a wise one. I am feeling surprisingly better. Perhaps I will survive longer than I thought. Will you come around and keep a sharp eye on my physicians for me?"

"I will do what I can." She would fix him one of her mother's herbal tonics. If nothing else, the tonic might stimulate his appetite.

Their conversation quite naturally went to Charles and Caroline. Maeve told him about their visit in Italy.

"I am glad they are happy together. Caroline will breed fine children. I am content that my immortality rests in good hands."

Maeve could not help forming a question aloud. "About your wives, when our hands touched, I had the distinct vision of violent death connecting you to them."

His misty eyes widened. "You cannot possibly think I would have harmed them?"

She did not immediately respond.

"Then that is your perception? Not that it matters overmuch, but I did not dispatch them to their maker. Rebecca died in childbirth, though cursing me, it is true. She gave birth to one stillborn after another. When I found Madeleine to be barren, I neglected her. She swallowed an overdose of laudanum on discovering I had a new mistress. I may have been a dreadful husband, but I assure you, I am not a murderer."

Maeve grimly perceived that he had surely been responsible for their deaths, if indirectly, but she kept that opinion to herself.

"Where is Adam?" the duke asked. "I thought the two of you inseparable."

"He had some business matters to which he must attend, and I needed to return to London. I wanted to do some shopping." That was certainly true enough, up to a point.

The duke smiled. "Ladies must always shop. It is their vocation."

Maeve was of the opinion the duke spent more time at his tailor than she ever would with a dressmaker, but she again reserved comment. She told him instead about her mother-in-law's visit, deliberately avoiding the more graphic details of the confrontation between Adam and his mother.

"I would very much like to locate Brianna and make certain she has a proper place to stay. She is an amiable girl and most deserving of consideration."

Rundwall viewed her shrewdly. "You want to know to whom Sophia might entrust her daughter?"

"Surely there must be someone."

Rundwall tapped his knee thoughtfully. "Most people gave Sophia the cut direct after what happened, and one can scarcely blame them. That was why she primarily chose to live on the continent. But there was a cousin, bit of a scoundrel himself, with whom she maintained a close connection."

Maeve was hopeful. "Could you possibly give me his name and direction?"

"Don't know that I know where he lives these days, but I have servants who might. I find they know the *on-dit* before I do. The more scandalous the nabob, the better informed they are."

The duke proved to be correct. After inquiries were made among the staff, it was discovered that one of the duke's footmen had walked out with the lady's maid of a certain Lizette Duvall, who happened to be the current mistress of Grenville Ogden,

Sophia's first cousin and supposed confidant. Maeve left the duke feeling hopeful that she would soon find Brianna and bring her home.

Adam's head felt as if it must surely explode any minute now. "For God's sake, stop making so much noise, Randall." He knew he sounded irritable but didn't care overmuch.

"Your butler said you have been ill for the past three days. It appears the chap has a gift for euphemism. I suppose he meant you've been in your cups since the funeral."

Adam groaned loudly. "Go away!"

"No need to be churlish, old man. And I've no sympathy for you. Some men do better avoiding strong drink, and you are certainly one of them."

"How insightful of you."

"No need for sarcasm. No way to talk to your savior, lad. It happens I know how to put together a certain drink, a restorative that will fix you up in no time whatsoever."

"Poison, I presume?"

Howard laughed. " 'Course not. An old family recipe. One taste of the stuff, however, and you'll never want to imbibe again, which is one reason I so rarely get ape-drunk myself. Where is your lovely bride?"

"Gone," was all Adam managed to croak out.

"Where?"

"I do not know her whereabouts precisely. Somewhere in London. She did not say much in her note."

Howard viewed him with obvious amusement. "Famous. Did you have a quarrel?"

"Not precisely." Adam eyed Randall warily.

But in the end, he told Howard the entire story while his friend listened in silence.

When he concluded, Howard leaned forward. "I doubt she has left you for good, old man, if that is any comfort."

"I cannot be certain that she has not taken me in disgust."

Adam could not bring himself to tell Howard what had run through his mind when he first discovered Maeve gone, how betrayed he felt, how lost and empty. He thought, *I am just like my father.* He did not know if he could be any stronger than that worthy if he too lost his wife. He spent the next three days drinking to forget her, alternately feeling anger and despair. One moment he was filled with rage and vowed never to see her again; the next he thought he might kill himself if she were gone for good. But now he was sober, with an intolerable hangover and eyes that refused to completely focus. Drinking for days had been foolish behavior on his part. Perhaps Howard was right; his heredity did not bode well for heavy drinking.

"Are you going after her?"

"And make a cake of myself? A man has to maintain some degree of pride and dignity." Adam straightened to his full, imposing height.

"Quite right. Well, old man, let me know if you are done with Maeve, I would not mind a'tall having a go at her myself."

Adam's reaction was sudden and unpremeditated; he lunged at Howard and punched his friend, one quick, punishing blow to the jaw.

Randall fell over with a shocked thud. Adam was himself appalled by what he had done. Such impulsive behavior was completely foreign to his nature. No, not at all like him. What was wrong with him? He didn't even have the excuse of being foxed anymore. He would have liked to blame his impulsive action on Maeve, but he knew better.

"Terribly sorry, old chap," he said, and extended a hand to Howard, who was now regarding him warily, as if he perceived a cobra ready to strike.

"A bit too handy with your fives." Howard moved his jaw tentatively. "Look here, old fellow, I was only joking. Anyone can see at a glance that Maeve is entirely devoted to you and would never consider being another man's paramour."

Howard's words gave Adam pause to reflect. His friend was completely correct. Maeve would be no man's bird of paradise. Hadn't she refused him? He could not persuade her for love or money. He remembered how she had described herself as a bird who would not be kept in a cage. Why, he'd even had to cajole her into marrying him. How had he ever forgotten?

Maeve was nothing like his mother. Maeve's heart was warm and loving. No woman had ever responded to his lovemaking with so much passion. She gave everything of herself to him, holding nothing back. She would never betray him. How foolish he had been to consider it for even a moment.

"Get up, Randall. I owe you a cold compress and an apology. I have certainly made a mull of matters. You can give me a ride back to London in your phaeton."

"Excellent notion."

"I do hope I can convince Maeve to come back to me. She has unfortunately discovered that I am not the paragon she thought me."

"I could have told her that."

Grenville Ogden's face was as red as a rare roast beef, and his hand, as he took Maeve's own, was as moist as a sponge. Instinctively, she found the man disquieting, even somewhat repulsive, and quickly withdrew her hand from his.

"Can I do anything else for you, sir?" The maid was a plump, apple-cheeked girl of perhaps sixteen.

"Tell Cook to prepare us some tea, love." He gave her well-padded rear end a lingering pat and the girl left giggling.

"Please have a seat." Ogden placed himself opposite Maeve and studied her appearance with such keen interest that Maeve was immediately uneasy.

"I have heard about you. You are certainly not an antidote. Such glossy black hair and striking gray eyes. I have seen gypsy women before and always found them swarthy and coarse. You are neither. And such elegance of form." His small, piggish eyes dwelt insultingly upon her bosom.

Maeve felt as if she had been touched by something slimy and revolting. "I have come here today with a particular purpose," she said pointedly.

"Now what is it I can do for you?" There was an undercurrent of insinuation in his voice, as if he expected her to make romantic overtures to him.

"You are my husband's second cousin, as I understand it. I am persuaded that my mother-in-law might have come here with her daughter Brianna."

Ogden leaned toward her and Maeve instinctively moved back. "Haven't seen either of them. Was there something you wanted with them?"

"I want to invite Brianna to stay with me."

"How nice for the girl. I will be sure to let Sophia know, when and if they happen to visit."

A strikingly attractive woman entered the drawing room of the lodging at that moment. She was dressed in an extremely low-cut, diaphanous gown. She wore no chemisette, not even a bit of lace, so that her breasts and nipples in particular were clearly outlined. Her cheeks were heavy with rouge and her hard eyes were lined with kohl.

"Lizette, my dear, meet my cousin's wife. Should we refer to you as Your Grace?"

"No, I do not care overmuch for formality," Maeve said.

"My, you are refreshing. Maeve has come

in search of my dear cousin, Sophia, and her daughter, Brianna. I told her as to how we have not as yet seen them."

Maeve picked up hopefully on what he had said. "Then they are expected?"

"Not to my knowledge. I did not mean to imply it."

Ogden put his arms around his mistress and ran his hand suggestively down the length of her body. All the time, his eyes were fixed on Maeve. "You must stay for tea. We should get to know each other better. I have always been very fond of my relatives."

Lizette gave Maeve a shrewdly appraising look while Ogden offered a venal smile from cupid lips. Maeve suddenly felt sick to her stomach.

"I must be going," she said, and rose quickly to her feet.

"But you must stay for tea! We even have excellent biscuits today."

"No, I have appointments to keep." She gave him her card. "If you happen to hear from Adam's mother, please contact me. I am concerned about Brianna's well-being."

The young, apple-faced maid had returned and was listening intently. It seemed to Maeve the girl would like to say something, but looking over at her employer, she lowered her eyes and put the tea tray down on an end table. Ogden turned to the girl. "Thank you, Doris. Why don't you place this card in a drawer for me?" Then he turned back to Maeve. "There, you see how lovely these are, quite luscious." He picked up a biscuit and bit into it hungrily. "Can I not tempt you?"

"Not in the slightest." These people had made her feel terribly uncomfortable. The worst part was, she had the distinct impression that Ogden was not telling her the truth. Sadly, she observed it might not be as easy to find Brianna as she had originally thought.

Adam's arrival at the ducal townhouse was greeted with a flurry of activity among the servants. He soon discovered that Maeve was not there, although their trunks from their trip abroad awaited them. Where had she gone?

The answer seemed obvious: Brockton's house. She had probably gone there to complain of Adam's cruelty. He groaned inwardly. He was not at his best and certainly in no mood to deal with Brockton, not one of his favorite people, to be sure. He decided on getting a good night's sleep and seeing Brockton on the morrow.

The following afternoon, dressed to the nines, his neckwear a la Byron, Adam was confident that he made a dashing appearance. Somehow it gave him the confidence to face an accusing Brockton and a teary Maeve.

But the meeting was not at all as he expected. Brockton received him civilly enough. "I am surprised you have come without Maeve," he said. "Where is the dear girl?"

Adam was so surprised, he could hardly manage an intelligible response. "Resting," he said finally. "She was tired."

"Well, tell her to drop by soon. Ginny and Mary are eager to see her. They've got some news to share." Brockton looked at him expectantly.

Adam wracked his mind for something to say. "Did Maeve tell you that Charles is Rundwall's heir?"

"We spoke of it briefly. Can't say I am a bit pleased about it, but the boy must make his own decision."

"Charles wasn't all that eager for it either."

"Didn't think he would be," Brockton said with a deep frown.

"But there is Caroline to consider. She does want it."

Brockton gave him a fatalistic nod. "The lad is a son to me, and I only want the best for him."

Their conversation came to an abrupt end. Brockton thanked him for visiting and Adam quickly left. He was gratified that Maeve had not gone running to Brockton for support, but there was still the matter of finding out where Maeve was staying. He found he could think of little else than being with his wife. The only thing he knew for certain was that he must find her as soon as possible. He no longer felt whole unless she was with him.

CHAPTER
TWENTY-TWO

Adam realized that the logical place to look for Maeve was at the house he had bought for her. She had lived there for a time before they married; it was not surprising she would want to go back there now. He took his phaeton, thinking that he would ask her out for a drive. But he met with disappointment. Rogers, the new butler there, informed him that Her Grace was in residence but happened to be out. Adam felt angry and frustrated; matters were decidedly not proceeding as he had hoped. His wife was much too unpredictable.

"Now look here, if she has told you to say that she is out, I refuse to be put off."

"Your Grace, Her Grace is definitely not at home."

"Just remember who pays the bills here."

"Yes, Your Grace," came the doleful response.

Adam regretted his comment as soon as it

left his lips. He had sounded childishly petulant, even to his own ears. "Do you happen to know where she is?"

Rogers gave him a negative response and he left feeling thoroughly thwarted. Where to go from here? He thought of Rundwall immediately. But he had no intention of asking his cousin's advice about women. The man was a valuable source of information on many things, but he had not done well with the fair sex at all. In fact, it might be wise to listen to Rundwall's opinions and then follow the exact opposite course of behavior. Adam decided to retreat to his club and consider the matter in comfort. Then he changed his mind. It was a perfect time for him to practice boxing at Gentleman Jackson's academy; of course, he thought grimly, a few of the young bloods might be the worse for it, considering his frame of mind.

Maeve had selected material for several new gowns appropriate for a woman *enciente*. Her breasts had clearly enlarged, and she felt uncomfortable in her current clothing. Unfortunately, the high-waisted style put the emphasis precisely on that particular bodily attribute. Hers, in fact, grew more eye-catching by the day.

On Bond Street, she ran into Lord Randall. She had a sense of *deja vu* as she recalled the last time she'd seen him there and shuddered at the memory of being threatened with death.

"I say, Maeve, Adam has come to town looking for you."

She lowered her eyes. "What is his mood?"

Lord Randall looked abashed. "Mood? Why, he's quite unhappy, actually. Why wouldn't he be? His wife, who is an incomparable, a diamond of the first water, has left him. He is sick at heart."

Maeve found herself flushing at the compliments Howard bestowed upon her. "Is that true or are you just flattering me so I will forgive him?"

Howard shrugged. "Perhaps a little of both. But he truly was physically ill, Maeve. There can be no question about that. Do take pity on the man. He adores you."

"If he comes to see me, I will talk with him. That is all I can promise for now."

Howard grinned broadly, transforming his homely features. "Of course, dear girl. That is all anyone could ask. Lovers' quarrels can easily be resolved when the lovers are in proximity."

She touched his arm. "You are, I am afraid, oversimplifying matters."

"Perhaps not. May I tell Adam that you will receive him?"

"You may."

Howard helped with her packages and then waved her off. Maeve was thoughtful on the short ride back to her house. Did she want to see Adam again so soon after their quarrel? Really, it had been nearly a week. And if the truth be told, she missed him terribly. She had been denying it, but every time she heard someone stop a horse or carriage near her house, she looked out thinking it might be Adam. He was always in her thoughts and her heart, much as she tried to deny it.

Adam returned to Maeve's townhouse that evening. This time Her Grace was in, and he was led directly into a small sitting room that Adam recalled as being quite feminine and cheery.

Maeve was sitting on a straight-backed chair looking over fabric swatches. She glanced up at him with troubled eyes. "Did Howard tell you we spoke this afternoon?"

"Haven't seen him today. Did your butler mention I was by earlier?"

"He did. I am glad you decided to return to London."

"So am I. Life was miserable in the country without you."

He drew up a chair beside her and took her hand in his. "I want you to come with me to live at the ducal residence."

"I would like that. I love you very much. I have also missed you exceedingly." She gazed into his eyes with warmth and desire.

He thought she looked tired, as if she were under a strain. Perhaps these days apart had been hard on her as well. He would certainly like to think so. He wanted to believe that she truly loved him, but how could he? She had run from him. Could she have done such a thing if she truly loved him?

He took her into his arms and held her close. The womanly scent of her aroused him like an aphrodisiac. There was a tight, clenching sensation that seized his lower body. He was hot and cold at once. He brought his mouth down on hers and nibbled on her lips with exquisite care. Then he kissed her with all the pent-up need that had built inside him during the past few days. He pressed his hard length against her softness. Her arms came up and she buried her hands in his hair.

"God, Maeve, I've missed you so. I hunger for your body. I thirst for your kisses. Let me take you upstairs."

She started to succumb then pushed him

abruptly away. "We must talk first."

"What about?" His voice was thick with passion.

"I have been searching for Brianna without any luck. I thought if you helped me, it would make all the difference."

"You know how I feel about that. Let us cease talking of the matter when it only puts a wedge between us."

She moved farther away from him. There was hurt in her eyes. He saw her slipping away from him again and wanted to howl like a dog baying at the moon in frustration.

"Why must you do this to us, sweetheart? Have I not made you happy?"

"I love you very much, Adam, but this just is not right. I implore you to help me find Brianna. She can live here, in this house. I will not insist that she be installed in your residence. However, we must have a care for her. I am truly afraid for the girl. I have a feeling that she is in horrible trouble. Please help me find her."

Adam turned away from Maeve. Clearly, they had arrived at an impasse. "You are very foolish. The girl is a stranger to both of us, and you would destroy our marriage over her. My mother was ever the actress. I am certain the girl is perfectly fine. Mother simply employed her theatrics to get her way, as ever."

Adam reached into his pocket and removed a velvet box. "I have a small gift for you. I passed a jewelry shop today and saw these exquisite earbobs in the window. They will be perfect for you." Adam opened the box and displayed his offering eagerly. The rubies and diamonds winked enticingly.

Maeve looked at them and frowned, then shook her head. "They are lovely, but I do not wish to accept your gift, at least not at this time. I should feel guilty if I did."

"You think I am trying to buy your good opinion of me?"

"You have in the past," she said.

What had he expected? She really did not understand his feelings. He was not of an inclination to discuss the matter further. Words of affection did not come easily to his lips. He was becoming much too angry for that anyway. His words when they came were stiff and formal. "Maeve, I will leave you for now. Perhaps we may talk again soon. Reflect upon our conversation, as I will." He was getting ready to leave when a thought popped into his mind. "I have seen Mr. Brockton."

She looked up at him, startled. "Did you tell him about our situation?"

"No, I thought it best that you should be the one to do so. Frankly, I was surprised you had not done so already. Ginny wishes to talk with you. Brockton tells me she has news for you."

Adam swallowed his pride, swept her into his arms and kissed her one last time. Her lips parted and he slipped his tongue into the warmth of her mouth. She tasted erotically sweet, like liquid chocolate. He gently lowered the bodice of her gown and rubbed one nipple then circled the other rhythmically with his forefinger. He heard a deep moan in her throat and felt himself begin to burn and finally go up in flames. Releasing her was near impossible, but he had to do it soon or die from need. He had wanted this to be a kiss she would not soon forget. However, Adam realized he would not soon forget it either.

"Goodbye, Adam," she said in a breathy voice.

"It need not be goodbye," he said, no longer trusting himself to touch her in a civilized manner.

"Just remember, I was once an orphan myself. And no one wanted me, either. I know how Brianna feels."

He groaned. "It is not the same thing."

She pulled away from him. "I perceive it

as such."

His anger flared again. "Why have you not used your famed second sight to locate her then?" he taunted.

The color rose in her cheeks. "I do not think now is the proper time to discuss that. Perhaps you were right when you said we are still strangers to each other." She lifted her skirts and rushed out of the room.

In a moment, he could hear her footsteps on the stairs. He left Maeve feeling furious with her. How could the woman be so opinionated, stubborn and wrong-headed?

Maeve visited Mr. Brockton in the afternoon when she knew he would be having his breakfast. Ginny and Mary were in the dining room with him. She was glad that she would be able to see all three of them together. She supposed it was time that she told them about leaving Adam, but it was certainly something she dreaded.

She had not slept well the night before. Twice she woke after particularly vivid dreams. In one, she had become Brianna. Sophia's vile cousin was leering at her. She was very afraid of him and what he might do to her. Maeve had woken up in a sweat and found it difficult to sleep again. Hours later, she finally slipped back into an unquiet repose. In the next dream, she was again in Adam's arms, and he was making love to her. It was a passionate yet marvelously gentle mating, and she knew he was truly the love of her life. Over and over again, Adam told her how much he loved her. She had been woken by a shattering climax. Realizing it had all been only a dream, she was bereft, reduced to sobbing into her pillow.

"Maeve, dear. Such a pleasure to see you." Mr. Brockton's words took her back to the present moment. "Ginny, Mary, see that we are served now."

After a quick hug, Ginny and Mary left Maeve alone with Mr. Brockton. His forehead wrinkled with concern.

"Maeve, is everything all right between you and your blue-blooded husband?" There was no way to hide the truth from Mr. Brockton; he knew her much too well.

"We are having some difficulties." She found it awkward to speak of her estrangement from Adam.

He took her hand. "I had that feeling when he visited me. But I thought it best to wait until I saw you. If that rogue has done anything to hurt you, he'll answer to me, Ralph as well, and then Charles when he returns."

"No, it is not what you think." She sat down and told him the whole story then. It felt good to confide in someone, especially in the man who had been like a father to her for so many years.

Mr. Brockton listened attentively. When she finished, he patted her head as if she were still a child. "I've no opinion to offer. Not my place to interfere. I know better than that. Give your man a bit of time, though. I believe he'll come around. As to this sister of his, I'll put out my ears. There's much that's said and heard in the establishment I run. Ralph and I will have a go at finding out more information. Speaking of Ralph, I ought to send him back to you. I don't like you living alone with no protector about."

She shook her head. "Ralph belongs with you. It is not as if my life is in danger anymore. Besides, there are good, reliable servants about."

"Well, if you change your mind, don't stand on ceremony with me. We're family, after all, my girl." He gave her a quick kiss on the forehead.

Ginny returned with Mary; the two young women carried trays of hot food.

"You didn't have to do the serving yourselves," he said.

"We wanted to do it." Ginny's smile was sunshine; her red-gold hair made her shine like a newly minted guinea.

"I have steaming hot chocolate for all of us," Mary said. Maeve noticed how Mary had filled out into a lovely young woman. The oval face with dimpled cheeks gave her charming warmth.

"Adam said something about Ginny having news for me." She looked from Mr. Brockton to her friend.

Ginny sat down at the table. "Well, you know how successful we've become at placing all our girls as domestics. It seems we have reached a point where the quality wants to pay us a fee for finding girls for them. We built ourselves a good reputation, Maeve. Your charity work is turning into a profitable business. Mary and I think we can make a go of it. What do you think about that?"

"I think it is a splendid notion."

"You've brought these two luck, as well as myself," Mr. Brockton said.

"They brought themselves the luck by their hard work and diligence, just as you did," Maeve said with true affection.

"I was the first girl you took from Beedle's house of hell," Ginny said. "I haven't forgot that. If not for you, I don't know what would have become of me. Nothing good, I'm certain of that."

"The same holds true for me," Mary said. "You've saved so many girls from lives of misery and degradation."

"I am certain there are those that would not agree with you on that," Maeve said dryly.

"There's always girls too lazy to do much else but work on their backs," Mr. Brockton said gruffly, "but at least we've provided as many girls as we could with some decent choices."

"I'm glad we could do it for them," Maeve said.

By the time she left her former home, Maeve was feeling considerably better. Perhaps soon Ginny and Mary would want to marry. They were wonderful friends. She wanted them to have full lives.

She might have told them about her child but realized she was not ready for that yet, not until she told Adam first. Last night had not been the right time. When would be the right time? Would they ever be together again the way they had been? With a deep sigh, Maeve thought about how perfect things had been between them in Italy and prayed they could be so again. She was certain that he loved her. Yet suddenly, she was becoming plagued with doubts.

Lust and love were not the same thing. Did Adam truly know the difference? He had married her, but then he always expected to pay for what he wanted. Perhaps he felt that marriage had been her price for living with him. And in a sense, he was right, wasn't he? But did he realize how much she loved him, really and truly loved him? She had to find some way to make him understand.

"Your Grace, there is a young person awaiting you. She is at present being fed in the kitchen. She insists that she must see you on an urgent matter. Although she seemed hardly better than an urchin, I allowed her in, since she had your card."

"Thank you, Rogers. You did just the right thing." Removing her spencer, gloves and bonnet, Maeve tossed down her outer apparel in the entry hall and hurried to the kitchen. Had Brianna found her? But surely no one would ever describe Brianna as an urchin?

Mrs. Widmore, the cook, glanced up and then gave a short curtsy. Maeve looked at the girl sitting at the large wooden kitchen table and recognized her immediately. The girl looked up from hungrily devouring a bowl of bread pudding.

"Good day to you, my lady, I've got something to tell you that I think you'll be wanting to hear."

Maeve could scarcely contain her excitement. Perhaps this girl had the answer to finding Adam's sister. Maeve could only hope so.

CHAPTER
TWENTY-THREE

"How are you, Doris?"

The girl gave her a look of startled surprise. "You remembers someone as lowly as me? Why, ain't that grand of you!"

"Did you come to tell me something about His Grace's sister?" Maeve was much too excited to engage in further pleasantries. The girl knew something; she was sure of it.

Doris looked down at her pudding regretfully, as if she wished she could simply continue eating and not have to speak at all. "Yes, I have a bit to tell you."

With that, Maeve dismissed Mrs. Widmore and the lad whose job it was to help with the lifting and carrying. When they were alone, Maeve turned back to Doris eagerly. "What is it you wish to tell me."

The girl regarded Maeve, head tilted to one side in a gesture of frank appraisal. "First, I got to ask if you will pay me what it's worth to know about the girl."

"Of course, I will," Maeve responded without hesitation.

Doris nodded her head with a look of satisfaction. "I wouldn't ask, but you're a toff and I got no money. You see, they left me high and dry, they did. Went off without so much as a fare-thee-well. It was true of all the servants. Only, I was a lot more than just a serving maid, if you catch my drift."

Maeve sat down opposite the girl, ready to listen patiently to all she cared to say. Maeve offered no comment but nodded her head encouragingly.

"I was with them two years, Mr. Ogden and Miss Lizette. Served them very well, too. Wasn't my fault he ran up such huge debts. Mr. Ogden has a nice income, you know, and an allowance from his family, but he can't manage to live on it. He's always gaming in the hells. I learned a little poem that fits him well: *Till noon they sleep, from noon till night they dress. From night till morn they game it more or less.*"

"I daresay that is the way with most of the upper ten thousand."

"I venture you're not like them, my lady. I seen you was different, that you cares about people."

"If that means believing those of sensibility should attempt to correct the injustices of the world as best they can."

"There, I knew it! You're nothing like Ogden and his whore. They care not a fig about others. Why, when his cousin brought her daughter to him, all he could think of was what good it might be doing him."

Maeve had not believed the man spoke truthfully to her, and now her suspicions were confirmed. But why had he felt it necessary to lie, and what had become of Brianna?

"Was Brianna at his lodging when I came?"

Doris looked up at her round-eyed. "Oh, no, miss, she were already gone. You see, it was like this. Mrs. Sophia were anxious to be on her way. I overheard Mr. Ogden say he couldn't take on the responsibility of another member in his household. Then she up and offers him some coin. He agrees finally, but says that she should sign over a guardianship agreement to him so everything will be legal and proper-like. Miss Brianna argued against it, but her mother wouldn't hear any argument. Nothing would serve but the girl stay with kin — though she did make Mr. Ogden promise he'd see the girl were taken care of. He had his eye on his cousin's fat purse and would have promised anything to lay his hands on it."

"How did Brianna react?"

"She cried long and hard, but it were no use. Mrs. Sophia left the girl with Mr. Ogden, who gave her over to Lizette. And I don't mind telling you, Lizette can be very mean at times."

"Mean in what way?" Maeve's heart beat rapidly with dread.

"I saw her slap the girl across the face and tell her to behave or it would go badly for her."

"What happened then?"

"Later I heard them talking, Mr. Ogden and Lizette. He said as soon as the guardian paper arrived, he'd figure out what to do with the girl. He had no real place for her, you see. He don't have connections, either. Mrs. Sophia used to be real close with him I heard, but she don't hardly know him anymore, being away mostly. He's not thought well of by anyone. So he couldn't introduce the girl around as her mother thought. Mr. Ogden was just plotting how he could get some blunt off her. That's his way, you see."

Maeve fought a wave of sickness in her stomach as fear grew within her. "Where is Brianna now? Do you know, Doris?"

"That's what I'm getting at. You see, Mr. Ogden might have let the girl stay a bit, but he was only one step ahead of his creditors. He was desperate for money. The night before you came, he invited someone to the lodging, not a very nice man." Doris took a huge spoonful of pudding.

"What man?" Maeve urged.

"I'm coming to it. He goes by the name of Dirk Foxworth. Don't think Dirk is his real name though; some say he got the moniker because he were so handy with a knife. Anyway, Mr. Ogden owes him a great deal of money, and the bloke threatened to cut his innards out if he didn't pay up. So Mr. Ogden offered him Brianna in payment."

"What!" Maeve jumped up in outrage.

"Oh, it were very straightforward. Mr. Ogden would sign over the guardianship paper and in return, Dirk would have her."

"For what purpose?"

Doris looked flustered and turned her eyes downward. "Well, the usual purpose I would imagine. Except . . ."

"Except what?" Maeve's teeth were clenched tightly.

"This person, he runs these houses."

"What sorts of houses?" Maeve was afraid she already knew the answer to that.

"Brothels. But he owns this very posh place too, and I heard him say something to

Mr. Ogden about how she'd do very well there indeed."

Maeve was horrified, yet somehow this was just what she'd expected. "And did the transaction go through?" She tried to keep her voice calm, but it was a close thing.

"I don't know for certain. You see, this Dirk fellow, well, he liked Brianna very well indeed, but he balked at the price. Mr. Ogden told him he wanted ten thousand pounds in addition to having his debts cancelled right and proper. The fellow tried to bargain about the price, but Mr. Ogden stood firm. Then old Dirk said he'd have to think about it and let him know in a day or two."

"And where was Brianna while all this was happening?"

"Oh, she was right there in the room."

Maeve was incredulous. "And she said and did nothing?"

"Well, as to that . . ." Doris cleared her throat awkwardly. "I believe Miss Lizette went and gave her a drugged cup of cocoa so she'd sleep through it all. But Dirk, he looked her over right and proper."

Maeve shuddered. She did not wish to consider what that might mean. "Where is Brianna now?"

"They sent me out shopping the next

morning. When I come back, she were gone."

Maeve's heart sank. "So you believe this dreadful person bought her?"

Doris shrugged. "Can't say for certain, ma'am. You see, after Dirk left, Mr. Ogden said something about another gentleman coming by and how maybe that fellow wouldn't be as clutch-fisted."

"And did this second man come to the lodging?" Maeve prodded.

"Don't know for certain, miss. You see, they went and sent me to bed. But I did hear the front door open later, and a deep male voice I never heard before was speaking. I opened my door and peeked out for a moment and saw a very tall gentleman with black hair. I didn't hear what was said and don't know what happened afterwards. So I guess I'm not as much help as you'd like."

"Actually, you have been a big help."

"Then you'll see your way clear to pay me? They left for the continent so fast, I never even got a character. And he left owing all of us money. Said he'd send it to us, but that's a bouncer, I vow. He won't be coming back, not with all the folks he owes. When I reminded him how he said he'd take me with him wherever he went, the man laughed in my face. Said he could hire servants just as good as me, maybe better, wherever he was to go. He ain't gentry as far as I'm concerned. No, Miss, Mr. Ogden ain't no gentleman."

"There we agree," Maeve said. "Stay right here, Doris. I am going to see that you are paid and that you obtain suitable employment."

Rarely had she ever felt this angry. Ogden had sold Brianna into slavery. Not only was such a thing immoral, but it was also illegal. Brianna was, after all, a free person. But before anything could be done, Maeve would have to find the girl and bring her to safety. That would be easier said than done.

Dirk Foxworth had to be located. Doris had provided a starting place, and it was up to her to follow through. Maeve had Rogers arrange for a hack. She'd sent the coach and driver to the ducal residence. She was on her way to Mr. Brockton's home with Doris in tow in a very brief period of time.

On the ride over, Maeve explained to Doris about the domestic service that was now run by Ginny and Mary. "You will be placed in a respectable position in no time at all. In the meantime, you will have a good place to stay and never want for a meal."

Doris was very pleased. She continued to talk and bubble over all the time they were in the carriage. Maeve was treated to a complete family history. She tried to listen with interest, but her mind was preoccupied. When they arrived at the house, Maeve asked the driver to wait. As quickly as possible, Maeve delivered Doris into Ginny's capable hands and went to talk to Ralph.

She found him in the courtyard grooming a spotted dog. "I did not know you kept a pet these days."

Ralph shrugged as if she'd caught him doing something he found embarrassing. "I saw him eating out of the trash. He had a wounded leg. I think someone tossed him out because of it. Anyway, he was all bones and snarled when I first approached him. I began feeding him and we've become good friends."

"He's a fine-looking animal. Have you given him a name?"

"I calls him Dog. It seems to suit him."

If it were anyone but Ralph, she might have laughed. The truth was, Ralph had a warm heart but little imagination.

"I wish to ask you about something. Someone, actually." She told him a little of what Doris had said about Dirk Foxworth. "Do you know where this person might be or the location of this fancy house he owns?"

Ralph's eyes narrowed. "You wouldn't be

thinking of going there yourself, would you? That would be a serious mistake."

"Of course not," she assured him. "I'll just set the runners on him. It's really no affair of mine."

"Well, if you're sure, because I don't want to see you in danger again."

"Naturally not."

It turned out Ralph did know about Foxworth. And he shared the information. There wasn't much that went on in London that Ralph didn't know about. "A good fellow to keep clear of, I'd say," Ralph cautioned.

"There is something you could do for me. Would you deliver a message to Adam? It really is important. I have written a note to him and would like him to see it right away. You are the only person I would trust to deliver it."

"Aye," he promised. "I'll find his worthyship, wherever he's had a mind to go."

"Thank you, Ralph. Time is of the essence."

When Ralph would have questioned her further, she quickly turned on her heels and hurried back toward the waiting hack. Ralph had given her Foxworth's direction; she now gave to the driver.

As they drove along, she tried to formulate

a plan for how she would deal with such a person as Foxworth when they met. She was a bit frightened but reasoned that an offer of gold would deliver Brianna from the fellow's clutches, if he had her. Of course, she had no personal wealth, but Adam would now see how critical Brianna's situation was. Knowing what happened to his sister would surely bring him to his senses and undo his prejudices. Maeve was convinced that Adam had a kind, generous heart. He would not let Brianna suffer. She had only to apprize him of the situation.

In the note she had quickly penned, Maeve wrote to Adam begging his intervention. She explained in the sketchiest terms the cruelty that had been perpetrated by Ogden. He would then understand why she had gone to the brothel. Ralph would drive him there. But she must find out if Brianna was actually a prisoner in that horrid place. If so, Maeve would begin negotiations. If not, perhaps Foxworth might have some knowledge of who the mysterious dark man had been. Maeve did not even wish to consider what might have happened to Brianna since the time she'd last seen and spoken to the poor, innocent girl.

"Driver," she called up, "can you not move faster?"

CHAPTER
TWENTY-FOUR

"Are you certain this is the address you wanted, My Lady?" the driver asked. His expression was dubious.

Maeve took a deep breath and steeled herself for whatever lay ahead.

"I am not certain this is the place, but I will pay you twice your usual fare if you will remain until I come out."

The driver, a bulky, middle-aged man smiled broadly. "Aye, Milady, that would do well indeed. I'll wait for you right here."

With that assurance, Maeve was ready to face whatever needed to be done. From the outside, the brothel looked no different from any other building in the flower district, although it was set back from the street and there was an ornate iron gate at the front. The impression was neither shabby nor elegant. Maeve had no idea what to expect. She realized that in spite of her early life, she had been rather sheltered. Although she had seen some of the worst and poorest of London's neighborhoods and rookeries, she'd never been inside a house of ill repute in her entire life.

She was not far from the theatre district of Drury Lane where unescorted ladies were unremarkable, in part due to the tradition of light skirts, actresses and opera dancers often found in the vicinity. Maeve wondered fleetingly if the location for the brothel had been chosen deliberately to capitalize on the number of young women who came to London looking for success in the theatre, only to be disillusioned.

When she walked up the stairs and knocked at the door, it was answered not by a butler but a young woman dressed in a low-cut, revealing gown of a gauzy thin poplin material. It was obvious at first glance that she wore no form of under garment. Her nipples were almost completely exposed. Maeve did her best not to stare. However, the girl's manners were not as good as her own.

"Did you want something 'ere?"

"Yes, I am looking for a Mr. Foxworth. I was told I might find him within."

The girl eyed her coldly. "Who wants him?"

"Is he here or not?" Maeve stepped forward, trying to glance around.

"Just stay where you are for the moment. I'll fetch someone to see you."

Maeve walked into the hallway and found herself in a large, opulent room. There were statues placed artfully about, white marble figures of men and women done in Greek and Roman style. But the figures were presented in many forms of erotic congress, vividly graphic. Maeve had never seen the like. Heavy purple draperies were pulled to keep out the light of day. There was thick, plush purple carpeting and comfortable chairs and settees all around the room. One wall was mirrored, and Maeve caught sight of herself in it. She thought how out of place she looked in such a room. When had she become so respectable, she wondered.

Suddenly, the girl was leading an older woman toward her. This woman was plump and wore heavy makeup. Her short, feather-cut hair was a bright, brassy red and she wore a damped down bodice, which proved revealing of her generously endowed bosom.

"You were asking for Mr. Foxworth?" the woman said as she eyed Maeve suspiciously.

"I was told I could find him here."

"You can, but I have to look you over first. If I don't approve, you're out the door before he considers you."

Maeve realized they had completely misunderstood her reason for being there. She was about to inform them of the error when the woman began to speak again.

"I haven't much time. We're having a number of important guests tonight, so let's be quick about this. I am Madame Louise," the woman lifted her head majestically. "I'm sure you already know who I am. The girls who work here are treated very well indeed. This is not your usual establishment. A girl must be very good to remain here. She must be of the best."

"Have you taken any new girls recently?" Maeve asked. Perhaps the madam could tell her if Brianna were here.

"We don't take many here. Mr. Foxworth judges all our girls. They must satisfy him first. High standards he has."

Maeve shuddered inwardly, thinking of Brianna. What would such a man do to an innocent like her?

"The clients who come here are of the quality. All well off, the cream of society, you could say. That's why you see such elegance all around you. And if these gentlemen want something a little different, well, we do our best to satisfy them. But then you must know all this, or you wouldn't have been sent here." Madame Louise suddenly placed her hand on Maeve's face and touched her skin. "You've got an unusual coloring. Are you a foreigner?"

"I am part gypsy."

Madam Louise looked at her more closely. "Well, there's some that would like a ride with a wild gypsy, no doubt. You look fancy enough. Take off your gown and let me see if your body's as good as your face."

This was going too far. She had no intention of disrobing and decided the charade had gone on long enough. She was just about to tell the madam who she was when a man's voice called out.

"Louise! Are you out there?"

The madam turned to the young woman beside her. "Go get him a glass of wine, and make sure it's our best port. You know how particular he can be. Hurry, girl."

They were soon joined by a man who was rather short in stature and rapier thin, but carried himself like a strutting rooster. His mode of dress was in the first stare of fashion. He had cold, light blue eyes that turned sharply to examine her own and probe their depths. "A new girl?" he asked Louise with interest. "We are missing a few tonight. Think she will do?"

"I haven't finished with her yet."

"I'll take it from here. You have a great

451

deal to do getting ready. We'll be busy in short order."

Before she could say a word, Foxworth had taken her arm and was leading her upstairs. He walked her down a long hallway where all the doors were closed and then surprised her by pushing her into a room. At once she realized that this was a well-appointed bedchamber. The first thing she noticed was the wall murals of nude male and female figures in classical design, arranged in a variety of erotic poses. In the center of the room was a large tester bed covered with a lush red velvet spread. The carpeting matched in color and luxury. It was gaudy and garish, yet the overall impression was amazingly sensual.

"I always put the girls to the test before they start working for me." Before she knew what was happening, Foxworth had placed his hands on her breasts. "Very nice," he observed. "These will please my customers."

She batted his hands away. "There has been a misunderstanding, sir. I am not what you think at all. I came to find my sister-in-law. I believe she may have been given over to your charge by an unscrupulous person. The fact is, Brianna is no more a whore than I am."

Foxworth stared at her in some amusement. Then he laughed loudly. "If a mistake has been made, it is yours. You are here, and I need an extra girl for the evening. After I have tried you out, I will let you serve my guests. Now cease your foolish prattle and remove your clothes so that I may see you naked."

Heat rose to her face. She decided the man must be stupid, for he had clearly not understood her. She would make her words more explicit. However, his behavior made her very uneasy, and her nerve endings were screaming out in fear. *Take hold of yourself; you've been in worse situations.* Unfortunately, at the moment, it did not seem so.

"I am Maeve de Viller, wife of the Duke of Clarmont, a Corinthian of the *ton*. I am here to discover the whereabouts of his sister, Brianna. I believe Mr. Grenville Ogden tried to illegally sell her to you. I am here to reclaim her. I am naturally willing to compensate you for your inconvenience. The duke is a very generous man. We can come to terms as soon as I have seen Brianna." She attempted to sound as haughty as possible, hoping to convince the man of the truth of her words.

At first Foxworth merely stared at her in total disbelief. Then he began laughing loudly. "What is that bastard Ogden up to now? Is this a jest? Does he think I won't have him killed because he sent you to me? You obviously have been about for a few years. So has that French whore of his. I told him I would take the girl. Then he up and sells her to someone else. Well, as far as I'm concerned, the girl was promised to me. It's a sign of bad faith to back out of an agreement as he did. I'll have his heart cut out for that. As to you, my girl, I've seen your kind before. You're a good actress. You'll do nicely here if I don't hear anymore of your lip."

She moved toward the door, convinced that the man was somewhat mad and certainly dangerous.

He seemed to have finely honed instincts, and pounced on her before she could reach the outside. He twisted her arm, his grip a painful vise. Then he pulled her toward him. He removed a long, sharp knife from a leather sheath that had been in his inside pocket. "I've another dagger like this that I carry in my boot when the occasion warrants. I'm very good with it, too. And I wouldn't want to cut up such a beautiful face as yours. So be a good girl and do just as I say."

■ ■ ■ ■

Adam was very worried. From what Ralph told him, Maeve had been making inquiries about a very dangerous ruffian. Her note to him was brief but clear. She had found out Grenville Ogden sold Brianna to someone, possibly this Foxworth creature. She was planning to discover if Brianna was the whoremaster's prisoner.

"Ralph, when did she leave you?"

"Why 'twas upwards of an hour ago. I looked everywhere for you. At your residence, they weren't certain where you were. I tried the boxing academy before I came here." Ralph had met him at White's in the fashionable district of St. James's.

"My God, she must be there already!"

Ralph gave him a look of amazement. "You think she went to see him?"

"I do indeed."

Ralph straightened his bulky frame. "But she promised to go on home. Said she was going to turn the information over to the runners and let the law handle matters. You don't think she's chasing after that blasted criminal herself, do you?"

"Knowing Maeve, she is there, and we'd better get over to that house immediately. I have heard that particular individual is a very nasty fellow."

Adam drove his phaeton through the rain slicked paved stone streets of London at a breakneck speed, narrowly missing an orange cart and a ragman. Ralph made no comment but held to the sides of the vehicle so tightly that his knuckles turned white. Adam cursed himself for being all kinds of a fool. Maeve was a wildly impetuous creature, emotional and loving to a fault. Of course, she would go all out to find the girl. Her own safety would be her least concern.

His half-sister left in danger and degradation? How was he to discern to what lengths his mother would go to ensure her own pleasures without interference? She had always been selfish and vain, an unloving, uncaring woman, but this exceeded even what he would have expected her to do. This time her actions bordered on the criminal.

He vowed to kill Ogden if he ever got his hands on the vile brute. Calling the man out was too good for him. He should be hanged, drawn and quartered. But right now, there were more important matters to consider. Fear for Maeve's well-being made his heart chill as if someone had placed ice in his chest cavity. Maeve was the person he cared about most in the world. He could not tolerate the thought of living without her.

Maeve silently castigated herself for being an idiot and a fool. She shouldn't have rushed here so quickly, and certainly not alone. Her thoughtless nature would be her ruin this time if she were not careful. She fought Foxworth as best she could, but for a small man, he was quite strong and wiry. She brought her knee into his groin just as Charles had taught her, and heard his grunt with satisfaction as she headed toward the door. But she hadn't done as much damage as she hoped, because he grabbed her at the waist. Then he'd threatened her with that horrid dagger again.

He forced her down on the bed, the dagger pricking painfully against her chest. Her arms were shackled, manacled to the bedposts before she even realized what was happening. She had never been more frightened in her life. The thought of the wretched man touching her was not to be borne.

She also thought about her unborn child and protecting it from harm. She could not allow Foxworth to rape her. But how was she to prevent it? As he leaned over to shackle her leg, Maeve brought up her free foot and kicked him hard in the stomach.

He raged at her like a bull.

But Maeve had a brief reprieve, because Louise called Foxworth downstairs. She let out her breath then, hardly aware that she'd been holding it for some time. She looked around the room but saw no escape. She lay there thrashing about for what seemed like forever.

When Foxworth returned, her heart began to beat like a hammer hitting against an anvil. Yet she kept herself as outwardly calm as possible, sensing that showing her fear was the worst thing she could do in this situation.

"I will have you handsomely rewarded if you release me, sir. I am who I claim to be and can prove it. My husband will be most generous with you. But you must release me now before any harm is done."

"That sounds real nice to my ears. In fact, if it's true, I can have both you and the money. You'll not tell your man I had you. If you do complain, I'll just have to kill you both."

"You are insane!"

He reached down, pulling her hair free from the pins that held it in place and wrapped it around his hand with a yanking motion that brought a welter of pain to her head.

"Lovely," he said, "ain't seen hair as shiny as this in ages. Feels just like silk." He leaned close to her now so she was forced to smell the foulness of his breath. "You'll do very well indeed." He tried to fondle her breasts, but she moved her body out of his reach. He simply laughed. "Soon enough you'll be begging for it. I'm known as quite a lover." Then he began lifting her skirts, pressing his hands none too gently into her sensitive inner thighs.

Maeve moved away from his revolting touch and then started to scream. She knew it was probably hopeless to think that anyone in this house would respond, but she prayed that Adam would reach her before the vile beast actually raped her.

"Stop that, or I'll be smacking you hard," Foxworth warned, his light blue eyes like a frozen lake in winter. He squeezed her mouth painfully.

Her legs still free, Maeve saw her opportunity, brought up her foot and quickly kicked him as hard as she could, catching him in the chest. He began to curse and tightened his hand into a fist, getting ready to strike her. She turned her head to the right and shut her eyes tightly. There was a great crashing sound at the door. She opened her eyes wide and lifted her head as best she could to look in the direction of the door and let out another shrill scream.

When the door burst open, she saw him. She hoped she wasn't merely imagining him. But no, he looked quite substantial indeed. "Adam, thank God you're here!"

Behind Adam was Ralph. Both of them looked as if they were ready to commit murder. Foxworth must have thought so, too, because he reached for his knife kept ever at the ready.

"Whoever you are, get out of here. I'm doing business in my own establishment."

Adam's dark eyes were totally black and narrowed now. He had never looked more lethal or dangerous. "You think that, do you? Perhaps we will have to have a bit of a chat about that matter. This is my wife. If she says you have harmed her in any way, I shall be forced to kill you."

"Not bloody likely," came the gruff reply.

At that moment, Adam came toward Foxworth.

"Be careful of his knife!" Maeve cried out fearfully.

Adam did not respond. He was moving swiftly around Foxworth, who suddenly lunged out with his weapon, swinging it in a wide arc. Adam appeared first to come directly toward Foxworth, then feinted to one side, out of the smaller man's reach, a boxer's strategy, Maeve realized, having seen Charles engage in fisticuffs occasionally. Instantly, Adam's right leg shot out and kicked Foxworth a hard, disabling blow to the groin.

Foxworth went to his knees, groaning loudly but still retaining possession of his knife, whereupon Adam caught him from the elbow and forced the weapon from his opponent's hand. There was a sound of cracking, and Maeve realized that Adam had broken his adversary's arm.

Foxworth lay on the floor alternately moaning and cursing. Adam kicked the knife to the other side of the room. "You will not be sticking anyone with this nasty piece for a while, we can assume," he said with some satisfaction. "Ralph, could you clear out the trash from the room? I want to have a talk in private with my wife before we leave this hellish place."

"Excellent skills you have, your grandship. Couldn't have done better meself." Ralph turned an approving smile on Adam. "But your eminenceship, those were street fighting skills you was using. Ain't they beneath a top-lofty gent like yourself?"

"One does what is necessary, and as you will recall, I was not dealing with a gentleman." Adam turned to Foxworth. "Oh, one other thing. I will have the key to these chains." Adam held out his hand to Foxworth.

When he proved too slow in reaching his pockets, Ralph took over, manhandling the fellow until the key was produced. Then Ralph unceremoniously lifted the man and threw him from the room, closing the door firmly behind them.

Tears of relief flowed down Maeve's face. "I am so glad you are here."

"I should think so." Adam stood staring at her, drinking in the sight of her.

"I was so afraid you would not get here in time."

"As I was. You and I must speak. It is past time."

"I quite agree. Please release me, Adam."

"Indeed I shall." However, Adam did not move. In fact, he stepped back slightly, leaned negligently against the doorframe and crossed his legs. His head was tilted to one side, studying her.

"What are you doing, Adam?" His behavior seemed peculiar and somehow unnerving.

"Observing you, my dear. You look quite

inviting with your long, thick black hair fanning out on that red velvet coverlet. I am remembering when you danced for me in Spain. You look just as erotic and seductive now. Red is really quite a good color for your full-blooded beauty, my love." He approached her and leaned over, running his hand over her cheek. Then he sat down on the bed and played with the skein of her hair. "Quite lovely." His hands moved lower and skimmed the tops of her breasts. Then without warning, he gently lowered the bodice of her gown and with a caress, removed first one rounded orb and then the other. He leaned over and commenced to kiss each berry-tipped breast. His thumbs teased and rubbed each nipple sending shafts of fire through her body.

"God, Maeve, you have become even more voluptuous in the past weeks." His hands lifted her skirts higher so that he could survey her lower body. "Magnificent," he said. Then his lips sought the small nub of her woman's desire and sucked it with exquisite gentleness.

Maeve thrashed her head from side to side breathing in gasps. "Stop this, please!"

He stood back from her for a moment and surveyed her thoughtfully. "You are quite the wanton in this pose, highly provocative.

Good God, Maeve, you are incredibly beautiful everywhere."

"I am demeaned and humiliated," she said hotly.

"It was not I who put you here. You must take the blame."

"Oh, must I?" Her face flamed.

"Yes, you must. You are too defiantly impetuous by half. You have also frightened the life from me. It would appear you are in need of a lesson."

"Not from you!"

"Oh, most especially from me." His voice was dangerously silky. "You see, you have this habit of not thinking matters through. You rush into situations that place you in jeopardy. I will not have that happen again. You are my life. The love of my life. There can be no other. And I will not let you destroy yourself and me. I simply, utterly refuse." He reached down to her again. His fingers moved rhythmically into her most private recesses.

She was experiencing a sense of powerful desire, an ecstatic rush of need that caused her to tremble uncontrollably. "Please stop," she begged.

"Not quite yet. As I was saying, I was terrified driving over here, and then when I saw that criminal ready to ravish you, I felt

464

the most extraordinary sense of outrage. Now, looking down at you, all that emotion has turned to lust. I feel like an alchemist who turns lead into gold. I believe I will ravish you myself."

"This madness has gone far enough. Adam, release me!"

"My love, that is exactly what I intend. And it shall be the most excellent release for both of us." He licked the rosy crest of each breast and abraded them gently.

"You are wicked and decadent." She could not prevent her chest from heaving with passion.

"I certainly hope so."

There was devilry in his eyes as he climbed onto the bed. First he turned the key on the lock that held her right hand in place, kissing and sucking on each finger in turn, then he did the same for the left hand. His kisses trailed down her face, her neck, the tips of her breasts, and then his hands were moving downward, rhythmically. Gently he touched the core of her and kissed her there again and again.

She could hardly catch her breath. "You are surely a depraved man."

"Quite so. But I have of late also been deprived." Then his hands moved downward until he reached her right leg. His long, lean fingers kneaded and rubbed. He pressed her feet against his hands and massaged them methodically. She had never considered her feet as the least bit sensual, but his actions caused a fluttering low in her belly, a quickening. She felt totally weak, shivering with desire and need for him. There was a languor in her body, a heaviness in her depths; she was all too aware of the moisture gathering between her legs.

His lips and hands moved upward now, pressing against her body. She let out a deep sigh of pleasure.

"Adam, this is too bad of you."

"As long as you cannot say it is badly done of me, my dear."

"Perhaps we have both made mistakes?"

Adam's expression turned grave. "I love you more than anyone or anything in this world. You are all that is generous and good. I could not bear it if anything happened to you, my darling. If you truly want me to stop, then I will. Perhaps I forced myself upon you when I was drunk. If I did that, I must apologize. I was not within my right mind. When you left, I had to come to terms with what I'd done. I will not do that now. I never want to lose you, to alienate you. Can you forgive me?"

As an answer, Maeve kissed him long and

hard, welcoming him.

Adam said no more, but took her mouth with his own, his tongue mating with hers, his hands cupping, lifting and pressing the fullness of her breasts.

She felt his erection swell and harden against her bare thighs. Her hands moved from his taut buttocks, to his firm stomach, down to the turgid thrusting proof of his desire. Unable to refrain, she lowered herself and kissed him intimately as he had done earlier to her.

She heard a groan from deep in his throat and then suddenly he was on top of her, and they were becoming deeply connected, totally as one. And when the sweet, wild oblivion reached out to burst upon them like starlight on a summer night, they were truly together.

CHAPTER
TWENTY-FIVE

There was a loud knock at the door and they disengaged.

"What is it?" Adam called out in a hoarse voice.

"Sir, I think we best be going. Foxworth is beginning to recover and making all sorts of nasty threats. I believe we must give him back his room or else pay rent on it."

Adam gave Maeve a quick kiss and helped her to her feet. "Where are your things?"

She pointed toward a chair near a drapery covered window. Adam helped her with her spencer. She straightened her clothing as best she could and slipped into her shoes.

"You had best wait in the phaeton," he said "I still have to talk to Foxworth about my mother's girl."

"Your sister, you mean."

Their eyes met, and he drew her close. "Never again will you place yourself in such danger. Are we agreed?"

She did not reply. "Foxworth said that Brianna is not here. Apparently, Ogden sold her to some other person."

"I am relieved she is not in this place."

"But Adam, I do not think he has any idea where she is. Only Ogden knows, and he is gone." Her mind clear now, Maeve was worried again about Brianna.

Adam took her hand. "What precisely did Foxworth say? Not that it really matters. I have every intention of interrogating him quite thoroughly as soon as you are safely home."

"He claimed that Ogden had promised he would have Brianna if he paid the asking price. Apparently, while Foxworth had gone off to think about it, Ogden sold her to someone else."

"When I find Ogden, he will sincerely regret ever being born."

Maeve recognized Adam's carefully controlled rage. "Ogden has left for the continent, according to his former maid."

"I shall have a word with her as well."

Maeve realized something that filled her with joy. "Adam, are you saying that you will personally be looking into Brianna's disappearance?"

He scowled at her. "Well, I cannot very well let you continue to do it, can I? I am certain I will be gray-haired in a manner of days if I let you go on like this."

"I am glad you are taking over, because I did not know where to turn next. Foxworth was my last hope."

Adam placed his arm around her. "First, the maid may know something more than she previously recalled. Second, if Foxworth knew that Ogden gave the girl to someone else, he might very well have some idea who that person was. It is obvious he must have returned and spoken to Ogden at a later time. Given Foxworth's unpleasant disposition, it is entirely likely he would have insisted on having further intelligence, since he obviously did want the girl. And last, if necessary, I am prepared to launch a thorough investigation into Ogden's flight to the continent. In any case, my man Pritchard is good indeed, and we will put as many runners on this matter as is necessary. I will spare no expense. I give you my word that we will find her. Are you satisfied?"

She nodded her head, not trusting herself to speak, and brushed her lips against his.

After paying the hackney driver, Adam drove Maeve to her own snug little townhouse but warned her that he would be coming for her in the morning. "We will not spend another night apart after this one. I shall let you rest tonight. You seem thoroughly exhausted. But on the morrow, we are moving you to the ducal house. You and I are not to be parted from each other, not ever again."

She smiled at his stern demeanor, not about to argue. That night, she slept the most peaceful slumber she had experienced since their time together in Italy.

In the morning, Adam woke her with a kiss from her sweet repose and placed a single red rose beside her pillow. "Sleeping beauty is quite desirable."

Before she knew what was happening, Adam had removed all of his clothes and was in bed beside her. His arms came around her and she snuggled into the comfort of his body. They pleasured each other with a thoroughness that was gratifying.

Later as they dressed, Adam told her about what he had done to locate Brianna in the brief time they were parted. Maeve was disappointed to hear that Foxworth had told Adam nothing they did not already know. But Adam assured her that he had every intention of interrogating Foxworth more thoroughly in the future.

"Did you manage to get any sleep?" she asked him with concern.

"Enough. I want to take care of this matter for your sake and mine. I have made you a promise, and I have no intention of reneging on it. We will find the girl, and soon."

Maeve smiled up at him. She had no doubt there would be positive results with Adam handling the matter. "When I was a small child working slavishly at the orphanage, I was crushed by sadness. One fine morning on a day in late spring, I carried some ashes out to the collier's bin. And there growing through all the ugliness of dispersed coal ash was the loveliest flower I had ever seen. It grew straight and golden yellow in the morning sun with a fine green stem. Well, being superstitious, I took that as a heavenly sign, an omen meant directly for me. I felt that I was being told something important, that I must not despair, never give up hope in any circumstance."

"You always do see the good in everything and everyone," Adam said and gently kissed her forehead.

She pressed her hand to his. "Of course, I did not realize that flower was but a weed. Nevertheless, weeds may serve a useful purpose. I know quite a few uses for dandelions. I prefer a good healthy weed to a hothouse flower any day. Even mongrel dogs may be healthier than those that are inbred."

Adam held her away from him for a moment. "Maeve, you are getting at some point I would hope?"

"Of course, Your Grace. I merely wish to note that just because a child might be born on the wrong side of the blanket does not mean he or she is the worse for it."

"Ah, I begin to see. You are talking about my mother's child."

"Your Grace, Brianna is your mother's child, just as you are."

He raised his aristocratic brows. "You wish me to accept her? That may take some time. I will have to know her first."

"Naturally," she agreed.

"You need not look so smug. I am doing what you asked of me only because I love you so much."

She gave him a satisfied smile that seemed to annoy him.

"What are you looking so pleased about? By rights, I should beat you. You've led me around like a trained lap dog with a panting tongue."

"You said you love me. You did mean it?"

"Never say things I do not mean, love."

She smiled happily. "I knew you loved me, that one day you would realize it and admit it. I told myself the words were unimportant, but still, they are very nice to hear."

"How could I not love a woman with bottom?" He looked suggestively at her derriere. "And such a lovely bottom at that."

She kissed his cheek. "You are a randy goat."

"But you like me that way. By the by, I am wondering about your so-called visionary powers. Will you allow they do not in fact exist?"

She let out a deep sigh and sat down on a chair. "I must explain. I truly have them. They do, or at least did, exist. I believe they will return in time. I know you are ever the cynic. However, the reason they are not available to me at present is because I am breeding."

"What?" Adam stared at her in amazement.

"You need not be so shocked, Adam. It would seem to be a natural result of our rather energetic coupling."

Now Adam lifted her from the chair, sat down on it himself, and then arranged her on his lap so that she faced him sideways. He put his arms around her waist.

"So you would give me an heir?" His face was singularly devoid of expression, and she had no idea what he was thinking or feeling.

She turned to face him squarely. "Possibly it will be an heiress."

"Quite so." His tone was misleadingly casual and disinterested.

"Would that displease you?"

"Not overmuch, I do believe," he drawled. "We would just have to try again." He gave her an ingratiating smile that showed his dimpled cheek to perfection.

"And if we get our heir the second time, what then?" She ran her fingers through his gold-tipped hair.

"Well, one can never beget too many heirs or heiresses, so we would just have another go at it, and another after that." He kissed her lips ardently. "Thank you," he said, "for loving me despite all my vices and flaws."

"I might very well say the same. However, you give me too much credit. You see, I cannot help loving you. You are quite irresistible, Adam."

His eyes touched hers and then his lips followed. "My love, I do believe I see a dandelion blooming through the ashes in the morning air."

ABOUT THE AUTHOR

Jacqueline Seewald graduated college magna cum laude and earned two graduate degrees at Rutgers University. She has taught creative, expository and technical writing at the university level, as well as high school English where she enjoyed teaching British Literature. She also worked as both an academic librarian and an educational media specialist. Nine of her books of fiction have previously been published. Her short stories, poems, essays, reviews and articles have appeared in hundreds of diverse publications such as: *The Writer, Sasee, Tea, Affaire de Coeur, Lost Treasure, The Christian Science Monitor, Pedestal, Surreal, After Dark, The Dana Literary Society Journal, Library Journal, The Erickson Tribune,* and *Publishers Weekly,* as well as numerous anthologies. Her romantic mystery thriller, *The Inferno Collection,* was published by Five Star/Gale in hardcover and Wheeler in large print. Her romantic mystery novel, *The Drowning Pool,* was also published by Five Star.

The employees of Thorndike Press hope you have enjoyed this Large Print book. All our Thorndike, Wheeler, and Kennebec Large Print titles are designed for easy reading, and all our books are made to last. Other Thorndike Press Large Print books are available at your library, through selected bookstores, or directly from us.

For information about titles, please call:
(800) 223-1244

or visit our Web site at:

http://gale.cengage.com/thorndike

To share your comments, please write:

Publisher
Thorndike Press
295 Kennedy Memorial Drive
Waterville, ME 04901